MEET THE MENAGERIE . . .

MR. DOYLE . . . Sorcerer and alchemist. A man of unparalleled intellect. When evil threatens to consume the world, he gathers those who will fight.

CERIDWEN . . . Princess of the Fey. Solitary and beautiful, she holds the elemental forces of nature at her command.

DR. LEONARD GRAVES . . . Scientist, adventurer, ghost. He exists in both life—and afterlife.

DANNY FERRICK . . . A teenaged demon changeling who is just discovering his untapped—and unholy—powers.

CLAY . . . An immortal shapeshifter, he has existed since The Beginning. His origin is an enigma—even to himself.

EVE . . . The mother of all vampires. After a millennium of madness, she seeks to repent for her sins and destroy those she created.

SQUIRE . . . Short, surly, a hobgoblin who walks in shadows.

More praise for the novels of the Menagerie

"Fast, fabulous, and thrilling."
—Tim Lebbon, author of *Dusk* and *Berserk*

"Rich, inventive stuff, with a new surprise on every page."
—Jeff Mariotte, author of *Witch Season: Winter* and *Angel: The Premiere Edition*

continued . . .

Novels of the Menagerie

THE NIMBLE MAN
TEARS OF THE FURIES
STONES UNTURNED
CRASHING PARADISE

CRASHING PARADISE

A NOVEL OF THE MENAGERIE

CHRISTOPHER GOLDEN
AND
THOMAS E. SNIEGOSKI

ACE BOOKS, NEW YORK

THE BERKLEY PUBLISHING GROUP
Published by the Penguin Group
Penguin Group (USA) Inc.
375 Hudson Street, New York, New York 10014, USA
Penguin Group (Canada), 90 Eglinton Avenue East, Suite 700, Toronto, Ontario M4P 2Y3, Canada
(a division of Pearson Penguin Canada Inc.)
Penguin Books Ltd., 80 Strand, London WC2R 0RL, England
Penguin Group Ireland, 25 St. Stephen's Green, Dublin 2, Ireland (a division of Penguin Books Ltd.)
Penguin Group (Australia), 250 Camberwell Road, Camberwell, Victoria 3124, Australia
(a division of Pearson Australia Group Pty. Ltd.)
Penguin Books India Pvt. Ltd., 11 Community Centre, Panchsheel Park, New Delhi—110 017, India
Penguin Group (NZ), 67 Apollo Drive, Rosedale, North Shore 0745, Auckland, New Zealand
(a division of Pearson New Zealand Ltd.)
Penguin Books (South Africa) (Pty.) Ltd., 24 Sturdee Avenue, Rosebank, Johannesburg 2196,
South Africa

Penguin Books Ltd., Registered Offices: 80 Strand, London WC2R 0RL, England

This is a work of fiction. Names, characters, places, and incidents either are the product of the authors' imaginations or are used fictitiously, and any resemblance to actual persons, living or dead, business establishments, events, or locales is entirely coincidental. The publisher does not have any control over and does not assume any responsibility for author or third-party websites or their content.

CRASHING PARADISE: A NOVEL OF THE MENAGERIE

An Ace Book / published by arrangement with the authors

PRINTING HISTORY
Ace mass-market edition / September 2007

Copyright © 2007 by Daring Greatly Corporation and Thomas E. Sniegoski.
Cover art by Christian McGrath. Cover design by Judith Lagerman.
Interior text design by Kristin del Rosario.

The Edgar® name is a registered service mark of the Mystery Writers of America, Inc.

ISBN: 978-0-441-01532-0

ACE
Ace Books are published by The Berkley Publishing Group,
a division of Penguin Group (USA) Inc.,
375 Hudson Street, New York, New York 10014.
ACE and the "A" design are trademarks belonging to Penguin Group (USA) Inc.

PRINTED IN THE UNITED STATES OF AMERICA

10 9 8 7 6 5 4 3 2 1

CRASHING PARADISE

A NOVEL OF THE MENAGERIE

PROLOGUE

THE demon Abaddon crouched, unseen, on the edge of a rooftop in the city of Basra and watched hatred blossom in the street below. The dirt road baked in the sun, the air shimmered with heat, and shouts echoed across buildings where no one dared come to the window. Curiosity was not worth their lives.

Two Jeeps and a delivery truck sat in the street, engines chuffing like panting dogs, idling, ready to flee. Three stripped-down motorcycles buzzed at the intersections nearby, riders standing sentinel, watching for any who might try to interfere. The demon knew that none would dare.

A handful of people scattered away from the Shiite mosque, moving swiftly along the dusty streets or into the darkened doorways of nearby buildings. They tried to be as unobtrusive as possible, like rats scurrying back to the sewers.

Abaddon smiled.

Their vehicles idling, twenty-two Sunni men ran toward the mosque, carrying an arsenal of assorted weapons. The demon saw assault rifles, grenade launchers, and antitank guns. The men wore ordinary clothes, many with an ironic Western influence. But they all had their heads covered in hijabs—some drab and filthy, others bright and clean and made from pretty fabrics—their scarves pulled across their faces.

Half of them took up position in front of the building, even as the others split up and ran along both sides, surrounding the place. The mosque had stood in that spot nearly a thousand years and, in a city leached of hope, its golden dome remained a beacon.

One of the Sunnis stepped forward and barked orders. He had a blunt, ugly assault rifle slung across his shoulder, its barrel clutched in his left hand. With his right, he gestured toward the front line of men. The grenade launchers remained shouldered, but the rest lowered their weapons and pulled the triggers. Staccato bursts of gunfire filled the air, echoing off every wall along the street. Bullets riddled the mosque, puncturing daylight into the shadows within.

Plumes of dust rose and drifted listlessly in the sweltering heat. There was no wind to carry it away.

Again the Sunni leader, whose hijab appeared to be a red-and-white-checked dishcloth, barked instructions. His men took up the shouting. More bullets were fired, but in short bursts. Time was of the essence now.

The leader signaled with his hand, and half a dozen of the mob ran up to the door. The two in the front fired several bursts at the door, then they kicked it open, wood splintering loudly.

Moments later they returned, propelling two staggering men before them. One was a young man, barely more than a boy, a head shorter than the two thugs who ran him out through the door, holding on to his arms. The other was a tall, thin, bearded man, who screamed and gesticulated wildly, calling them all pigs and devils.

Abaddon smiled, recognizing him. The man was the highest-ranking Shia cleric in the city.

The Sunni in the red-and-white-checked hijab marched over to the screaming cleric and the frightened boy. His men held the two Shiites as he bent to whisper something to the cleric.

The holy man fell silent.

The Sunni leader turned his assault rifle around and smashed the butt into the young Shia boy's temple. The young one crumpled to the ground, dangling in the grip of the two Sunnis who still held him. At a gesture from their leader, the men dragged the young man back through the door of the mosque. They were lost in the shadows within only a few moments before emerging without him.

The cleric began to scream again.

On the roof ledge across the street, the demon Abaddon laughed softly. He had expected a show today, and he was not disappointed.

A soft whisper reached him on the motionless air. The demon turned his heavy, horned head and looked up into the sun. Silhouetted there he saw a dark, slender figure descending upon white-feathered wings that seemed to spread across the sky.

A moment later, when the angel Jophiel alighted beside him, the wings faded like a mirage, shimmering away on the heat of the desert city. The angel wore a long, elegant, black silk jacket over an untucked white shirt, more L.A. than Iraq.

"All right, Abaddon. I've come," Jophiel said, golden eyes gleaming. His perfect, androgynous features were framed by ringlets of black hair. The angel personified beauty the way Abaddon did ugliness. Appearances could be deceiving. They both desired the same thing.

Survival.

"What are we here for?" the angel asked, one eyebrow raised. "We've already established that the Garden Gate is not in Iraq. The theologians may speak all they like about the place where the Tigris and Euphrates meet, but it isn't here."

He brushed at the sleeves of his jacket, as though the dust of Basra would dare to touch his person.

Abaddon smiled. "We're here on a recruiting mission. I thought you should observe the latest candidate to add to our little troupe."

Jophiel glanced down at the men in the street, a dubious scowl on his perfect features. The Sunnis who had taken up position around the mosque were coming back now. At a signal from their leader, two of the men ran into the ancient holy place carrying small, dirty knapsacks.

A moment later, they emerged empty-handed. No one else had come out of the building. The Sunni leader barked orders, and all of the men began to run back to their vehicles, climbing into the back of the truck and into the Jeeps, the barrels of their weapons jutting out.

The two who held the cleric dragged him, screaming, toward the truck. The leader strode beside them in his red-and-white-checked hijab. The cleric continued to scream, even as the men forcibly turned him to face the mosque.

The Sunni leader spit in the cleric's face even as the man cursed him. The two armed men—faces still hidden; always hidden—drove him to his knees, where the leader kicked him once in the side.

Choking on dust and his own screams, the cleric vomited in the street.

Then the mosque exploded.

Abaddon felt Jophiel flinch beside him, and grinned. The force of the blast was mostly absorbed by the ancient walls, which burst outward, rubble tumbling into the street. The roof collapsed, and in moments, through the rising dust, all that could be seen were jagged teeth of still-standing wall, the ruins of the place.

In the cloud of dust and dirt that swirled like fog around the wreckage, the Shia cleric screamed to his god and sobbed. He turned and railed at the man who had led those responsible. The Sunnis let him go, and he started to rise.

The leader leveled his assault rifle at the cleric and pulled the trigger; a short burst that ripped the man's head apart in a spray of blood, bone, and brain. His corpse slumped into the dust.

"What do you think?" the demon asked.

Jophiel sniffed. "Him? Vicious or not, he's just a man."

Abaddon glanced at the angel and saw the doubt in those golden eyes. "Is he? I think not. These men came in vengeance, today, for the destruction yesterday of one of their own mosques and the murder of seventeen men, women, and children, by a Shia militia squad. The cleric who was just killed? He was said to have led that attack."

The angel tilted his head in birdlike curiosity. "He didn't?"

The demon smiled and shifted, black wings shushing against his back, hooves crumbling the ledge beneath him. He pointed one long, red-black talon at the Sunni leader below, his red-and-white hijab still visible in the rising cloud of dust that roiled off the destroyed mosque.

Through that fog, the engines of the motorcycles whined as their riders drove off. The Jeeps rumbled away as well.

The truck waited for the Sunni leader; but he strode away from them, climbing over the rubble of the mosque, disappearing into the dust and debris.

But just as the angel and the demon could not be seen by anyone in the city, simply by choosing not to be visible, so could they make out the figure that picked its way among the ruin of the mosque.

"Yesterday," Abaddon said, "*he* was the cleric. Or so he appeared."

Engines roared, and shouts were raised in the distance. The police coming, Abaddon knew. Now that the trouble was over, they at least had to create the appearance of having responded to this fresh horror.

"What are you talking about?" Jophiel demanded.

"We have gathered several useful allies, old friend," the demon said, gazing down with admiration. "But none who shall prove quite so useful as this one. Watch."

As the angel complied, the figure moving through the dust and rubble emerged. But the red-and-white hijab was gone, replaced by a billowing, black abaya that covered the entire body. Yet the clothing was not all that had changed. Despite only the eyes being visible, the shape beneath the abaya made it obvious that this much smaller figure was a woman.

Jophiel narrowed his golden eyes. His exquisite face took on a cruel edge, and his lips turned up in a smile. "That was not simply a change of clothing."

"No. It wasn't," the demon replied.

"You cannot mean—"

Abaddon laughed. "Oh, yes. The Clay of God, Jophiel."

The angel paused a moment, then his upper body moved in an almost sensual shudder, and white wings unfurled so wide that they blocked out the light of the sun.

"Well, then, we ought to have a talk with him, don't you think?"

The demon nodded, black wings unfolding with a leathery slither. "Indeed. I have a feeling that the Clay may be the most vital of our allies. Once we find the Garden Gate, all we'll need is the key."

Jophiel laughed as they both took flight and began to follow the black-sheathed Iraqi woman across the ravaged city of Basra, invisible to all eyes below.

"The key is the easy part," the angel said. "We know just where to find her."

1

ARTHUR Conan Doyle stood upon the ancient, chalk white wall encircling the Croatian city of Dubrovnik, gazing out over the peaceful calm of the Adriatic Sea and marveling at the calmness of it all.

He could have stood there for hours, soaking in the beauty of the turquoise waters, growing a deeper, darker shade of blue as the sun began to set, using every distraction that he could find to avoid dwelling on the imminent danger that threatened the existence, not only of this beautiful place, but of the entire world.

And all of the worlds beyond it.

The Devourer was coming; drawn to the life, vitality, and magic of the world like a shark to blood. *But its hunger will not end there,* Conan Doyle reminded himself, looking up into a cloudless, robin's egg blue sky—imagining the skies on hundreds of other planes of existence at that very moment, each of them threatened by the inexorable approach of the Demogorgon.

A lesser man would have given in by now, accepting his fate—the fate of his world—for it was written that nothing could repel the hunger of the Devourer once it had fixed its attention upon a particular prey. But Arthur Conan Doyle had never allowed himself the luxury of accepting fate, not even when death had come for him.

A flurry of movement drew his eyes from the deceptive tranquility of the view, and Conan Doyle looked down to see that a small bird had alighted upon the wall, looking up at him with a quizzical tilt of its head.

"We're ready for you, Arthur," said a familiar voice that issued from the bird's open beak.

Momentarily startled, he scrutinized the tiny creature. It wasn't a thing of flesh and blood but a complex, mechanical device, designed to be almost as real as the actual thing. It appeared that Velimir—the ancient monk who had helped him organize this evening's congregation—had become even more adept with his hobby since the last time the two had met.

The artificial songbird's eyes flashed briefly before it took flight, the mechanism's magical power source giving it the appearance of life. Conan Doyle followed its path, walking toward the steps that would take him down from the great wall encircling Dubrovnik into the city streets.

They're ready for me, Conan Doyle mused. *As I am for them.*

It had taken Velimir close to a month to put together this conference at Conan Doyle's request, and he did not want to keep those who had answered the invitation waiting.

At the foot of the stairs stood an aged and hunched figure, wearing the dark brown, hooded garment of his religious order. Velimir leaned on a cane carved from the gnarled branch of some ancient tree. Conan Doyle knew that his lover, Ceridwen, could have told him the name of the tree from which it had come in any number of ancient tongues. He missed his Princess of Faerie, longed to hold her lithe and powerful body tightly in his arms. In her, Conan Doyle found the strength to go on—the strength to fight—even when things looked hopeless.

She made it all worth fighting for.

"I wasn't about to walk up there to get you," Velimir Dragoslava said, his accent thick, a friendly smile upon his lined face as he pulled back his hood. The mechanical bird fluttered down and perched on the old man's shoulder, trilling happily.

"I wouldn't expect you to, my friend," Conan Doyle said, reaching the bottom. "I was just gathering my thoughts before the conference."

Velimir nodded, reaching up to take the mechanical bird from his shoulder. "Do you like her?"

"Very impressive." Conan Doyle gently stroked the head of the delicate machine. Then the old man placed it in a leather pouch that he wore tied to his waist. "For a moment, I believed it was real."

"The next best thing," the wizened monk said. "An actual bird's life energies provide the source of power, giving it the semblance of life."

The two started to walk across the Placa, the city's main promenade. Conan Doyle had not been to Dubrovnik in years, but he had heard much about the civil war that had raged in Croatia less than twenty years before. Bombs had fallen upon the ancient, beautiful city—a place so lovely that it might well have been the capital of some Faerie nation— but there seemed no trace of those ugly days of war. The Placa and, indeed, all of the alleys and streets of the old city that meandered within those ancient, white walls, were clean and neat. The people smiled and chatted happily, and the storefronts gleamed with fresh paint and new windows.

Velimir did have some trouble with the cobblestone streets, however. The cane was useful, but the old monk was unsteady on his feet, and his cane might catch upon the odd, uneven stone. Conan Doyle held his arm as they walked slowly past the exquisitely elaborate Onofrio Fountain on their way to the fourteenth-century Franciscan monastery that would play host to this evening's congregation. On Conan Doyle's behalf, Velimir had summoned representatives from numerous realms, including some of this world's most powerful magical beings—and many from worlds beyond.

"I have been thinking, Arthur, that someday, in the not-too-distant future, I may create a similar device—fashioned after a man—to contain my own life energies. Such a mechanism would enable me to perform my function as mediator many years after this rotting carcass has fed the worms," Velimir said.

Conan Doyle glanced at his old friend, his suspicions about the advancements in the man's hobby suddenly sharpened.

"Perhaps, then, I could be of service to you, and to the world in its approaching time of need," the monk added.

The implication of the old man's statement was startling. Just how close had Velimir come to perfecting his mechanized creatures? He wished they could continue the conversation, but there were more pressing matters to attend to.

The church bell tolled six o'clock. Visiting hours were over, and a steady flow of tourists streamed from the monastery as Conan Doyle steered his friend through the foot traffic to enter the ancient structure. A security guard standing just inside the door took note of their arrival but largely ignored them as he continued to usher visitors from the building.

Conan Doyle had been here only once before. He could recall with great clarity the conference that had been called after the mysterious disappearance of Sweetblood the Mage. When a magic user, especially one as powerful as Lorenzo Sanguedolce, went missing, everyone within the supernatural community took note. During that last congregation, those summoned had been more concerned with filling the sudden power vacuum left by the archmage's vanishing than in discovering where he had gone. Conan Doyle hoped that this conference would be more productive.

Velimir led him deeper into the building, toward an elaborate reading room whose walls were covered in bookcases. Upon those shelves sat ancient, leather-bound manuscripts. Conan Doyle recalled that this part of the monastery had been destroyed by fire after an earthquake in the late seventeenth century, and painstakingly refurbished by a friar of the same secret Franciscan order as Velimir.

The holy man did excellent work.

The old monk pulled away from Conan Doyle's supportive grasp. Moving through the library, he eyed every corner of the large room, making certain that all of the day's visitors had vacated the premises. The mage followed the old man as he went to the rear of the room and stopped in front of a section of bookcase. The venerable monk reached out, removed a particularly fat volume, and set it down upon a nearby table. From the same leather pouch where he had stored his mechanical bird, Velimir produced a long, golden key, and inserted it into the lock located behind the ancient text.

He turned the key sharply to the left and stepped back as a section of bookcase slowly swung open to reveal a stone staircase descending beneath the monastery.

Gesturing with his cane, Velimir motioned for Conan Doyle to precede him. The stairway was lit with lanterns that burned with an eerie, pulsing incandescence. The last time he had been here, flaming torches had lit the way.

The section of wall swung closed behind them with the sound of stone grinding against stone. Velimir followed Conan Doyle down, the tip of his wooden cane striking each stone step as he carefully descended.

The staircase ended in an antechamber. Twin wooden doors, weathered with age, led into a much larger chamber beyond, where Conan Doyle would be addressing those who had gathered at his behest.

Silently, the two men entered the chamber. The old man went to a wooden chest resting on a high table in the corner and, using the same golden key, opened it. He reached into the box, withdrawing a mask and placing it on his face.

The mask was of two halves—two visages. One half depicted the common man—the unaware—the other half almost animal in its depiction of the unnatural. This half represented those touched by the paranormal and forever changed by it, as well as those who were not human and had never been so.

Behind the mask, Velimir Dragoslava no longer existed. Now there was only the Mediator of the Franciscan Order of Conciliation. The Order had begun during the early fourteenth century and had been the first of the Church's orders to recognize the existence of the supernatural not as a threat, but as a force to be studied and accepted as part of God's grand design. The Mediator existed in both the human world and the supernatural world and acted as an arbiter over matters of concern to both.

"Are you ready, Arthur Conan Doyle?" the Mediator asked, his voice sounding completely different from Velimir's.

"I am."

The Mediator walked to the double wooden doors, no longer needing the help of a cane, and threw them wide, striding down a stretch of wooden planking and onto a circular dais in the center of a timeworn amphitheater.

Conan Doyle waited patiently in the doorway, his mind reviewing all that he wished to say.

"Brothers and sisters of the weird, I am the Mediator," the masked figure announced as he slowly turned on the circular platform, addressing all those who were present. "I have summoned you here at the request of one of your own, to listen to his pleas for solidarity in this time when a terrible shadow falls upon us all."

The Mediator paused.

"Will you hear his words?"

From where he was standing, Conan Doyle could not see the number of those who had answered his call, but he heard their answer to the Mediator, their voices joined as one as they agreed to listen.

"Come forward, Arthur Conan Doyle, and address this conference where all are equals."

Adjusting the fit of his tweed jacket, Conan Doyle marched down the walkway. The Mediator stepped to one side, allowing him to stand in the center of the stage. At first he said nothing, gazing about the room, studying the faces of those who sat on the wooden benches surrounding the dais, committing those in attendance to memory, as well as marking the absence of those who hadn't bother to attend.

He wasn't at all surprised that Sanguedolce was nowhere to be found. Since his reemergence into the world, Sweetblood had pursued his own ends secretively and to the detriment of others. Yet Conan Doyle was astonished to see the grotesque visage of Nigel Gull staring up at him from the back of the theater, eyes afire with an unnatural hatred. He and Gull had learned sorcery together under the tutelage of Sanguedolce himself, but his former friend had chosen darker paths than Conan Doyle, and their mutual admiration had turned ugly. But tonight all of their history would be put aside. There were other matters—*matters of grave importance*—that eclipsed their hateful feelings, and he was glad to see that Nigel had the good sense to understand this as well.

Conan Doyle acknowledged the hideously disfigured master sorcerer with a barely perceptible nod. Gull responded by wiping a dribble of saliva away from the drooping corner of his malformed mouth. Perhaps the expression upon that horselike countenance was some kind of smile, but it was impossible to tell.

The others in attendance met his gaze with a mixture of disinterest, fear, hate, and curiosity. Most them he knew by name—practitioners of all the mystical arts, good and evil, but some were new to him, and he made it a point to remember their faces. The unnaturals, those in attendance who were not human, clumped together on one side of the auditorium, enshrouded in a shifting black shadow of their own creation, and he paid them the same level of respect as given to all others.

Conan Doyle stroked his graying mustache, then cleared his throat and began. "I'm sure the majority of you are fully aware of the reason why this convocation was called." His eyes touched those of each member of his audience. "One can sense it in the air, in the ground beneath our feet. It is the soft rumbling of an approaching storm off in the distance—miles away—but still coming."

He paused.

"Make no mistake about that." He put a hand to his ear as if listening to something in the distance.

"The storm is coming."

THE conference had gone exactly as he had expected.

Even though most in attendance could sense the abnormal shifts in the ether—see the increased levels of violent, paranormal activity—the majority still did not want to believe.

Conan Doyle paused on his way down a narrow, winding street, at last on his way to the house he had rented outside the walls of the old city, up on the high, mountainside road overlooking the harbor. He had been walking since the end of the conference, replaying the evening in his mind.

A night bird screeched as he reached into the inside coat pocket of his tweed jacket to retrieve his traveling pipe. Much smaller and less cumbersome than his Meerschaum, Conan Doyle often brought the dark Briarwood along when away from home. He stuffed the wooden pipe bowl full of an

English tobacco blend from a small leather pouch, then muttered a simple spell of conflagration, igniting the tobacco
with the tip of his index finger. Smoking the pipe helped him
to think, and even though the conference was over, there was
still much to dwell upon.

He continued on his way, pipe smoke billowing, the sweet
smell of his favorite tobacco stimulating his thoughts.

They had wanted to know what he intended to do if the
threat of the Demogorgon became reality. He'd wanted to
laugh, but it was too damned pathetic. There he was, the
caller of the conference, and still they dallied with the possibility that he could be wrong. He had explained that he, and
his agents—his Menagerie—could only do so much, that
they all would have to contribute to the effort if they were
going to turn away the inevitable threat. The convocation
hadn't cared for that in the least.

Conan Doyle nibbled upon the stem of his pipe, anger
flaring as it had then. In his mind's eye he could still see their
blank stares and emotionless faces. Few of them truly com-
prehended the magnitude of his warning. Gradually, they had
all risen from their seats, ready to return to the lives they had
left, as if nothing had changed.

He had screamed at them, then, screamed that whether
they stood on the side of righteousness or shadow, they must
unite against the coming threat. The Demogorgon's approach
was not some wild theory. It was fact, supported by the words
and actions of Sweetblood himself. Yet each of those who attended had been the object of fear themselves, once upon
a time, and could not conceive of something that could destroy them all. They refused to imagine something so terrifying that even the terrors and nightmares of a hundred worlds
ought to be afraid.

Only then, as they listened to the fury in his voice, perhaps seeing a spark of madness caused by the beginnings of
desperation, had they begun to listen. At last his apocalyptic
warnings began to permeate their narrow minds. Having finally gotten their attention, he had stressed that if the earthly
realm were to fall, there would be nothing to stop the other
dimensions from falling as well. The Demogorgon would run
roughshod over the many realms that branched away from

the human world—what many other peoples called the Blight. Their lands would fall like dominoes.

A sharp chill rode up his spine, making the hair at the back of his neck stand painfully on end. Its icy prickle sent a spasm through his body. Conan Doyle sucked upon his pipe, attempting to calm his troubled state, but saw that the tobacco had been extinguished.

Only then did he realize how incredibly cold it had become.

Unnaturally cold.

He tensed, a spell of defense ready at the tip of his tongue. He stood beside a small café, closed for hours now. On the other side of the narrow street was a florist, also shut up tight for the night. A growing sound, like the rushing roar of the tide, seemed to come from all around him, but it wasn't the nearby Adriatic that he was hearing.

It was screams—the wailing cries of frightened children—calling out from their beds, clasped in the grip of terror.

Above the sounds of the children's cries, a raspy chuckle drifted on the freezing night air.

"Show yourself!" Conan Doyle commanded, planting his feet, weaving a defensive spell. A rush of magical energy flowed through his body and down his arms to crackle from the tips of his fingers.

"The door flew open, in he ran," whispered the dry, singsong voice. "The great long Red-legged Scissor-man . . ."

Conan Doyle started at the mention. How long had it been since last he'd heard that foul bogeyman's name?

The Red-legged Scissor-man had been one of the first violent, supernatural threats he had ever faced, back in the winter of 1922. He had been summoned to London's Infant Orphan Asylum by a former medical associate who had shared his interest in the paranormal. The man had requested his aid in investigating what had appeared to be an epidemic of self-mutilations—the children were cutting off their own thumbs as they slept.

The memory of his tour of the orphanage rushed back to him with startling clarity, as if it had happened only yesterday. He recalled the look of absolute terror on the suffering

children's faces, most of them in a strange, fear-induced catatonia. Only one little boy—*Timothy*—had had the strength,
and bravery, to speak the name of the creature that had
haunted his sleepless nights, and the nights of all the other
children for close to a month.

The Red-legged Scissor-man.

Conan Doyle watched as a lantern made from the skull of
an adolescent emerged from a nearby pool of ebony shadow,
clutched in the hand of a creature he had believed banished
from this plane of reality over eighty years ago.

"Snip! Snip! Snip! The scissors go," the hideous creature
sang as it languidly unspooled from the patch of darkness,
swinging the lantern from side to side. "And Conrad cries,
Oh! Oh! Oh!"

The Scissor-man was tall, his body clad in a filthy waistcoat with tails, his naked lower body stained red with the
dried blood of innocents. Around his long, emaciated neck he
wore an elaborate necklace made with the thumbs of his
young victims. In the other spidery hand, clad in a black
leather glove stiff with gore, he held a pair of the largest scissors Conan Doyle had ever seen. The shears were nearly
black with blood. The grotesque figure cut the air, doing a
strange little dance as it continued its song.

"Snip! Snip! Snip! They go so fast, that both his thumbs
are off at last."

Conan Doyle raised his hand, afire with preternatural
power. The bogey shied away from the purity of Conan
Doyle's magical light, jerking back so quickly that it dropped
the skull lantern. It shattered in the street, extinguishing its
flame. The Scissor-man's flesh was the gray of the recently
deceased, its eye sockets empty except for the squirming lar-
vae of insects. As it recoiled from the radiating light in the
mage's hand, its waistcoat swung open to reveal an exposed
rib cage, a wild-eyed crow fluttering frantically within the
confines of human bone.

"Oh, Doyle, is that anyway to treat a mate you've not seen
in such a while?" the creature asked with a clucking chuckle,
shielding its face from the burning light.

"I admit I am surprised to see you, beast," Conan Doyle
said calmly. The mage tapped the tobacco from his pipe on

the side of the building, returning it to safety inside his jacket. He then moved toward the cowering Scissor-man. "If I remember correctly, you were banished to a pocket dimension, with no chance of escape, never to bother anyone, or anything, ever again—at least that is what I believed."

The mage extended his arm farther, dispelling the pool of shadow the bogey used to travel in a stinking, oily cloud. The Scissor-man attempted to pull the tails of its stained coat over the exposed areas of its foul flesh to protect it from the burning glare of his magic.

"So how is it that you confront me here and now?"

Conan Doyle was perplexed at the appearance of this creature, beginning to wonder if the Scissor-man had somehow responded to the invitation for conference. *But that's absurd,* he thought. A creature such as the one cowering beneath him had no concept of anything other than its own perverse needs.

But, then, why is it here? And how has it managed to escape from the prison I made for it?

He didn't have time for this. His frustration flared, and he touched a burning finger to the bald head of the cowering Scissor-man.

"Tell me," he demanded.

The foul beast's body began to tremble with what Conan Doyle at first thought was a mixture of fear and pain. Then he realized that wasn't the case at all—the Scissor-man was laughing, turning its face and body into the searing light thrown by Conan Doyle's hand, with no adverse effect.

No effect at all.

"Snip! Snip! Snip!" the creature screeched, lunging toward his outstretched hand, the bloodstained shears opened like the beak of some predatory bird.

The scissors closed, severing Conan Doyle's index finger. It fell to the street, blood dripping down between the stones.

"They go so fast," the Scissor-man hissed, snatching up Conan Doyle's finger and shoving it into its exposed rib cage for the crow to greedily consume.

Clutching the injured hand to his chest, the mage bellowed his fury. A wave of magic exploded from the fingertips of his uninjured hand, engulfing the bogey and hurling him, screaming, against wall of the flower shop.

"Damn you!" Conan Doyle roared, raising his bloody hand to his face, staring at the bleeding stump of his finger in shock. *How is this possible?* his mind raced. *Has my brain become so obsessed with the Demogorgon that even this childhood bogeyman can get the better of me?*

He had expected to see the burning body of the Red-legged Scissor-man stretched out upon the cobblestones, but it was not to be. The beast still stood, looking down at its bloodstained legs, nearly as surprised as Conan Doyle.

"Seems that either my benefactors have refashioned me of sterner stuff," the nightmare-stalker said with a growing smile of jagged, jack-o'-lantern teeth, "or the passing years have made you far weaker."

Despite the blinding ache in his hand, Conan Doyle set his jaw against the pain and began to summon a spell that would show the beastie just how "weak" he was, when he heard footfalls approaching. He cursed beneath his breath. As if he didn't have enough to concern himself with at the moment, now he had to worry about some unknowing pedestrian blundering into the midst of their battle.

"Stay back," he cried, and the lone figure hobbling down the street came to an abrupt stop.

"Oh, I'm sorry," an all-too-familiar voice responded. The twisted form of Nigel Gull slowly emerged from the shadows.

"I didn't mean to interrupt."

Conan Doyle stared at him warily. "I should have known you'd have something to do with this."

But then the Scissor-man was on the move, bloody shears raised to strike.

"Arthur, what's going on?" Gull asked, putting on an air of surprise.

"Spare me, Nigel," Conan Doyle said.

With a twist of his fingers and a flick of his wrist, he sent forth arcs of cracking, blue magic that skewered the advancing bogey—but again, did not destroy it. The Scissor-man shrieked, wisps of oily black smoke trailing from the empty caverns of its eye sockets as the maggots writhing within them began to burn.

"I don't understand, Arthur," Gull said, his twisted frame stepping closer. He cocked his head and studied the melee unfolding on the street, the blood and magic spattering ancient stones. "Have I done something to offend?"

Conan Doyle ignored him a moment, though his nostrils flared with anger. He had to focus on the Scissor-man. The mage reached deep within himself and drew upon the magic that churned at the core of his being, increasing the deadly power of the spells he cast at the Scissor-man. Its body twisted, wracked with pain and sorcery, but still it did not fall. There was no way that this beast should have been able to withstand a casting of this magnitude, and it made Conan Doyle seethe.

"Your very presence offends, Nigel," the archmage said, not even bothering to hide his anger and disgust from the disfigured sorcerer. "I was willing to look past all that—past our history—to come together in the spirit of unity to defeat a common foe, but I guess I was foolish to think *you* were capable of such camaraderie."

The Scissor-man let out an unearthly howl, attempting to use the blades of its shears to deflect the arcs of humming, preternatural force that skewered its body.

The scissors closed upon the bolts of magical force, causing an explosion that repelled both Conan Doyle and the bloodstained bogey, the crow cawing and fluttering about inside its rib cage.

Spots of color danced before the mage's eyes as he picked himself up from the street to face his attacker again.

"I haven't a clue what you're going on about," Gull said indignantly, even closer now, and Conan Doyle fought the urge to begin an attack against him as well. As long as Gull did not assault him directly, he would not open up a second front to this battle.

"Are you suggesting that I have something to do with . . ." Gull looked toward the Scissor-man, who was now in the process of picking up hundreds of thumbs that littered the street. In the ruckus with Conan Doyle, its necklace had broken.

"Are those thumbs?" Gull asked.

"You bloody well know what they are," Conan Doyle spat, clutching his injured hand to his chest.

Gull was silent as Conan Doyle advanced toward the first of his foes. The Scissor-man was beside himself, muttering names—*the previous owners of the liberated digits,* Conan Doyle guessed—as it attempted to pick them all up.

"James, Carolyn, Bartholomew, Richard, sweet little Betsy," the Scissor-man whined, holding his treasures against its chest.

Conan Doyle hovered over the bogey, the power of the magic he now mustered radiating from his body, stirring the very elements around him. His silver hair moved atop his head as if disturbed by a strong wind.

"I've had just about enough of this, monster," the archmage proclaimed in a thunderous voice.

A blast of green fire knocked the collected thumbs from the Scissor-man's hands.

"You will tell me how you came to be free," Conan Doyle said, his patience at its lowest ebb. "And then you will tell me of the benefactors you spoke of—who they are, and why they would use you to do me harm."

Infuriated by this indignity, the Scissor-man sprang up, its large shears ready yet again to sample Conan Doyle's flesh, but the mage was ready, or at least he believed he was.

The Scissor-man struck the barrier of magic that surrounded the mage and became stuck like a fly within a spider's web. The creature thrashed wildly, its body attacked by the magic Conan Doyle had conjured to protect himself. It cried out in pain and frustration, its frantic movements only making its agony all the more pronounced.

"Tell me what I want to know, and I'll make it stop," Conan Doyle said calmly. "Who is responsible for this attack?"

The Scissor-man began to laugh horribly. "They know you oh so well," the monster chortled, its voice trembling in pain. "But you have not a clue as to who they are."

"Tell me!" the mage demanded, increasing the level of power within the protective aura, inflicting even more hurt upon the captured bogey.

The Scissor-man screamed. "They spoke to me from the shadows of my captivity." The nightmare-beast thrashed in the grip of the power that trapped it. "Promising that I could hurt you . . . that I could see your pain."

"Who? Are? They?" Conan Doyle growled through gritted teeth.

"Angels of mercy, they were," the Scissor-man replied.

It shifted its position and thrust its thirsty shears—suddenly unhindered by the power of the mage's conjuration—toward the soft flesh of his throat.

This is not possible.

Before the archmage could react, there came a sudden arc of blistering magic that tore the Scissor-man from Conan Doyle's web.

"No!" the Scissor-man shrieked, struggling to be free of this new sorcery.

Conan Doyle spun to find Gull standing there, manipulating the forces that now held the monster aloft.

"You actually believe I would ally myself with *this*?" the deformed mage asked, the hint of annoyance in his voice.

The Scissor-man's shears began to work on Gull's magic, cutting it away. Conan Doyle said nothing as Gull raised a gnarled hand and sketched at the air as ancient words, dripping with power, left his distorted mouth.

The Scissor-man barely had time to scream as its body was suddenly assaulted from all sides. Its limbs were broken before Gull's magic wrenched them from their sockets. The savagery intensified, the nightmare bogey torn into pieces that momentarily hovered in the air before dropping wetly to the stone street.

"You don't know me as well as you think you do," Gull sneered. He wiped his still-sparking hands on the front of his dark suit, turned on his heel, and limped off into the darkness.

The threat averted for now, Conan Doyle breathed in the cool night air and attempted to isolate the pain of his hand. He walked toward the haphazardly discarded remains of his attacker, eyes scanning each and every bloody piece. The bogey had already started to decay, its rotting flesh beginning to smoke, smolder, and stink.

Conan Doyle was looking for the bird—the body of the crow that had flapped its wings wildly within the cage of the Scissor-man's ribs.

He needed to retrieve his finger.

2

THE Equinox Festival organizers had set up on a vast, open sprawl of scrub brush, skeletal trees, and red clay earth a few miles outside Sedona, Arizona. To the east and north were ragged cliffs of layered rock, red-orange at the bottom and white at the top. In the early afternoon, the sun shone on those cliffs, and the colors were so vivid that they seemed almost unreal, as though they came from some otherworldly place.

To Katie Matthews, their beauty was half the reason to hold the Spring Equinox Festival here. The landscape had a rugged beauty, unlike the lushness she knew characterized so much of Faerie, but it was that surrealness that made the Red Rock Secret Mountain Wilderness outside Sedona the perfect place for the fest.

There's magic here.

Even hardened skeptics who came to visit this place went away with their cynicism challenged, quieted. Katie made the trip once a year, leaving her bookstore in Cambridge, Massachusetts, in the hands of two friends who'd been working for her part-time since she had first opened the store. The Equinox Festival filled her with such a sense of peace and wonder and magic that it restored her spirit for another year.

Yet it was more than a simple pilgrimage. It was also the one time every year that the Daughters of Ceridwen gathered. Katie had followed the folktales of Ceridwen for almost twenty years—since even before she had opened the bookstore—but it had only been when she'd joined the rest of the world on the Internet that she'd discovered others also were fascinated by the stories of the Princess of the Fey, an elemental sorceress who had fought in the Twilight Wars and saved many worlds from darkness. Most people—even the modern pagans and other believers in Faerie—paid little attention to recent folktales about the Fey.

As if something has to be old to be true, Katie thought, smiling at the narrow-mindedness of the idea. But there were women in the Daughters of Ceridwen—a group that had come together because of the Net—who had claimed to have met Ceridwen themselves, even some who claimed to have set foot in Faerie.

Katie's heart fluttered at the thought of visiting that fabled land, but it had not happened yet. However, she did share a secret with the other members of the group . . . Ceridwen was no folktale. Katie had met her, had seen her magic firsthand, had been astonished by her beauty. The sorceress seemed to dance on the air, even when she walked, and her eyes were a shade of purple unlike anything seen in the human world.

So even here, at the Equinox Festival, among the wiccans and pagans and neo-druids, the Daughters of Ceridwen had their own magic—their own truth. They joined in the singing and the creation of art. Some of them went topless or nude and danced around evening bonfires there under the moon in the shadows of the red rocks, calling out to goddesses of fertility and nature and rebirth.

But much of their time was spent gathering together, apart from the several thousand others who had come for the festival. The Daughters of Ceridwen had their own prayers and rituals. There were nearly one hundred of them, and they had come from all over the world—teenagers and housewives, writers and ecology crusaders and artists and musicians, but also a handful of professional types, doctors and lawyers and a biologist from Geneva. Once a day, during the festival, they gathered to drink wine and laugh together and focus their positive energies on the elements and on spiritual support for Ceridwen and all her works.

Together, they practiced magic. It was small magic, certainly, creating a bit of elemental fire or a breeze where none had been. Several of the women, including an eighteen-year-old British girl called Seraph and Katie herself, could do somewhat more—they could sculpt things from the dirt and rock. Seraph had created a figure and made it move. Katie was better with fire.

Ceridwen herself had taught them these small magics. In the past year they had seen her more and more. She had entered the world, leaving Faerie behind for now. From time to time she spoke to them. They would see her face in the bark of a tree or the surface of a pond or the crackling fire in the hearth, and she would talk to them.

Katie was grateful for the other Daughters of Ceridwen. If not for them, she might have thought she was insane. Even the day when Ceridwen had come into her bookstore, traveling between Faerie and Earth through the pages of a book, had seemed afterward too much like the richest, most vivid of dreams to be real.

But it had been real, and she cherished it.

Now she sat outside the camper she shared with Arielle Pardue, a twenty-six-year-old woman from Phoenix. Katie had flown out to meet Ari, and the two had traveled north in Ari's camper. It was hot as hell inside, even with the windows open, but this time of year there was no reason to be inside the huge beast of a vehicle. The sun was warm, but the air was sweet and pleasantly warm and the breeze gentle. The camper had a canopy that unrolled from one side, and it was open now.

Katie sat in the shade of the camper with her journal open on her lap, recording the beauty of the gathering around her. She could see an older couple walking hand in hand, and a young, Asian woman painting a goddess portrait in blues and oranges, even as two men nearby were busy painting one another. From somewhere not far away, she smelled something delicious cooking. Guitar and flute music filled the air, and though she could not understand the words, she heard voices raised in song.

The journal felt good in her hands. It had been handmade by Guin Schiffman, another of the Daughters of Ceridwen. Guin was from Orcas Island, in Washington state. She cured and stretched the leather herself, and even made the leather strap that held it closed and hammered out the brass button the strap attached to.

She was also the most psychically sensitive woman in the group. Guin had never met Ceridwen in person, but the elemental had been in contact with her through ice and flame and wood more than any other of her human followers. It was Katie's theory that Guin had more than a little Fey blood in her family.

Maybe they all did.

A smile touched her lips as she wrote this in her journal, going further with her speculation that perhaps that was why they had been so drawn to Ceridwen, and she had attempted to help them learn a bit of elemental magic.

A pleasant spark lit in her heart. Katie loved the idea that there could be a bit of the Fey in her.

Someone called her name. She looked up from her journal to see Ari hurrying toward her, past a big tent that had been put together with bamboo posts and silk sheets of elegant colors, like something out of *Arabian Nights*. A trio of twenty-something wiccan women called out to Ari as she went by, and she gave a quick wave and hurried on.

A ripple of concern went through Katie. Ari nearly always had a smile on her pretty face—sometimes a happy, ready-to-dance kind of smile, and sometimes a sleepy, musing sort of smile—but at the moment she looked very serious.

Katie tied the leather strap over the brass button on her journal and stood up.

"Ari, what is it? Is something wrong?"

The younger woman did not slow down. She took Katie by the wrist and led her up the steps into the camper. Ari slipped the journal and pen from Katie's hands and set them on a table.

"What?" Katie demanded. "You're scaring me."

Ari tucked her blond hair behind her pixie ears, her blue eyes sparkling, and a kind of mad grin split her face. Her hands shook.

"Guin sent me to get you and spread the word," Ari said, practically giddy. "Everyone's supposed to gather on the top of the hill in half an hour. Oh, goddess, Katie . . . She's coming here to talk to us. Ceridwen's coming!"

•   •   •

THE air swirled around Ceridwen, caressing her with a gentle lover's touch. She clutched her rowan staff in her right hand and closed her eyes, letting the wind carry her forward. When she had returned to the human world, she had crafted a tenuous alliance with the elemental spirits of this place. Air, Earth, Water, and Fire—and all of the spirits that comprised the elements—were her allies when she walked the land of her birth. In Faerie, the elemental forces were still almost pure; primeval. But there was a reason the Fey called the human world "the Blight." Nature here was tainted.

At first, the elemental spirits in this world had been hesitant when she reached out to influence them. She could force them, but if they resisted, her sorcery would have been diminished at best, and dangerously volatile. But the elements of the Blight were tethered by ancient kinship with Faerie, and Ceridwen was an ally to nature.

The elements served her willingly.

Now those spirits carried her on a traveling wind she had summoned to transport her to the Arizona desert. Fire and ice danced on the wind as it whirled around her. Weightless, she slipped through a magical, elemental passage in the world. The wind in Boston delivered her into the grasp of the hot, Arizona breezes.

Her feet touched hardscrabble earth, and Ceridwen opened her eyes. A shudder of pleasure went through her as the living cyclone of elemental winds spun around her. Dust rose from the ground. The wind began to diminish so that she could see the shapes of figures gathered around her and a ridge of cliffs jutting up from the earth not far away. Her thin cotton dress clung to her body and swirled in all the hues of the ocean around her legs, then swayed gently as the wind dissipated.

The last of the dust her arrival had raised swept down off the hill on a breeze. Ceridwen touched the bottom of her rowan staff to the ground, and the traveling wind was gone. The top of the staff was a sphere of ice, within which danced a ball of fire.

All around her were gathered the women who called themselves Daughters of Ceridwen. Though she was young

compared to many of the Fey, the sorceress had been alive for
centuries. Still, how strange it was for her to have women
who appeared far older than she to call themselves her
daughters. Arthur had teased her about it many times, calling
her his "old thing." But it was gentle teasing, full of love. And
as she regarded the faces of the dozens of women gathered
around her atop that hill, she felt full of love and adoration,
both that which they gave her and that which she returned to
them.

Some of them were unfamiliar to her—women who had
devoted themselves to her but whom she had neither met in
person nor seen in a scrying pool. Others she had known for
many years, and they were precious to her. The tiny red-
haired Moya, from Edinburgh; the Canadians, Emmy and
Kiera, who had met because of their devotion to her, and recently had become lovers; young, willowy Seraph, from
Norwich, England; voluptuous Arielle, from Phoenix; Katie
Matthews, the bookseller from Boston. There were more than
ninety of them, all together, beautiful women of varied age
and shape and race. Their faces glowed with benevolent feeling, and they watched her expectantly.

Off to the left, behind two older women from Vermont,
stood a woman with dark ringlets of hair and freckles
splashed across her deeply tanned face. Unlike most of the
others, she seemed almost too shy to look up.

"Guinivere," Ceridwen said.

The psychic raised her eyes and smiled sheepishly. She
had become such an asset in a short amount of time. Sensitive
as she was—both to the human heart and to the elements—
Ceridwen had understood immediately how valuable she
could be. They had not met in person, but through scrying
pools and candle flames they had looked upon one another
and talked of magic and love and the future. Conan Doyle
had even forced Ceridwen to use the phone to call her several
times, though the lack of any spiritual connection in this
mode of communication had troubled her.

As she had with many of the other women who had devoted themselves to following Ceridwen's example, she had
given Guinivere guidance in learning small bits of elemental
sorcery. It was important that these women know how to tap

into nature, to offer their respect to those spirits, and thus earn their goodwill.

Ceridwen walked over to Guinivere. Seeing that the sorceress's eyes were focused on her, the others moved aside. Ceridwen brushed several dark ringlets away from her face and bent to kiss Guinivere on the forehead.

"Daughter," she said. "It is a great pleasure finally to meet you face-to-face. If all of your sisters truly wish to be of assistance to me—and to this world—in the difficult times to come, then you will have a significant role to play in that effort."

A murmur went through the gathered women. Moya stepped toward Ceridwen and bowed her head. "All of our faith is in you, majesty. Whatever help we can be, you've only to ask."

Many of the women nodded. Katie opened her hands and spread her arms.

"We're all here for you, Ceridwen. For the earth and the air, for the water and the flame."

In unison, they repeated the words. "For the earth and the air, for the water and the flame."

Ceridwen took a deep breath of the warm desert air, rich with the smells of the earth and clay. She glanced beyond the women at the thousands of people gathered on the land that spread out at the bottom of the hill for the Equinox Festival. Among the scrub brush they had created a tribe on the red earth, in front of the face of the red rock cliffs. Their flags fluttered in the breeze, and their songs filled the sky.

These people were the heart of the world.

The smile faded from Ceridwen's face. It filled her with joy to have the company of these women, but there was darkness on the horizon, and the news she carried was not at all pleasant.

"My friends," Ceridwen said, the warmth of the sun enfolding her. "Thank you for coming, and thank you for your faith in me and in the earth beneath your feet. Knowing that you would all be gathered here today, I felt compelled to come and speak with you. I wish I had come only to see and touch you, to share with you the hope and beauty of the equinox. But as many of you already know, even as we speak, whispers travel, and the worlds tremble with dreadful anticipation. A terrible power threatens your world, and my allies and I believe it represents a danger to all of the realms connected to the—"

She'd been about to call their world the Blight. Ceridwen tried to avoid using the term with these good women. They were among those who wished to alter the Earth for the better.

"To this plane of existence," she said.

"The Demogorgon," Katie Matthews said.

"Goddess," Emmy whispered, shuddering. Kiera put an arm around her and held her close.

Ceridwen nodded. "Yes, Katie. That's correct. Some of you are already aware of this and know what that could mean. Others are perhaps hearing the name for the very first time. Suffice it to say that the Demogorgon is called by many names, one of which is the Great Devourer. It exists, and it has turned its horrid attention upon this world.

"It is the equinox, when we celebrate the rebirth of spring, and fertility, and all of our hopes for the future. I am no different from any of you in that respect. I have my hopes for the future, just as you do. I love, and am loved in return. I have everything to lose.

"I tell you this not so that you will lose that hope, or so that you will cease your celebration. That would mean a catastrophic loss of faith. Instead, I want you to hold that hope close to your hearts in the coming days and months. It may be years before the Demogorgon arrives, but I fear we do not have that kind of time. When the Devourer comes, I and my allies will stand against it. Some of the most powerful mages and monsters in this world will defy the Demogorgon.

"On that day, will you stand with us?"

Arielle reached down and caught Katie's hand in her own, but she lifted her chin. "Of course we will, Ceridwen. You know we will."

A chorus of assent was raised. The benevolent smiles had gone from their faces, and the women nodded grimly.

Ceridwen turned to Guinivere, whose gaze seemed to be searching for something. "And what of you, Guin? Will you stand with me?"

The woman glanced away a moment before meeting Ceridwen's eyes. "You know that I'm devoted to you. It's just that this thing . . . it seems so huge. You're a sorceress, with all of the elements at your fingertips. What can we do against something like the Demogorgon? I can barely wrap my mind around the idea of something so terrible."

Ceridwen laid a comforting hand on Guin's shoulder. "What can you do?" She looked around at the women who had gathered on that hill to greet her and knew that all of them were thinking precisely the same thing. "Some of you have already begun to commune with this world's elemental spirits, to connect your hearts and souls to the natural forces of the Earth. Among you there are those with the potential for real magic. I will not say that you can perform the kind of sorcery that is possible in my world, but you can tap the power that is here. And with that magic, and the valiant hearts I know that you all possess, you can fight."

She turned to Guinivere again. Their shadows stretched across the red earth of the hill, merging into one, all of those women standing together.

"Those among you whom I've already begun to teach, I will continue to visit as often as possible. And you will all have to help one another to nurture whatever touch of magic you can find within yourselves. Guinivere is going to be my voice among you."

"What?" Guin asked, a shy smile on her face as she looked down. "Me?"

"You have a gift, Guinivere. You can feel the hearts and thoughts of others, and you sense the other worlds that exist so close to your own. You can see into those worlds if you focus enough. You've told me so yourself. I will guide you as best I can," Ceridwen said, turning to survey the formidable women arrayed around her once more. "All of you. But there are other threats to be combated, and I will not always be able to be with you. Guinivere will guide you. She is the axis upon which all of our efforts must turn. Learn what skills you can. Love one another and share what you learn. If there is any way to turn the Devourer away before it reaches this world, it will be done. And if there is no way, then I will stand with you all on our darkest of days."

Ceridwen fell silent. For long moments none of them spoke. Music rose from the festival below, with voices and laughter and the whisper of the wind. The sun played upon the ragged cliffs, bringing out myriad shades of red and white from the clay and rock and earth. In that place of quiet beauty, Ceridwen felt sure the quiet that had come over them all was a moment of prayer.

"We're with you, majesty," Guinivere said, her gaze steady and strong. Ceridwen had known such courage was in her.

"I'm a princess of the Fey, Guin. But here, I'm just Ceridwen. We stand together. I offer guidance, but from among you, not above you."

Guinivere smiled.

Ceridwen nodded, proud of them all and satisfied that she had set something in motion. Fear danced along her spine, but she stood tall and did not let it show upon her face. The Demogorgon would come, and the world's most powerful mages would stand against it, alongside sorcerers and warriors of Faerie and all manner of creatures. If the battle was so desperate that these bright, good-hearted women were needed, the world would probably already be doomed. But she would never give them the slightest hint that she harbored such doubts. For on that day, when so many would undoubtedly die, there was no telling what might happen. And if they had to die, at least this way they would die fighting. It was a gift she was giving them, really—a noble death, and a chance to make a difference, in the end.

"Your courage gives me strength," she told them, walking among them now, her dress flowing around her legs, the blues and greens startlingly vivid against the rich, red soil. The women reached out for her as she passed them, and Ceridwen touched them as she moved, brushing her fingers against their hands and arms and faces, bringing the peace of Faerie to them all, at least for a moment. Their eyes were alight with love and determination, and the fire of purpose.

She stopped to whisper congratulations to Kiera and Emmy on the love they'd found with one another, and again to apologize to Katie for not having visited, since her bookstore was in Cambridge, not far from where Ceridwen lived with Arthur Conan Doyle in Boston.

When she had passed a word or a moment with them all, she paused and glanced out across the extraordinary landscape. Much of Faerie was lush and green, but the lovely serenity of this place reminded her of home. She felt as though she could see the ghost of the primordial world, here, out across the rough landscape. It was nothing but ancient land, as far as her eyes could see.

"Ceridwen?" Guin ventured.

Shaken from her momentary reverie, she turned. Guinivere had been made the voice of these women, and already she inhabited the role.

"Yes?"

"What of Faerie?"

A sad smile came to Ceridwen's face. "You all would know better than I," she said, and raised her staff. "Gather round, sisters. For that is what you'll be from now on. Not Daughters, but Sisters of Ceridwen. Gather round."

They did, moving closer, shuffling together until their circle was intimate, in spite of their numbers.

"You've all brushed up against Faerie in some fashion," she continued. "Some of you have seen the Fey in those places where my kin sometimes cross over. Others, I know, have known the street fairies, my distant cousins who've chosen to live in this world. Most of you know Faerie only through me, and through the stories you've heard and read and breathed in, and the truth you've found for yourselves. But the whispers are out there, with the street fairies and other creatures who keep one foot in the doorway back to my world. Some of you have told me of rumors you've heard on the street or on the Internet.

"Keep listening. That's all I ask, right now. And when you hear things that are worrisome, let me know. My focus is here, now; in this world. This is the battlefront. If we cannot hold against the Demogorgon here, there is no hope for Faerie. My uncle would have me return, but I cannot, no matter how many whispers I hear of trouble brewing, or what kind of cryptic messages the Harper brings."

Moya gasped. "The Harper?"

Ceridwen frowned.

"He's real?" Katie asked.

"Yes," Ceridwen said. "He's real. And just as handsome as the legends say."

A ripple of nervous laughter went through them, lightening the mood.

"Now, then," she went on, "I'll count on you all to let me know whenever you hear anything of Faerie. Meanwhile, you've all got a difficult task ahead, tapping the elements, learning from one another. This may be the single most important thing—"

Guinivere cried out as though a dagger of sorrow had been thrust into her heart and fell to her knees on the rough ground. Arielle and Seraph reached for her, but Ceridwen was quicker. She crossed the space that separated her from Guin as though she herself was the wind and knelt by her side. Guinivere had one hand covering her eyes.

"Seer, what is it?" Ceridwen asked, one hand steady upon her staff, while with the other she clutched at the woman's arm.

When Guin looked up, her pupils were fully dilated, despite the sun, and Ceridwen felt as though the seer was looking right through her.

"Goddess, I've never felt such malice."

Ceridwen felt it, then, a *presence* spider-walking up the back of her neck and along her arms. She stood and spun toward these women who'd put such faith in her. Blue mist and orange flame spilled out from the sphere at the top of her staff, and she scanned the crowd gathered around her.

"Go!" she commanded them. "Run from here. I'll find you all soon. But now you must go!"

Eyes wide with fear, they began to stumble away, to hurry down the hill toward the festival below, where revelers continued their celebration without any inkling that trouble had arrived. Most of the women she knew well—those with a particular affinity to the elemental spirits of this world—hesitated.

"Run!" Ceridwen roared, raising her staff higher.

The wind swirled around her, lifting her several inches off the ground, even as the hill began to tremble. Loose soil shifted, and cracks spread across the red earth of the hill. Kiera stumbled backward and fell. Emmy gripped her by the arm and pulled her up, and the two of them began to hurry away. Moya followed, though she kept glancing reluctantly back up the hill. Katie and Arielle helped Guin rise, but they stood with Seraph, brave but foolish, perhaps thinking they could help. Why could they not understand that the best way for them to help was to live through the day?

The ground erupted as something burst from beneath it. Red dirt swirled on the wind, then, a moment later, Ceridwen saw the creature whose malice Guin had sensed. He stood a dozen feet tall, with bright gold eyes and long, copper hair, run through with a streak of white. His flesh was like rough brown leather, and his ears as pointed as the three-inch incisors that jutted up from his lower jaw. Tribal markings were tattooed above his left eye and on his left arm, and he wore black-red chain mail and thick wool trousers.

In truth, he looked just the way he had the last time Ceridwen had seen him. Half-Drow and half-Fey, he had once been her greatest enemy.

"Duergar!" she snarled, hovering on the wind.

Before she'd even gotten the name out, Duergar lunged at the women who had not yet fled. Quicker than Ceridwen remembered, or could have imagined, he grabbed Seraph in his enormous hands and lifted her up. Ceridwen screamed and sent rippling elemental fire arcing toward him, but she was too late. Duergar broke her up in his hands like dry kindling and tossed her aside.

The fire struck him, and he roared, but there was no pain in that sound. The fire seared his face, but he grinned through its ravages. It had been a battle cry.

The rest of the women Duergar ignored. He had come for Ceridwen.

Hatred filling her heart, she rushed to meet her ancient enemy.

HUMAN beings had always been afraid of shadows. Yet it was not darkness they feared; it was the threat of what might lie waiting within. They craved the sunshine, but the brighter the day, the deeper the shadows. In the modern world, people scoffed at their fear of the dark, at the anxious glances they found themselves giving to the darkened corners of their lives. But in their hearts they still trembled at the thought of what might lurk under the bed or in the closet, or in the back of the garage, among the tools and the lawn mower, and the dark.

But, in ages past, humanity had known that there was reason to fear the shadows, that races of inhuman creatures lived in those patches of darkness. Very few, however, had understood that the shadows were not simply the absence of light . . . they were the black substance of another plane of existence. All the shadows in the world were connected; each one was a door into a place of endless dark called the Shadowpaths.

Once, many creatures had been able to travel the Shadowpaths. Some even lived there, never able to emerge into the human world, or only able to do so after dark. Time and war had caused most of them to become extinct or flee for other realms. A small scattering of Norse *svartalves* still lived within that shadow world. There might be a rare tengu or another creature with a gift for shadow walking. Otherwise, the Shadowpaths were home only to hobgoblins. In another age, they had numbered in the thousands—the hundreds of thousands. Whole communities had existed. Now there were pitifully few hobgoblins remaining in the human world or within the Shadowpaths, and nearly all of them lived solitary lives. Whatever family or community had once existed was gone.

Lonely in the darkness, they could only wait for their race to become extinct.

In his workshop in a hidden corner of the shadow realm, with the darkness flowing and pulsing all around him, Squire stood before his forge. He pumped the snorting bellows with one hand while with the other he turned the blade he was making in the fire, admiring the way it glowed red with heat and magic. The Shadowpaths swallowed nearly all light, but the furnace was enchanted, and its light would have shone in the deepest cavern.

He stared at the sword blade, letting his mind wander again.

Normally he liked being at the workshop. When he wasn't at the forge, he allowed himself to be light of heart. He'd spent years working for Mr. Doyle as driver, valet, armorer, and weaponsmith—though this last was his true calling. But out in the human world, he loved all of the worst of their culture—junk food, bad television, and trashy women. Nobody liked a good time more than Squire.

At the forge, he normally liked things quiet. Making a weapon was serious business. But of late, his visits to the workshop had not been pleasant. On his own, he would drift into dark ruminations on the future, and on the past. Even now, thinking about how detached he had become from any others of his kind, he felt a melancholy that was entirely unlike him.

Squire was in a foul mood. Which made him all the more grateful for Shuck. The huge shadow beast was curled up just out of reach of the sparks that flew from the furnace, huge eyes watching Squire's every move. Shuck was not a dog, but out in the world, that was how people perceived him. Their minds couldn't explain the beast any other way. Squire had brought him into the human world to help deal with some serious trouble a few months back, and since then Shuck had just stuck around at Conan Doyle's house, becoming a sort of mascot to the Menagerie almost by default. Really, it was Squire and Eve who took care of him. Eve acted like she couldn't stand the mutt's presence, but she loved Shuck in spite of herself.

"I know, I know," the hobgoblin said to the beast watching him. "Get to work."

He laughed humorlessly and drew the white-hot blade from the fire, then moved it to the anvil. Not long ago he had made a double-bladed handheld weapon he called the Gemini Blade. One side was made of iron, which was deadly to fairies and their ilk, and the other crafted of silver, which poisoned vampires and werewolves and many other creatures of darkness. Recently, he'd taken the concept further. Conan Doyle was a master of many sorceries and sciences, and alchemy was among them. With an enchantment from his employer, Squire had been able to create a metal alloy that was a perfect blend of iron and silver, and he had set to work.

The Demogorgon was coming. When it would arrive, none of them could say for sure, but they had to be ready. Weapons would be necessary. Whether or not iron or silver would have any special effect upon it, Squire had no idea. But the armory of weapons he had made for the Menagerie—swords and axes, bows and crossbows, pikes and daggers and katars—needed to be bolstered, regardless. Many had been lost or broken. And if Conan Doyle was correct, when the Demogorgon came, they might have new allies to equip for fighting.

In the meantime, there were other menaces to be faced. And for most of those, the silver-iron alloy would do quite nicely indeed. So Squire had been hard at work replenishing the armory with the finest, lightest, most elegant, and most deadly weapons he had ever crafted. From the sound of this Demogorgon thing, he wasn't going to be a whole lot of help in the fight. But his weapons might be a different story. It helped to feel like he could contribute.

He picked up his hammer and brought it down on the now cooling, red-hot metal of the new alloy sword. Again and again, with the clang of metal upon metal resounding through the workshop and out along the Shadowpaths, he hammered the sword's blade, flattening its edges, perfecting its shape.

This was the legacy of his kin. Hobgoblins knew metalwork and weapons the way they knew how to travel the shadow realm. Squire could see the blade in the metal even before it was forged, the same way his eyes could find the right path through the shadows to emerge wherever he wished in the human world.

On a rack nearby hung four such swords, two new battleaxes, and a set of seven daggers made from the silver-iron. He'd put his runic signature in each blade, and their handles were ornate and intricate. Squire was proud of his work and saw no reason for it not to be as beautiful as it was deadly. A hundred arrows tipped with the alloy lay on a wooden table nearby, along with a bow he had fashioned out of ironwood. Metal wasn't the only thing he could craft. He'd even been known to dabble in explosives, though not of any ordinary sort. As a creature of the shadows, he'd found the best such weapons to be magical—grenades that exploded with the light of sunrise.

The grindstone sat nearby, quiet and dark. The sword wasn't ready for sharpening yet. It needed more time with the furnace and the hammer. Once again he moved it to the fire, holding it there as the metal heated.

On the floor, Shuck shifted, suddenly alert. The beast raised his enormous head and gazed at Squire.

"What's up, pal? You hungry again?" the hobgoblin asked. "I think I've got a couple of bags of Oreos somewhere. Or I could heat up some of those microwave burritos if you promise not to stand upwind after."

Squire grinned, baring rows of shark teeth.

Shuck crouched low and began to growl, the shadow hound's hackles rising. Squire stared at him, then glanced around the workshop, peering into the shifting, breathing darkness of the Shadowpaths. The mutt wasn't growling at him; he was sure of that. A little teasing about the effect burritos had on him was nothing new.

No, Shuck had the scent of something that wasn't supposed to be here.

Squire listened, his hearing even more acute than his vision in this place. His fingers loosened and then tightened their grip on the handle of the silver-iron blade still thrust in the flames of his furnace. He wished he could have gotten to the rack of finished weapons, but there was no telling what stalked him, now, and he didn't want to take any chances.

In the pulsing shadows to the left, past the grindstone, there came a whisper of something in motion. Even as Squire spun to face it, blade still in the fire, Shuck let out a thunderous roar and bounded past the hobgoblin.

A wave of oily black shadow darted, serpentine, into the light of the furnace. Only those eldritch flames illuminated the thing's jaws as they opened wide, revealing long ebony teeth, black upon black. Squire pulled the unfinished sword from the flames, liquid metal spattering the forge and anvil and the floor, still on fire.

Too slow. The thing's jaws opened wider and it thrust at his head.

Shuck rammed into the shadow serpent, jaws closing on its oily hide. It hissed loudly as it fell to the ground, and then it shook the length of its body, which disappeared into the darkness in woven coils, at least twenty or thirty feet long. It threw Shuck off—the hound crashing into the grindstone and knocking the wheel over. Shuck cried out with the impact, and Squire raged at the sound of his pain.

The mutt had bought him precious seconds.

The shadow serpent tensed, then sprang toward Squire again. But the hobgoblin was faster than he looked, and he sidestepped, slashing the unfinished sword at the snake's head. The blade glowed with heat, and the silver-iron was still soft from the fire. It cut the dark substance of the monster's hide, and bent as it did, the burning metal flowing and molding itself to the thing's flesh, searing itself into the wound even as it cut.

With a shrieking hiss, the thing rose and slammed its body on the ground. It thrashed and coiled and threw itself into the shadows, writhing in pain and trying to dislodge the melted metal. Squire would have gone for more weapons then, but the serpent was between him and his new armory.

"Shuck!" he called. "Come on, boy! We're out of here!"

The beast leaped up and ran at his side, the two of them racing along the Shadowpaths together. Squire looked over his shoulder, his heart pounding and his thoughts racing, terror and superstition moving through him faster than poison.

"Can't be," he whispered into the roiling, living darkness around him, the shifting clouds of black and gray. "No fuckin' way."

The Murawa's dead. No one's seen one for three hundred years.

But what else could it be, Squire wondered, if not the shadow serpent that had stalked hobgoblins along the Shadowpaths since the shadows had first coalesced? The Murawa was the bogeyman story hobs told their little 'goblins to make them behave.

But it was dead. It had to be.

Squire ran blindly through the shadows, keeping to the solid paths beneath his feet, careful not to slip into the shifting void on either side, but paying little attention to destination. Getting the hell away from the workshop was his only concern at the moment. Shuck ran with him. Tendrils of darker shadow, the living blackness that comprised this place, reached out as though to slow them down. Shuck growled low in his massive chest, and the shadows withdrew, giving them a clear path.

But the whisper of motion came from behind them. The serpent was wounded but not dead. Squire just wasn't that damned lucky. It was after them, and picking up speed.

If the Murawa doesn't exist anymore, then what the hell is that thing?

The answer was obvious. The rumors of the hobgoblin-eater's death had been greatly exaggerated.

"Shit," he grunted, and redoubled his speed. His chest ached. His hands opened and closed as he wished for a weapon.

A path opened to his left. Squire didn't hesitate or bother to consider where it would lead. He'd get back to Conan Doyle's house in due time. Right now, he and Shuck just had to get out. Maybe he could double back along another path, get to the workshop and find a way to defend himself. Not that he was worried about the forge or the weapons he'd made. The Murawa didn't have any hands. It wasn't going to be picking up a sword.

Except the one I buried in your ugly head!

Shuck started to growl again as he ran, low and angry. Squire shushed him. His lungs burned with exertion. He peered through the shadows, trying to figure out where he was, get his bearings so he could find a good spot to exit.

A hiss seared the air, too close.

Squire glanced behind him and saw the Murawa sliding and darting along the curving path behind them. The hot metal imbedded in its flesh still had the tiniest glow as it cooled.

Way to go, the hobgoblin thought. *Now you really pissed him off.*

"Shuck!" he called, and darted to the right.

Shadows swirled around them. The path was soft beneath his feet, but he had to find some way to escape the Murawa. The shadow serpent hissed and charged into the maelstrom of darkness in pursuit. It was faster than Squire, by far. Faster than Shuck, and the mutt ran like hell followed after.

Squire muttered curses under his breath, covering his fear with profanity, trying to hide it even from himself. He heard the Murawa's jaws snap closed and then a gentle sigh as it opened them wide. He called out to the hound again as he hurled himself to the left. Shuck followed, just as the shadow serpent lunged at them. It tried to twist to snatch them, but its momentum carried it past, into the black nothing of the void. Its body slithered past them, and for a moment, Squire thought it might spill entirely into the forever abyss that lay waiting for those who strayed too far from the solid paths. But its body was too long. It coiled back in on itself and started after them again.

The hobgoblin and his shadow beast had kept running. The Murawa had lost ground, but it would gain quickly. Up ahead, a trio of paths split off from the one they were on. He took the left fork, and it spiraled downward. He and Shuck raced along the curling path. Above them, the Murawa hissed again. Squire heard its jaws clack.

It would have them in a moment.

"Fuck it," he said, glancing at the hound. "No more time to be picky."

A gray patch of lighter shadow wavered off the path to his right. He had no idea where he was, but he called to Shuck and leaped through it. The hound came after him.

Squire backpedaled away from the shadows. Shuck circled around him, staring at the place where they'd come back into the human world. The ground was rocky and inhospitable but he paid little attention to their location, standing back, staring at the shadow cast by a ridge of stone and earth. Beyond it was the rising sun, so the shadow was long.

In the dark, Squire felt sure he could see the Murawa squirming, and imagined he could still hear its hiss. It thrust again and again toward him, but could not escape the Shadowpaths.

He let out a long breath of relief as it disappeared, and the shadow was just a shadow again. With a laugh of horror and amazement, he took another step back, lost his footing, and splashed into cool water.

Sputtering and waving his arms, he dragged himself up and looked around. In the soothing light of dawn he saw a pair of sampans with torn and dirty sails moving lazily along the river. Shuck made a sound that might have been a bark or a laugh, and Squire shot him the middle finger.

"Enough outta you, muttley. Not funny. You know I hate bath time."

Still, he had to smile as he climbed onto the riverbank and stood up, glancing around at the sampans and the river and the mountains in the distance.

"So," he said. "China."

Then he looked once more at the shadows where they had emerged. The snake showing up might have been random, but it didn't feel that way. Squire needed to inform Conan Doyle as soon as possible, and that meant he didn't have time to find another way home. Once he'd had a rest, it looked like he was going to have to enter the shadow realms again. He wondered how long he could evade the Murawa.

"Fuck."

3

DANNY Ferrick held a plastic DVD case in his hand, staring at the profiled headshots of the man and woman gazing intensely into each other's eyes, mere seconds away from a passionate kiss. The movie was called *Casablanca*, and it was supposed to be some sort of film classic.

Danny thought it looked like crap.

"It was one of my favorites, back before I passed away," the ghost of Dr. Leonard Graves stated, his specter hovering in the air beside the couch where Danny was sitting. "I actually attended its official premiere in 1942."

He looked up from the case, focusing on the ghost. The phantom's translucent substance softened, and then grew sharper, as if phasing in and out of existence.

"Yeah, but is it any good?" Danny asked with a petulant snarl. He had suggested a Japanese horror movie import that he'd gotten off the Internet, but his mother and the ghost weren't quite in the mood for the horrible—*thank you very much*—especially after what they'd gone through recently with him when his father, a demon who feasted on human experience, had returned to the human world looking for a reunion.

Danny cringed inwardly at the images that filled his mind. He squeezed his eyes tightly closed for a moment—he knew he had his father's eyes—and attempted to banish the memory of what his father had done, and what he had done at his father's request.

The demon boy opened his eyes to find the ghost watching him.

"At a glance it is a masterfully told tale of two men vying for the love of the same woman set against a wartime backdrop of political and romantic espionage," Dr. Graves said. "But upon closer examination it is also a film that expertly depicts the conflict between democracy and totalitarianism."

Danny looked down at the case in his hands and snarled. "Sounds like ass," he said sourly.

An emanation of frigid cold flowed from the ghost, a sure sign that Graves was annoyed. Before he could reply, Danny's mother came into the room.

"Are we set?" she asked.

Danny turned to see that she had a large bag of microwave popcorn and two unopened cans of soda in her arms. She smiled as she handed him the bag.

"I guess," he grumbled, digging into the popcorn, pushing one kernel into his mouth at a time. "We got a real exciting one about democracy fighting totalitarianism—whatever the fuck that means."

His mother frowned and slapped his leg as she dropped down on the sofa beside him. "Danny. Enough with the language."

He rolled his eyes.

She set the cans of soda down on the coffee table and picked up the DVD case. "*Casablanca*. Bogart and Ingrid Bergman. It's one of my favorites."

Danny glanced over at Graves and saw an uncharacteristic smile on the ghost's face.

"Figures."

His mother was really starting to get on his nerves. She'd come to live with him in Mr. Doyle's Beacon Hill brownstone after their old house in Newton had been destroyed during the confrontation between Conan Doyle's Menagerie and Danny's own demon daddy.

Julia Ferrick had actually found a condo in Brighton, and would be moving in a couple of days. The day couldn't come fast enough as far as Danny was concerned. He loved his mom, but having her around twenty-four/seven was getting old.

"So, are you game?" she asked him, wiggling the plastic case in front of his face.

"I don't care," he said with a shrug. "Don't know why you'd want to though, both of you have already seen it."

"But you haven't," his mother said cheerily, getting up from her seat to put the DVD into the player. "Excuse me, Leonard," she said to the hovering phantasm, and the two shared a certain look before Graves drifted out of the way.

That little glance they shared made Danny want to puke.

It wasn't bad enough that he'd found out that his real father was an evil son of a bitch. Evil with a capital E. Not bad enough that his physical changes were getting worse just about every day, making him less and less human and more and more demon. Now he had to worry about his mother crushin' on a ghost. Life didn't get much weirder than this.

At least Graves is a pretty cool guy, he reflected, *and it could be a lot worse—she could have the hots for Squire.*

Danny stifled a smile that threatened to crack his typically sour demeanor as his mother returned to her seat.

The movie started with a series of ads that he quickly advanced through to get to the actual DVD menu.

"Ready?" he asked, with as little enthusiasm as possible, pointing the remote at the television. As he laid his head on the overstuffed arm of the sofa, he saw his mother motioning to Graves to sit beside her on the couch.

"I'm fine here," the ghost said, glancing at the television screen. "Really."

"It's distracting," his mother said.

Dr. Graves looked at her, his nearly transparent features etched with confusion.

"The floating," Julia said. "It's very distracting."

The ghost hesitated momentarily, but soon succumbed to his mother's wishes, drifting over to sit on the other side of her. He could not actually sit, of course, but managed to create the illusion of being seated, just as he often appeared to be walking, though his feet never touched the ground.

"Now, isn't this comfy?" Julia said, leaning back in her seat.

"Give me a fucking break," Danny mumbled, hitting the PLAY button on the remote to start the movie.

His mother sighed at his language but didn't correct him this time. Then the movie began to play. He just about shit when he saw that it was in black and white. Danny hated movies that weren't in color and made his displeasure known with heavy groans as he dropped his head back against the sofa.

"Give it a chance," his mother said, and patted his leg affectionately. He considered swatting her hand away but thought better of it, catching himself before the damage could be done. She already had issues with some of his recent behavior; no reason to add to the list.

Danny slouched down in his seat, arms folded defiantly across his chest and watched the movie he was certain was going to suck moose dick.

Half an hour into it—much as he hated to—Danny had to admit he'd been wrong. *Casablanca* didn't suck moose dick. In fact it didn't suck any kind of dick at all. It was really good . . . especially for an old, black-and-white movie that starred people who had been dead since way before he was born.

But he wasn't about to let his mother and Graves know that.

"Well, what did you think?" Julia asked, when the film had finished. She rummaged through the bag of popcorn for the last of the crumbs. "Wasn't it wonderful?"

Danny shrugged. "It was all right. I don't know if I'd call it a classic though." He picked up his soda can, tipping it toward his mouth just in case there was anything left. There wasn't.

He felt Graves's eyes on him, a creepy feeling that could only be compared to the first uncomfortable sensation you feel when breaking out in a nasty skin rash. And from all the physical changes he'd undergone the last couple of years, he knew a thing or two about skin rashes.

"And how exactly would you define a classic?" Graves asked. "I'm curious."

Danny shrugged, thinking about the question. "I don't know. Maybe something that isn't so freakin' old?"

Graves nodded, seemingly understanding where he was coming from.

"I see," said the ghost. "So a motion picture . . . perhaps in color . . . would have a better chance of reaching the status of classic?"

"Exactly," Danny said. "And it would also have to have a lot more action." He nodded, thinking about his criteria. "Yeah . . . color, action, and sex. It's gotta have a hot sex scene."

Julia threw up her hands. "That's it," she said. "Think we've talked enough about the classics."

Danny liked to see his mother squirm, especially in the presence of her new boyfriend . . . or whatever the hell he was. Normally she would have just rolled her eyes and ignored him, but since Graves was there, it made her suddenly uncomfortable, like he'd think she was a bad parent or something.

He was about to ask her why she was blushing when Conan Doyle's doorbell began to chime.

"Who could that be at this hour?" Julia asked, glancing at her watch.

"I'll see," Danny said, springing off the couch and jogging toward the doorway. "It'll give you two a chance to be alone."

He started to laugh again, knowing that if he'd looked at his mother, her eyes would have been shooting daggers at him. She and Graves had been flirting around with each other for weeks now, but if confronted with the suggestion of her interest in the ghost, his mother immediately dismissed it as nonsense.

Danny saw the way they looked at each other, listened to how they spoke. Everybody in the house knew that something was definitely on the verge of going on, even though his mother and Dr. Graves seemed either oblivious or determined to hide what they felt. It was about time that they knew that the little dance they were doing wasn't fooling anyone.

The demon boy stopped at the front door, leaning in toward the peephole for a look. He was surprised to see Clay—a friend, and a member of Conan Doyle's Menagerie—standing on the front step. The shapeshifter wore his favorite face today, the one he most often used to walk among ordinary people.

"What the hell?" Danny said, unlocking the door and pulling it open.

"Can I come in?" Clay asked, attempting to look past him and into the house.

"Duh, you live here," Danny said, turning his back on the shapeshifting creature that he had learned to call friend. "Why didn't you just use your key?"

There was a rustling behind him, the sound that he had come to associate with his friend's shapeshifting.

I can become anything ever created by—or even thought of by God, Clay had once told him.

As Danny turned to face his friend, he saw the last moment of Clay's transformation into a thing that looked as though it had been shat out by the world's worst nightmare. He grinned, about to ask Clay what kind of god would even think of something as nasty as that.

He never got the chance.

Clay lunged at him, claws ripping the air, and Danny had no more questions—only the instinct to stay alive.

CERIDWEN remembered.

Horrid images of the past collided with the immediacy of the present.

Like a grizzled warrior gazing at the raised, silvery scarring from what had once been a near-fatal wound, she recalled her first encounter with Duergar.

It had nearly been the death of her.

THE blizzard in the Northern hills was relentless; blinding. Icy snow rode the shrieking gusts like tiny blades of shattered glass. Even through the white sheets driven by howling wind, she could see that they were dead.

The Twilight Wars had caused thousands of elfin refugees to flee their homes, seeking sanctuary in the mountains and caverns of Tullanah, perhaps the most inhospitable region of Faerie.

Some of them never made it there. Ceridwen had stumbled upon them—hundreds of women and children, most elfin but some Fey as well—horribly murdered and mutilated. The mangled bodies were stacked in a pile, dark blood seeping out from around the base of the mound, steaming in the snow. Already the bodies were being covered by a blanket of white, as if the elements were part of some vile conspiracy to conceal the horror of the loathsome act.

Ceridwen, Arthur, and their allies were determined to wait out the fierce storm in the refugee camp, perhaps partaking of a warm meal and drink before continuing with the hunt for their elusive quarry. But there would be no respite, no brief moment of peace in which they could temporarily forget the atrocities perpetrated by the one they pursued.

"Form a circle!" Ceridwen commanded over the wailing winds, tearing her gaze from the sight of the stacked bodies, soon to be covered up by the storm.

Conan Doyle and the soldiers under her command did as they were instructed, weapons at the ready.

"He will not have gone far," she added, squinting through the whipping snow, searching for a sign of the barbarian's passing.

She knew the dark heart of this enemy all too well. Duergar would have stayed behind to see their reaction to this latest act of cruelty. He would still be here, somewhere. The Twilight Wars had changed all who had fought in them, whether on the side of light or darkness. Duergar had been a monster before, and the war had made him into something worse.

Much worse.

"Damn the storm," Conan Doyle growled, shielding his eyes with a leather-gauntleted hand.

Ceridwen had been about to speak the language of the mountain storm, requesting a brief lull, when over the wail of the winds she heard a different sound.

A child's cry.

They all heard it, but the wind distorted the sound, making it nearly impossible to locate its source.

Their circle remained tight. Again they heard the pitiful cry. This time it seemed to come from within the ravaged elfin encampment.

Is it possible? Ceridwen wondered, turning toward the collapsed and broken walls of the shelter. Had someone managed to survive Duergar's cruelty?

Then she saw it; movement from the pile of mangled corpses. Accumulating snow dropped from the bloodied bodies, revealing the expressions of terror that had been frozen upon the victims' faces in death.

Again the cry—a high, keening wail—and Ceridwen gasped as two tiny hands pushed out from beneath the corpses, followed by the squirming body of an elfin child. Like some macabre birth, the bloody little girl emerged from a womb built from the dead. The child was hysterical, her body wracked with a terrible trembling.

They all reacted as one, the circle breaking as they each moved to comfort the wailing toddler.

Ceridwen faltered, squinting through the snow.

Why is she alive?

She had seen the half-blood's other kills, and those sights had caused her many a restless night. Though he had the build and strength of a Drow, he had the cleverness of his Fey ancestry. A cunning monster was Duergar.

"Stop!" Ceridwen shouted, just as one of her soldiers—Fendarith—squatted down in front of the child, pulling her shaking body to him and wrapping her in his scarlet cloak.

Conan Doyle must have sensed her unease. Blue eldritch energies began to spark at his fingertips.

"It is all right, Princess Ceridwen," Fendarith said, turning toward her with the child. "I have one at home just this age and—"

The sentence would never be completed. The pile of corpses seemed to come alive, bodies erupting in all directions as Duergar surged up from his hiding place beneath the mountain of death.

Time slowed to a crawl.

It was Fendarith's first instinct to protect the child. He turned his back to their enemy, seeking to shield her. Duergar snatched him up from the ground as though he, himself, was a child. Fendarith had dropped the girl, who scrambled away, screaming, as the towering half-blood monster raised the soldier over his head and in one fluid movement dashed his body to the cold, frozen earth, never to move again.

The Fey soldiers drew their swords as Ceridwen and Conan Doyle summoned deadly magics with which to combat the barbaric creature. The elemental sorceress raised her staff, and the storm began to bend around her, lashing at Duergar, whipping him with stabbing ice. Conan Doyle thrust out his hands, and a burst of vivid yellow light arced from his fingertips and struck the monster in the chest, burning through his armor, searing his leathery flesh.

Duergar staggered backward two steps. Only two. He dropped to his knees, thrust his fists through the snow and into the ground, and the frozen earth beneath them began to tremble. Then he charged. In that single moment when they were caught off guard, the swift half-blood snatched the child up in one of his enormous hands. Fingers as thick as tree limbs wrapped tightly around the body of the squealing little girl, keeping her close to shield himself from attack.

"Hold!" Ceridwen cried over the howling storm, stifling the magic that was about to flow from the end of her staff, pulling it back inside of her. For the sake of the child, there was no choice. From the corners of her eyes she could still make out the crackle of magic that danced upon the fingertips of her lover's hands, and smell the faint aroma of burning flesh as he held back its release.

The most terrifying aspect of their enemy's monstrous countenance was not the tribal tattoos on his face and arms, or the yellow tusks that jutted from his lower jaw . . . it was his eyes.

She had looked into the gaze of many a monster; of murderers too numerous to count. It was like looking into the eyes of an animal caught in the grip of madness. But in Duergar's yellow eyes was a terrible intelligence. Malignant. Evil.

The elfin child cried out as he brought her closer to his broad face.

"Such a wonderful girl," he growled, eyes unblinking as his gaze darted from one enemy to the next. "Did exactly as she was told." He kissed her then, his large cracked lips pressing to the child's bloody face. "A good friend, she is, a good friend indeed."

"Release the child," Ceridwen commanded, the sphere of ice and fire atop her staff glowing with a fierce, white light.

"Are you a good friend, my pretty princess?" the monster asked.

His eyes glittered happily. She did not want to hear him, see him, anymore, wanted nothing more than to unleash the full fury of her rage.

But the child . . .

Duergar gave the elfin girl a sudden, vicious shake and she cried out, reminding them all of how fragile his captive was.

Ceridwen felt her soldiers' eyes upon her. She had hand-picked this group, and their bravery, loyalty, and fierceness in battle had become nearly legendary. With their skill and Arthur at her side, she knew she could finally put an end to Duergar's evil. They waited for her reaction, ready to do her bidding at a moment's notice.

"What do you want?" she asked, hating the words as they fell from her mouth. Hating herself for uttering them.

Duergar laughed again. "You surprise me, pretty princess." The half-blood reached up and stroked the girl's head. *"But that is what is so special about this life we live . . . the surprises."*

He grinned, jagged teeth tinted red from the blood of his victims.

"Set the child free, and go," Ceridwen said, her voice booming over the moans of the wind.

"Just like that?" Duergar asked, obviously amused. *"I give up this child to you, and you let me go free?"*

Ceridwen nodded, her next words nearly causing her to choke. "You have my word."

Duergar gazed at the child in his hand. "Such a quandary I face," he murmured, stroking her dark hair, flecked with snow and ice. *"I give you to them, and I'm allowed to go free, losing myself in these mountains until it is time for me to scratch another itch . . ."*

The monster glanced at the bodies that littered the ground around him. His smile faded, and he raised his eyes to gaze at Ceridwen.

"And then you come for me again."

He tore the little girl's head from her body, turning the

stump of her neck toward them so that they were sprayed with the gore that erupted from her body.

"Where's the fun in that?" Duergar roared, eyes wild as he popped the little girl's head into his gaping jaws and began to chew, crunching her skull in his teeth.

4

THE distant memories seemed so fresh that Ceridwen could still feel the melting snow upon her face and taste the bitter bile of rage in her mouth. Years had passed, and now she faced Duergar again, and his fists were stained with the blood of innocents once more.

With a cry of fury, the Fey sorceress raised her staff and summoned the wrath of the elements down upon her foe. The glorious blue desert sky turned nearly black, a sudden storm whipped into a frenzy by her magic and her rapport with the spirits of the air. The rain punished the ground, falling in prickling sheets, and the thunder growled like some great primordial beast.

"It's been some time, pretty princess," the monster said over the hissing of the downpour.

Hatred flowed through her body and into the wood of her staff. Fire danced with her rage inside the ice sphere atop it. With a scream that echoed the one torn from her lungs when she'd watched the half-blood murder that small child, Ceridwen called down the fangs of the storm upon him.

Lightning arced down from the shifting black sky, the storm eager to please this mistress of the old ways. But Duergar was fast—far faster than something of his size should have been—avoiding each strike with an animal litheness, as if somehow sensing where the wrath of the storm would fall.

The half-Drow creature danced among the lightning bolts,

a hideous barking laugh joining with the growls of thunder, as he made his way closer to her.

"Come now, princess, this is not the reunion I'd hoped for," Duergar called, his coppery skin beginning to smolder; for even though the lightning had not found him, the ground beneath his feet was charged with the storm's fury.

Ceridwen leaped into the air, and the wind gusted behind her, carrying her toward him with such speed that even Duergar could not ward her off. She descended upon him and whipped her staff around to strike his face with such force that his head snapped viciously to one side.

Duergar caught her delicate ankle in one huge, filthy hand. Blood like tar trickled from a vicious cut above his urine-colored eyes. She reared back with her staff, ready to strike him again.

"So strong, so beautiful . . . and yet so soft and frail."

The monster sneered, savagely yanking her from the sky and flinging her away before she could do him further harm.

She crashed against rain-slick rocks, and the air was knocked from her lungs. Bright explosions of pain danced before her violet eyes, but she climbed to her feet. The slightest moment of weakness would mean her death.

Duergar was almost upon her, his large hands covered in thick, yellowing, dirt-caked callus, eagerly reaching. Ceridwen crouched, laying her own hand upon the earth, beckoning to the dirt, rock, and sand beneath her fingertips to answer her call.

The spirits of the earth responded, flowing upward and grasping at the monster's thick legs, stopping him in his place.

"Come now, princess," Duergar barked. With a grunt, he tore his legs free from the solidified ground. "You can do better than that."

"True," she snarled.

Ceridwen jammed her staff into the dirt and a formation of rocklike gigantic shark's teeth exploded from the ground beneath the half-breed's feet, hurling him into the air. The instant he was aloft, she called upon the winds, which swept around him, pummeling the half-blood creature as he hung in the air.

Duergar roared in pain. Ceridwen orchestrated the storm, exacting vengeance for the torture, rape, and murder of hundreds of her kin and other races of Faerie. She had no intention of stopping until he had paid for his crimes in full, and only then would she allow him to die.

A voice called her name. Ceridwen turned to see three of her human sisters emerging from behind a newly birthed formation of rock. They were soaked to the bone and shivering from the maelstrom that she had unleashed. Their eyes were lit with fear, but they had steeled themselves against it and now bravely sought to join the battle. Ceridwen was about to tell them to seek cover when she felt searing pain explode in her right shoulder.

Her concentration shattered, disrupting her magic. Duergar tumbled from the sky and landed with a grunt, twenty feet away.

Ceridwen cried out, reaching back to find the handle of a dagger jutting from the meat and muscle only inches from the top of her spine. Had the blade struck true, it would have been the end of her.

The half-blood rose to his feet, a savage smile upon his primitive features. His terrible strength had been such that he had thrown the knife, even with the storm beating against him.

"I believe you have something of mine," he said, reaching out a beckoning hand.

Ceridwen positioned herself between her foe and the three women who had been unable to reach safety, her gaze never leaving his. She reached back and tugged the blade from her flesh.

"This, abomination?" she asked. "Have it, by all means."

She hurled the blade back to its owner riding on a ferocious slipstream of air. Duergar was swift, but even he could not dodge entirely. The blade cut off the tip of one of his pointed ears. He turned his head slightly, blood streaming down the side of his face, watching the knife as it rocketed past him.

"My father gave me that blade," Duergar said, casually bringing his fingers up to his ear, his squared-off fingertips coming away covered in gore. "Just before I cut his throat. Sentimental value, it had."

Ceridwen raised her staff and whispered summonings to the elements, preparing for a final assault. Movement drew her attention, and she glanced over to see Guinivere, Kiera, and Moya taking up a position to join the attack, to aid her in this struggle.

As family . . . as *sisters* would do.

"Your courage gives us strength," Guinivere said, and the air became charged with their accumulated power, little as it was. Their unity was like a thing alive, and Ceridwen added its strength to her own.

Several of her other human sisters began to encircle Duergar, emerging from the storm. The monster stood perfectly still, blood still dripping from his ear onto his shoulder to stain the already tarnished mail of his tunic.

"You cannot destroy us all," Ceridwen said, gripping her staff. The sphere of ice burned as brightly as the noontime sun, dispelling some of the darkness of the storm.

Duergar dropped to a crouch, grabbed up a handful of the muddy, red soil, and plastered it on his ear to staunch the bleeding.

"Another time, pretty princess," Duergar said.

Pitching himself forward, he shoveled his hands into the earth. In seconds he was gone, tunneling deep into the stratum.

Silently Ceridwen thanked the elemental spirits that had answered her call, even as her gaze found the broken body of Seraph lying lifeless upon the muddy ground.

"Ceridwen," Guinivere said softly beside her. "You're hurt . . . let us . . ."

She felt them try to move her away and stopped them with a glance.

"That can wait," she told them. "See to Seraph."

Some of the women responded, walking to where their sister had fallen.

Guinivere remained beside her, assimilating the role of leader much quicker than she had ever imagined.

"What are we going to do?" the woman asked, standing rigid and raising her chin. Sorrow filled her eyes, but

Ceridwen saw no fear in her. She would lead the others well in the days to come. Ceridwen knew, then, that she had chosen well.

"I need to communicate with Conan Doyle," she replied, suddenly, irrationally—*it is Arthur, after all*—fearing for her lover's safety. "He must learn of this at once."

An icy chill crawled up her spine, causing the fine, downy hair on her arms and the back of her long neck to stand on end.

She needed to hear his voice.

To know that he was safe.

"WHAT'RE you, high?" Julia Ferrick heard Danny yell from down the hall. "What the fuck are you doing?"

A horrible sound punctuated his shouts, like something very heavy being smashed against the floor. The impact had such force that she felt the thump in the wood under her feet, even though she stood in Conan Doyle's den and her son was all the way at the front door of the brownstone.

Julia looked wide-eyed at the ghost of Dr. Graves, who was staring toward the arched doorway that led into the hall.

A scream of pain cut the air, then. Julia's heart froze. *Danny.* She found herself running for the door. An icy cold numbness seized her upper arm, and she looked around to see Graves standing beside her.

"Stay here," he told her firmly, letting go of her arm.

It took sheer focus of will for the ghost to grasp living flesh, but intensity was not something Leonard Graves had ever lacked. Twin guns materialized in their holsters under his arms. He drew the phantom pistols as he drifted toward the wall and passed through it to the hallway beyond.

Straining to hear over the hammering of her heart, Julia listened. The house had gone deathly quiet. Despite the ghost's warning, she found herself gradually moving toward the door.

Maybe he's just playing a prank, Julia thought, knowing she was wrong.

Booming gunshots rocked the first floor. Julia let out a scream, running out into the hall. For a moment her brain couldn't even comprehend what it was that she was seeing. Dr. Graves hovered in the air of the grand foyer, guns aimed, firing in rapid succession.

But at what?

The intruder changed its shape in rapid succession, the ghost's ectoplasmic bullets rippling across constantly shifting flesh—feathers, fur, and scales. When she thought she understood what she was looking at, it changed from one species of beast to the next, sometimes the forms mingling together into something of nightmare.

Something monstrous.

Her son snarled as he threw himself at the thing, even as it shifted its form again. It became a huge, white-furred ape and roared as it spun to face him, its mouth opening wide to show rows of wicked teeth. Danny roared back, delivering a savage blow just as the intruder morphed into something huge and gelatinous. A thick, dark green tentacle whipped out and snared him, throwing Danny against the wall. The plaster buckled, and he dropped to the floor.

"Danny!" she screamed, starting down the hall toward the boy, not realizing what she was doing until it was too late.

The shapeshifting monster noticed her. In a space of a heartbeat, it assumed a human guise—a face that she had become only too familiar with over the last year.

"Clay?" she whispered, not believing what she was seeing, thinking that surely she had to be mistaken.

With a snarl the intruder morphed into a silver-skinned animal the likes of which she was certain had never existed upon the earth.

Dr. Graves darted in front of her, keeping the beast at bay.

"Leonard, what's going on?" she cried. "Is that Clay . . . what's wrong with him? Why is he doing this?"

Graves fired his phantom pistols into its face, driving it back against the broken door, which hung crookedly to one side on a single, twisted hinge.

"Get out of here, Julia!" Dr. Graves shouted.

The unknown beast slashed at the ghost's immaterial form and Graves let out an anguished cry. The ghost drifted to the floor, clutching at his chest. A kind of translucent mist slid from the wound in the specter's substance, and a tremor of panic went through Julia.

Is he bleeding? Is that possible?

"Leonard!"

The silver-skinned beast loomed above the ghost, its bullet-shaped head dipping down toward her fallen friend. Multiple arms unfolded from its flesh, and each was tipped with hooked barbs that rose up, prepared to strike at Graves.

Julia snatched a vase from a small table in the foyer.

"Clay!" she shouted. "What the hell's wrong with you?"

The vase shattered off the shapeshifter's head. It reared back with an ear-piercing hiss.

"Why are you doing this? Why are you attacking your friends?"

Again it changed shape. With the liquid sound of flowing flesh and the loud popping of reconfiguring bones, it transformed into some kind of large, predatory cat—*a sabertooth, maybe*—something that hadn't stalked the earth for eons. But here it was, and it was coming for her. It crouched low to the ground with a throaty growl, beginning to pad slowly toward her.

She could tell that Clay enjoyed this shape.

Julia kept her eyes on the great cat as she backed up. Its elongated canines glistening wetly in the flickering light of the hallway. From the corner of her eye she could see that Leonard was standing again, hand still pressed to his chest.

Somehow Clay's last form—the silver-skinned beast— had been able to injure the ghost, and it appeared that he was having great difficulty in recovering.

The spectral adventurer raised a single pistol, firing into the great cat's side.

The animal roared and shot a warning glance toward the spirit, then continued down the hallway toward her. Julia could see the muscles beneath its fur bunch and tense, and she knew it was about to pounce. Julia thought about running, but knew it would drag her down.

A throaty whine grew in the feline's throat, its emerald green eyes locked upon her—its prey. Her whole body shook with fear and despair, but she steeled herself. She would fight, no matter how useless her struggles might be.

Grave's guns boomed.

Julia and the shapeshifter both spun at the sound, and she stared in confusion when she realized that Graves was not firing at the great cat this time, but at her unconscious son.

When those phantom bullets struck him, Danny's eyes opened and he began to scream in rage, scrambling to his feet in a cloud of plaster dust.

"Help your mother," Graves hissed, slumping forward again and sinking through the floor.

Danny snarled, twisting around and locking eyes with Julia.

The cat leaped toward her. Julia screamed and jumped backward, stumbling and falling to the floor. The saber-toothed tiger landed mere inches from her. The beast lifted one of its large paws, its movement an orange blur as it swiped at her.

The pain in her shoulder was excruciating; the front of her blouse tore away as the animal's claws dug deep furrows. The smell of her blood filled her nostrils, and Julia felt herself begin to grow dizzy. *If I'm lucky,* she thought, *maybe I'll black out before it starts to eat me.*

The great cat's face loomed closer. Its jaws opened, and its mouth began to descend.

Danny slammed into the beast, tackling it and hauling it away from her. He struggled with the shapeshifter on the floor of the hall.

"Get out of here!" she heard her son growl as he attempted to keep the beast from rolling out from beneath him.

Julia staggered to her feet and leaned against the wall. Her head swam, and she could feel warm rivulets of blood as they ran down her skin beneath her tattered blouse. As she started down the hall, Danny and the great cat careened across her path, twisting on the wooden floor, blocking her way.

Danny looked her way, holding the snapping jaws of the cat away from his face.

"Get ready to run," he grunted. Then, with a roar, he drove the squealing animal back against the wall with all his might.

"Go! Go! Go!" Danny screamed, holding the struggling monster even as it abandoned that form and changed into something else.

Julia didn't look to see what it was. Using the wall that supported her, she pushed off, running down the hallway as fast as she was able, hurtling toward the kitchen. At the door she turned to make sure her son was following her and screamed at the sight of a gigantic tentacle undulating toward her. Danny was in the midst of a struggle with a thing that could only have been some kind of giant squid, though how it survived out of the water she could not guess.

She stumbled backward into the kitchen, crashing against the marble-topped island and knocking the wind from her lungs as she dropped to the floor. The tentacle slithered into the kitchen, and she watched in disbelief as a bulbous, blood-shot eye grew from its slick skin.

It's looking for me, she thought. *But Clay could never do that.*

The orb saw her, and the tentacle reared back, preparing to strike. Julia grunted, the pain in her shoulder like fire as she forced herself to her feet, searching for a way to defend herself. A knife rack sat on the counter. Leaning across the cold marble, she withdrew a kitchen knife. Squire liked to keep the blades sharp. Julia spun just as the tentacle reached for her.

She lashed out with the knife, gashing the thick tendril. A squeal of pain echoed through the house. The horrible limb recoiled, then tightened into a kind of fist.

The air around her dropped to frigid temperatures, as though she'd been touched by some icy winter wind. Ghost hands gripped her for the second time that day and pulled her aside just as the muscular limb came down, shattering the marble island to pieces.

Julia looked up into the gauzy eyes of Leonard Graves.

"You're all right?" she asked.

"Better," the ghost said.

Now that the moment had passed, his hands passed through her flesh. She shuddered at his touch, and not only from the cold. Graves aimed one of his phantom guns and fired at the writhing tentacle, shooting the bulging eye.

"Quickly, now, we need to get out of here."

He led her toward the cellar door, avoiding the thrashing limb as it withdrew from the kitchen.

"What about Danny?" she asked, halting.

The ghost turned on her impatiently, but she saw in his eyes a fear for her safety that made her catch her breath.

"I'll go back for him," he told her. "There's an exit at the back of the cellar. Get to your car. We'll catch up."

They stood at the top of the stairs. She hesitated only a moment.

"Be careful," she said. "That thing can hurt you."

"Careful as mice," he said in a whisper, disappearing into floating wisps of ectoplasm as he turned away from her.

Julia hurried down the stairs. The basement appeared far larger than it should be, and it took her a moment to get her bearings. She moved toward the far wall, avoiding shelving units and boxes stacked to form aisles.

Something started to hum nearby, and Julia instinctively jumped back, only to realize it was some kind of refrigerator. *What's that for?* she wondered as she bumped up against a heavy, metal shelving unit, and she spun around to steady the shelves of what looked to be multiple burial urns.

Moments later, she found the wooden door that Graves had been talking about. She slid the rusting metal bolt aside and turned the skeleton key. Taking a deep breath, Julia plunged into darkness, moving toward what seemed to be a speck of light in the distance and eventually coming to another wooden door. This too was locked, with a sliding bolt and key. She undid them both, exploding out the door into the brisk, spring night.

The small backyard seemed to provide storage for gardening tools and trash barrels. Julia ran to a wooden gate, pulled it open, and darted down a narrow stone passage between Mr. Doyle's brownstone and the neighboring home.

Flowers of pain blossomed before her eyes as she ran, each step jostling her wounded flesh. As she found her way to the front of the brownstone, her foot caught upon something on the ground. She managed to catch herself before she fell, and glanced down at whatever had tripped her. The ground was covered with dead cats, their black fur making them nearly invisible in the dark. She had seen the cats roaming around Conan Doyle's home upon her comings and goings, and felt a pang of sadness, wondering why anyone would do such a thing.

Julia ran toward her Volvo wagon and stopped short, staring at the vehicle with an intensifying hate.

My keys.

She spun around to gaze at the brownstone. Her keys were inside the house. The door hung crookedly from the frame, the sound of battle leaking out from within, and she had to wonder if Conan Doyle had done something to his building to mask anything unusual happening there from the eyes of those who lived or passed nearby.

The door exploded outward, her son riding what appeared to be a plume of fire. Danny landed in a roll, his T-shirt in tatters, smoldering on his back.

"Oh, my God. Are you all right?" she asked, helping him to his feet.

Something roared inside.

"Fucking dragon," he said, shaking his head. "He turned into a fucking dragon."

"But dragons aren't real," Julia whispered.

"Let's get the fuck out of here, Mom," Danny said, dragging her toward her vehicle.

"I don't have my keys," she said.

Her son swore under his breath, looking back toward the house. She knew what he was considering.

"No, you can't go back," she warned him. Julia could hear the hysteria creeping into her voice and wasn't too sure how much more she could take.

Gunfire erupted from within the house. They looked up to see the ghost of Dr. Graves shoot out of the building backward, guns aimed at the front door as he continued to fire.

"Get in the car, both of you!" the specter ordered, firing those phantom guns again and again.

"But I don't have the—"

"Get in the car!" he screamed, and she saw the human form of Clay standing in the doorway to Mr. Doyle's home, his eye blazing an unearthly red.

Julia pulled open the driver's side door, ecstatic that she'd been unable to break the normally foolish habit of forgetting to lock it, and unlocked the back door for Danny. She clutched the wheel in both hands, waiting for Graves.

The ghost flowed into the vehicle, his eyes riveted on the top of the brownstone's front steps. Clay stood in his human guise, unmoving.

"We have to get away from here," Graves said, from the passenger seat. She was about to protest again that she'd left her keys, but the ghost reached past her, his hand disappearing into the steering column.

The engine turned over, the instrument panel in front of her coming to life.

"Go!" Graves snapped.

As she put the car in drive, she could see Clay slowly descending the steps. *Why isn't he chasing us?*

Julia stepped on the gas, pulling out of her parking space with a squeal of tires. In her rearview mirror she saw Clay reach the sidewalk, watching them as they drove away.

All was silent within the car as Julia drove down Mount Vernon Street, not having a clue as to where they were going and not caring, as long as it was away from there.

"Would somebody explain to me what the fuck just happened?" Danny asked from the backseat.

And the silence went on.

5

IN the Garden, the wind dances around her, one breeze carrying the sweet scents of oranges and ripe peaches and the next caressing her with the aromas of the loveliest flowers. The rich smell of earth and green life lies beneath it all.

A deer appears in the trees. It tilts its head to watch her, then looks up as several others run by, pursuing one another playfully. She sprints after them, and soon runs alongside, laughing as she crashes through branches and leaves.

They burst from the trees on the edge of a stream that burbles over rocks and tumbles down a hill ahead. The deer race off in another direction, but she stands, mesmerized, and gazes down at the glistening water as it splashes down over smooth black rocks, spilling into a waterfall. From the pool below, the stream continues, winding off into some distant corner of the Garden. A bear stands on a rock in the stream, thrusting massive paws into the swift water, hoping for a fish.

All around the waterfall, and on both banks of the stream below, color is in bloom. Blossoms of gentle red and blue and white, and vivid purple and green and orange, hang in tangles from the trees. The flowers are such a mélange of color that her breath simply stops.

She basks in the beauty and the scent, and the sound of the cascade of the water below.

Mice and voles caper across her path as she descends the hill alongside the waterfall. Soft brown birds explode from the trees around her, an entire flock taking off as one, as though some shift of the wind has carried them out of the branches and into the air. They move together, one mind, one heart, and she watches as they settle into the high branches of another tree, not far away.

A fish in its jaws, the bear wanders off into the trees. Farther along the stream, she sees a pair of black horses emerge from the wood, nuzzling one another's necks.

The pool at the base of the waterfall splashes her with cool water. One corner of the pool eddies lazily, away from the current of the rest of the stream. Tiny fish jump, there, silver things that flash in the sunlight. She laughs to see them and hugs herself, bumps rising all over her bare skin at the chilly touch of the water droplets that splash her.

The wind urges her toward the water. It is morning, and the stream still quite cool at the early hour, but she cannot resist the pull of the water, the playfulness of the fish, and the urging of the wind. Surrounded by the delicious, sweet scents of the Garden, she wades into the pool, then dives beneath the water.

The chill embraces her, and her spirit soars. She bursts up from beneath the water, giddy, as damp strands of hair cover her face. She pushes that wet curtain of hair away from her eyes and sees the colors of paradise all around her, and, above, the perfect blue-white sky.

She spins, trailing her fingers in the water, splashing, then she wades over to stand beneath the waterfall. The sensation of the pressure and rhythm of the water streaming down onto her is ecstasy.

She feels him behind her before he touches her. Out of the corner of her eye, she sees movement, and she knows it is he. Then his hands caress her arms and back and he slides his arms around her, embracing her from behind. He kisses the back of her neck, and she sinks into his strong body just as she had given herself over to the waterfall.

It is bliss.

In the Garden.

Then he is gone.

Darkness falls around her. The sound of the waterfall recedes to a distant drip, drip, drip and all that she can feel is the cold of the water enveloping her, and a deep, powerful

*ache in her belly. She moves, and the pain is so sharp that she
cries out.*

*She forces herself to inhale, but the sweet scents of fruit
and flowers and the rich earth have vanished. All she can
smell now is blood.*

The taste of it is in her mouth. It is thick in her throat.

And it is not hers.

Again, she moves. Again, the twist of pain.

Her eyes flutter open . . .

WITTENBERGE, GERMANY, A.D. 1627

HER skin was on fire.

Eve opened her eyes in a hiss of pain. Yet there was something exhilarating about this pain. Her skin prickled as
though flames were crackling all over her flesh, but she
looked down the length of her body and saw no fire.
Whatever seared her was *inside* her body.

The blood tingled on her lips.

She narrowed her eyes. The searing, wonderful pain was
a distraction, but now, as she shifted, a terrible ache twisted
in her abdomen, and there was nothing pleasurable about it.
She touched her hand to the wound there, felt the rapidly
cooling blood. Beneath her back were hard ridges of stone—
marble steps. Above her was a vaulted ceiling sixty feet up,
with beams of dark wood.

In the Garden . . .

Eve squeezed her eyes closed. Vivid colors splashed
across her memory. In her mind's eye, she saw the Garden,
and she remembered the sweet scents and the peace of her
heart as she wandered its paths and ran with the wolves and
deer. In that place of bright recollection, she could still feel
Adam's hands on her, and the blissful contentment that had
been all she had ever known. All she ever would have known,
if not for the serpent.

A spike of agony shot through her skull. Images cascaded
across her thoughts. *The serpent, whispering. The fruit of the
Tree. The taste of knowledge. That first day, when she had
known shame; that first night, when she had learned fear.*

And Adam—sweet, innocent Adam. She had given him to eat of the fruit because she was afraid to be alone in the intimate knowledge of fear.

The Voice of God. The screaming of angels. Burning swords. The Gate of Eden closing behind them, leaving them lost in the vast wilderness of the world, with the bliss and peace and safety of the Garden denied them forever. Cast out of the Garden, they were easy prey for the demons.

Where were the angels then?

"Angels," she whispered, squeezing her eyes more tightly closed. Her fists clenched with hatred.

Her tongue ran out, and a shiver of pleasure went through her as she tasted the blood on her lips. Her hands shook, and a cold trickle of blood began to weep from her eyes. Thousands of years had passed. Hundreds of thousands of years, perhaps. Or more. Driven from the Garden, abandoned by God, she had been dragged down by the demon, her mind and body raped, her flesh tainted and transformed.

Eve had been made a new kind of monster. She had given birth to the children who would go forward and propagate the human race. And then she had become the tainted, viral evil, the first vampire, and she had become mother to a second race, which preyed upon the first.

She had relished every kill. Every drop of blood. Her off-spring had begun as a tribe, then spread around the world, and she had rejoiced with each new vampire she created. Humans feared the shadows because of her. They feared graveyards and alleys and the darkness beneath their beds. Eve celebrated, bathing in their blood, slashing flesh with her claws, stalking them without mercy.

Her children slaughtered her children.

And she had never known.

When the demon had violated her flesh and spirit, twisting her into this dark beast, all her memories of the Lord and of Eden, of purity and sweet innocence, had been swept away. An eternity of blood and murder had followed.

Now she remembered both.

She threw back her head, skull cracking on the stone beneath her, and screamed in anguish. Bloody tears slid down her face. Her entire body shook, and she twisted her head from side to side, trying to deny what she knew to be the truth. Eve remembered both lives, now, the bliss of the Garden . . . and the bliss of the slaughter.

"God, what have you made of me?" she whispered to the darkened place, to the stones in the walls and the wooden beams above. "Was my sin so great?"

Flashes of fresh memory spilled across her mind. The demon pursuing her, dragging her down, forcing the icy sharpness of itself inside of her. Her own screams were so loud that they echoed in her mind even now.

It had happened on a plain not so very far from Eden— close enough that the angels guarding the Gate must have seen. They had seen, those jealous, beautiful creatures with their fiery swords. They had seen, and done nothing to save her.

Angels.

"Jophiel," Eve whispered.

Her eyes opened. Shaking, she forced herself to rise. Her mind was awash with these images—memories lost to her for so long—but still she felt the shock when she at last understood where she was. She had lain on the marble steps just below the altar. Beyond it, on the rear wall, hung the cross, upon which was a carved figure of the Christ, in all of His glorious suffering.

A church.

The mother of evil stood in the House of God.

She hissed and flinched back, lowering her eyes. Then her brow furrowed. The image of the Christ had caused her no pain. Merely entering a holy place, dedicated to the worship of the Lord, should have boiled her flesh. Yet she stood there in the shadow of His Son, washed in colors shone by moonlight through stained glass—stood on His altar—and was unharmed.

"How can this be?"

Her skin still prickled with the delicious burning pain she'd felt before. Her whole body felt alight with it. She glanced around the church and she saw the angel, Jophiel, sprawled across the pews. One of his wings looked broken. He twitched and tried to stir, but consciousness eluded him, for now. His throat was torn open, and glistening crimson blood dripped to the stone floor.

Again, Eve licked her lips.

He'd nearly killed her, with his sword. Jophiel—her ancient enemy—had dragged her across the sky. One of the stained-glass windows, near the front doors, had been shattered. That had been where they crashed through. He'd intended to kill her, bringing her into the church. Eve had nearly defeated him, and Jophiel's last hope had been to bring her onto holy ground, where the divine presence of the Lord would destroy her, or weaken her enough that the angel could cut her down with that flaming sword.

But as Jophiel wrapped an arm around her, twisting the sword in her belly, Eve had filled her fists with his golden hair and dragged his throat to her jaws. She'd torn the flesh of an angel, and drunk deeply of the blood of the divine.

It raced through her now, the fire of an angel's blood, the taste of divinity, and she knew that must be the answer. Somehow, the blood of an angel had awoken the memories within her of the last time she had encountered such purity— her memories of the Garden of Eden.

Revulsion and self-loathing filled her at the thought of what she was, and all of the terror and death she had wrought upon the world. But Jophiel's blood had given her self-awareness, and, with it, a choice. Despite her hunger, she did not have to be a monster anymore.

A spark of hope ignited in her cold, dead heart. Could this be a second chance for her? Had the Lord given her this awakening so that she could seek redemption?

Then, as quickly as it had ignited, despair crushed that spark. How could she redeem an eternity of wading in death? She clutched a hand over the wound in her abdomen, which was already healing. The hunger still gnawed at her. She was still a monster; that had not changed. The Garden would never be hers again. Such innocence had no place in this world.

But perhaps there was peace to be found beyond this world. For an eternity she had been the devil's unwitting tool. Given a choice, now, could she make amends for all of that blood? Could she become the Hand of God? Could she find her way back to Him?

Shivering, Eve turned to face the crucifix. She gazed at it. And then she closed her eyes and tried to remember the Voice of God. She pictured herself in the Garden.

"They are the children of my blood and cruelty," she whispered, "the monstrous get of my rape by Abaddon. I will scour them from the face of the Earth, and the demon as well. I only pray that it will be enough."

The vow made, she paused a moment, wishing for the intimacy that she had felt with the Lord in the Beginning.

In the church, there was only silence.

But silence was enough for her, that night. It would have to be enough. Monster or not, she had been given a choice.

Eve went to stand above the unconscious Jophiel. The angel began to stir. She knew what he would see when he opened his eyes—the mother of all vampires. The plague of evil. The angel would never understand, for forgiveness was not his to bestow. And his kind had ever been just as cruel as their fallen brothers.

Eve spit on him.

Then she walked from the church and out into the moonlight, a crusade begun.

VILLEFRANCHE still had a medieval feeling about it. Eve had last traversed its cobblestoned streets and breathed in the perfume of its flowers 327 years before. Now, in the twenty-first century, little about the place had changed, except for the preponderance of tourists and the cafés and restaurants that serviced them.

The beauty of the Cote d'Azur reached its pinnacle in Villefranche. From the sandy beaches of the seaside to the way the shore extended its arms outward to create a natural bay, protecting the town from the elements, it seemed a tiny sliver of paradise. The cobblestoned streets crisscrossed back and forth up the steep hillside upon which the town was built. Terraced steps and paths and alleys separated blocks of terracotta, brick, and stone.

Eve stood on the main road, high above, and looked down

over the red-tiled roofs of the Old Town and at the Mediterranean beyond. The moonlight was her only illumination. She could only imagine how astonishing the view must have been during the day, with the sun picking out the colors of the architecture and the flowers, and the sky clear above the deeper blue of the sea.

"It's breathtaking," Clay said, behind her.

She turned and glanced at him. "I don't have any breath to take."

He smiled. "Even so."

Eve nodded. She liked to bust his balls. Clay was a good sport about it, which made him good company. Joe Clay wasn't his real name. The truth was, he did not have a real name. Word was, he was the Clay of God—the real thing—the actual material that He had used to design all of the creatures who had ever walked the Earth. When God was done, He'd just thrown the clay away, left it there on the new world.

If that was true—and she had no reason to doubt it—that made Clay the only creature in the world older than Eve.

"You ready?" he asked.

She frowned. Fucking stupid question. She'd spent the better part of four hundred years ready, tracking down every vampire she could get her hands on and exterminating the vermin. Her children. The darkness still cloaked her, just as it had when she was a monster, like them. But ever since that night when she had tasted Jophiel's blood and her memories had come back to her, it had been the vampires' turn to be afraid. She had become their bogeyman, the thing that they whispered about and warned each other to watch out for. Some did not believe she existed, until the very moment she was tearing out their dead hearts.

From time to time, one would rise among them as a leader. Whenever that happened, Eve made a special effort to track and kill it. She did not want the vampires to have hope. It was also convenient, because whenever some leech got arrogant enough to want to be the boss, lots of the others gathered around. She could destroy dozens of them in one fell swoop.

"Let's go," she said.

Side by side, Eve and Clay started down through the maze

of terraced paths that was Villefranche. In her Caroline Herrera top and white cotton pants, she was the picture of the wealthy tourist. She might have been an Italian model or a Brazilian heiress. Even here, where the rich and beautiful were merely part of the landscape, she drew attention. And, yet, with Clay at her side in his blue jeans and T-shirt, she blended.

People sat at outdoor cafés, drinking wine or coffee on patios. Lovers walked hand in hand, some curled against one another in acrobatic marvels, even as they strolled together. An old woman watered her flowers with a rusting can. Two men walked a dog, the three of them fashioning some kind of family. A stunningly handsome man with thin, Gallic features and piercing eyes stood on a corner and played the violin for all those who might appreciate his music.

He was a vampire.

The violinist caught sight of her, and the smile vanished from his face. He turned and began to make his way down a steep alley that curved down toward the Mediterranean amidst shops and restaurants. Laughter and the tinkling of wineglasses erupted from an open door. The vampire continued to play his violin with every step, moving slowly, capering a bit as he entertained those he passed.

"Him?" Clay asked.

Eve smiled. "Him."

The shapeshifter reached out and twined his fingers in hers. Eve resisted the urge to pull her hand away. Instead, she gave him a look full of warmth and love. In this form, Clay was ruggedly handsome, with his dark hair and stubbly beard and those ancient eyes. But they were not lovers. Their intimacy was for appearances' sake, so that they would blend with their surroundings. Eve had entertained the idea of becoming Clay's lover.

Fucking him, you mean, she thought.

A small chuckle escaped her lips, and Clay looked at her strangely. The odd thing was that fucking was not what she thought of at all when she considered the possibility of sharing a bed with him. And perhaps that was why she had not allowed herself to get any closer to Clay. Anytime Eve wanted a man, she took what she wanted. They never argued. She would take them for a ride, and sometimes there would be wounds, and sometimes there would be blood—always voluntary. But it was always on her terms.

Clay knew who and what she was, but he was probably the only creature in the world who was not intimidated by that knowledge. He had been even closer to the Creator, in his way, than she had been, in her days in the Garden. The loneliness and confusion that ached in him was like a beacon to her. Clay had been discarded by God, just as she had been. He understood her in a way no one else could. The idea of becoming more intimate with him frightened her.

Eve didn't like the feeling. It pissed her off. All of which was a good way to mask how she really felt. All of her fighting and fucking and laughter kept her distracted, when she wasn't hunting vampires. Her crusade had been going on for four centuries, and not once had she received any sign from God that He had noticed.

Yet she kept working toward her redemption. She had felt His presence and heard His voice, so long ago. Eve had faith that God would not have allowed her to continue to exist without giving her the chance to redeem herself, to cleanse the horrors from her soul. If she allowed herself to get too close to Clay, she would dwell too much on the callous way in which the Creator had abandoned him, and she would be forced to wonder if she had been wrong, to wonder if redemption was beyond her reach.

They were close, Eve and Clay.

But she would not get closer.

If she had to kill every vampire, eradicate the last leech on the face of the Earth, to earn her redemption, then that was precisely what she would do. Even if it took her until the end of time.

Which brought her back to the question that had been plaguing her for the past few years. What if eradicating vampirism was not enough? What if there was some key that she was missing, some task that she had to perform in order to earn her redemption? Was there some wrong she could set right, some evil to be destroyed, or some fated moment when by her actions she might call the Creator's attention down upon herself and *force* Him to forgive her, to heal her, to let her rest?

Sometimes she hated God more than the vampire filth she had spawned, more, even, than the demon that had made her a monster.

"You all right?" Clay whispered.

Eve glanced at him, at those eternal eyes, and she nodded. "Fine."

"I'm getting the idea you wish I hadn't come," he said, keeping his voice low and amiable as they walked down the cobblestone steps. "I know this crusade is pretty personal—"

"No," she said, dismissive. "I'm glad you're here. No way to know how many of them there'll be."

But that was the big question, wasn't it? Why had she asked him to come? Eve had slain thousands of vampires since her awakening from evil. She didn't need a partner. The redemption she sought was for herself alone.

The violinist disappeared into a side alley ahead. Eve picked up her pace, hand still linked with Clay's. Once they entered the alley, she let him go. Shuttered windows hung open, and there were sheets and clothes hung to dry over windowsills. A man passed them in the other direction, smoking a pipe, tobacco so rich and redolent that Eve could not help but think of Conan Doyle. Then a boy raced past them on a bicycle, calling out ahead of him so that people dodged out of his way. He had a small horn on the front, and he honked it several times as he rattled over the cobblestones, reckless with his own safety but somehow still worried about those who might be fool enough to get in his way.

A slender man and woman ran their hands over one another, leaning against a wall, just out of reach of the light thrown by a lantern that hung from a bracket on the wall.

Of the vampire and his violin, there was no visible sign. And yet . . .

"Do you hear it?" Eve asked.

"Yes. Just ahead."

The music continued, luring them on. And she had no doubt that it was a lure. The violinist wanted them to follow. Surely he would reach the nest in Villefranche where he and others of his kind rested during the day, and where they brought their victims at night. The new leader that had sprung up, a Spaniard called Orjo, would be there as well.

Eve smiled.

Clay hesitated. "He's the bait."

Eve flipped her long, raven hair back and glanced at him, wearing a smirk. "No, babe, he only thinks he's the bait. We're the bait . . . and we're the trap, too."

They followed the music through another alley, and beneath several vaulted passages, where archway tunnels led beneath houses. The sense of going back in time, of walking the Medieval town, only grew as they explored the Old Town. They crossed small squares, one in the shadow of the tall church at the center of Villefranche, even as the church bell chimed eleven.

And then they came to another vaulted passage. Eve and Clay paused at the entrance to read the name engraved on the entrance. RUE OBSCURA. Eve thought it aptly named. As they entered, they were leaving the rest of Villefranche behind. Several other people were walking ahead of them, chatting in fascination, gazing around at the stone construction of the passageway. The Rue Obscura ran under several blocks of houses. Its many archways and stone walls comprised a long tunnel through the heart of the town. Iron lanterns hung at intervals from the high ceiling, bright lightbulbs burning from within metal grills.

The violin music seemed to come from everywhere and nowhere along the Rue Obscura, drifting like mist along the masonry walls. Eve and Clay walked along the passage, glancing warily in both directions each time they came to an open arch on either side. To the left, the openings led uphill, and they could see people and hear laughter. The openings on the right led downhill, along stone steps, and over the red-tiled roofs they could see the Mediterranean, calm and beautiful.

Clay glanced at Eve as they walked deeper into the Rue Obscura. His body language had changed entirely. His muscles were tensed and ready for a fight. She nodded. There was little need for pretense, anymore.

Just as she thought this, the music grew loud and brash. They moved beneath a stone arch and into a new section of the dungeonlike tunnel, and the violinist waited for them just ahead. He leaned against the wall, just as the lovers had earlier. With a final stroke, he ceased playing his instrument and lowered the bow, watching them openly, with a languid, almost bored sort of stare.

Eve bit into her lower lip, just to taste the blood on her tongue.

"Now," she whispered.

But it was not a signal to Clay. It was her prediction. And it was correct. Even as she spoke that single syllable, shutters clacked open on the windows down in that vaulted passage. Dark, lithe figures leaped from open windows. Others dropped down from the ceiling above, unfolding from where they had clung to exposed wooden beams and the iron chains that held lanterns aloft. Like giant spiders, they landed on the cobblestones and scuttled into position. Still more emerged from the side passages.

A middle-aged German couple had been coming along the rue toward them from the other direction. Eve and Clay could only watch as the vampires swarmed them in near-total silence and tore their throats open. Blood sprayed, and the vampires drank.

The moment was broken.

Clay roared his righteous fury, enraged not at their savagery, but at his inability to stop them from killing. Eve watched in fascination as he surged toward them, changing with his first step. His flesh flowed like liquid, and she could hear the pop of bones shifting inside of him as he shifted into his primal form, his natural self. Clay must have been nine feet tall, his flesh a brownish orange in the lanternlight, cracked and split like dried earth. He had no hair, and was clad only in an Egyptian-style kilt.

The first of the vampires clawed furrows in the rough earth of his flesh. Clay moved quicker, even, than these vermin. He snatched up the vampire by her throat and drove her upward at the iron lantern above. The metal broke through her back and burst through her chest, destroying most of the withered organs inside, her heart included.

She exploded in a cloud of ash that sifted to the ground.

Then the fight was on.

The vampires swept in. From the sheath at her back, hidden beneath her blouse, Eve withdrew the Gemini Blade that Squire had made for her. One side of the curved blade was iron, the other silver. Either one would do for her purposes.

Eve leaped into the air, spinning, and kicked the nearest vampire so hard that its skull shattered and it fell to the cobblestones. It would heal, if she let it. Coming down, she grabbed a fistful of the long, greasy hair of a male and twisted, using the leech for leverage as she kicked out again, knocking two others back.

She landed on her feet, and swept the Gemini Blade to the right, decapitating a fat, pustulant thing that lunged at her. It burst in a flash of cinders, even as she turned, gripping the Gemini tighter, and punched the iron edge at the face of a grinning, dark-skinned woman. The blade cut off her head above the lower jaw, leaving the bottom fangs gleaming in the lanternlight.

Perhaps a dozen feet away, they swarmed around Clay again. He was so huge that he made a large target. Six or seven vampires had their hands on him, but there was nothing they could do to him. The shapeshifter could not be made one of them, and in this form, he could not even be made to bleed. They gouged at his clay flesh, tore chunks of it away, but he would rebuild himself. And as he did, he destroyed them.

Clay reached up and snapped a centuries-old beam from the ceiling, a narrow crossbar that splintered as it broke off. He tossed three vampires away. Two of them crashed into the stone wall, and the third landed on the stone floor. With a grunt, Clay turned and plunged that splintered beam into the heart of a vampire. Faster than they could have known, he pulled it out and struck the next, and the next, and the next. A breeze swept through the Rue Obscura, and the ash of vampires danced along the cobblestones.

Eve kept killing. This was her crusade. This scourge upon humanity had begun with her, and it would end with her.

A vampire grabbed hold of her long hair. Grinning, she spun, and sliced off his arm with the silver edge of Gemini. The poison silver coursed through the vampire, and it screamed, just before she swung the blade a second time, severing its head with a crunch of spine and gristle.

The one she had first thrown to the ground, shattering its skull, began to rise. She drove one sandaled foot down onto its chest and punched the Gemini down like a guillotine blade. More dust swirled around her.

A trio of teenaged girls, civilians, came walking into the Rue Obscura from one of the side passages. When they saw Clay murdering vampires, and two of the vermin started toward them, the girls screamed and ran. Only one of the vampires followed, but there was nothing Eve could do, as the rest of the tribe was still swarming them.

Impatient, now, Eve punched her left fist through the chest of a towering vampire and tore out his withered heart. As he fell away to cinders, she crouched low, spinning around with the Gemini ready. The vampires around her hesitated now, not wanting to throw their lives away.

"You didn't know who it was, coming for you," she said.

Their eyes gleamed in the lanternlight, down there in the dark passage. But they were skittish now, and she knew she was correct. They were only just now beginning to realize.

"Oh, yes," she said. "It's me."

"Eve," one of the vampires said, anxious.

But he didn't run. Eve frowned. Why wouldn't they run? What could give them such confidence against her? All she could think of was that this new leader, the Spaniard, Orjo, had made them believe they could destroy her. Time to put a stop to that.

"Orjo!" she called, in a singsong voice. "Come to Mama!"

One of the vampires laughed. That unnerved her.

"What's so fucking funny?"

"Orjo's dead, bitch. You already dusted him."

Eve frowned, and the vampires began to close the circle around her once again. She watched as Clay lifted a hulking leech above his head and tore the vampire apart with his bare hands. The shapeshifter could have turned into a lion and bitten their heads off, or a bear, and snapped them into kindling. But in this form, they could not draw blood. He grabbed another vampire and swung it at the wall. Its head burst like an overripe melon.

We're killing them. They don't stand a chance, she thought.

"Are you just fucking dense?" Eve demanded, glancing from one vampire to the next as they circled her. She tightened her grip on the Gemini's handle. "Why aren't you afraid?"

Even as she spoke, another couple came along the Rue Obscura. Eve saw them, then saw the sling the mother wore across her chest, and the baby sleeping within.

A thin, ugly vampire with a crooked nose took a step nearer, almost daring her to attack.

"It doesn't matter if we die, as long as you die with us," the vampire said, a giddy little laugh bubbling out of his throat. "And with the allies we have tonight, you *will* die."

"Not before you," Eve snarled as she leaped into a spinning kick that shattered the arrogant vampire's face and that crooked nose.

Before she could finish it off, four of the leeches broke away and raced for the couple and their baby. The woman screamed, holding the baby against her in its sling as she backed away. Her husband started to shout, full of male bluster, trying to hide his fear. The first vampire to reach him grabbed him by the hair and slammed his face into the stone masonry of the wall. He cried out for his wife to flee.

"Clay!" Eve called, turning to see him pulping a leech's head against a stone archway.

"Busy!" he snapped. Five of them hung from him. One had attached itself to his back, elongated claws thrust into the earthen flesh, jaws clamped on his neck. The thing gnawed him like a dog, and Clay barely seemed to notice.

Eve shot an elbow into the face of a vampire trying to grab her from behind. Bone broke and fangs snapped on impact and the vampire roared in rage and pain. He would recover, but Eve wasn't waiting around. A thin little blond girl raced toward her, no more than twelve years old when she had been turned. She looked like a whore, painted eyes and sheer blouse and lipstick so bright it gleamed red in the dark.

"Enough," Eve growled, and she ran at the little girl.

The lithe blond vampire reached for her when they were about to collide. Eve punched the Gemini Blade at her chest.

The girl tried to block it with her arms, but the blade cut through muscle and bone, hacked off her right hand, and split her torso between her breasts. Eve had cut her heart in two.

She tore the Gemini out of the girl's chest with a wet snap, and rose, glancing around, feeling the feral rage rising up within her. Her fingers lengthened and tapered into twelve-inch talons, the nails like blades themselves.

The mother screamed. One of the vampires tore the sling from her with a rip of fabric. The baby wailed in terror. Eve cried out in return, as though it could understand her answer. Two vampires dragged the mother to the ground in the yellow lanternlight.

"No!" Eve snapped.

Clay was otherwise occupied, and she was closer.

Eve ran toward the vampires as they tore into the parents. The leech who'd grabbed the baby unwrapped it from its sling with a sickening grin, like a hideous child opening a candy bar. A long rivulet of pink saliva drooled from its mouth.

Beyond them, a solitary figure stepped into the Rue Obscura from one of the alleys that crossed through it.

"Stop!" he commanded.

Pure, white light flashed as he lifted his hands. Eve cried out as the light seared her skin, and she threw up her hands to protect herself. The vampires who had been attacking the couple shrieked, and she heard them collapse on the cobblestones.

She lowered her hands, eyes slitted against the diminishing light, and vile, poisonous hatred bubbled up inside of her. The new arrival had taken the screaming infant from the vampire's hands. The leeches had fallen to their knees around him, hiding their faces.

"No babies," the angel Jophiel declared, white-feathered wings unfurling behind him. His stern, too-perfect features were pale and gleaming in the divine light that streamed from within him. His golden hair hung to his shoulders.

Stylish prick, Eve thought.

The vampire who'd had the baby in his hands whined. The others laughed softly and went back to murdering the child's parents. They tore open the mother's abdomen and pulled out coils of her intestines with a slippery sound. A red-haired female vamp ripped her uterus from the gaping wound and began to gnaw on it.

Now she understood why the vampires had not run. They hadn't come alone. This whole thing had been a setup. A few vampires circled her warily but did not make any further attempt to attack. They were waiting for Jophiel to give the word.

"Wow, saving babies," Eve said, glaring at her ancient enemy. "You're a fucking hero."

Jophiel grinned at the irony, spreading his wings farther. He loved to show them off. Eve had ripped them from his back once, but they'd grown back.

"You've got strange taste in friends," she snarled.

For some reason, Jophiel thought that was very funny. He laughed and shook his head, then sighed. "You have no idea, darling."

"Clay!" Eve shouted, without turning to look at him. "The baby!"

"Coming!" the shapeshifter called, and she heard the crack of bone and shriek of pain from a vampire that had stood in his way. The cobblestones shook as he made his way toward her. "What the hell is going on?"

He'd seen the angel. Still, Eve didn't bother to turn.

"Unfinished business," she drawled. "And the time's come to finish it."

"Not today," Jophiel said, kissing the baby's tender skull. The child had stopped crying and gazed up at him with love. His golden eyes gleamed as he looked up at Eve again. "Not to worry. I'll leave him in human hands."

"You'll put him down, or we'll take him from you," she replied, sliding the Gemini Blade back into its sheath at her back. Her long talons were enough to tear the angel apart, and that was what she wanted—to do it with her bare hands.

Jophiel arched an eyebrow, caressing the baby's scalp. "Who's we?"

Wary, Eve risked a quick glance over her right shoulder at Clay. The massive shapeshifter reached over his shoulder and peeled the vampire from his back, hurling it aside. His dry, cracked, clay flesh was already filling in where it had been

torn away. Lanternlight gleamed on his bald pate. His eyes
shone green in the shadows of the Rue Obscura.

Vampires still lunged for him, but he paid them no mind.

Together, Eve and Clay would take down Jophiel, and as
many vampires as the turncoat angel wanted to throw at
them. Finally, the bastard had shown his true colors. Down
across the millennia he had pretended that his hatred of Eve
was in the righteous service of God, but she had known he
was a sadistic shit all along. Allying himself with vampires
was all the evidence of his hypocrisy she would ever need. It
had lifted her heart to see, because there was no longer any
doubt in her mind. Jophiel didn't speak for God. He had divine essence in his blood and flesh and the light of God in his
hands, but he was just another flawed creation.

"You get the baby," she told Clay. "I kill the angel."

"Done," he replied, not questioning her for a moment. She
felt absurdly grateful.

Then a shiver ran through her, and the very air in the Rue
Obscura seemed to ripple. Several of the unbroken lanterns
went quietly dark, and her skin crawled with the attentions of
a thousand spiders. A stink filled her nostrils, and it was familiar.

The vampires began to laugh.

Jophiel sneered at her.

Eve had thought the presence of the angel filled her with
hatred. But that was a tiny candle flame compared to the infernal rage that filled her now. Stomach twisting with revulsion, she turned to see the hunched, hulking figure coming
along the Rue Obscura behind Clay. The vampires scurried
from the demon's path. His hooves clacked on the cobblestones, and he moved so swiftly that Clay barely had time
to turn before Abaddon reached out his giant hands, gripped
the shapeshifter by the head, and hurled him back along the
vaulted passage.

Clay slammed into an arch. A massive slab of stone shook
loose and crashed down on his right shoulder. He grunted and
went down face-first on the cobblestones. Clay started to rise,
but then the vampires swarmed him, all of them at once, tearing and beating at him and shrieking in pleasure.

Abaddon stood taller than Clay. Even crouched on his

haunches, he had to bend to stride through the Rue Obscura. Bones jutted from the top of his spine, sharpened yellow spikes. His wings were pinioned behind him, and his crimson flesh was such a dark red that the shadows turned it black. His eyes burned hot as coals, fire licking up from the corners, and his two, massive horns curved back away from his skull and dragged up sparks when they brushed the stone ceiling.

Eve stood between the angel, cradling the baby, and the demon. Images flashed across her mind of the days, the months, she had spent as Abaddon's plaything. She could still feel his vile touch, the pain as he violated her, tearing her, ruining her, and now his insinuating laughter filled the Rue Obscura, and it was as though only moments had passed since his terrible ministrations had transformed her into this. His blood, his seed, had infected her, and created of her a new monster.

Eve's scream tore up from her throat. She lunged at Abaddon, ancient madness overtaking her.

Abaddon opened his arms to embrace her. Eve plunged her talons into his flesh, tearing, digging. Black blood spilled.

"I've missed you," the demon whispered into her ear, nuzzling her hair, breathing her scent.

Eve shrieked, but Abaddon held her so close and so tightly in his grip that she could not break his hold, could not withdraw to tear at him again. She forced her talons deeper. If she couldn't pull away, she'd push all the way through and rip out his spine.

But then she felt the searing of her own flesh and saw the brilliant white glow that told her the angel was close. Jophiel came up behind her and touched her hair, just as he had the baby's. She despised him even more for that.

"Come on, Eve. Time to take you *home*."

THE vampires squirmed above him like a nest of vipers. Clay tore at them, crushed their heads, ripped out their hearts. They could not kill him—he didn't think so, anyway. But there were so many that even he began to grow weary. The ash from all those that he had killed swirled in the air, dust devils eddying in the breeze along the cobblestones.

As he reached down to pick up his severed finger, a gust of wind rose within the cottage, a swirling mass beginning to take shape.

He'd hoped to have his finger reattached before any communication with his operatives, especially with Ceridwen. But the cell phone, which was to be used only in the case of absolute emergency, had started to ring before he'd had the chance to gather his wits and prepare the healing spell that would allow him to reattach his severed digit.

The wind grew in intensity, forming a swirling vortex of dust and dirt in the center of the living room. Conan Doyle stepped back, raising his uninjured hand to protect his eyes from the tiny specks of flying debris. A familiar figure appeared within the maelstrom of dust and dirt, ruffling curtains and sliding furniture, knocking over a floor lamp. Ceridwen had arrived, riding the traveling wind from Sedona to his side.

He would have preferred that she stay exactly where she was until he had a better understanding of what had befallen them, but still Conan Doyle found his pulse racing at the sight of her. A smile lifted the corners of his mouth.

The wind ceased as abruptly as it had been aroused, and the Princess of Faerie stood before him, her flowing cotton robes stained with the dirt of the desert and spattered with what could only have been blood.

"You were injured," Ceridwen stated, her violet eyes finding his.

Like a small child caught in an act of disobedience, he put his injured hand behind his back.

"Nothing to concern yourself with, my dear," he said, trying to slip the bloody handkerchief containing his finger into the pocket of his jacket.

"Why am I having such a difficult time believing you?" she asked, leaning her staff against the wall before crossing the room toward him.

"Truly there was no need for you to have—" Conan Doyle began, but she stifled his explanation with a hungry kiss. He brought his arms around her, ignoring the throbbing pain in his hand, lost in the feel of her against him.

She gripped the wrist of his injured hand and lifted it up for her to see.

Conan Doyle sucked air through his teeth, the injury throbbing beneath the makeshift bandage he'd made from a dishrag.

"Is this what I've no need to concern myself with?" she asked, carefully pulling the rag away to reveal the blood-caked stump of his finger. Ceridwen gasped, a Dannaaini curse leaving her lips at the sight of the injury.

"It's not as bad as it looks," he said, pulling his hand away and making his way toward the kitchen table. "I was just about to reattach the finger when you called."

He took the handkerchief from his pocket as he pulled out a chair to sit down.

"You say a bogey did this to you?" she asked, and he could hear the disbelief in her tone. If the situation had been reversed, he would have doubted it as well.

"A bogey whose abilities have somehow been increased tenfold," Conan Doyle said as he carefully unfolded the handkerchief to expose his severed finger.

Ceridwen moved to stand behind him. "And while you were dealing with your foe, I was confronting mine."

"Exactly," he said, picking up the finger, examining it to make sure that none of it was missing. He was pleased to see that it was intact.

"Do you think there might be a connection?"

"A distinct possibility," the mage said, bringing the bloody end of the finger up to his mouth. In the ancient tongue of Fey healers, he spoke to the severed flesh, coaxing it back to vigor. He stared at the drying gore of the finger's trunk and blew gently upon it.

The dried flesh grew suddenly moist, the cells and capillaries reinvigorated by his incantation. He could still recall learning that spell during the Twilight Wars. Gleaw the Wise would coax those who should have bid good-bye to life back to health so that they could continue the battle.

Conan Doyle hissed between clenched teeth as he rejoined the finger to his hand. He continued to speak the ancient language of healing, convincing the still-living flesh, blood, and bone to accept what had been removed. The living flesh protested, having little interest in allowing the dead matter to be rejoined with the still thriving. Feeling himself growing tired, Conan Doyle focused his will and repeated the incantation, demanding that his flesh acquiesce.

Then he felt her hand upon his shoulder, her voice in unison with his—*her magic joined with his*—and he felt the pain as his body began to heal. Bone fused back to bone, tendons reconnected, blood flowed through capillaries. His flesh knitted itself together, thanks to the power of their combined magic. Conan Doyle knew that he was one of the world's most powerful mages, but with Ceridwen by his side, her strength added to his, the enormity of what he felt flowing through him left him in awe.

His finger tingled painfully, but he was able to move it. The faint bloody line where it had been bitten away and rejoined had already begun to fade.

"How does it feel?" she asked him.

"Whole," he replied, rising from the chair, wriggling all his fingers, glad to be complete again.

She took his hand in hers and brought it to her mouth, softly kissing the once-injured finger. "As good as new," she said.

They both smiled at the Fey princess's use of the vernacular. Gazing into her eyes, Conan Doyle saw all the reason he would ever need to continue with the struggle against the encroaching darkness. That war had come to define his existence, but in the years that they had spent apart, he had become numb and hollow. She had brought him to life again, reminded him what he was fighting for.

"What of your own injuries?" he asked.

"I'm fine," she said, her voice no more than a whisper, eyes still locked upon his. "Bumps and bruises that have already begun to heal."

Conan Doyle cupped her face in his hands, bending down to kiss her. It unsettled him to know that he cared so very much for anyone. Love made him vulnerable, but he could not—and would not—combat his own heart.

Just as their lips were about to touch, the two of them lost in one another, his cell phone began to ring.

• • • •

" I 'LL be there as quickly as I can," Dr. Graves said, then the connection to Dubrovnik was broken.

The ghost could have held on to the phone, but it required sustained concentration for him to grasp solid objects. Instead, Danny had dialed and held it up for him to talk, and to listen to Conan Doyle. Now he nodded to the boy, and Danny set the receiver back in its graffiti-incised cradle. They were standing in the dark beside a pay phone outside a convenience store off the Jamaica Way. The streetlight above them had been broken, and the darkness was welcome.

"Well, what did he say?" Danny asked.

"His suspicions were already aroused," Graves replied, watching as Julia came out of the store, removing the cellophane wrapper from a pack of cigarettes. She'd been so upset by what they had just experienced that she'd scrounged together the necessary change from inside the car to restart a habit that she had quit over ten years ago.

Long dead himself, in life the ghost had been a medical doctor. He wanted to say something to her, but knew that this was not the time.

"Both Conan Doyle and Ceridwen have been attacked as well," Graves said, looking back at the demonic boy. Danny had thrown on a hooded sweatshirt that he'd found in the backseat of his mother's car, helping to hide some of his more disturbing attributes.

"Clay attacked them, too?" Danny asked.

"No, two foes from their past."

"Who was attacked?" Julia asked, shaking out the match she'd used to light her smoke and letting it drop to the ground. She nervously puffed on the cigarette.

"Ceridwen and Mr. Doyle," Danny answered.

Julia looked at Graves, fear in her eyes. "Are they all right?"

The ghost nodded. "They're fine, but Conan Doyle cannot imagine the timing of the attacks being coincidental."

"Did you tell him that it was Clay who attacked us?" Danny asked.

"I did, and he suspects there is something more to *this* as well."

"What's to suspect?" Danny growled. "Our fucking friend tried to kill us."

Julia put her arm around her son. "It's all right," she tried to reassure him, careful not to let any of the loose ash from her cigarette fall on him.

"Arthur isn't convinced it was Clay," Graves continued, concentrating on keeping his ghostly form as material as possible, so as not to draw attention from the people coming and going from the store. It helped that it was dark. He knew his body seemed more substantial in the shadows.

"Then tell me who it was," Danny said. "We saw him, Doc . . . *you* saw him. It was fucking Clay. Who else could it be changing into *Animal Planet*?"

The boy grunted and stalked away from them. Dr. Graves could see that Danny was attempting to control his anger, to keep a tight rein on the violent, demonic nature that was his legacy.

"All right, Danny," Graves said. "Losing your temper won't benefit anyone right now."

Julia reached out to Danny, rubbing his shoulder. "Leonard's right, kid," she reassured. "Deep breaths and all that."

The boy glared at his mother, his eyes glinting yellow from inside the shadows cast by the hood over his head. "Sure, I'm sorry," he finally said, sighing. "I'm still a little worked up. I trusted the guy, y'know?"

"We all did," Julia said. "I'm still a little wound up myself."

"Can I have one of those?" Danny asked, gesturing with a clawed finger toward her cigarette. "It might help calm my nerves."

Julia seemed stunned by his request. "Certainly not," she said, taking a final puff before dropping the remains to the ground and grinding it into the concrete.

"Oh, but it's okay for *you* to start again," he chided her.

"After what I've been through lately, smoking is the least damaging of the vices I have to choose from."

"What's it going to do to me?" he asked, the tension back in his voice. "Do you actually think anything worse could happen to me now?"

Graves placed himself between them. The nearness to him was chilling, and they each backed away, reacting to the sudden drop in temperature.

"That's enough of that," the ghost told them. "If Conan Doyle doubts that it was really Clay who attacked us, let's leave it a question mark until we learn more."

"Yeah, yeah, yeah," Danny said, folding his arms across his chest. "So what now? Is Doyle coming home or what?"

Graves thought carefully about what he was going to say next.

"I have instructions to join him and Ceridwen in Dubrovnik as quickly as possible."

Danny narrowed his eyes. "And what about us?"

"Per Conan Doyle's instructions, I'll accompany you back to Louisburg Square to make sure the intruder is gone. Once we've secured the house, you'll remain there to watch over the brownstone and your mother."

"What?" Danny shouted, baring his needle teeth. "You've gotta be fucking kidding me! Is he crazy?"

"He was emphatic," the ghost explained. "Squire will apparently be along soon to join you in keeping watch. Look, Danny, Conan Doyle doesn't think you're ready to rejoin the Menagerie in battle just yet. Frankly, I agree with him."

Fire sparked in the demon boy's golden eyes. "If I'm going to be left on the fucking sidelines, why am I even hanging around?"

Graves reached out, willing his hand solid, and gripped Danny's arm. "Listen to me very closely. In recent months you've given all of us reason to doubt your self-control. I have faith that you're going to learn to really control the darker side of your nature. But we're in crisis, now, and we can't gamble with our lives. Until we're sure you're ready, we won't run that risk."

Danny snarled, pulling his arm away. "Yeah, I'm a roll of the fucking dice. But you've got faith, Doc. I'll be ready any day now, right?" He stomped toward the car.

Julia had stepped away, allowing them their exchange of words. She was smoking another cigarette as Graves glided toward her.

"Are you comfortable staying at the brownstone with him?"

She was silent for a moment, gazing at the car between puffs. "Sure, I'm fine," she said, looking at Graves, a weak smile on her face. "Why wouldn't I be? He's my son."

Dr. Graves returned to the car with her, choosing to open the passenger-side door and close it after himself as if he were still of flesh and blood, just in case anyone was watching.

Julia snuffed out her latest cigarette in the car's ashtray and turned to him.

"Could you do the honors again?" she asked, motioning toward the ignition.

Dr. Graves complied, placing his hand within the steering column, using his ghostly substance to turn the engine over. Car running, she put the vehicle in drive, made a U-turn, and drove from the parking lot.

"What if he's right?" Danny asked, from the backseat of the Volvo.

The ghost looked into the rearview mirror to see the boy's luminescent eyes glowing in the darkness.

"What if it wasn't Clay . . . but shit, how can that be possible? You saw the same thing as me . . . you both did. There couldn't be two like him . . . could there?"

Dr. Graves pondered the question. If there was anything he had learned since becoming a part of Conan Doyle's strange group—his Menagerie—it was that no concept or theory was too outrageous to be considered.

When dealing with the ways of the weird, anything was possible.

"I don't know, Danny. But we're going to find out."

UNNOTICED by the constables of Villefranche, the gray mouse skittered along the stone foundations, losing itself in the cool shadows of the medieval structures.

The mournful wail of an ambulance siren filled the early-morning gloom as the tiny creature paused, looking back momentarily toward the murder scene. Frenzied law officers were attempting to cope with the brutality of what had transpired in their normally tranquil city.

Knowing that there was nothing more it could do, the mouse continued on, moving along the cobblestoned streets, searching for a place away from prying eyes.

In a deep patch of shadow, Clay assumed his human guise—the delicate rodent form abandoned for his mask of humanity. The shapeshifter emerged from the shadows, cautious eyes scanning for any sign that he had been noticed. Finding none, he continued on.

Every instinct told him that he should be searching for Eve, but intuition assured him it would be a fruitless task. Wherever she had been spirited off to, it would not be nearby. A nagging voice inside his head told him that what had transpired here was no simple vengeance upon her. Had they wanted only to take revenge, they would have slain Eve, not taken her away. This had to be bigger than that.

His mind's eye was seared with the image of Eve held between the angel and the demon as though they were children fighting over some prize won at carnival game. Clay felt an apprehension the likes of which he had never known before.

He picked up his pace, striding quickly down the cobblestoned street toward the lodging that he and Eve had acquired for their stay in Villefranche. His cell phone had been destroyed in combat with the vampire swarm, but he knew he had to contact Doyle immediately to let him know what had transpired and that Eve had been taken.

Clay altered the structure of his eyes to improve his vision, and the gloom of the early-morning hours appeared to him like full daylight. He searched the shadows for any potential threat, but the city streets were as quiet as the grave.

The Grand Hôtel Du Lion D'Or was nestled in a nearly hidden corner of a residential street. It resembled a medieval castle, its stone walls concealed in a verdant covering of ivy. The concierge at the front desk had instructed them when they'd checked in that the doors of the hotel would be locked promptly at midnight and that their room keys would grant them access to the building. Clay searched his pockets, found his key, and let himself inside. The structure was eerily silent except for the gurgling of a watercooler from the darkened office behind the vacant front desk. Not wanting to wait for the antique elevator, he climbed the stairs to their adjoining rooms on the third floor. He glanced at the door to Eve's room and again turned over the riddle of the night's chaos.

Heaven and Hell, acting in unison.

Such a thing was momentous. Their purpose must have been as well.

Clay entered the room, not bothering to switch on the light, his eyes still augmented to see in the darkness. As he approached the phone resting on the nightstand, he heard a noise.

From Eve's room.

He approached the locked connecting door, and as he had done with his eyes, he did to his ears. Gripping the cold metal knob, Clay tilted his head toward the door and listened.

There were two voices, creatures speaking in excited whispers as they went through Eve's belongings. Even though they had planned only to be away for two days, Eve had still insisted on bringing two full suitcases, as well as a carry-on bag.

I need my stuff, she'd told him, and he'd shaken his head in dismay.

The memory acted as a kind of spark. Crushing the metal doorknob, Clay broke the lock, charging into the other room. What he saw inside enraged him all the more.

A pair of vampires—one male and one female—stood among the refuse of Eve's emptied suitcases. The female was holding one of Eve's silk blouses against her body, a startled expression on her gaunt, undead face as Clay barged in.

She hissed at him, long slavering fangs bared as he came at her.

"That does not belong to you," Clay growled as he shed his human guise, resuming the towering, earthen shape that was his true form. He wrapped his hand around the female leech's throat, choking away the hiss of ferocity, squeezing so tightly that the pathetic creature's head popped from her body before she exploded in a shower of ash.

Eve's blouse fluttered to the floor.

The male knew that it was futile to fight him.

"You were supposed to have been killed," the vampire

shrieked, scrabbling across the room floor on all fours, making his way toward the drawn, velvet drapes that covered the windows.

But Clay was faster. He dived, grabbing the vampire's ankle in a grip that pulverized the bones beneath the pale, undead flesh.

The vampire shrieked, rolling over onto its back, slashing at him with razor talons. Clay reached down and picked the squirming predator off the ground by his leather vest.

"In case you haven't noticed, your friends failed," Clay said, giving him a savage shake.

The leech threw himself forward, burying his fangs in the shapeshifter's cheek.

"Stop that!" Clay roared, pulling the creature off, the vampire coming away with a large mouthful of the dark soil that was his true flesh. The clay.

The night-thing thrashed in his grasp, choking and coughing as large chunks of mud dropped from his open mouth. Clay tore off the vampire's arm. The leech's scream was ear-splitting. Clay tossed the arm aside.

"You son of a bitch!" the vampire cried in fury and agony.

Clay responded the best way he knew how—by ripping the other arm from its socket. Over the vampire's screams, he tossed that one on the floor as well.

"Have we established who holds the upper hand?" the shapeshifter asked.

The vampire squirmed in pain, moaning loudly as thick gouts of stolen blood spewed from the ragged stumps where his arms had been.

"I have some questions I'd like to ask you," Clay said, holding the vampire close to his face.

"I don't know a thing," the vampire hissed, his crimson eyes wild.

"Too bad," Clay said.

Digging his fingers deep into the flesh and muscle, he tore off one of the creature's legs. The limbs came away with no more difficulty than the arms. Clay grinned.

"I'm going to ask you anyway."

Clay tossed the vampire's mangled body up against the

wall. The creature was completely crippled, flopping around in its own fluids, begging for Clay to kill it.

"Not until after we talk, and after I've made a phone call. See, your pals took someone I care very much about. Every second that goes by, I worry more about what might happen to her. And for every one of those seconds, I'm going to hurt you unless you tell me what I need to know."

He sat on Eve's bed, the springs creaking noisily. He reached for the phone and, reading the instructions printed in six languages on a plastic information card, dialed Conan Doyle's cell phone number. It rang only once before he heard Conan Doyle's unmistakable voice.

"Yes?"

"It's Clay," he said, and started to recount the story of the evening's ambush. When he'd finished, the silence on the other end of the line went on far too long.

"Is something wrong?" he asked.

"You're only the latest of us to be attacked," Conan Doyle said.

"Is everyone all right?"

"They're fine. However . . ."

"What is it?" Clay prodded, troubled by the mage's hesitation.

"If I'm to believe what Dr. Graves has told me, it was *you* who attacked the brownstone in Louisburg Square, almost killing Danny and his mother."

Clay blinked and shook his head as though he'd been slapped.

"Me?" he asked, standing up from the bed. "Arthur, I'm here in France."

"Yes, you are," Conan Doyle replied, and Clay could practically hear the grinding of gears inside the man's head as he attempted to unravel this riddle.

"What the hell's going on?"

"I'm not certain. But at a guess, I'd say it has something to do with Eve and her abduction."

"We have to find her," Clay said. He and Conan Doyle shared a rich history with the woman who was the mother of mankind and vampires alike.

"Of course we do. And when we have done so, our mystery will be solved."

Clay stared at the vampire squirming upon the floor in agony. The stumps of his missing limbs had stopped bleeding and had actually begun to regenerate.

"Stay where you are, Clay. Ceridwen will come to collect you and we'll gather here in Dubrovnik."

"I'll be waiting," he said.

He hung up the phone and stared at the leech writhing on the floor in agony.

"You're going to tell me everything that you know. If it's helpful, I'll end your life and your pain right now, quickly and with mercy."

The vampire sneered, eyeing him defiantly. "Why would I tell you anything?"

Clay reached down, pulled the vampire's tattered remains up from the floor, and directed him toward the curtained windows. Although the room was still dark, it was evident that the morning sun had risen in the sky and that it was a gloriously bright day outside. Beams of yellow light could be seen along the hems of the heavy curtains.

"Because slowly and without mercy is your other option, and something tells me that you're not quite up for that."

The vampire stared in horror at the strip of sunlight radiating out from beneath the velvet window treatments, then looked back to Clay with fear-filled eyes.

"Am I right?" he asked.

The vampire began to speak.

7

CLAY showed the vampire the mercy he had promised, tearing out its heart with a single, swift blow, and crushing it in his hands. The foul creature didn't even have a chance to scream.

Long ago, Clay had learned the art of swift, efficient killing. He had mastered those skills through the long years of his existence, but those abilities had been honed to peak efficiency during a time when he had not been himself, when he had been captured by covert organizations within the U.S. government and his mind altered. His memories had been twisted and erased over and over, and reprogrammed. His history had been glorious, but they had turned him into little more than a weapon.

They had made him a monster and, when necessary, he could still let the monster out.

Clay walked into the bathroom, turning on the faucet to wash his hands clean of the residual remains of the vampire he'd just slain. He caught his reflection in the mirror and found himself staring at his ancient, clay features, at the cracks that lined his earthen face.

A monster no more, he thought, touching his dampened hands to his orange flesh. He could recall so clearly the day that the fog had been lifted from his mind, the day that the techniques of his oppressors had been overridden and he had remembered who—and *what*—he really was.

She had been responsible.

Eve.

Clay left the bathroom. He sat down upon the bed, waiting for Ceridwen to arrive, and his thoughts drifted back to the time when he had been sent to murder Conan Doyle.

And she had set him free.

THE PLAZA HOTEL, NEW YORK CITY, 1988.

CLAY had entered the old hotel as a fly.

Flying up through the elevator shaft, he had found the floor, then the room, gaining access by assuming the shape of a dust mite and crawling through the thick jungle of carpet beneath the locked door and into the suite on the other side.

His debriefing had been extensive; his handlers stressing how dangerous this individual—this Arthur Conan Doyle—could be. He was a sorcerer, one of the world's most powerful, and he needed to be eliminated. Which was why they had sent Clay. That was his purpose—to kill quickly and efficiently.

Doyle didn't stand a chance.

But the intelligence he'd received had been incorrect. Instead of one subject in the room, there were two: the target and a female.

It did not matter to him. Two could be killed just as easily as one.

He would catch them unawares, assuming the shape of something swift and savage. First he would take out the target—ripping out his throat before he could even react—then he would deal with the female witness. He couldn't imagine it taking any more than two minutes . . . three at the most.

Conan Doyle stood beside a dark, cherrywood desk, going through his briefcase. The woman fell onto the bed, bouncing up and down as though testing it out, trying to get comfortable.

They did not suspect a thing.

His prey seldom did.

From microscopic insect, the assassin assumed the guise of a Dire Wolf, one of the most ferocious beasts ever to walk the planet. His flesh flowed like water, bones popping and growing. In the blink of an eye he became a monstrous beast, jaws snapping. Clay sprang at his prey, anticipating the feel of the man's neck in his mouth, his jaws breaking it, the gouts of blood as he tore into the flesh.

It would be over in moments.

The man spun as Clay descended upon him, one hand glowing as if aflame. The sorcerer's eyes crackled with some sort of inner power as he uttered the words of an incantation. Searing, crimson light erupted from the target's hands, hurling Clay backward toward the door. He snarled in anger and surprise, shifting fur and flesh to something that would absorb the brunt of the impact.

Crashing against the door, he glanced down upon the dark brown shell that had replaced the thick fur of the wolf. *Something reptilian,* the killer thought, the bones of his body reconfiguring into a primordial creature.

He scrambled to his feet, a hiss upon his tongue, a spiny tail waving furiously behind him.

Conan Doyle stood defiantly at the center of the room, both hands now crackling with unearthly energy. The mage hovered above the floor, his feet not touching the ground.

At least that part of the intel was right, the assassin thought to himself. *A sorcerer without a doubt, but a dead man nonetheless.*

The woman—the unexpected witness—crouched on the bed, staring in shock. She seemed about to act, but Clay paid her no mind. She posed no danger. Her moment would come soon enough.

He sprang, evading the dark power that arced from the man's hands. He shifted from one shape to the next, from one size to another, leaping around the room with such speed that his intended victim could not get a bead on him. This adversary was good, a challenge. It had been too many years since an assignment had challenged him. It excited him.

He clung a moment to the ceiling, then lashed out with hooked, bony claws. The sorcerer attempted to evade his attack, twisting as he summoned a blast of magical power from burning fingertips. But this time Clay was faster. Like the snap of a bullwhip, the bone claws raked across the man's chest, clothing and flesh tearing away with ease, the smell of spilled blood suddenly filling the air.

Conan Doyle fell.

The killer dropped down from the ceiling, momentarily assuming his natural form as he stalked toward his prey. The bone claws exuded a powerful neurotoxin. It would be only seconds before the man was completely helpless.

The sorcerer went rigid on the floor, his body going into spasms.

Clay could not remember the last time his pulse had quickened during an assignment. He knelt down beside the man.

"Thank you for the challenge," he whispered, reaching out a powerful hand to crush the man's throat, ending his life mercifully, and as quickly as he could.

The sorcerer deserved no less.

"I wouldn't do that if I were you."

Clay frowned. He'd been so caught up in the challenge of his prey that he had forgotten the room's other occupant. *The woman.* He would deal with her next. Frowning, he grabbed hold of Conan Doyle's throat.

His arm was pulled backward with such fierce strength that he nearly lost his balance. He spun to face the woman, who now held his wrist in her hand.

Not a woman. Something else. So much for intel.

"I said no," she said, and she twisted his wrist. The sound of breaking bone echoed in the room like a gunshot.

He leaped away from his prey, cradling his arm even as he willed the molecules to flow, repairing the injury in an instant.

The way the woman stood, the glint in her eyes, made him realize he was in the presence of a predator. Her hands had become razor-sharp talons, and she sneered at him, revealing pearl white teeth and long, razor-keen incisors.

"Vampire," Clay said, even as he transformed again, taking on the shape of a Bengal tiger. He sprang across the room, claws ready to match hers in combat.

She met the attack full on, catching him in midpounce and flipping him onto the floor.

"Do you know how much I hate that fucking word?" she snarled, raking her claws across his exposed belly.

The killer roared in pain, the wounds burning like fire.

The tiger vanished in an instant as he shifted again, diminishing until he became a dragonfly. He flitted out of her path as she tried to claw him again.

Before she could react to that transformation, he darted behind her and became a mountain gorilla, raising huge arms and smashing down upon her with bone-shattering force.

Clay chanced a quick glance at Doyle, who had propped himself up against the wall, obviously still feeling the effects of the toxin in his veins. The sorcerer smiled, and Clay was filled with an overpowering sense of dread. He had to end this now. Glancing across the room, he was startled to see that the female did not lie in a crumpled heap against the wall, but instead clung there spiderlike.

"My turn," she said, springing at him.

He became an enormous Kodiak bear as she leaped on him, roaring his displeasure as he attempted to swat the vampire away. She clung to his thick fur. The killer thrashed, driving his own body against a nearby wall in an attempt to crush her. She spun herself out of harm's way.

Then she was behind him. Her hands clamped on either side of his head with such strength that he thought she might tear it right off. Instead, the vampire pulled his head back, exposing his throat.

He didn't have a moment to react. She darted her open jaws toward him and sank her fangs through fur and layers of bear fat. Blood spurted into her mouth and onto her face.

The vampire began to drink. No matter how he struggled, or thrashed, he could not dislodge her.

The assassin felt himself growing weaker, unable to focus his thoughts or even rely on instinct to change his form. He stumbled around the hotel room as the leech clung hungrily to him, draining the blood from him. He felt the world around him begin to grow dim. His legs gave way beneath him, and he slumped to the floor.

It can't end like this, he thought, fighting to remain conscious—fighting to stay alive. He could hear her feeding, the awful sucking sound as she pulled the life from his veins.

Just as he was about to slip into the abyss, it happened.

It felt as if his mind had been encased in amber, and now it began to crack. He did not fight it. He allowed it to break—

to shatter—and from within the shell they emerged, a deluge long kept dammed up, suppressed.

Memories.

He let them wash over him and immersed himself in the sea of what had been hidden from him for so long. The memories flowed around him, images of his past. He remembered his capture during the Second World War, taken by the United States Army from a French village that had been under his protection. They had thought him nothing more than a monster, something to be used . . . his talents exploited. Their scientists and their torturers had taken control of his mind and stolen his memories.

Turning him into a weapon.

A killer.

But he was more than that.

So much more.

The assassin slumped to the floor, bombarded with the memories of the history he had lived before his capture . . . of the people he had known, the lands he had visited. He had seen the rise of civilizations and, in some instances, had a hand in their demise. He had invented himself over and over, warrior, hero, monarch, and serf.

"Eve, let him go," a distant voice said, and he felt the vampire's fangs leave his throat.

He lay powerless on the hotel room floor. Barely able to lift his head, he stared at the sorcerer—Conan Doyle—as he was helped to his feet by the woman. Her lips were stained crimson with the blood she had taken from his veins.

Involuntarily, he felt his body change, returning to its true, earthen form. It was like being caught beneath an avalanche, the eternity of lifetimes he had lived falling into place.

And when it seemed as if he could take it no more, he remembered the Garden, and the hands of the Creator. He remembered what he was, the thing from which all life was formed.

The Clay of God.

His mind at last whole, and belonging completely to him, the Clay of God rose slowly to his feet, his eyes upon his would-be victims. The sorcerer stood unsteadily on his own, the vampire attentive at his side.

Conan Doyle lifted his hand. The tips of his fingers started to glow with an unearthly light.

"I believe this concludes our business," the Englishman said.

Someone started to pound at the door, voices on the other side demanding to be let in.

Clay looked toward the window, his body shifting into that of a bird. Orange flames trailed from behind his wings as he sailed toward the closed window and crashed through the glass in an explosion of fire.

He had taken on the form of the phoenix.

For he had been reborn.

CONAN Doyle breathed in deeply, inhaling the lingering scent of his lover. Ceridwen had just departed in the swirling embrace of a traveling wind, and already he felt the ache of her absence. He knew it was a liability, becoming so dependent on anyone, but he could not help himself. Nor did he wish to. He'd cast himself completely into the abyss of his love for her and would gladly pay any consequence. Come what may, he was hers.

He flexed his hand, wincing at the pain that still ached in his reattached finger, but was glad to see that he had regained almost all mobility. The discomfort would pass over time, and he had other more pressing matters to concern him.

All around the world, the Menagerie had been attacked. And now Eve had been abducted. In his mind, he drew together all the skeins of this strange web of events. Simple deduction said that the attacks were meant to be a distraction from the actual goal, which was the abduction of Eve.

But for what purpose?

The question rattled around inside the mage's skull as he stepped into a patch of shadow thrown by a large armoire.

"Squire, can you hear me?" he said, speaking into the shadow. "I require your presence at once."

He had attempted this form of communication with the hobgoblin several times already. As before, there was no answer. Conan Doyle felt a twinge of apprehension. Squire was the only member of his Menagerie who remained unaccounted for subsequent to the attacks. If whoever was responsible for choreographing them had been thorough, it seemed likely that Squire had been assaulted as well. Since he had not been at the brownstone when the ugliness there had unfolded, Conan Doyle could only surmise that he was likely at the forge, his workshop in the Shadowpaths.

Another ripple of dread went through him as he wondered what enemy their unknown assailants would have sent against the hobgoblin. To say that Squire had ruffled a few feathers over the years would be an understatement. The only comfort he could take from this train of thought was that it seemed likely the shadow hound, Shuck, was with Squire at the forge. Perhaps together, they would survive.

He went to his coat, hanging from the back of one of the wooden kitchen chairs, and fished around the inside front pocket for his pipe and tobacco. A smoke would help soothe his frazzled nerves and help him to think more clearly, or at least that was what he told himself.

Stuffing the pipe bowl full, he lit the tobacco and eagerly began to puff upon the stem.

If anything, the hobgoblin is resourceful, he told himself, pacing the small cottage floor. Conan Doyle recalled the numerous times that Squire had helped to pull victory from the jaws of defeat. His ability to travel through shadow was the perfect tool in their war against the encroaching darkness.

"He's fine," the mage found himself speaking aloud.

But as he stared off into space, a tiny voice in the back of his mind whispered back. *What if he's not?* Conan Doyle quickly silenced the thought, turning back to the shadow beside the armoire. He went to it again, removing the pipe from his mouth to call down into the shadow.

The darkness itself surged up to attack him, a roar filling his ears and driving him backward.

Under attack from the Shadowpaths themselves, Conan Doyle whispered a simple hex and churning, crackling magic writhed around his fist, powerful enough to destroy almost anything emerging from the realm of shadows.

He hesitated as he heard a snuffling noise, and the great beast—dripping in darkness—emerged from the pool of shadow. Conan Doyle stayed his hand. There was something familiar here.

"Shuck?" he asked.

The beast began to shake. Spatters of darkness flew from its body to dapple the floor and walls with shadows that quickly dispersed when exposed to the morning light. The animal made a soft, mewling sound as it fixed its dark gaze upon him, turning around to stare into the darkness from which it had just emerged.

Conan Doyle's pulse raced. "Where is he, Shuck?" the archmage asked, coming to stand beside the animal. "Where is your master?"

As if on cue, a hand emerged from the darkness, followed by Squire's large head. The hobgoblin gasped for air as Conan Doyle reached down to help pull him from the black pool.

"Thank the gods," he said beneath his breath as he hauled Squire out of the shadows.

"Bet I had you worried there," the hobgoblin said, gulping at the air as he wiped liquid shadow from his eyes and mouth. "Stuff tastes like shit," he muttered, the spatters already dissolving to oily whips of smoke as it was exposed to the light coming into the room.

"There have been attacks upon the others, I was concerned that—"

"Us, too," the hobgoblin said, patting Shuck, who had dropped to the floor to rest. "Somebody sicced a fuckin' shadow snake on us."

Conan Doyle frowned. "The Murawa? It hasn't been seen for centuries."

"Yeah, well we've been jumping on and off the paths for hours trying not to get our asses eaten. So, apparently, it's back."

Squire walked across to the window and into a pool of morning light. The oily, shadow stuff that clung to him began to dissolve.

"Had to leave the established paths and swim through the primal stuff. Made a pit stop in the Orient. Obviously, I wasn't walking home from there, so we dived back in. Shucky was the one that heard your voice and led us here."

Squire crossed the elegant living room and went to the kitchen, smiling as he spotted the refrigerator purring in the far corner. The shadow beast scrabbled to his feet, following his master.

"Got anything to eat?" Squire asked, pulling open the door. "I'm famished."

"There's no time for that now," Conan Doyle replied.

Squire emerged from the refrigerator holding a wedge of cheese.

"What's up?" the hobgoblin asked, taking a large bite from the wedge. Pieces of cheese dropped to the floor, where Shuck promptly licked them up.

"I told you that we've all been attacked over the last few hours, a distraction I believe from the real objective."

"Which is?"

"They've taken Eve."

Squire froze and looked up. Shuck began to emit a low, dangerous sound deep in his chest.

"Who the fuck's done that?" the hobgoblin asked, leaving the kitchen, Shuck trotting at his side.

"A motley collection of enemies," Conan Doyle said, continuing to puff upon his pipe. "A horde of vampires. A demon. An angel. All working together."

"That ain't good," Squire said through a mouthful of cheese. He gave the last bite to Shuck and wiped his grubby hands upon the front of his pants. "So what are we doing now?"

"I'm awaiting Ceridwen's return with Clay. I need you to go back to Boston and see to the brownstone. Danny and Julia are there. You're to stand sentinel there against further attacks. Bring what weapons you can."

Squire nodded in understanding. "What kind of attacks are we talking about? Anything special that I should know in choosing weapons?"

Conan Doyle thought about Graves's description of the brownstone's attacker. "It appears that whoever is attacking us has acquired the cooperation of a shapeshifter. And not some ordinary were-beast. A true shifter."

"No shit," the hobgoblin said. "Does Clay know about this?"

"He does, yes. And there's the twist, old friend. Dr. Graves, Danny, and Julia initially believed that it was Clay who attacked them. The shifter gained entry by wearing his face. But Clay was in France with Eve when they, too, were attacked and Eve taken."

"Beautiful," Squire grumbled, rubbing his hand across the rough skin of his chin. "I don't like the sounds of this one."

"No," Conan Doyle said with a shake of his head. "Nor do I. You'd best hurry along. I'm aware the Shadowpaths are dangerous at the moment, Squire, but if you'll brave them once more, we'll find a way to destroy the Murawa as soon as Eve is back among us. Return to the house, check the wards to see if they're still holding, and provide Danny and his mother with a means to protect themselves."

Squire looked away. "So I guess I'll see ya in a while," he said with some apprehension.

"Yes, you will," Conan Doyle said. His pipe had gone out, and he tapped the burned tobacco remains into his cupped hand. "That is, unless you're eaten by a shadow snake." The archmage looked up to fix him in his gaze.

"Ain't you a fuckin' barrel of laughs," Squire snarled, leaping into the pool of darkness, Shuck following right behind him.

"Be careful, old friend," Conan Doyle whispered, certain that only he could hear. "Be careful."

THOUGH she lay deep beneath the desert sands, she knew the sun had set. She could feel it.

In the utter darkness of her daytime resting place, under the shifting dunes, Eve opened her eyes. The gnawing pain in her belly urged her to awaken.

To emerge.

She squirmed in the embrace of the cool, desert sand, turning herself toward the surface, and began her ascent. She dug her way upward toward what had once been a sun-baked sea of dunes and dust but had become a more fitting environment. Suited for what she had become.

Fragmented memories of days long ago flashed through her mind, so alien to her now that they could have just as eas-

ily belonged to another. She found the recollections annoying, a distraction, and pushed them to the back of her mind, where she hoped they would eventually become lost, then forgotten.

All that concerned her was the hunger, and the hunt that preceded it. She swam through the rough, desert sands toward the surface, driven by the need for blood. The higher she ascended, the warmer the ocean of sand around her became, a stinging reminder of the warmth that rained down from the sun, absorbed by the desert sea.

As deadly as fire to her now.

Her hands were the first to break through, emerging from the desert like strange vegetation, urged to blossom and reach toward the rays of moonlight. The rest of her followed, her senses coming alive as she hauled herself from the sand. The night winds caressed her, carrying the scent of what had originally brought her to this place.

Prey.

Eve blinked away the sand and grit from her eyes, a transparent membrane sliding across the surface of the delicate orbs, protecting them from the harshness of the environment.

She looked out over the sea of shifting sand, searching the broad expanse of nighttime wasteland for what had drawn her there. Tilting her head back, she searched the air for the scent again and found it almost immediately.

Not so far off, nestled in the embrace of night, she could see it, dark and squatting, asleep until the coming of dawn.

A city.

No, it was far too small to be called that, but she was sure that if it had the time, it would grow.

If it had the time.

Eve closed her eyes, pulling the scent of civilization into her nostrils. She could practically see them: the young and old, men, women, and children, most of them asleep in their hovels of mud, clay, and straw.

Awaiting a dawn that they would never see.

Her stomach gurgled noisily, eager for sustenance from those in the settlement ahead, more than enough to slake her voracious thirst. But she could not think only of herself; those selfish days were long past, and she now had many mouths to feed.

Turning briefly away from the settlement, she looked out over the broad expanse of desert behind her and saw that her children had also been awakened by the hunger brought on by nightfall.

She watched as they climbed up from their desert nests, their animal eyes glinting red in the light thrown down by the moon and the stars. Their number had grown since last she took notice; the offspring that her insatiable hunger had transformed, now responsible for the creation of their own thirsty spawn.

One after another they crawled up from the sand, many with their heads already tilted back, smelling the night air. She did not recall the last time the tribe had fed, when they had begun their trek across the ocean of sand in pursuit of food.

Her children, and her children's children, anxiously licked their dry, cracked lips in anticipation, awaiting a sign from her that it was time for them to feed. She was the matriarch of the hungry pack, and they would not act—no matter how voracious they were—until she showed them that it was time.

She nodded, turning away as they surged forward to follow her across the desert sands, and toward the sleeping settlement.

To feed.

8

EVE woke to the rotten-meat stink of vampires. Her nostrils flared, and she simply stopped breathing. Inhaling another breath of that stench would make her vomit. Her entire body throbbed with a terrible ache, and she began to stretch, feeling the muscles sliding over bones, wondering if parts of her were broken and somehow unhealed.

The sensation of motion carried her along. She heard the rumble of a truck engine and felt the jarring bounce of its tires over a rutted surface. The dry heat suggested a desert, though she could not feel the strange prickling of her skin that afflicted her whenever the sun was out. Night. In the desert. This time of year, it could only be Africa.

A scritch-scratch voice, like nails on a chalkboard, spoke in French and several other voices joined in laughter. Her mind translated. "Isn't that sweet? Mommy's awake."

The leeches were talking about her. Eve wanted to tear all of their throats out with her teeth and rip their faces off. The urge felt good; it helped to wake her up. She opened her eyes and found herself surrounded by eleven vampires, each more sneering and arrogant than the last. They were amused, these creatures, but this was not the swaggering foolishness that so often went along with the recently undead. These were old, powerful leeches who'd earned a bit of arrogance. Their kind usually tried to avoid her at any cost, knowing what she would do to them.

Now they relished her captivity and debasement. To them she was traitorous, a pariah, but also the scourge of their kind. The vampires—male and female, of mixed race and language—regarded her with quiet glee, eyes slitted, the edges of their mouths upturned.

Hatred suffused her entire being, and Eve tried to rise. She could not. A terrible weight lay across her. When she managed to lift her head and crane her neck to look down the length of her body, she saw that a thin crimson chain had been bound around her shoulders and legs and kept her wrists pinned together behind her back. They looked as though they ought to weigh nothing, but she might as well have been buried a thousand feet beneath the earth.

"Wrought by demon's hands," said a thickly accented vampire, a female who slid from the bench in back of the truck and crouched beside her, tracing the lines of Eve's face with sharp nails, like a sensuous lover. "Chains made from the blood of angels."

Another leech laughed. "Of one angel."

Jophiel, Eve thought. And she wondered how long the bastard had been in league with the demon Abaddon. Whatever they were up to, how long had they been planning it?

Eve closed her eyes again, seething, shutting out the sight of the vampires just as she had their stink. What had prompted the angel and the demon to use her blood-children as their pawns, she had no idea. Perhaps they knew how difficult it was to think with so many vampires nearby; the rage and the need to destroy the filth whipped her into an almost bestial frenzy.

But the chains bound her, and she could do nothing at the moment. She forced herself to lie still, to close out the world, save for the rumble of the truck across that rutted road. The canvas flap that covered the back of the truck did not entirely prevent the dust that rose from their path from infiltrating the rear of the vehicle. It drifted in and eddied about like the ghosts of the desert itself.

The truck bounced in a dip in the road. Eve's head struck the floor. In that moment, she understood that they had left the road—if indeed they had ever been on a real road at all.

"Traitorous bitch," came a whisper.

Eve's eyes fluttered open almost against her will. The vampire male had the features and complexion of a South

Sea islander, and his eyes were different colors—one blue and one the deepest brown she'd ever seen. Eve recognized him immediately.

"Palu," she rasped.

The Samoan grinned, revealing his fangs. Eve had not turned him herself, but as far as she knew he was one of the oldest surviving vampires in the world, perhaps third-generation. Twice she had been within feet of him, and he'd managed to escape her.

"It's been a long time, mother," he replied, still in a whisper. Palu rarely raised his voice above that level.

"What the hell are you doing, all of you working together?" she asked, for the older vampires tended to hate one another and despised one another's company.

The truck bucked twice, rolled a dozen feet, and the engine went silent, the vehicle popping and ticking as it began to cool.

Palu stood, reached down, and twined his fingers in the chains that bound her—the blood of angels, wrought by demons—and lifted her effortlessly. He brought her face up to his, and the grin vanished.

"Survival of the fittest, Mother," he whispered.

Another leech whipped back the canvas flap, and Palu hurled her out of the truck. Eve braced herself as best she could, but the chains dragged her down so heavily that when she struck the ground, for several seconds she lost consciousness again.

Powerful hands lifted her. Her eyelids fluttered as she tried to refocus, clear her mind. It occurred to her that the goddamned leeches were ruining her outfit—the jacket had cost her nearly a thousand dollars, and must be completely ruined, and the blasted desert landscape would be hell on her Manolos. She prayed to God—though she knew He probably hadn't listened to her since her last day in Eden—that she would be able to kill them more than once.

Eve inhaled deeply. Now that they were out in the chilly desert night, the stink of the vampires was not so terrible, and she enjoyed breathing. It made her feel not so far away from all the things she wished she could be, and do, and have. Humanity. Forgiveness.

"Where the fuck are we?" she asked.

The vampires escorting her around the truck stiffened at the question. She wanted to ask them what they were worried about. They were basically carrying her. She hung between them, dragged toward the ground by the chains that weighed nothing to them, and more than Atlas's burden to her.

"Libya," that intimate whisper said behind her.

"What the hell are we doing in Libya?"

Palu only laughed.

The vampires gathered around her. Another truck rattled up twenty yards away, and more of the leeches poured out. They dragged her forward and dropped her. Eve went down hard on her knees, the blood chain breaking her left clavicle with the impact. But she remained on her knees. The chain didn't prevent her from looking around, but there was little enough to see. Aside from the night and the desert, the two trucks and the wraithlike undead they'd disgorged, the only feature of the land around her was a single structure, a one-story, nearly featureless building that might have been mosque or monastery. Its front doors were the only thing that caught her eye, tall and arched in a vaguely Moorish style, with large iron rings for handles.

Her clavicle pained her. The bone kept trying to heal, but the weight of the chain would not allow it.

Eve glanced around, full of questions without answers. The vampires ignored the little mosque, gazing up at the night sky. A rustle came from above, and she glanced up, following their fascination, to see Jophiel and Abaddon arriving. The demon's red-black wings gleamed wetly, and the desert sand seemed to ripple in revulsion as his hooves touched the ground. The angel circled once, perhaps purposefully allowing Abaddon to arrive before him to avoid any possible conflict with the vampires.

Then they stood side by side, white, Heaven's wings next to Hell's most hideous vulture. Palu slunk toward Abaddon, the Samoan vampire wearing his trademark grin. Even in the dark his one blue eye seemed to sparkle, until the demon turned and fixed him with a glare and a dismissive sneer. Palu hesitated, then lowered his gaze.

The leeches don't get a seat at the table, Eve thought. That meant they were following Abaddon. And why not? If she was their mother, then he, most assuredly, was their father.

The angel and the demon whispered to one another. Eve could do nothing but wait. The chains Abaddon had made from Jophiel's blood would not allow her to attempt to fight, or to flee. For now.

Once again the ground began to tremble. The vampires glanced around nervously. Eve frowned and stared at the desert floor. Grains of sand sifted and danced before her. Around the mosque, things began to force their way up out of the sand, ugly, troll-like things. Whatever Eve might have started to think was going on, these new arrivals wiped her mind of any assumptions. These weren't vampires or demons or angels. They weren't anything to do with Heaven or Hell, and they weren't from the human world at all.

A few feet away from Abaddon and Jophiel, a monster burst from the sand. It erupted from the ground with a spray of sand, a twelve-foot warrior creature that bore some resemblance to the somewhat smaller things gathered around the mosque. But she could see the dark intelligence in its eyes and the arrogance in its carriage. The warrior was clad in red-black armor and had long golden hair, but his face was monstrous and his flesh like leather.

"Welcome, Duergar," Abaddon purred. "Your mission went well, I hope."

Eve had heard Conan Doyle speak the name. She knew what Duergar was—who he was—but why he would be here, with the rest of these horrors, she could not begin to guess.

"She still lives," the monster spit. "It is not to my liking."

"You weren't required to kill her. Only distract her," Jophiel said, flicking his hand as though brushing the half-Drow, half-Fey creature away. "There'll be more than enough time to destroy them, if you're foolish enough to put the destruction of your enemies ahead of your own existence."

A rumble of hatred came up from Duergar's throat. A heavy axe hung at his side, and he reached for it. Abaddon touched his arm and shook his head slowly.

"That isn't the way it works. We're allies."

Duergar sniffed in amusement at the idea. "The key?" he asked.

Now the angel Jophiel smiled, and for the first time since alighting upon the desert sands of Libya, he turned toward Eve. He gestured toward her.

"We have her."

The Drows—huge, lumbering trolls clad in scraps of wool and carrying heavy maces and axes—began to close in around the mosque. The vampires clustered impatiently, rustling like dry leaves, but did not dare approach without Abaddon's approval.

Duergar hocked something up from deep in his throat and spit a fat, black wad of filth into the sand. "Why are you both just standing here?"

Abaddon rose up on his hooves, wings spreading wide. He did not like Duergar's tone, that was clear. Then the demon subsided and his aspect altered, revealing a slender, olive-skinned man in a perfectly tailored suit and scarlet tie. He gave a razor of a smile.

"Waiting for you, my friend. You wish to walk through the Garden Gate with us? You and your dim-witted friends must open those doors."

Duergar spit again. "You try my patience, hellspawn. Perhaps the weak things of the Blight fear you, but you would be making a mistake to think that is true of Duergar. We are allies. Our shared interests draw us together. I am not your lackey."

"Stinking, lumbering fool," Jophiel said, wings spreading, suddenly as tall as Duergar himself. Eve expected him to draw a sword, but he did not. "We serve each other to serve ourselves. Open the godforsaken door!"

"Ah, if only it were godforsaken, we wouldn't have this trouble," Abaddon replied.

Duergar looked back and forth from angel to demon. The Drows began to moan their displeasure with the way their master had been spoken to, and they began to move toward Abaddon and the angel, until their half-blood kin raised a hand to halt them.

In that moment, anything might have happened. Bound by ancient power, Eve could not move, but she quietly rooted for the three of them to murder each other, there on the sand. The pain in her shoulder and the crushing weight of the chains had grown worse. A burning hunger had begun in her gut, a gnawing need for the taste of blood. It had been too long.

She started to laugh.

Abaddon spun to glare at her. Jophiel whipped his head around, long hair reflecting starlight just as brightly as his wings. Duergar took a step toward her, the canines that jutted up from his lower jaw making him look barbaric and also vaguely like a walrus. His green eyes gleamed in the dark. The white stripe in his copper hair drew Eve's gaze almost hypnotically. The vampires hissed at her, and even the numbskull Drows seemed agitated by her laughter.

Eve snickered, leaning forward, surrendering to the weight of the blood chain, and it tipped her over. She grunted as she struck the sand, and rasped a bit as she kept laughing.

"What do you find so amusing, Eve?" Jophiel asked.

She sighed, trying to stifle her laughter, and stared at him. "Who, me? What the hell do I know? I'm not part of your little club. Nobody's talking to me, or even really acknowledging I'm here. Which is fine by me. You're all fucking ugly, evil fucks, and I'm planning to fucking kill you as soon as fucking possible. But, all that aside, I do think the whole scene's a giggle. I've put it together now. I don't believe it, but I get it. One of you morons actually thinks somehow you're going to use me to open the Garden Gate, right? How stupid are you? I mean, the fucking troll, okay, but you other two twits were there when God banished us. I'm tainted, you pricks, and I haven't been forgiven for anything. Not the first sin, and not the last. That Gate isn't going to open for me."

Duergar turned angrily upon Jophiel and Abaddon, both of whom ignored the massive, savage warrior.

"We shall see," the angel said.

His smile said he knew something Eve did not. That troubled her deeply enough that she stopped smiling.

"Duergar," Abaddon began.

"The doors," the half-blood creature said. He marched toward the mosque with a speed and power that Eve could only admire, muscles rippling beneath his golden flesh.

Duergar reached out with his massive hands and gripped the iron rings on the doors of the shabby little building. He began to pull. The hinges shrieked and the doors opened, just a crack.

They exploded outward, sheared in two by a blade of fire. Duergar stumbled backward and fell to one knee, copper hair flowing around him. The thing that burst from within the tiny structure was impossibly large, far taller than Duergar himself. Once, it might have been an angel, for its wings spread so wide that they were broader than the squat little building. Naked and amorphous, it shone with a brilliant white radiance that made the vampires scream in pain and sorrow. Its head seemed too large for its body, and its face was etched with madness and anguish. Its radiance seared Eve's flesh, and it nearly crippled her just to look at the Guardian of the Gate, but she also could not look away. This was divinity.

Yet it was also tainted.

The Guardian's eyes were missing; in their place were black hollows, as dark as the angel's radiance was bright. Somehow, in the eternity that had passed since mankind had been banished from the Garden of Eden, the Guardian had been blinded. Eve wondered if its eyes had been torn out in some prior battle to protect the Garden Gate, or if the Guardian had removed its own eyes.

It howled in rage and despair and lunacy. The Guardian raised its sword of fire and listened. Duergar began to rise. The Guardian twitched, hearing the noise, and the blade swept downward. With a roar, Duergar shot to his feet and began to raise his axe, but Eve could see that he would be too late.

One of the Drows, huge and ugly with its misshapen face and yellow tusks, stepped between the blind, burning angel and its master. The sword of fire sheared the lumbering bone-eater in two, searing the flesh as it cut through the Drow. Duergar raised his left arm, and the fiery blade scored the crimson-black armor with a clang and a hiss of melting metal, but the sword did not cut through. Cleaving through the bone and gristle of the Drow's body had slowed the blow enough.

Duergar turned the blind angel's attack away even as the two halves of the dead Drow spilled wetly to the sand around them. He swung the axe and hacked off the Guardian's arm, which fell to the ground still clutching the flaming sword. A low roar of triumph issued from the mouths of the Drows, and they closed in around the burning angel, battering it with maces and hacking with axes. Duergar choked it with his bare hands, and Eve could smell his flesh burning. But from where she lay on the ground, she could see the burning sword and brilliant white light of its amputated arm turn to blazing liquid and flow back to the angel. In that same moment, when it touched him—flowed into him—the Guardian manifested a new arm and sword, and the burning blade began to swing.

Drows shouted death cries as the angel struck them down, and Eve's cold black heart soared. A part of her wanted desperately to see Eden again, and always had—but not like this. Jophiel, Abaddon, and all of their allies ought to be scourged from the face of the world, and she only prayed she would be chosen as God's instrument for the task. If not, she'd do it just for fun.

The ground shook. Duergar bent to touch the earth, and the sand swept up and began to drag at the angel's legs, slowing it down for a moment. But whatever Fey magic the half-blood commanded, it would not stop an angel of the Lord. The blind Guardian tore free. Maces bludgeoned its face. Another axe blade severed its sword hand at the wrist, and Eve began to think the battle would last for eons. But attrition had begun to eat away at the Drows. They might injure the angel time after time, but its essence came back together almost instantly. They couldn't destroy it. Yet each time it attacked, the Guardian killed at least one of the Drows. Soon, Duergar would have no more Drows to serve him, and the vampires weren't going to be any help. Palu and the others—even the most ancient and powerful among them—couldn't even approach a being radiating with the touch of God.

The weight of the blood chains seemed to have grown. It felt as though the flesh on her left shoulder had torn, but she ignored the pain, studying the angel Jophiel and Abaddon. The Hell-Lord maintained his smooth, exotic façade, but Jophiel seemed to grow. His angelic aspect expanded, wings spreading wide, a radiant whiteness coming from within, laced with a tint of red. Side by side, angel and demon began to move toward the slaughter taking place in front of the little mosque-style building, out there under the nighttime desert sky.

What are you two thinking?

Even as the question entered her mind, Abaddon stepped sidewise and vanished within the white radiance of Jophiel's angelic presence. Eve could see a man-shaped stain deep inside Jophiel's brightness. Silently and swiftly, Jophiel circled around to the Guardian's right. The towering, hollow-eyed angel slashed viciously at one of the Drows nearby, then blocked at attack from Duergar, even as Jophiel darted toward him without a sound. The Guardian noticed nothing, and Eve understood.

Somehow, Jophiel had masked Abaddon's presence. The Guardian didn't sense the demon approaching.

"No," Eve rasped. Then she bucked against the blood chains. Despite the weight of their magic, she rose an inch off the ground. Where the skin had been torn on her left shoulder, the chains cut deeply and pulled, ripping through her jacket and blouse and pulling the skin away. The wound seeped tears of dark, viscous blood and the chain slid into her flesh. If she moved, it would saw deeper.

"Guardian!" she shouted, trying to keep as still as possible. "Abaddon is here! The demon attacks to your right!"

The vampires swarmed her, kicking and punching and twining their fingers in her hair. Palu stripped a light cotton jacket off a female leech, wadded it up, and forced it into Eve's mouth.

The towering angel had responded to the sound of her voice, whipping his blazing sword to the right, face upturned as he tried to sense the presence of the demon. But now as Eve managed to peer between the vampires who bludgeoned her, she caught a glimpse of Duergar taking advantage of the Guardian's distraction. The half-blood swung his battle axe and buried it in the back of the gigantic angel. The Guardian threw back its head and let out a scream of pain. Fire erupted from the wound in its back, and the axe melted and fell to the sand, burning black.

The angel Jophiel stepped around behind the Guardian, even as his blind brother screamed out to God in a language that predated the world itself. Abaddon emerged from within Jophiel like some phantasm.

Vampires clawed at Eve wherever the chains did not protect her flesh. The blows tugged on her bonds, and the demon-forged chain slithered deeper into the wound on her shoulder and began to cut across the tops of her breasts and her calves. She just lay there, taking the violence, not feeling, not caring, watching as the demon Abaddon cast off his human face and stood once more in the grotesque grandeur of his infernal nature. The demon's flesh looked purple-black in the darkness, but it glistened bloodred in the radiance of the mad Guardian's presence.

The giant, blinded angel had a grip on Duergar's throat, sword raised high, his touch searing the half-blood creature's flesh. But the moment that Abaddon took on his true form, the Guardian raised his head as though catching his scent. He sensed the demon. Hurling Duergar away from him, the Guardian spun to face Abaddon.

A tiny voice in the back of Eve's mind urged the demon on—the whisper of a serpent, so familiar—and she hated herself for the knowledge that it was her own voice. She yearned for the Garden Gate to be opened, and if the pitiful, eyeless creature that guarded it had to die, that small part of her cared not at all. Her heart and mind attacked such thoughts at once, eradicating them, but she could never deny them.

Abaddon moved too swiftly. Even as the Guardian brought that blade of fire around in an arc that would have removed the demon's head, Abaddon stepped in close. He reached up with both hands, leaving himself vulnerable to attack, and plunged long talons into the black, empty sockets where the angel's eyes should have been. With an obscene grin, Abaddon tore the rest of the Guardian's face away, leaving a gaping hole that seemed a window into some dark void, an endless abyss.

Eve whimpered. She had wanted to be welcomed back to Eden someday, not to return like this.

The demon reached his arms deep into the angel's ruined face and continued to tear, widening the rip in the fabric of the world. Abaddon bent the Guardian backward, opened his jaws, and vomited black blood and hellfire into the void where the angel's face had been.

Jophiel screamed in triumph, and in that moment, when Eve glanced at the beautiful angel, she saw that there was in him even more iniquity than in Abaddon, though the demon had violated her, tainted her soul for eternity, and driven her to madness. Jophiel still wore the façade of an angel, but within, he had more of Hell in his heart than the most perverse of demons.

A terrible ripping noise filled the air, rolled out across the desert, then the pure white radiance of the Guardian flashed so bright that the vampires screamed and dropped to their knees. Even Abaddon roared in agony. Eve squeezed her eyes closed against that pure light, wishing it would burn the monster out of her—take the obscene hunger away. With her eyes shut, she could hear the moaning of the surviving Drows and even of Duergar.

A cool breeze passed over Eve, easing the pain of her wounds, and she caught the scent of lilacs on the air. Slowly, hope fluttering in her chest, she opened her eyes. As she did, she realized that she no longer lay upon sand. Beneath her was sweet grass. Nearby she heard the burble of a stream. Her eyes beheld rolling hills and distant woods. For a moment, she let herself believe that somehow all of her enemies had been destroyed.

Then she heard the dark laughter of the demon and the giddy cry of the angel Jophiel's delight. She shifted her head and saw the vampires and Drows rising. Duergar limped as he moved to join Abaddon and Jophiel. The three of them stood before the true Garden Gate, a gleaming wall of polished wood with marble posts. There were no slits in the gate, no way to see into Eden, and Eve knew by instinct that neither the angel nor the demon would be able to fly over the Gate—or if they did, they would find only more hills and woods on the other side—and the Drows would not be able to tunnel under it.

They existed now, all of them, in some strange limbo realm outside the Garden of Eden. Through some divine power, the Garden had been removed from the earthly plane and existed in this place, this perfection that Eve sensed all around her. It had remained here, untainted by the sin of the human world. The Guardian had defended the door, but some past intruder had blinded the angel, tainting him at the same time. Perhaps Abaddon had done the deed himself in a prior attempt to gain entry. Regardless, it must have given the Guardian a vulnerability it had never possessed before, a strange kind of rot.

And perhaps the Guardian itself had been the door into this limbo . . . so that they could now stand before the Gate of Eden.

The vampires roused themselves, simply staring at the Gate, both terrified and elated. Jophiel's face was etched with a passion akin to lust. Abaddon stared at the Gate a moment longer, then turned and strode toward Eve. He reached down, wrapped his fingers in the chains, and carried her back toward the marble-and-oak Gate. The blood chains bit farther into her flesh, and she clamped her teeth together, refusing to cry out in pain.

The demon held her aloft as though she were some small child. He reached out, and tore away the chains, which snapped like twine and fell with Eve to the grass. She grunted as she struck the ground, hissing in pain and hatred. The chains became angel's blood once more and soaked the grass around her.

"Open it," Abaddon said.

Eve climbed to her feet. Where the chains had cut into her flesh, already she had begun to heal. The skin and muscle would knit quickly. She flexed her fingers and stared up at the seething, pustulant face of the demon.

"I don't think so."

Jophiel's wings enclosed him a moment, and when they unfurled, the glory had gone from his aspect, and once again she saw him as the effete, elegant, arrogant creature who had dogged her for so many centuries.

"Eve, you want to see beyond the Gate as much as we do," the angel said.

"Not like this."

Abaddon laughed. "You still hope for your pathetic redemption? Forgiveness. You had smeared your own soul with the stink of shit before I ever touched you. You're filthy with sin, cunt. I ruined your body, and took great pleasure in it, though I'd no idea the plague I would begin. But the spirit— that was your doing."

"He gives forgiveness to those who are worthy of it, who truly desire it," she whispered, fingers hooked into claws, canines elongating.

"Oh, yes, it's easy to see how much you desire forgiveness for what you've become," Abaddon replied with a laugh.

Duergar laughed softly, stepping up behind the angel and the demon. Palu and the vampire horde laughed as well, a susurrus of insidious mockery. The Drows were too dull-witted to laugh.

Jophiel gestured toward the door. "Open it, Eve. You believe yourself indestructible, but you cannot possibly hope to defeat us all. Open it, or we'll rip your heart out, end your life, and you will never have the redemption you seek."

Hatred burned in her, but she heard the truth in the angel's words. She approached the Gate, staring up at them. Her dead heart could not beat, but she imagined the racing of her pulse. Fear took her over. She did not want to know if the Gate of Eden would open for her, if she had earned that much.

But if she did not try, she would never know, and she would never be able to try again.

The Gate of Eden was not locked. Anyone could push it open if they were pure. Eve put her hands on the door and pushed.

Nothing happened. She had been banished at the beginning of time, and nothing had changed since. Horror filled her unlike anything she had felt in millennia. All of her sins, as a woman and a demon, fell upon her with more crushing weight than the chains that had bound her. Once more she dropped to her knees, staring up at the Gate of Eden.

IN her mind, she slips back to that moment when she had awakened, not far from the Garden. The demon had fallen upon her and violated her in every way, pouring his blood and his hellish seed into her, breaking her bones, tearing out her hair, beating her, tasting her flesh and her blood. For hour upon hour, day upon day, night after night, he had pierced her, feeding her only bits of his own flesh, sips of his own blood, subjecting her to every obscenity he could imagine while using his infernal will to keep her alive. She had been cast out of the arms of Heaven, but Hell received her in a warm embrace.

Now she wakes and finds that her soul is stained with the blood and lust of Abaddon, but her body is not broken. She can still feel his filthy touch, still feel the way he'd torn her up inside, the tearing of her scalp, the massive, sharp phallus with which he'd fucked her every orifice, and created new ones.

Madness rises up inside her. She feels it happening, feels her mind breaking again, just as it had during the eternity she'd spent in his grasp. But with the madness, there is something else—the hunger. The taste of his blood is still in her mouth, and she must have more. If not Abaddon's blood, then the blood of man.

Adam's blood.

Her mind screams at the thought. The tiny shard within her that is still Eve reels from the horror of it, and she staggers to her feet. Adam is not far away, she knows. He will be searching for her. His scent is carried to her on the night wind. All she has to do is go to him and her hunger can be sated.

Eve cannot. She flees, screaming at the moon, racing as fast as she can away from Adam, knowing that there will be others. The hunger is clawing at her soul and gnawing at her gut. She can taste the blood on her lips and in the back of her throat.

She is lost. The floodwaters of madness rise around her, and she begins to drown in them. Eve is a beast, then. A monster.

It is an eternity before the madness will recede, and she will be alone for all of that time. God has turned a blind eye to her.

EVE blinked and looked around, barely aware that she'd slipped away, wondering how long her mind had wandered—

how far. Only seconds, she thought, from the expressions upon the faces of her most hated enemies. The memory had been so strong it had overwhelmed her, just as sorrow took her now.

God had turned a blind eye to her at the dawn of mankind, and still she was beneath His notice.

"As I told you," Jophiel said to Abaddon, "the Gate will not open for her."

Duergar snarled at them, the axe still in his hand, rising slowly. "What is this, godlings? Vows were made."

"And will be kept," Abaddon snapped. And then he smiled. "We are prepared."

The demon raised a claw and beckoned toward the vampires. One of them pulled away from the others, a pale creature unfamiliar to her, with eyes an icy blue. As the vampire walked toward her, his flesh rippled fluidly, and he began to change.

Eve had seen such a transformation hundreds of times before, but she had only ever seen one creature perform it. The vampire grew larger, flesh altering, turning to a rich earthen clay, dry and spiderwebbed with cracks. Despite his clay flesh, he was human in every other aspect, eight or nine feet tall and massively broad of shoulder. He wore a short garment in the Egyptian style.

She knew him. Eve knew him so very well.

Fresh horror flooded her mind, but then he moved closer to her, a smile on his face. Eve stared into his eyes, studying them, and she knew. Not a speck of tenderness existed in those eyes.

"You're not him," she said. "You're not Clay."

9

THE ghost of Dr. Graves lingered on a marble balcony overlooking the Adriatic Sea and the walled Old City of Dubrovnik. The whitewashed walls and buildings had an almost spectral glow, and the orange roof tiles turned red in the moonlight. When the gathering had been planned, Conan Doyle had acquired this house high on a hill above Dubrovnik's old port, but its purpose had changed. It had been meant as a place for him to rest. Now it was their war room. An unlikely and beautiful place for such endeavors. Often, particularly of late, he wondered about Arthur's methods. But he never doubted the man's resourcefulness.

The Mediterranean breeze whispered across the tropical landscape, and Graves wished that he could feel it. He held up one spectral hand and studied the city below through his gauzily transparent flesh. When he lowered his arm, the rich beauty of Dubrovnik filled him with a terrible longing. That obscured view seemed more appropriate for one such as he— out of focus, intangible. It seemed wrong, somehow, that Graves could see all the vibrant life and color of the place and not be able to take part in it.

He yearned to step off that balcony, to drift across the harbor—the Adriatic still vivid blue, even after dark—and walk the streets of that old, dignified city. But for what purpose? If he intended to remain here, in this world—and his heart winced at the idea of departing, of leaving Julia behind in the tangible plane—then he vowed never to linger among flesh-and-blood beings simply to haunt them with his longing.

Diaphanous curtains billowed around him, and Graves turned to see that the breeze that blew them came from within the house. It could only be Ceridwen, carrying Clay back from France on a traveling wind. Dr. Graves bristled, a tremor passing through his ectoplasmic form. Conan Doyle claimed that Clay could not have been the one who attacked them at the mage's Louisburg Square brownstone in Boston, and perhaps that was true. Still, Graves would be on guard.

He moved in through the open French doors—feigning a stride, though he did not actually need to walk—and passed through the curtains as though it were they that were insubstantial.

Conan Doyle stood with Ceridwen and Clay in the center of the room. The mage seemed no worse for the trials of the previous twenty-four hours. He smoothed his mustache idly with one hand as he listened intently to whatever Clay had to say. Graves paid no attention. He focused on Clay's face—on the shapeshifter's eyes. *No, not his face,* the ghost reminded himself. *His true face is not human.* They were friends, the ghost and the malleable being who was, in truth, the oldest creature on the face of the Earth. Or, at least, Graves had thought them friends after Clay had helped the ghost to solve his own murder, sixty years after the fact.

But he'd once considered Conan Doyle a trusted friend. Of late, he'd begun to realize that he had a tendency toward naïveté that was embarrassing. Conan Doyle remained an ally but could not be trusted. He thought himself too clever by far and kept his confederates in the dark, keeping his own counsel, far too often.

Ceridwen and Doyle looked up as the ghost came across the room toward them. Clay turned slowly, a strange and uncertain regret in his eyes.

"Leonard," the shapeshifter said. "I'm told you have some questions for me."

The specter drifted a bit from side to side, studying Clay's eyes. Something in those eyes seemed true and real and present in a way that the eyes of the assassin who'd tried to kill Danny and Julia had not.

"Do you have an explanation for what happened in Boston?"

Clay shook his head. "There's only one of me. There are bits of sorcery that can change form and appearance, but nothing like me."

"The thing altered itself at will, fluidly. I didn't have the sense there was any magic to it at all. In that moment, I felt sure it had to be you. We all did."

Conan Doyle and Ceridwen had fallen silent, just watching the exchange, letting the two of them work it out on their own. Clay spread his hands wide, his gaze sorrowful.

"I was in Villefranche with Eve, Len. I can't be in two places at once. That's not possible, even for me."

"You're sure about that?" Graves asked.

Clay arched an eyebrow. "Entirely."

"It's a shame Eve isn't here to back up your story. A cynic might say that was awfully convenient."

The shapeshifter seemed to deflate, disappointment coloring his gaze. "Are you that cynical, Dr. Graves?"

The ghost hesitated. He glanced at Ceridwen and Conan Doyle, both of whom studied him with a kind of clinical detachment. He'd never realized how perfect the two were for each other until that moment.

With a sigh, the phantom shrugged. His manifestation had been nearly complete, a full body of spectral substance, but now he faded slightly, his anger dissipating.

"Not yet, apparently. If not for these other attacks, I might be harder to convince. But for the moment, I'll give you the benefit of the doubt. You've earned that, at least."

Clay nodded. "It's appreciated. What worries me, though, is that if we're all here, the house is unprotected."

Conan Doyle strode to a side table and picked up a small wooden case, in which he kept his pipe.

"Not entirely. Daniel is there. He makes a formidable sentinel. And I've sent Squire back to—"

"To do nothing," a voice said, from a shadowy corner.

The hobgoblin stepped out of the darkness. He never looked good—his kind were some of the ugliest creatures in any world—but his leathery flesh seemed pale, and his eyes were wide with fright that he was trying hard to hide.

"What are you doing here?" Ceridwen asked.

Squire sniffed. "'Scuse me, your highness. Just didn't wanna miss the touching reunion."

Conan Doyle took out his pipe and set down the case. "Ceridwen is correct, Squire," he said, setting the pipe between his lips. "I sent you back to Boston for a reason. You and Shuck can be most helpful to us—"

"Crap," Squire replied.

Conan Doyle flinched. The ghost of Dr. Graves could not but smile.

"I beg your pardon," the mage said, gripping the back of a chair.

"You just don't want me traveling the Shadowpaths cuz of the snake slithering around in there. I appreciate the thought, but we're under attack, boss. You need all the help you can get. I can't let a shadow serpent scare me off a fight."

Ceridwen glanced incredulously at Clay and Graves, then turned to Squire. "You hate combat."

"Nah," Squire replied, brushing at the air. "I hate getting hurt. I don't mind combat when I'm doing the hurting. Look, you're going to need the weaponsmaster in action. Someone's got us in their sights. I'm going to have to play armorer, even if I'm not actually fighting. So far I've been able to give the shadow snake the slip. If I'm lucky, I'll stay two steps ahead of him, never go through the same patch of darkness twice. Meanwhile, Shuck's back at the house with Danny and Julia. If there's any trouble, he'll come fetch me."

Dr. Graves slid through the air toward the hobgoblin.

"I'm not sure that's a good idea, Squire. Particularly with this shadow serpent searching for you every time you travel through the dark. Shuck may not reach you, or you may not get back in time if something goes wrong."

Conan Doyle lit his pipe with a purposeful flourish, as though the sound of the striking match was meant to interrupt them. Graves felt sure that had been his intention.

The mage puffed on the pipe to get it going and looked at the gathering of his Menagerie. Ceridwen wore a grim expression that somehow made her all the more beautiful, her hair wild and her violet eyes bright and alert. Clay seemed ordinary, but his every muscle tensed with the desire for action. Squire had gone uncharacteristically quiet.

They all waited on Conan Doyle.

"I suspect that our friends in Boston will be perfectly safe for the moment," the mage said. "The attacks were coordinated too well to be coincidental. Old enemies resurfacing. The Red-legged Scissor-man, Duergar of the Fey, and now comes word that the vampires that attacked Clay and Eve in France were merely a distraction so that the true enemies might get their hands on Eve."

"True enemies?" Graves asked.

Conan Doyle puffed on his pipe. "Clay discovered two vampires looking through Eve's things at their hotel in Villefranche. He dealt with them and made certain inquiries."

Squire sneered. "I hope you tortured the fuckers till they begged for mercy."

Clay crossed his arms and leaned against the wall beside the fireplace. "They received none, I'll tell you that."

Ethereal and lovely, Ceridwen moved among them. Her gaze seemed far away, and her gown rustled as though the elemental spirits who provided her traveling wind had not completely released her from their grasp. She looked at Squire a moment, and then turned to Dr. Graves.

"Jophiel, an angel who has long plagued our Eve," the Faerie sorceress said, "and Abaddon, the demon responsible for turning Eve into a—"

Ceridwen stopped herself from completing the sentence.

Dr. Graves stared at her. "A monster."

"Abaddon is the thing that caught Eve after she was banished from Eden, that made her what she became," Conan Doyle said.

Squire sat down heavily in a chair and pressed his palms against the sides of his head as though afraid it might fall apart. "Son of a bitch. You're saying these two fuckers are working together?"

Everyone in the room looked at Clay. "So it appears."

"And you've no idea about this other shapeshifter?" Ceridwen asked.

Clay narrowed his eyes in annoyance. "I've said as much, time and again."

"Did the bloodsuckers tell you anything else?" Squire asked.

Graves studied Clay, moving nearer to him. "Yes. Was there anything else, anything about what the angel and the demon planned to do with Eve, why they wanted her in the first place?"

Conan Doyle clenched his pipe in his lips a moment, then took it out and held it in his hand. "They were foot soldiers, you said. Not involved in planning, more than likely, but their type listen carefully, searching for any bit of information that might help them advance in the hierarchy. Anything they said might be important."

Clay crossed his arms, brow creasing. "I'm well aware of that. Contrary to opinion, you didn't actually invent deductive reasoning."

In spite of his own concerns about Clay, Dr. Graves couldn't help but smile. Conan Doyle's arrogance was as much a part of him as his soul or intellect, but that did not mean it could easily be forgiven. Clay had reminded the mage of his shortcoming, and the ghost silently applauded him.

"My apologies," Conan Doyle said, with a curt nod. "No offense intended."

Clay brushed the words away. "Never mind. I know we're all on edge with what's happened to Eve. Finding her is our only priority. As for the vampires in Villefranche, they couldn't tell me much beyond the names of a handful of the old ones they've been working with and the identities of the angel and demon behind it all. There is one other thing that you might be able to make something of."

Conan Doyle and Ceridwen regarded Clay expectantly. Squire stood beside the ghost of Dr. Graves, tapping his foot. After a moment, he threw up his hands. "Spit it out, already!"

"When I tried to get them to tell me where to start looking for Eve, where Jophiel and Abaddon might have taken her, they were clueless."

Dr. Graves felt a tremor go through his spectral essence. He narrowed his eyes. "What else would they say?"

Clay shot him a hard look. "Trust me, Leonard. They were not attempting to mislead me. If they knew where Eve was, they would have told me. It's far from the first time I've had to get information from someone who didn't want to give it up."

"Go on," Ceridwen said.

A crackle of energy—tiny slivers of lightning—sparkled in her violet eyes.

"My point is, they didn't know where Eve would be taken. But I did get them to backtrack for me, providing a list of everywhere they'd journeyed with Abaddon since he started recruiting vampires for this assault. We've got to start checking out those locations and see if we can find the trail, or better yet, find Eve."

The gauzy curtains billowed with a breeze that swept up from Dubrovnik harbor. Down in the old city, the church bell rang. The five of them stood in that dimly lit room, the nighttime encroaching at the windows at French doors, and gazed around at one another. They were five creatures of different breeds and worlds with nothing in common but friendship and a willingness to put themselves between innocence and the evil that threatened to destroy it. Conan Doyle had christened them the Menagerie for a reason.

The mage gestured toward Clay with his pipe. "Is there a pattern to their travels?"

"I'm not sure. The two I dealt with hooked up with the group in the Ala-dagh Mountains in Turkey. They mentioned a river in Belgium, a city in Iraq, Sri Lanka, Ethiopia, and the Seychelles."

Ceridwen held her wood-and-ice staff and studied Conan Doyle's face.

"What the hell's all that about?" Squire asked, patting his pockets as though looking for his wallet. A second later he pulled out a chocolate bar and tore the wrapper. "Vampire world tour? These guys torch in sunlight, and they're running around some of the hottest, sunshiniest places on Earth. Doesn't make any sense."

Dr. Graves felt another ripple pass through him. He studied Clay, then looked at Conan Doyle.

"Actually," said the ghost, "it may make complete sense."

"Agreed," the mage said, reaching up to stroke his mustache with his free hand. While his true age would never show, in that moment his eyes and the lines on his face made him seem older than he'd looked in years. "There's only one thing I'm aware of that connects all of those places. Combined with the abduction of Eve, I fear that something terrible is imminent."

Ceridwen touched his arm. "What is it, Arthur?"

"Yeah," Squire said, "don't keep us in suspense, boss."

Graves and Conan Doyle stared at one another.

"Eden," said the ghost.

Clay stared at him. "What are you talking about? Eden hasn't touched this world since shortly after the dawn of man. Don't you think I would have traveled there if I could have? There's no way to get into Eden from the human plane."

Conan Doyle crossed to the French doors and gazed down onto the city below. "That may not be entirely true. Certainly, it appears that neither Jophiel nor Abaddon believes it. The Scheldt River, near Antwerp, is a landmark for one story of the Garden's location. Other claims are as varied as a town in Florida and the island of Java, but include all of those places Clay named. It would seem that Abaddon and Jophiel were searching for the original location of Eden and, I presume, the placement of the Garden Gate."

Ceridwen reached up and, with a gesture, the moisture in the air formed a small sculpture of ice showing a massive gate of stone and wood. Graves studied it.

"The Garden Gate is known to the Fey," the sorceress said, but she narrowed her gaze when she turned to look at Conan Doyle. "But it doesn't exist on this plane, either."

"No," Graves agreed. "But though historians and theologians disagree on the location of the historical Eden, many of the stories conclude that there must be some kind of entry point still here in our world."

Clay shook his head. "I'd sense it. I would know."

"Would you?" Conan Doyle asked. "How can you be certain? It would be well hidden, of course, and it would be guarded carefully."

Ceridwen waved a hand, and the ice fell to the floor in a sprinkle of rain. "Oh, it is. I don't know if a passage exists between the Blight and the Gates of Eden, but the plane upon which Eden rests is not unfamiliar to my people. The Fey have walked between worlds many times. But there is a

Guardian—it may be part sentinel and part barrier—which keeps anyone from even approaching the Garden Gate, or even entering the realm where the Gate stands."

Conan Doyle smiled at her. "So we don't need to find the door in this dimension. If we can find a dimensional matrix point we can use to journey into Faerie—difficult enough in itself these days—we'll be able to find a door from there?"

"A door, yes. But how we'll get past the Guardian, I have no idea."

"We don't have to get past it," Squire said. "We just have to make sure the assholes who took Eve don't get past it, either."

The ghost of Dr. Graves drifted toward Conan Doyle. "You think they took Eve because they believe that she can help them get past the Guardian?"

"Or through the Gate. Or both," the mage replied. "And with the allies they've brought together on this, Duergar and the shadow serpent and whatever the thing was that mimicked Clay's abilities, it's obvious to me that they've been planning this for quite some time."

Clay seemed to have deflated. His distant gaze drifted, as though once again he was seeing into some other world, perhaps all the way back to the Creation itself.

"The Guardian will stop them. But we can't take any chances. They can't be allowed to enter Eden. Their evil would taint the place forever."

Dr. Graves studied him, still not entirely trusting. "Clay, it seems to me there's been evil in the Garden before, and it survived just fine."

"No," Clay said. "It survived barely. Just barely."

Squire licked chocolate from his fingers and crumpled up the candy bar wrapper. "So the fuckers are crashing paradise. They've got brass ones, I'll give 'em that. I take it we're going to track 'em down, get Eve back, and trounce on their heads."

Conan Doyle smiled. "You can rest assured, my friend. There will be copious amounts of trouncing."

Graves glanced at Squire and Clay, then studied Conan Doyle and Ceridwen closely. "Last I'd been aware, most points of entry into Faerie had been closed off. Do you plan to unseal the door in your home back in Boston?"

Ceridwen seemed about to answer in the affirmative, but Conan Doyle shook his head.

"I think not. Entering that way will undoubtedly draw the attention not only of King Finvarra, but whatever enemies trouble him presently. We can't afford to become embroiled in the difficulties brewing among the Fey as yet. No, I've an old friend who lives not far from here, just up the coast, who ought to be able to guide us along another path. If I'm correct, we won't even need to enter Faerie at all."

"Which old friend?" Ceridwen asked. "Not Jelena."

Conan Doyle tapped out his pipe, set it on an end table, and smiled. "Hold my hand, love. A traveling wind for us all, I think, if you can manage."

Ceridwen took his hand, but she did not look at all pleased. Squire had long expressed a dislike for traveling via magic, but with the shadow serpent awaiting along the paths, he seemed to have gotten over his fear. He stood beside the elemental sorceress as she raised her staff and began to summon the spirits that would create the wind. Squire clutched a handful of her dress. Clay took her other hand.

"Leonard?" Conan Doyle asked.

"I'll make my own way," replied the ghost, his substance fluttering like the curtains that rustled in the night breeze. "Call to me, and I'll find you."

"So be it," the mage said.

The wind swirled around them. Within the ice sphere atop Ceridwen's staff, a tiny ball of fire churned. A rushing noise filled the room, and the four of them were plucked from the ground by a massive gust of wind that drew them upward for just a moment before they vanished entirely.

Alone, the ghost stared at the place where they'd stood, and wondered what would come of all this. Of late he had doubted whether or not he could trust Conan Doyle, and now his trust in Clay had been called into question. Graves wondered if he could truly trust any of them. The thought disturbed him. If the Menagerie could not rely upon one another, they could not stand side by side against the horrors that preyed upon humanity, and certainly would never be able to combat the Demogorgon when it finally arrived.

It worried him. Even a dead man could feel fear.

THE world transformed into a rush of blue and gray, the wind propelling them forward even as it encircled and held them aloft. Conan Doyle squinted, wishing that for once he could get a clear view of the world around him as the elemental spirits hurtled them toward their destination. Glimpses of towns and forests and a bit of ocean were all he could manage. He had never been certain if those fragmentary images were real and tangible—that the traveling wind simply rushed Ceridwen through the physical world—or if the elemental spirits transported her into their own realm, a place of wind and storm, and those glimpses were windows. He suspected the latter, but even Ceridwen did not know for certain, and her rapport with the elements far exceeded that of any ordinary human sorcerer, no matter how accomplished.

In the grasp of the wind, Conan Doyle tried to force himself to relax, to surrender to them, but he had never been comfortable with giving over control to others. Squire liked it even less. He could hear the hobgoblin cursing as though far, far away, the words stolen away by the gale, lost in their trail. Conan Doyle tried to glance back, but the 'goblin was little more than a dark blur. He felt Ceridwen's grip tighten on his hand and looked at her, then past her, at the heavy, golemlike figure of Clay. He had reverted to his natural form, and the wind scoured away bits of dirt, eroding his face to a strange smoothness.

His jacket whipped around him, snapping like a flag. Conan Doyle heard Ceridwen shout at Squire. Apparently his questing hands, in search of a more substantial grip, had slipped beneath her dress. The mage could not help smiling. Then he felt one of the hobgoblin's hands clutch at his arm, and he nearly lost his grip. Conan Doyle cursed, trying not to imagine where he might land if Ceridwen were to lose track of him in the midst of the traveling wind.

They slowed. The blur of air twisted around them in a kind of cyclone. Arthur could not help it—every time

Ceridwen transported him this way, he waited for the drop, for the impact of his feet upon solid ground. Yet as ever, the traveling wind began to dissipate, and he felt only the weight of his own body settling once more, and found himself standing in the midst of a thick forest whose trees were like things out of legend. Their trunks were thick with gnarled bark, and their branches twisted up into the night sky. The trees towered above them ominously, as though they might come to life at any moment.

But this wasn't that kind of forest.

The wind whispered through the leaves and across the forest floor, and only the natural breeze remained. The air held the scent of the ocean, only miles to the west.

Ceridwen released his hand, perhaps a bit too quickly. Her blond hair was wild from the wind and her violet eyes gleamed with a preternatural light. He saw disappointment in those eyes.

"Here we are," she said.

Conan Doyle's expression became grim. He reached for her hand, fingers brushing against hers. "It will be fine. The time is coming when we will need every ally who will stand with us. That's why I conducted the conclave in the first place."

"Don't concern yourself," she replied.

Yet he could not help but be concerned.

Ceridwen wandered away from him, staring up through the trees at the night sky and peering into the trees around them. The fire inside the ice sphere atop her staff glowed a deep blue that spread its light around them, the trees casting sinister shadows.

"Where the fuck are we?" Squire asked.

Conan Doyle spun on him. "Would you, for once in your life, attempt to speak plainly and without profane adornment?" he said, far more sharply than he'd intended.

Squire blinked. "Where the *hell* are we?"

The mage sighed. "Still in Croatia. Looking for that old friend I mentioned."

Clay stood several feet away. His face, arms, and chest seemed to have been partially worn away and a scattering of fresh dirt the color of his body lay on the ground around him.

He shuddered, then changed form, flesh fluidly shifting into the human face he so often wore.

"Are you all right?" Conan Doyle asked.

"I am, thanks. An odd experience, though. I thought traveling in that form might be less unsettling, but it's far worse. I won't do that again," Clay vowed. "What about Leonard?"

Conan Doyle nodded and looked up into the night, as though he could peer into the ghost world with ordinary, human eyes. "Dr. Graves! Leonard Graves! Join us, if you will."

Squire looked around. "No sign. Maybe we need a Ouija board."

"He'll be here," Clay said.

"Arthur," Ceridwen called.

Conan Doyle and his companions turned as one to see Ceridwen holding up her staff and moving off through the trees.

"Ceri, wait!" the mage said.

"This way," the Faerie princess said, continuing on.

The three of them watched her go a moment, then Conan Doyle scowled. "I suppose Dr. Graves can catch up to us."

"What's eating her?" Squire asked.

Conan Doyle shot him a dark look.

"Someone named Jelena, apparently," Clay replied, as if the mage wasn't there at all. "I'm beginning to think she's not everybody's 'old friend.'"

"Save your speculation," Conan Doyle warned. "You'll meet her soon enough."

The mage strode after Ceridwen, leaving Clay and Squire to follow in his wake. They did so in surprising silence, given that the hobgoblin rarely kept quiet for more than a few minutes at a time unless there was a television present. Ahead, Ceri could be seen bathed in the pale, blue light, and soon enough the three of them caught up with her.

For perhaps twenty minutes they made their way through the forest, following paths rarely trod by human feet, over roots and low hills, always beneath the web of tree branches, so that they seemed lost in an endless, primeval forest. If not for the perfectly ordinary cast of the night sky, with its infinite pinpoints of celestial light and the scimitar moon, he might have thought they were no longer in the human world at all. Ceridwen paused and backtracked, adjusting her course several times.

At last she slowed. Conan Doyle gestured to Clay and Squire, and when the hobgoblin began to whisper some question in a hoarse rasp, the mage pointed at him, freezing him with a stern look. Squire held up his hands in surrender and pretended to zipper his lip. Conan Doyle considered doing it in reality.

The rush and tumble of a river filled the night. Ceridwen picked up her pace again, and the rest of them followed suit. In moments they emerged from the trees before a crumbling stone structure that had once been a mill, its wheel half-rotted by time and mold, but still dipped into the water that flowed by beneath.

"What is this?" Clay asked, voice low. "There isn't a trace of any settlement here. Who'd build a mill out here in the middle of nowhere?"

Conan Doyle turned to him. "It wasn't built in this world. It shifted here, long ago, the way things sometimes do."

Squire sighed. "What does that even mean?"

Ceridwen raised her staff, and the blue light brightened, drawing their attention. Eerie shadows danced across the broken, cracked, collapsed face of the mill. Some of the shadows seemed to exist on their own, without any object to throw them.

Halfway across the space that separated Conan Doyle from Ceridwen, the ghost of Dr. Graves manifested in near silence, only a kind of low static marking his arrival. Anyone else would have thought the sound a part of the river's hiss.

"You might have waited," the specter said. His appearance had altered somewhat. Graves seemed more solid than usual, and beneath his arms hung the twin holsters for the phantom guns that he had managed to fashion from his own ectoplasmic substance over the years. The ghost could also control other elements of his appearance, and at the moment appeared clad in a collarless shirt and dark tweed trousers with suspenders. He often appeared in this fashion when he thought there might be a fight.

Squire hushed the ghost, perhaps a bit too enthusiastically, having been warned to silence himself.

"No need for stealth now," Ceridwen said, addressing all four of them. "Come, Arthur. We're here, now. This is her lair. You'd best call her. Eve and Eden both require our aid."

Conan Doyle hesitated a moment. It had been a very long time since he had last seen her. The eyes of his Menagerie were upon him, full of curiosity and expectation. With one final glance at Ceridwen, he took a step closer to the ruined mill and cupped his hands around his mouth.

"Jelena!" he called. "Jelena Kurjak!"

His voice echoed off the stones of the mill and from the trees behind them. The river seemed to whisper in reply.

When Conan Doyle looked over at Ceridwen, he found her gaze averted from him. He ignored the others and turned to face the forest, calling out for Jelena again.

"Show yourself!" he shouted into the night black woods. "It's Arthur Conan Doyle, come to call!"

Nothing stirred in the forest. Not a night bird sang, nor rodent scurried. Even the wind seemed to have died. Only the river continued its low commentary.

Conan Doyle turned again, facing the mill. He cupped his hands and shouted her name.

"Jelena Kurjak!"

A low growl sounded from the trees off to the right. As one, the Menagerie turned. Conan Doyle held his breath as the wolf padded silently out of the forest and paused at the riverbank, illuminated by starlight and that sliver moon.

The ghost of Dr. Graves moved soundlessly forward. The wolf growled deep in its throat and glared at Graves with golden eyes.

"Arthur?" Clay ventured.

The mage raised a hand to forestall any intrusion by his companions.

As they watched, the wolf stretched and rose on its hind legs. It stood. The massive beast reached up and gripped the fur at her throat, pulling it apart . . . ripping it open with a wet, slick sound. The wolf stripped its skin away, slipping out of her fur and stepping away from it as seductively as though it had been an evening gown. Jelena Kurjak stood before them, her body exquisite, olive skin gleaming damply in the starlight, as though a light sheen of sweat covered her. Otherwise, she was entirely nude, her slender form powerful and tall, her breasts perfect, her dark hair hanging around her shoulders. With the exception of those golden eyes, the she-wolf had vanished.

Only she had not. The she-wolf stood before them.

Arthur could not breathe.

He heard Squire mutter some words of appreciation, so awed that he'd forgotten to be vulgar for a moment.

"You know," Jelena said, striding warily toward them, gaze darting between Ceridwen and Conan Doyle, "you don't have to shout. I am not deaf."

Though she spoke English well—he'd taught her himself—her accent seemed thicker than the last time they'd met.

"Apologies," Conan Doyle said, remembering to breathe. He had been witness to great beauty in his life. Ceridwen managed to steal his breath nearly every day. But there was such majesty in Jelena that he could not pretend it did not affect him.

"I wouldn't trouble you at all if it weren't important," the mage went on. "You know that."

Jelena crossed the space between them, brazen in her nakedness. If she saw how it affected the others, she gave no sign. Even Clay could not tear his gaze from her. The she-wolf ignored Conan Doyle a moment and went to Ceridwen.

"Good evening, princess," Jelena said, and the words were almost a purr. "We did not part on the best of terms. Do you come to ask my help?"

A breeze whipped around the Fey sorceress that seemed only to touch her, and no one else. She met Jelena's gaze with her own bright, violet eyes, staff in her hand, and now Conan Doyle realized the powerful sway of the she-wolf's presence. How could he have thought for a moment that she was more majestic than Ceridwen, who carried herself with all the command of her heritage as a Princess of Faerie.

"On behalf of a friend who is in grave danger, and of a world that might be similarly imperiled, I do indeed plead your help and indulgence, Wolf's Daughter."

Jelena gazed at her with golden eyes and smiled. She

bowed her head almost as though submitting to Ceridwen's royal status, and turned to Conan Doyle. Clay, Squire, and Dr. Graves had gathered around him, now, and the she-wolf seemed to take them in for the first time.

"You are a handsome lot, aren't you?" she asked.

Then all trace of amusement left her, and she focused on Conan Doyle. "Arthur, it is I who should apologize. You summoned me to your gathering in Dubrovnik, and I did not come. I could not. I do not like to go into the cities anymore, or to travel beyond the forest. The world has changed. The Blight has become uglier. More and more, I find myself reluctant even to cross over into your world. I prefer the Wildwood."

Grimly, Conan Doyle nodded. Jelena stood only an arm's length away, and he had to resist the urge to reach out to lay a comforting hand upon her. This was her power, not only over him, but over all men, and many women as well.

"While I'm glad to find you here, you might well wish to return to the Wildwood after tonight," the mage said. "I had called for that conclave to discuss an immense danger that even now approaches the world of men. Honestly, Jelena, I cannot say for certain if you'll be safe from the Demogorgon's power, even in your own dimension. But it must be safer than being here in man's world."

Unconsciously, the she-wolf crossed her arms across her breasts, not out of shame, but the instinct to protect herself. "The Demogorgon. I have heard the legend. I thought it was only a story."

Clay transformed into his primal form, the towering, earthen man. "There's no such thing as 'only a story.'"

Jelena appraised him openly, whispering some appreciation in Croatian. The ghost of Dr. Graves floated nearer, and now the she-wolf studied him. She knew well what ghosts were, Conan Doyle recalled. What she might make of Squire, he had no idea. The hobgoblin had not yet ceased to leer at her.

"Before you retreat to safer ground," Ceridwen said, the blue fire in her staff's ice sphere blooming brighter, casting the entire riverside in its light, "we would ask your indulgence."

The she-wolf turned to look at her. "What is it you wish, princess?"

"Safe passage into, and through, the Wildwood."

"And where will you go from there?"

"To a place that many believe is the beginning of man's world, to save the life of the mother of all humanity."

Jelena cocked her head a moment, confused, golden eyes alight. Then she gave a deep bow, with a flourish of her hands. Watching the way her body moved mesmerized them all for a moment—all save Ceridwen.

"By all means, princess. You've brought me warning that may have saved my life, and that of my kin. I will help in whatever way you wish. I am your servant."

Ceridwen narrowed her violet eyes. The she-wolf had agreed to help, but Conan Doyle thought that his lover did not look at all impressed, or pleased.

THE forest seemed impossibly quiet.

Squire liked the weight of the Gemini dagger he carried on his hip, and wished he had the time to return to Boston and bring the whole damned armory back here. With the serpent lurking along the Shadowpaths—and no doubt keeping an eye on the forge—it would be difficult for him to retrieve weapons from his workshop. But there were plenty of killing instruments back at Conan Doyle's house.

Time wouldn't allow it. Not for the moment, at least. The train was leaving the station. The she-wolf, Jelena, picked up the wolf skin she'd shed and strode toward the ruined face of the old mill and went to the door, which sat at odd angles in a crooked frame. Squire paused a moment to admire the way her muscles moved under her skin, which shone in the moonlight. Mostly, he was just staring at her ass. The view from the back was breathtaking; nearly as delicious as the front.

"We've got work to do," Clay said as he strode past, following Jelena, Ceridwen, and Mr. Doyle up to the door of the mill.

Squire watched the she-wolf as she pressed her hands against that awkward door—a door that couldn't possibly open—and muttered words in an unfamiliar tongue. The hob-goblin didn't think it was Croatian, particularly as it involved a lot of guttural snarling. He couldn't have missed the inter-play between Ceridwen and Conan Doyle as this bit of spell-casting went on. The mage tried not to look at Jelena—a nearly impossible task, giving the way her breasts rose and fell as she moved her hands over the door—and Ceridwen stared at him the entire time, ignoring her.

It made him wonder if his boss had ever had a thing with the she-wolf. Some guys had all the luck. Though Squire wouldn't have wanted to trade places with Conan Doyle now—not with the harsh looks Ceridwen kept shooting in his direction.

Something shimmered just to Squire's left, and he glanced over to see the ghost of Dr. Graves standing there, arms crossed, studying him with obvious disapproval. The hob-goblin knew that Graves had lived a life of adventure and danger, but half the time, he had trouble believing it. Graves could be the ultimate buzzkill.

"She's beautiful," the specter said.

"And naked," Squire replied.

The ghost sighed and nodded slowly, as if talking to a slow-witted child. "Yes, Squire. She's also naked. Do you think you could set aside your diminutive lothario act long enough for us to keep Eve alive?"

The hobgoblin blinked several times. "Act?"

"Squire."

"Okay, okay," he said, raising his hands in surrender. "Jeez, Doc, give a guy a break. You put something that yummy on my plate, I'm gonna salivate, right? Ask Pavlov. Just can't help it."

"Pavlov worked with dogs," the ghost replied.

"Your point?"

"Eve is your friend."

Squire nodded. "Evie loves me. She's also gorgeous. Though not naked nearly as often as this chick, from what I gather."

The ghost of Dr. Graves shook his head and started toward the broken-down mill. Squire smiled. More than anything, he missed Eve because most of the other members of Conan

Doyle's Menagerie were so fucking serious all the time. Once in a while, he just couldn't help busting balls.

But maybe Graves was right. The sight of Jelena naked like that, with her olive skin and that long hair, half made him forget his name—never mind what it did to other parts of his body. Squire figured he owed Eve more than that. He had been telling himself that everything would be all right. Now, the time had come to turn that prophecy into truth.

"Squire!"

He looked up sharply. Conan Doyle stood just beside the mill's door. It hung open, now. Ceridwen, Clay, and the she-wolf must have already gone through, and even now, he saw the phantom figure of Dr. Graves slipping through into darkness. Magic had to be involved, because as off kilter as that door had been, there was no way it could just open. He hadn't figured the she-wolf for a mage, but some bits of magic didn't require much mastery—just the right words at the right time. Hell, there were a thousand kinds of magic in the pandimensional worlds. It just made him feel a little hinky when he didn't know the person dabbling in sorcerous acts.

But if Conan Doyle trusted Jelena, he figured that would have to be enough.

"Coming, boss," he called, hurrying toward the mill.

The river that ran behind the wooden structure grew louder as he approached the door. Then he realized the rushing sound came not from the river but from the darkened doorway, and he faltered a bit.

"Hurry up, damn it!" Conan Doyle snapped, his jacket flapping in a sudden breeze that kicked up. "It only stays open a minute or two!"

Squire felt a tremor of fear pass through him—not fear of any danger to himself but of being left behind, of not being there to help Eve—and he ran toward the door. Conan Doyle stepped aside to let him pass.

Without further hesitation, the hobgoblin ambled through the warped frame and into the darkness. His feet splashed in cold water that soaked through his shoes, then hit wooden floor. Blinking, he saw light ahead, in the shape of another warped door, and the silhouettes of figures waiting beyond it. A few steps later, and he found himself standing in another forest, in another world. So much seemed the same, but also different. The trees were taller and thicker, ancient things whose branches spread imperiously overhead. The stars were a vast field, their multitude seemingly even greater than anything he'd ever beheld. The moonlight shot through the branches and fell across the forest floor in shafts of liquid gold, giving an odd, ephemeral hue to everything.

The others had arrived before him, all except for Conan Doyle, and that strange glimmer shone upon them all, giving the weight of myth to their presence. They seemed like ancient heroes. Olympians. Titans. In that moment, knowing he was one of them, Squire believed that the Menagerie was capable of almost anything.

Clay and Graves stood side by side in a clearing of ragged, wild grass. The she-wolf lingered at the edge of the clearing, peering into the trees, her entire body rigid with attention. She had tied her wolf skin around her throat. Squire felt certain that if she were in her wolf form, instead of just wearing the fur like a cloak, her ears would have been cocked.

Ceridwen seemed to emerge from shadows off to his right, and he had the idea she'd been down by the river. The elements of any world spoke to the Fey sorceress, and Squire had seen her in action enough times to know she would want to establish a rapport with this world before attempting any magic here.

Now, though, her expression was stern. "We've no time for hesitation or daydreams, Squire," she said as she approached.

The hobgoblin grew irritable. "I get it, okay? We focus on the nightmares. Let's move on."

"Indeed," came a voice from behind him.

Squire turned to see Conan Doyle emerging from the crumbling mill through what appeared to be that same skewed door. He closed it behind him. The mill looked precisely the same in this world as it had in the other, but otherwise their surroundings had altered. The forest and the now-rushing river all seemed primeval. This made sense to Squire. If you couldn't get to Eden by way of a world where the wild still ruled and nature grew unhindered . . . well, hell, it just felt like they were closer, here, than they'd been in the human world.

"Jelena?" Conan Doyle asked.

At the edge of the clearing, the she-wolf turned. Even partially hidden behind the fur that hung across her back and shoulders, her body was gloriously rounded, arms and legs taut and sinewy. The golden glow that suffused this world gave her the presence of an animal, even though she presently wore human skin.

Ceridwen stepped in front of him, blocking his salacious view. He glanced up guiltily, trying not to notice the curves of Ceridwen's body beneath her thin, silky dress. He expected her to be glaring at him, but found instead that she gazed at him with gentle, caring eyes.

"You worry me, Squire," she whispered. "Please do try not to get your head chopped off because you couldn't keep your mind on the job."

He grinned. "I'll do my best."

By then the others were already moving out. Conan Doyle and Jelena had evidently had some kind of conversation about their destination. They started off through the forest, picking their way among the trees. No path existed here, but there were places where the Wildwood was thicker than in others. Jelena led the way and chose for them the easiest available route.

Conan Doyle and Ceridwen followed the she-wolf together. The tension between them shimmered almost as brightly as the moonlight. Squire felt pretty confident that it was an ephemeral thing—it would pass. They loved each other enough to fall all over again when they had gotten back together after so many years apart, and pissed off. Whatever chemistry the boss had with Jelena, Ceridwen had to know it wouldn't go anywhere.

Unless it already did, way back when, Squire thought.

He would have to keep an eye on all of them.

Clay hung at the back, watching their flank. Squire wondered why he hadn't shapeshifted into some animal form to blend better into the Wildwood, or into his natural form to seem more formidable. He made a mental note to ask later, but a fragment of insight occurred to him; perhaps Clay didn't want the denizens of the Wildwood to perceive him as some kind of pretender. If he took animal form, it might be seen as some kind of insult.

Then again, maybe not. Squire had never been all that perceptive when it came to social niceties.

"Do you see them?" the ghost of Dr. Graves asked.

Squire flinched and turned to find the ghost striding along beside him. Or pretending to stride, in that ghostly, never-touch-the-ground sort of way.

"Doc, could you please not do that? You're gonna give me a fuckin' cardiac arrest here. I don't wanna be flopping around like a drooling simpleton in front of everyone—especially not the hot wolf chick. And I really don't want to die here. If I've gotta go, it ought to be in the arms of my one true love—Angelina Jolie—after hot and sweaty sex."

If ghosts could twitch, Graves did. One of his eyes closed halfway, and his upper lip curled in a sneer of disgust.

"Is there some kind of curse on you, Squire, that requires you to vomit up a certain amount of profanity and vulgarity in any given hour, or some dreadful fate will befall you?"

The hobgoblin grinned. "Nah. I'm just a pig. Normally, Eve gets to hear all my cleverest bon mots, but since she's otherwise engaged, you're the lucky benefactor of her absence. Oh, and check it out, I can talk like I'm uptight, too. It just sounds so fuckin' silly coming from me."

Again, Graves scowled, but Squire thought he caught sight of a slight grin on the specter's features as well.

"Anyway, what were you saying?" the hobgoblin asked.

Dr. Graves gave a nod, indicating the forest off to their right. "I wondered if you'd seen our new companions. We appear to be attracting more and more attention with every step."

At first Squire didn't know what the ghost was talking about. He studied Jelena, Ceridwen, and Conan Doyle, who were making their way through the trees ahead, then glanced back at Clay. But when he turned to look at the ghost again, he saw something dart among the trees. His view was obscured because the glimpse he'd gotten had been through the translucent form of Dr. Graves himself. But then he understood what he was looking for.

All around them, branches swayed and underbrush rustled. A fox dashed behind the splintered stump of a lightning-struck tree. A pair of large owls hooted softly, eyes alight in the darkness. A dark form lumbered along to their left. At first, Squire thought it was a bear, but then it shifted and the moonlight splashed across the figure and he saw that it was a massive, savage-looking man wearing the head and fur of a bear like a shaman's garb.

No, Squire realized. It wasn't a bear or a man, but a creature like Jelena. One of the spirits of the Wildwood. Perhaps every one of the beasts that paced them as they made their trek through the forest was one of those woodland spirits.

"Cool," Squire whispered to the ghost. "As long as they don't decide to eat us."

Graves actually did laugh, then, though softly. "Jelena is our guide. I suspect they will defer to her in this. At least for now. I wonder, though, if Arthur had more than expediency in mind by passing through this place on the way to the Garden Gate."

"Like what?" Squire asked, furrowing his leathery brow.

"I'm not sure. But we'll need allies in the days to come. Knowing Arthur, nothing is by accident. A display like this will alarm them, let them know that there's trouble brewing, and that we're on the case."

The hobgoblin glanced at him. "You think this is all a show?"

"No. But I'd be willing to bet the show is no accident."

Squire thought about that. Maybe Graves was right, but that didn't make Conan Doyle's intent malign in any way. If he wanted a little *sturm und drang* to rally the troops, where was the harm? They were certainly going to need all the help they could get when the Demogorgon finally reached the human world. That ugliness would spill through a hundred dimensions. Could be none of them would be safe, then. Any creatures in these pocket realms who thought they'd be safe—that the destruction wrought by the Demogorgon would only touch the Blight—would be fooling themselves.

The ghost's tone made it clear he didn't like the way Conan Doyle manipulated situations to his own advantage. Squire understood why. Graves had been manipulated by

Conan Doyle himself, even though the mage thought he'd been doing the ghost a favor, saving him from a truth too painful to endure. But then Graves had learned the truth, and he'd endured. And had it really been Conan Doyle's business?

Not at all.

But Squire knew Conan Doyle's mind—his cunning—might be the only thing standing between survival and destruction when the Demogorgon arrived. If that meant a little propaganda, Squire was all for it.

"What about the Fey?" he asked. The people of Faerie had been on his mind a lot, recently. Ceridwen had been visited by messengers from her uncle's kingdom, asking her to come home. Trouble was brewing there. Maybe even war. And the creature who'd attacked her—who'd been working with Eve's abductors—had been an old enemy from that world.

"What about them?" the ghost asked.

"They've got problems of their own. I don't know why all these sprites and fairies and trolls and shit want to beat the crap out of each other when there's an enemy on the way that'd like to scrape them all off the ass of the world. You think they're going to lend a hand when it all gets ugly? When the Demogorgon hits town?"

"We may find ourselves with all manner of surprising allies," the ghost replied.

Squire nodded. "I hope you're right."

His stomach grumbled. He hadn't had anything to eat in hours, and with no hope of chocolate, Doritos, or any of his other favorite junk foods on the journey ahead, he had started to feel even more irritable.

They marched through the forest. More and more of the creatures of the Wildwood accompanied them.

"Feels like we're following the freakin' Yellow Brick Road," Squire muttered to Graves.

The ghost arched an eyebrow. He didn't get it.

Squire only sighed and kept on. Another twenty minutes of hiking, and they came to a small hillock—maybe an ancient burial mound or something, from the look of it. In the distance there was only more forest, nothing but the Wildwood. But obviously the spot had some kind of arcane significance for Jelena.

The she-wolf turned to face them all. Squire couldn't help being mesmerized by her naked form, cloaked in fur. He shook himself and tore his eyes away. So he couldn't have candy or Cheetos and he couldn't stare at the extraordinary rack on the stunningly gorgeous naked wolf chick. What was the point of living?

"This is where the walls between worlds are thinnest," Jelena said. "There is no door into the limbo place you seek, but you have powerful magic. You will get through."

Conan Doyle took her hand, a gentleman's courtesy. "Thank you, Jelena."

Ceridwen's eyes flashed, and she raised her elemental staff. The wood seemed darker than Squire had ever seen it. The sphere of ice on the top gave off a cold mist that glowed in the moonlight, and within the ice, the flicker of fire turned to a tiny, raging conflagration.

"A traveling wind will carry us there," she said.

Clay had kept back, watching all of the wild creatures who had followed them. Now he snapped his head around as though he'd heard a gunshot.

"What? I told you an hour ago I wasn't doing that again?"

Conan Doyle gave him a hard look. "Eve awaits. You can accompany us, or remain here."

The shapeshifter narrowed his eyes. Squire didn't think he'd ever seen Clay pissed off at the boss before. The guy had lived since the beginning of time—he was literally older than dirt—and usually it seemed to give him perspective. Not tonight.

"Make it swift, then. I don't like being cast adrift like that."

Ceridwen nodded. "Swift it shall be."

Jelena stepped toward her, pulling the wolf skin around to cover her nakedness. "I would come with you."

The whole forest seemed to hold its breath.

"I'm not sure that's—" Conan Doyle began, glancing worriedly at Ceridwen.

"The best news I've had all week!" Squire declared, grinning broadly.

They all turned to stare disapprovingly at him.

"Oh," he said. "Did I say that aloud?"

Jelena glanced from Conan Doyle to Ceridwen, her proud gaze somewhat softened. "I would help you, if I can. For my people, and for the Wildwood. If you seek to stop the Demogorgon, then I am with you."

Ceridwen stared at her a moment, then looked at Conan Doyle. Some unspoken communication passed between them. From what Squire could tell, it wasn't pleasant. Conan Doyle reached out and touched the Fey sorceress's cheek, and Ceridwen nodded.

"We would be honored."

Squire blinked in surprise, then glanced at Dr. Graves. The ghost didn't look at him, focused instead on the strange trio at the peak of the burial mound. Squire glanced at Clay, who had his arms crossed, watching with interest.

Politics, the hobgoblin thought.

Whatever issues caused the tension among those three, the survival of their worlds took precedence.

Wonderful. This oughta be loads of fun.

Ceridwen began to whisper to the elemental spirits, calling up the winds, blowing leaves across the ground and making branches sway. The traveling wind had come.

Squire took one last glance around, but except for Jelena the creatures of the Wildwood had departed.

The Menagerie were on their own again.

10

EVE felt addled and exhausted, her body one enormous bruise. Nothing seemed to make sense to her. She stared at the creature standing in front of her, the shapeshifter who wore Clay's face.

"You're not him," she said again, repulsed by the creature's masquerade.

Over the years they had known one another—and especially recently—she and Clay had grown close. They were friends. It sickened her to see her friend's face on this monster.

Eve mustered the strength to stand, feeling the talons of her hands elongate with indignation. The vampires leaped upon her like the vermin that they were—her own offspring, down across a thousand generations of leeches—and they forced her to her knees in front of the impostor. Palu, the ancient Samoan bloodsucker who'd always despised her, held her wrists behind her back in an iron grip as the others laughed and snickered among themselves. They relished the sight of the one they most feared humiliated by their efforts.

The cracked clay figure smiled though, his teeth like marble.

"No, that's true. I am not *he*," he said, voice a deep rumble. He spread his arms and began to slowly turn. "I am Legion."

His body changed as he turned, one form to the next, his malleable flesh shifting from animal to human to insect. If it walked, swam, flew, or crawled upon the earth, the imposter—*Legion*—was able to take its shape. He was like Clay in almost every way, and Eve wondered how it was possible that there could be two such beings in this world. Clay had always been unique—crafted by the Creator Himself. So where had this creature come from?

She was mesmerized by the transformations, a myriad of life-forms in the blink of an eye, so fast that one blurred into the next.

Jophiel cleared his throat, his powerful wings beating loudly in the silence before the Gate, commanding their attention.

"If we might proceed," the angel began, his impatience evident in the way he licked at his thin, perfect lips, snatching quick glances at the impenetrable Gate to the Garden. "Eden is waiting."

Legion halted his succession of shapes as some sort of ape. He bowed his head to the angel and assumed his earthen form. "As you wish, brother of Heaven."

Duergar stalked forward, axe in hand, his Drow followers at his side.

"What rough beast is this?" the half-blood warrior demanded, pointing his blood-encrusted blade at Legion. The Drow grumbled and whispered among themselves, mirroring their master's displeasure. "And who invited it to join us?"

Still on her knees, Eve watched Abaddon. The Drow-Fey half-breed seemed to be getting on the demon's nerves. The evil one seemed to consider the feral warrior beneath him, somehow, and—with a sigh—dismissed him as a fool. One look at the dark, ugly intelligence in Duergar's eyes told Eve that Abaddon was making a mistake. All of the members of this terrible alliance were equally dangerous.

Abaddon pinched the bridge of his nose as if attempting to be rid of a headache.

"It was not necessary for me to make you privy to my every decision," the demon stated, barely suppressing his exasperation. "But let me assure you, Legion is a welcome and beneficial addition to our flock."

Duergar glowered, and Eve smiled inwardly. She hoped she would survive long enough to take advantage of their disharmony.

"Shall we proceed?" Legion asked, directing his question to Abaddon.

The demon continued to stare at Duergar, as if awaiting a further challenge to his plans. But the half-blood warrior only nodded, waving away the Hell-Lord's oppressive gaze, and barked something in the guttural language of his kind as he and his small army stepped away.

Eve sensed that the vampires at her back had let their hold grow slack, as if they believed she had given in to their superior numbers, that they had driven the fight from her.

In their dreams.

She let her body sag heavily in their grasp as though she were losing consciousness. Then she surged upward, driving the back of her head into Palu's fat Samoan face and twisting out of his grip.

The leeches didn't know what hit them.

She spun, swiping her talons across the exposed throats of three who blocked her way. Her claws scraped newly exposed spinal columns. She turned to run, to lose herself in this strange, forested limbo realm between the earthly world and the Garden of Eden.

She was not fast enough.

Abaddon's hand clamped around the back of her neck, yanking her toward him.

"Going someplace, darling?"

She slashed at his chest with a growl as he drew her toward him, digging deep furrows into his flesh. The bloodred demon gave her a vicious shake, like a terrier thrashing a rat, and she felt her neck give way with a muffled snap.

"Enough of that," he spit. "You are a part of this whether you care to be or not."

Her body went numb as she dangled in his grasp. She could see in his eyes that he enjoyed her helplessness, probably reminiscing about the days when he'd first had his way with her.

"Of all the meat I've sampled in my many years, I've always remembered you as the most succulent." He brought her closer, rubbing his coarse lips against her throat, inhaling the smell of her. Then he whispered in her ear. "The softness of your flesh . . . the smell . . .

"The taste."

Eve felt his mouth clamp down on her neck, his teeth biting through the flesh as he yanked a ragged patch of skin away. She grunted, more in horror than in pain. Abaddon twisted her so that the scarlet mist hissing from the wound in her throat was directed toward Legion. Her blood sprayed the shapeshifter's earthen body.

Legion opened his mouth, taking the dwindling spray onto his tongue. "Ah, that's it," he said, rubbing her blood into the deep, jagged cracks of his dry flesh.

Abaddon let her drop to the ground. From where she lay, Eve could still see what transpired before her, even though a part of her wished she could not.

Legion's flesh flowed, the way she had seen Clay's transform a thousand times. But what he'd become was no monster, no beast. Legion stood above Eve now as a beautiful, exotic woman, entirely nude, her breasts heavy and her curves catching the light.

Eve stared at herself.

Yet this was not entirely herself, not a precise duplicate. What stood before her was a copy of the woman she had been in ancient days, at the dawn of the world, from the time before she had disobeyed the Creator, before she was driven from the Garden. Staring at that image of herself, still alive and pure, broke her heart. She wished that her neck wasn't broken so that she could have turned away.

The angel Jophiel began to clap. "Bravo. A lovely parlor trick. But to what end? Why would you presume that a duplicate could work better then the real thing?"

"Your kind lacks imagination," Abaddon replied. With a flourish, he directed their attention to Legion.

The shapeshifter, the naked, sensual form of young Eve herself, had begun to shake. Arms wrapped around herself, the false Eve bent over in pain. She shuddered, wracked with violent spasms, then she—Legion—vomited a thick, oily black fluid onto the grass at his feet.

"Lovely," Jophiel said. "Something he ate?"

Abaddon smiled. "In a roundabout fashion, yes."

He gestured for the angel to come closer as he stood above the puddle of steaming black vomit. "She ate from the tree, partaking of the forbidden fruit. That indulgence introduced into her body—and into her blood—that which came to be called original sin. A taint. An impurity that altered her for eternity, even before *I* had my way with her."

The angel tilted his head to one side, gazing at the puddle. "Are you saying that's—"

The demon bowed. "Original sin, purged from her blood."

Legion admired his female form. "My flesh existed at the beginning of the world, untainted by original sin, but my inhumanity would never grant me access," the shapeshifter said, admiring Eve's young form. "But as the first woman, untouched by the blight of sin . . ."

"Is it possible?" Jophiel whispered, staring at Legion, at Eve, then at the Garden Gate.

Eve wondered the same thing as she watched herself walk naked toward the Gate, wishing there was some way for her to be that woman again.

Legion glanced over one shoulder at them before placing both hands flat upon the polished wood. At first there was no reaction, and Eve breathed a sigh of relief that Abaddon's scheme had met with failure. But then the air grew suddenly still, and she felt a violent tremble pass through the earth where she lay. She could sense the fear of the vampires, as the victims of her earlier escape attempt leaped up from the ground, hands pressed to the slowly healing tears in their throats.

Eve could feel her own spine mending and the sensation of pins and needles in her limbs, but she remained perfectly still on the ground, watching with a perverse mixture of excitement and utter dread.

The Gate to Eden opened inward, a sound like the inhalation of some great breath filling the air. The lush jungle fauna waved in a breeze ripe with the scent of life in bloom, beckoning them to enter.

It was what she'd always desired more than anything. To return.

But not like this.

Legion was the first to enter, followed by Abaddon and Jophiel. It looked as though neither wanted the other to pass through first, and the two entered the Garden at the same time. Duergar went next, cautiously, axe in hand, flanked by his Drow soldiers.

Not like this.

Palu stood above Eve, his face stained with blood from his broken nose. He wanted to end her, she could see it in his eyes, but there was also hesitation. What if they still needed her for something? He wouldn't kill her unless Abaddon authorized it. Eve wanted to smile up at him in the worst way, but decided not to tip her hand. It wouldn't be long until she could move again, and she wanted it to be a surprise.

The leech reached down, taking a handful of her thick, raven hair and began to drag her toward the entrance, the other vampires cautiously following. The sharp pain from her healing neck intensified, the muscles in her legs and arms starting to twitch spasmodically. But the vampires didn't notice, they were too entranced by the sight before them, by the ultimate violation they were about to perpetrate.

Palu paused, and Eve knew exactly what was happening. The vampire was standing at the Gate, ancient survival mechanisms kicking in, attempting to discern whether or not it was safe for his kind to enter such a holy place and not be instantly destroyed.

The other leeches huddled together, watching their elder with fear-filled eyes. Waiting for him to make his move.

The thought of creatures as vile as these entering Eden filled Eve with a rage she could barely contain. She wanted to kill them all, not only for what they had done to her, but to protect the Garden from the taint of their evil—an evil that she had been responsible for.

She didn't want to despoil this wonderful place again.

Slowly, cautiously, Palu began to walk again, passing through the open Gate. He paused just inside, waiting to see if he would die, then continued into the Garden itself. He let Eve drop to the ground, and she listened as he offered words of encouragement to his brethren—ordering them to enter with no fear.

A ripple of power shot through her, a kind of electricity that came up through the moist earth, coursing through the grass under her back and into her flesh—pulsing through her body. It was as if a black curtain that had enshrouded her thoughts had been whipped away—like the trick of some vaudeville magician.

She remembered.

Eve remembered her time here in the Garden. The exquisite details flowed across her brain, bringing tears to her eyes.

The Garden knew her, and welcomed her back. Eve wanted to pull her knees up, curling into a tight ball, reveling in the freshness of memories long since driven from her mind. But there was no time for that.

She surged up from the ground.

The vampires moved to restrain her, but they might as well have been moving in slow motion. Eve swatted their grasping hands aside, plunging her claws into their chests, tearing out their black, stunted hearts. There was just enough time for her to show them the stinking hunks of muscle before they erupted in an explosion of ash.

She spun to deal with the others, even as Palu started to scream.

"She's awake!" he bellowed.

Duergar and his Drow soldiers charged from the jungle, raising their blades and hammers.

Eve felt almost completely healed, but not well enough to take on an entire army. Instead, she turned and dived into the embrace of the thick jungle. As she ran, she could hear them behind her, calling out her direction to one another as she weaved through the dense foliage, the blissful vitality of being back in this place fueling her flight.

It wasn't long before she lost them, so deep into the primordial jungle that it appeared night had fallen. She found a cool, dark place beneath the large, overhanging leaves of verdant undergrowth. Entirely drained of strength, she crawled beneath the plants, curling into a tight ball, and was almost immediately asleep.

And dreaming.

SHE remembers Paradise, and how easily it can be lost.

The taste of bitter fruit is in her mouth.

She doesn't want to remember this part, preferring the bliss she felt before the serpent.

Before temptation.

But those recollections are chased away by the hissing of a reptile, and she sees it all as clear as day, climbing up into the tree at the serpent's urging, reaching for the fruit that dangles there. It would bring her closer to Him—to her God—the whispering serpent promised.

Afterward, scared and alone in her sin, she went in search of her mate, so that she would not have to bear the burden on her own. She acted as the temptress to ensnare him—her beautiful Adam—in her guilt.

She remembers the screams of angels as they were driven from Eden's sweet embrace. The howling winds, the swords of fire raised to chase them through the Gate to a place beyond the eternal forest—an inhospitable place that would be their punishment for disobeying His holy Word.

Eve struggles in the grip of the dream, not wanting to go on. She tries desperately to awaken, to pull herself from the raging river of memory, but the current is too strong, and she is carried helplessly along.

The land was harsh, dry, and barren. Many a night they went hungry, not knowing how to fend for themselves in such an uncaring place. But eventually they learned to work the land, and to sustain themselves on the paltry bounty that they received from their hard work.

They made a life for themselves beyond the Garden, tamed the land, raised children, but Eve never forgot her sin.

Never forgot what had been taken from her.

It was worse when she dreamed; the smells of the wonderful place would come to her and she was back there with Adam, her sin somehow forgotten.

Now Eve stirs fitfully in the hold of the past.

On a night when the dreams were more vivid than ever, a voice called to her from the wilderness. She'd heard it before, out there in the desert, a whisper very much like the hissing of a snake. Normally she had the strength to ignore it, moving closer to her sleeping husband, listening to the rhythmic sound of his breathing, and eventually drifting back to sleep.

But not this night.

The voice called to her, and she answered.

Eve left the safety of their hovel. The night was as black

*as pitch, the usual brightness of the stars in the nighttime sky
somehow neutralized.*

*She remembers now that she almost turned back, that
night, to curl up against her sleeping mate. But the voice
called to her again—her name drifting on the desert winds.*

"Eve."

*And she left her home, her husband, and her family, going
out into the desert to find the one who called her name.*

*There was something strangely seductive in that voice that
hinted of things past. For the briefest of moments, as she
pulled the veil of her robes up over her face against the fierceness of the desert winds, the smells of the Garden came back
to her, almost as if it were somehow close by.*

*She couldn't recall how long she had walked across the
expanse of sand, her safety all but forgotten. She had to find
the one who called to her. Somehow he knew about the
Garden, and perhaps he could help her to get back there.*

*One moment there was only a sea of sand, as far as the
eye could see, then suddenly he was there.*

"Eve."

*He was wrapped in the thick robes of a desert nomad, a
hood and thick scarf over his face to protect him from the
fiercely blowing sand. She wondered if he was real, or a fig-
ment of her imagination, driven by her longing to return to
Paradise.*

*"I hear your dreams, child of the Garden," the figure said,
whirlwinds of dust whipping about the unmoving figure.
"They call to me across the sand, summoning me to your
side.*

"You yearn for Paradise."

*She caught a glimpse of red from within the shadows of
the stranger's hood.*

"You hunger to return to what has been taken from you."

*Again she smelled it—thick and fragrant riding upon the
winds—the blossoming flowers, the ripening fruit, the moist,
damp earth. Eden was somehow close by, and she moved toward it.*

Closer to the stranger.

*"How bitter you must feel," he said, the words drifting
from within the deep black of his hood. "To have something*

so wonderful snatched away—to be punished for wanting to be closer to Him."

His words were true. All she had ever wanted was to be closer—for her and Adam to be closer—to the Creator.

"He drove you from the bosom of Paradise because you loved Him too much."

She felt her bitterness ignite into a burning flame of anger. What sort of God was it that punished His children for their adoration?

Eve moved closer to the stranger, hands clenched into fists.

"He will never allow you to return," the stranger hissed, his hooded head moving from side to side. *"He is a stubborn Maker, a stranger to forgiveness. Perhaps it is time that He was taught a lesson. Perhaps it is time for Him to be punished for His cruelty toward us—toward you?"*

The scents of Paradise were suddenly gone, the Garden taken from her again, and Eve felt her anger toward her Father—toward the Almighty—flare like the desert sun.

"Yes," she agreed. For taking away her beautiful Garden, she wanted to make Him pay. *"He needs to be punished."*

The stranger began to laugh, a horrible sound, devoid of joy, as he reached out and pulled her to him with clawed hands the color of dried blood. Eve looked into the darkness of the stranger's hood and saw that he wasn't a man at all who had drawn her out into the night, across the merciless desert.

Merciless.

EVE awoke in the cool darkness, a scream upon her lips.

She could still feel Abaddon's touch, and her body remembered all too well the degradations heaped upon her then fragile, and still-human, form. Now, as she emerged from the shadows of Eden's undergrowth, she felt unclean—unworthy to set foot once again in Paradise. For all of the eons she longed to return, it simply felt wrong to her. Her thoughts were abruptly filled with images of water—a river to wash away the filth. The Garden was reading her, feeling her emotion, and she darted from her place of concealment, knowing exactly where the water could be found.

As she traversed the Garden, Eve became aware of the animals scrambling and skittering through the brush and in the branches above, many curiously peering from their hiding places. Allowing herself to breathe, she inhaled the humid scent of the nearby river and immediately began to remove her soiled clothes. Her bloodstained jacket and blouse were first, and she let them lie where they fell. She burst through a thick wall of huge fronds and found herself at the edge of the river, at a place where rocks had created an eddying pool where the current languished. Desperately she undid her jeans, kicking off her boots and shucking her pants like a serpent sloughing off its skin.

Eve sprang from shore, her naked body plunging into the cool embrace of the pool. She found a soothing calm beneath the water, gradually sinking toward the bottom. Beneath the river, she lay in silt and mud, her mind filled with memories of the past. Not too long ago Eve had bemoaned the fact that so much of her early life was lost to her, but now, as her memories returned, she at last understood that remembering was far more painful than forgetting.

Knees tucked beneath her chin on the muddy bottom, Eve let the past wash over her. It wasn't long before the life within the river scuttled and swam closer to examine her. Some of them nipped at her, but they could do her no real damage. She imagined their eager mouths eating away her sins, consuming the residue left behind by Abaddon's filthy touch. Perhaps once her transgressions were eaten away, she would feel at ease in Eden and again experience the grace of God.

A dim, muffled sound reached her there at the bottom of that eddying pool. Eve flinched, scaring away the fish that had been investigating her. She heard the high-pitched squeal again, knifing through the tranquility beneath the river.

She turned her eyes to the surface. Planting her bare feet, she sprang off from the river bottom, her naked body cutting through the water. As she broke the surface, the cry of terror filled the air again. Eyes just above the waterline, she searched for the source of the bloodcurdling cry.

On the other side of the river, struggling at the bank, Eve watched in horror as a large, gray-skinned animal—some sort of ancient pachyderm—was attacked by a horde of vampires.

"Fuckers," she swore under the water.

The vampires swarmed upon the flailing animal, their teeth and claws ripping away bloody chunks of its flesh. The smell of its blood filled the air, and she felt an awful hunger stir.

The animal tried to defend itself, slamming its body against the nearby trees. But the leeches clung fast, drinking away its precious life-stuff, eventually weakening the beast's struggles.

Eve wanted to look away as the animal's knees began to buckle. It flopped upon its side, crushing three of the bloodsuckers as it fell, but it did not kill them. Disgusted, she watched as they freed themselves, slithering up onto the beast, dragging broken and pulverized limbs behind themselves to feed with their brothers and sisters on its dying form.

Her hunger at its peak, she could no longer hold back. She swam silently toward the opposite bank of the river. Eyes riveted to the awful sight, she felt revulsion at the grotesque tableau, and at the very thought of creatures such as these—creatures like herself—existing within the Garden.

Eve emerged from the river and stood naked, staring in fury at the vampires as they drained the last bit of life from the once-regal beast.

She'd seen enough.

She cleared her throat, and the vampires snapped around to hiss at her, their hungry mouths stained crimson. Eve charged, not giving them a chance to react, scaling the body of the fallen pachyderm, slashing with deadly efficiency, her every strike doing the most damage possible.

The vampires barely had any opportunity to fight back. Bodies bloated with the blood of the kill slowing their reactions, they died without even the time to scream, and the air was filled with their drifting, ashen remains. Eve perched upon the elephant's haunches, eyes scanning the area for further prey.

Satisfied that she had slain them all, she leaped to the ground. She placed a hand upon the side of the great animal. Its flesh was still warm, and the knot of hunger in her belly grown more painful and gnawing.

It would be a sin to allow its blood to spoil, she told herself, bringing her mouth to a soft spot behind one of the animal's large ears. Her fangs pierced its leathery hide, and she sucked upon the wound, gouts of its still-warm blood filling her mouth and pouring down her throat.

At last sated, Eve pulled away from the wound in the dead elephant's neck, stepping back from its massive corpse. The blood of the animal had done her well, filling her body with vitality and giving her new clarity.

She returned to the river, wading back into its embrace, washing away the blood that spattered her naked body and face. Still naked—the way she had been before temptation, before shame—she stood on the riverbank and tipped her head back to the gentle breeze. As usual, the smell of the place was wonderful, rich with the smell of life in full bloom, but there was another aroma present now. It was a scent completely out of place here, and one that she was going to do everything in her power to eliminate.

There was evil in the Garden. Eve wondered why the Creator had not yet intervened, smiting those that had invaded Eden. She darted into the thickness of the Garden, moving toward the offending scent. *Free will,* she thought. *God's bear trap.* He would be waiting to see how this would all turn out before getting His hands dirty. When events had run their course, He would get involved.

And *He* would judge them all.

11

DANNY sat in the darkened living room of Conan Doyle's brownstone. He'd brushed crumbs off the sofa, remnants of Squire's last marathon of old *Dawson's Creek* DVDs. The hobgoblin liked junk TV almost as much as he liked junk food. On the floor, Shuck watched Danny's every move. When the demon boy pulled one sneakered foot up underneath him, the shadow beast looked up and shot him an inquisitive look.

"I'm just getting comfortable," Danny snarled.

A low rumbling emanated from somewhere inside Shuck, like a powerful engine turning over.

"Why did Squire have to leave you here anyway?" Danny asked under his breath. "You hate me . . . lot of good you'll do me if we're attacked again. Probably help whoever it is take me down."

Shuck lowered his strangely shaped face down between two massive paws, his deep dark eyes never leaving Danny.

"Can't you just look over there?" Danny yelled, getting up from the couch and plopping himself down again in another position. "Fucking Squire."

The goblin had returned with Shuck over an hour before, emerging from a hall closet covered in what looked like some kind of oil, but Danny learned was actually pure shadow from the outskirts of the Shadowpaths.

Fucking freaky.

The goblin had been all business as he stalked from the closet, wiping away the shadow stuff that clung to his body, and Danny had seen something in his friend that he'd never noticed before. Even his mother had noticed.

Squire had seemed nervous—jumpy, even—as he'd told them that Eve had been taken. All the while he'd kept looking back to the closet, to the shadows, as if he half expected something to be following him.

He'd told Danny that Conan Doyle wanted him to stay at the house, protecting it, just in case. Shuck would be left there with him, the meanest guard dog in history. It bugged the shit out of Danny that Conan Doyle had benched him, and that he and the mutt were supposed to hold the fort. But when Squire advised his mother to leave right away—that for her own safety, she ought to be anywhere else—that had really pissed Danny off. It wasn't as if she was going to protect him or anything, but it was cool to have somebody around to talk to. The goblin had smiled and said that was why he was leaving Shuck behind.

Squire hadn't given Julia a chance to argue, and Danny hadn't made much of a fuss. If the Menagerie were under attack, the truth was that she would be safer at her new Brighton apartment. As much as he'd miss the company, she'd already been hurt, and deep down, he didn't want to take the chance of something even worse happening to her. He couldn't risk losing the one person in the world who helped him stay human.

Once she had left, Squire had gone to work fixing the front door so it could be closed again and checking and double-checking some of the magical bullshit that was supposed to keep the bad guys from being able to get into the house.

Fat lot of good that *seemed to do.*

Now, Danny watched an old war movie on Retroplex, mind unable to focus. Shuck got up with a grunt and ambled over to the corner, where the open door cast a patch of shadow. The beast sniffed at the darkness and whined.

"What, do you miss your friend?" Danny asked. "Why don't you go and find him. I won't mind. Go on, go find Squire. I'll be right here, watching the house, like the useless piece of crap they think I am."

Squire had finished fortifying the house, then disappeared

down the cellar for a bit, finally returning with a golf bag filled with weaponry. "Just in case," he'd grumbled, switching off the light and closing the door behind him.

Now, here Danny sat, bored out of his mind, being baby-sat by something that might've been a dog in some serial killer's worst nightmare.

Shuck whined again, returning to his spot and dropping his bulk to the floor with a sigh.

"Fine, be that way. Stay here and be miserable with me."

He leaned his head back upon the couch, thinking about how fucked up his life had become, wondering if it would ever be normal again. It was like looking down a really long tunnel, that tiny dot of light way in the distance, the times before the Menagerie. Danny closed his eyes. He knew it would never be normal, but wondered if life would ever get back to that place where Mr. Doyle and the others could trust him. Graves had said it was just a matter of time. But Danny wasn't so sure.

His father had awakened something in him, something completely unpredictable, and no matter how hard he tried to ignore it, he could sense that it was always there, waiting for its opportunity. Waiting for him to screw up again. And the light of normalcy at the end of the tunnel grew that much dimmer.

Shuck started to growl, and Danny lifted his head to see that the shadow beast was looking toward the doorway out into the hallway.

He spun around, half-expecting to see somebody standing there. "What is it, boy?"

Climbing to all fours, Shuck stalked toward the door, and Danny followed. His mind raced. *What now? Has the evil Clay returned to finish off whatever the hell he'd been here for? Or maybe it's just the fucking Jehovah's Witnesses.*

Shuck slunk around the doorway into the corridor with Danny right behind him. The animal padded down the hallway toward the front door, stopping partway, and again started to growl.

Danny stopped, listening to the sounds of the brownstone. He didn't hear anything out of the ordinary, but there was a smell.

A scent that he'd come to associate with powerful magic.

The recently repaired door at the end of the hall suddenly opened without a sound, slowly swinging in to admit a large figure that stood upon the doorstep.

"Holy shit," Danny said, not quite sure what he should be doing.

The acrid, magic stink became stronger as the man entered the house.

With a throaty roar, Shuck propelled himself at the intruder. Danny gasped, certain that the bloodshed to follow with be completely heinous. But the man simply held out his hand, bringing the beast to a sliding stop before him. Within seconds, he was petting Shuck's square head, the shadow beast leaning into the stranger, hungry for affection.

"That's just so messed up," Danny muttered, startling himself as he realized that he'd spoken the words aloud.

The man was wearing a long, gray raincoat, unbuttoned to reveal a dark, three-piece suit that screamed expensive. Still petting the shadow beast, he removed a stylish fedora from his head with the other hand, and Danny recognized him as the only person in the world who could have just walked right past the magical defenses into the brownstone.

"Conan Doyle, changeling," Lorenzo Sanguedolce commanded. "Bring him to me. I need to see him at once."

Sweetblood the Mage, they called him. The guy was a dick, but according to Mr. Doyle, he was the most powerful sorcerer in the world. Danny didn't know what to do. His thoughts raced as he stared at the magician at the end of the hall.

"Are you simple, boy?" the archmage asked, disdain dripping from his words. There was a hint of an accent in the man's voice. Danny hated accents. "Announce to Conan Doyle that I am here and waiting. There isn't much time."

Danny was infuriated by the magician's tone and was sorely tempted to tell him to go fuck himself. But he didn't think that would be too smart and held his anger in check. Dr. Graves would be so proud.

"He's not here," he managed instead.

Sweetblood stopped petting Shuck and came down the hall toward Danny.

"What do you mean he isn't here?"

Danny smirked. "Are *you* simple? He isn't here."

Sanguedolce stopped short. Danny was startled by how tall he was up close, but he didn't back down. Staring defiantly at the mage, Danny noticed that though he was well-groomed and expensively dressed, the man himself looked exhausted—worn around the edges. His skin was pale and there were dark circles beneath his eyes.

"Insolent pup," Sweetblood snarled, the air around him crackling with dark magic. "But I suppose that is to be expected if you are to travel the path to your destiny."

The words were like a bucket of cold water dumped over his head. "What are you talking about?"

Sanguedolce waved the question away, leaning back against the wall with a sigh. He closed his eyes.

"Do you know something about my future?" Danny asked, feeling his heart begin to race.

The archmage opened his eyes slowly. "The future is ever uncertain. You have much maturing to do, yet, boy. You will be there for the final battle, but your role in the grand scheme remains to be seen."

Danny grabbed him by the arm. "I need to know—"

A powerful jolt of energy coursed through his body, knocking him back. Danny yelped, striking the opposite wall, his entire body painfully tingling as Shuck trotted over to investigate.

"Where is he?" Sanguedolce asked, eyes narrowed. "Our time grows short."

In the sorcerer's voice there was a hint of something that could have been mistaken for desperation. The realization distracted Danny from questions of his future. Sanguedolce's unexpected visit signified something big.

Demogorgon big.

"Somebody's taken Eve," Danny blurted out.

"The temptress?" Sweetblood asked, tilting his head to one side with curiosity.

Danny couldn't hold back, compelled somehow to spill the beans. "Yeah, she was taken by some demon connected to her past . . . and there's an angel, too."

Sanguedolce pushed himself away from the wall, motioning for Danny to continue.

"Mr. Doyle figured out where she was being taken, and he and the others have gone to rescue her."

"And did he share their destination with you?"

The crackling aura had returned around Sanguedolce. It seemed stronger, what little remained of the hair on the back of Danny's neck standing on end.

Danny felt sort of stupid saying it. The place had been just as real to him as Never Never Land until a few hours ago.

"Eden," he replied, averting his eyes. "He said the demon was taking her to the Garden of Eden."

A dreadful silence fell upon the house. Danny looked up to see that Sanguedolce was rubbing his chin, a hint of a smile playing upon his lips.

"Of course," he said, replacing his hat upon his head.

Danny could have sworn that the mage seemed more alive than he had mere moments ago, filled with a sudden energy.

Confident.

Without another word, he strode down the hallway. The door had closed behind him after he had entered, but now swung open at his approach.

"I'll tell Conan Doyle you were looking for him," Danny called after him.

"Oh, yes. Please do," Sweetblood replied.

The door slammed shut behind him.

ALL she had to do was wait for them to get hungry.

A small fraction of the vampires recruited by Abaddon, either unwelcome or uninterested in the activities of the others, had set up a camp of their own. Eve stayed hidden within the verdant Garden and watched as several strayed from their group in search of food. They seemed hungrier here, needing to feed more, and she wondered if it had anything to do with the fact that they didn't need to hide from the sunlight.

For, while there was light, there was no sun in the sky above Eden.

She gazed up through the canopy of thick leaves and fronds at the sunless sky, and wondered for the first time where the light that shone down upon the Garden originated. When Eve had lived here, she had never thought about such things, but now it was different. If she ever had the opportunity for a sit-down with the big guy upstairs, it would be one of the first things she asked Him.

What's up with the light in Eden? Where does it come from?

She was about to go out after the five or six that had wandered away from the others when she heard it.

Eve flinched, suppressing a gasp as she felt blood begin to flow from her nose, down her face. Her head filled with the most horrible sounds, a message of some kind broadcast directly into her brain.

An invitation to come to Eden.

She heard it in the most ancient of the vampire dialects, a language spoken only by the oldest of the leeches. Gazing from her hiding place, she saw that the vampires at the encampment were reacting as she did, their noses streaming red as they nervously looked around.

Wiping the blood from beneath her nose, she slipped from her hiding place, leaving the vampire encampment, going off in search of the source of the message.

It wasn't long before she found the clearing where the others had set up their base of operations. The ground had been charred black, the rich greens and colors of the Garden burned away. Drow warriors had set up a perimeter around the encampment. Tents were being erected by vampires all around the edges of the sprawling camp. Other tents had been pitched closer to the center, made from some sort of thin, richly veined animal skin. Just beyond those she observed the pulse of an unearthly light.

Eve would have loved to stay and play with the Drow soldiers a bit, but she found that she was getting hungry again. Still, she had a suspicion as to the source of the message being broadcast into her skull that needed to be confirmed.

The message continued to blare, the invitation repeated over and over. It took all of the concentration she could muster not to curl herself into a tight little ball until it was finished. Crawling through the thick underbrush, she moved around the outskirts of the camp for a better view of the source of the strange, pulsing lights.

Eve peered through the tall grass, her suspicions verified. In a private area, behind the skin tents, the angel Jophiel hovered in the air, his wings slowly beating with powerful strokes to keep himself aloft. He held a sword of fire in his hand, pointed toward Heaven.

A messenger of God, Jophiel was using his angelic voice to deliver a message that was the ultimate blasphemy. The sword of the angel was like an antenna, broadcasting the invitation from Eden out into the ether.

But who are they attempting to communicate with?

Abaddon stood beneath the hovering angel, gazing upward with eyes that glinted with excitement. Duergar had dropped to his knees, his large, calloused hands covering his ears, but that was little protection from a message delivered directly into one's brain. Legion stood off to the side, eyes closed, swaying in the gentle breezes of Eden. It was as if he were listening to the chords of the most beautiful symphony ever played.

A shudder of revulsion rippled through the earth upon which Eve knelt, Eden practically begging her to evict these cancerous beings from its heart. She fought to restrain herself, knowing that it would be suicide to attack them now. No, she would wait for a more opportune time, when there was a better chance for doing them harm. For now, she would watch, and learn.

The message built to a painful crescendo, and she bit through her lower lip to keep from blacking out, the warm taste of her own blood flooding her mouth. Then, just as quickly as it had started, the communication was over. Jophiel drifted down to stand before the demon Abaddon. The mother of all vampires could have heard a butterfly's wings from that distance, so listening to their conversation posed no challenge.

"It is done," the angel said. He appeared wan, tired, as he wished the flaming sword away in a flash of brilliance. "The solicitation has been sent."

Legion opened his dark eyes and applauded. "Bravo," he cried, an unnerving smile forming on his craggy face.

Duergar rose to his full height, dabbing at his ears with hands dirty and callused. "It surprised me to hear you speak in the voice of the Drow," the half-blood said, observing the blood that had leaked from his ears onto his fingers. "I wouldn't have believed that one of your nature would sully yourself with such a guttural tongue."

Jophiel gazed at Duergar with complete disdain. "It is a gift of my kind," the angel stated haughtily. "Our message is heard in the most familiar tongue of the species listening."

The angel studied Duergar as the warrior dug a finger into one of his ears, digging furiously.

"Even something as lowly as the Drow," the angel added.

Hatred flared in Duergar's eyes at the insult, and he started for the angel.

"There will be none of that," Abaddon said, placing a hand between them. "It is a time for rejoicing. Soon our numbers will swell, an army the likes of which has never been seen coming together under my command."

Duergar fixed him in a suspicious stare. "*Your* command, demon?"

"A mere slip of the tongue," Abaddon apologized. "*Our* command, of course."

Duergar grumbled, and Legion began to laugh. It was an insane sound, one that seemed to make even Duergar uncomfortable.

"Why do you laugh, shifter?" the monstrous half-breed asked.

The shape changer looked around. "Can't you feel it?"

The ground began to tremble, then to writhe as if in pain.

"The first to answer our invitation have arrived."

From her hiding place, Eve watched in horror as the air around them began to shimmer, to bend and stretch. Large rips formed in the very fabric of Eden as passages from other, far more horrible places were opened.

Eve wanted to scream, but knew that she would be immediately set upon. All she could do was watch, as demons and other abominations spilled from the jagged holes like diseased internal organs freed from the bellies of monsters.

The creatures chattered and squealed as they touched the blessed soil, fouling it immediately with their mere presence.

The earth beneath her recoiled in agony.

Eve sank her fingers down into the cold, trembling earth, holding on to keep from being thrown from her hiding place. She felt the screams of the earth beneath her—the plants and flowers, every blade of grass—as it was infected by these creatures' foul presence.

The Garden of Eden was dying.

She wasn't sure if she'd ever experienced anything quite so painful—quite so sad. The earth ceased its spasms, and she removed her fingers from within its cold, dirty skin. Eve stared at her filthy hands, stained with the blood of the soil, watching as they changed to deadly talons. She was nearly blind with her rage, the emotions of a dying and frightened Eden reverberating through her form.

Something had to be done—somebody had to be punished.

She looked out to see that the monsters were still arriving, and her thoughts reeled from the insanity of it all.

What are they doing? Why have these abominations been called here?

Her eyes fell upon Jophiel. Eve could see by the look on his perfect, heavenly features that he was as repulsed by the new arrivals as she was. The angel stepped away from the accumulating number that Abaddon was welcoming with open arms. Jophiel spread his wings, soaring up into the air, flying away.

Eve again stared at the encampment, furious that there was nothing she could do. But she then turned her nose to the sky, smelling the divine scent of the angel, drifting on the Garden winds.

She followed.

Perhaps there *was* something she could do after all.

I T was as if the Garden were helping her.

Just as she believed she had lost the angel's scent, a sudden breeze would kick up, the smell of the messenger's trail there for her to follow.

Eve moved through the thick forest like a shark through water, stalking her prey. She climbed up and over fallen trees larger than the greatest redwood, and waded across bubbling lagoons frothing with aquatic life. The stink of the angel that had evicted her from Paradise and that had plagued her for the subsequent years, fueled her pursuit. As did the plaintive, psychic cries of the Garden in agony.

As the angel's stink grew heavier, a terrible foreboding struck her. Eve glanced about, searching for signs of danger, only to realize there was no imminent peril. Instead, it was the part of the Garden she had just entered that filled her with such dread.

She had been here before.

As she pushed aside a wall of hanging vines, her eyes confirmed that suspicion. Yes, she had been here before—on the day she had fallen from grace.

The Tree of Knowledge stood as it had those many millennia ago. Now, though, its base was ringed with a thick, high wall of dark bramble, which prevented access to the tree and its ripe, dangling fruit.

Jophiel stood before the tree. Tentatively, he reached into the growth, attempting to tear away the obstruction. The angel cried out, the air suddenly rich with the scent of his blood. Eve crouched at the edge of the clearing, watching as Jophiel pulled back. The angel gazed woefully at his blood-covered hands. The thorns of the bramble were razor-sharp, uncaring about who or what they bit.

"Do not deny me this," she heard the angel say, gazing up toward the heavens.

The smell of his blood made her stomach ache.

"Who are you talking to?" the temptress asked, coming into the clearing around the Tree. A stream ran past it, and it washed over her bare feet as she stepped into the water.

Jophiel turned, red-stained hands held out before him.

"You."

"Blood on your hands," she snarled, feeling her canines elongate within her mouth. "How fucking apropos."

The angel sneered. "I will not be judged by the likes of you," he spit, his wings nervously flapping as he wiped his hands on his shirt.

Eve shook her head disapprovingly. "What have you

done, Jophiel?" she asked, eyes boring into his. "What the hell have you done?"

He seemed to think about her question a moment, his perfect features slack and unemotional.

"Times such as these create the most unusual bedfellows," he said. He held out his hand, and a sword of crackling fire ignited in his grip.

"I believe He intends for us all to die," the angel said, the flame of his blade dancing in the darkness of his eyes. "I came here . . . to the Tree, thinking that perhaps it might hold the answers I seek."

"What are you talking about?"

"The Devourer is coming, and I don't think even Heaven can stop it."

Jophiel's movements were lightning; one moment he stood, back to the brambles, the next he was beside her, the burning sword slashing through the air.

Eve barely avoided the blade, feeling the heat pass dangerously close to the flesh of her neck as she dropped to the ground.

"It's self-preservation, Eve," he said, watching her with mad eyes. "Worlds will die, and I will do everything in my power to make sure that the same thing doesn't happen to me."

"Selfish prick," she hissed, knocking his feet out from beneath him with a sweep of her leg.

The angel went down on his back with a grunt. Eve dived on top of him, pinning his wrists to the ground. His wings flapped as he attempted to stand, kicking up bits of debris that stung her eyes and flesh, but she held fast, grinning as she sat astride him.

"You'd betray everything just to save your own ass," she said, bearing down on him with all her strength. "Now why doesn't that surprise me?"

He tried to use his sword, to lift his hand, but she had found power in her rage and believed that it partially came from Eden itself.

"Listen to you." Jophiel thrashed beneath her. "The temptress speaks to me of morality."

The angel began to laugh, a high-pitched braying that felt

like steel spikes being driven into her brain. He had laughed very much like this as she and Adam were chased from the only home they had ever known, out from within the bosom of His protection, out into the wasteland.

Looking down at the angel, helpless beneath her, there was nothing Eve wanted more than to rip the perfect flesh from his face, to reveal the monster beneath.

But he bucked again in a surge of anguish and broke free of her grip, hurling her off him.

Eve landed against the brambles encasing the Tree of Knowledge.

That fucking Tree, as she had learned to call it over the countless millennia. The thorns hungrily pierced her flesh and she could feel rivulets of warm blood running down her back as she fell to the ground. She looked up to see the fearsome shape of Jophiel standing above her, burning sword in hand, ready to pass judgment upon her.

Just like the old days.

"I think it's time that somebody put you out of your misery," the angel sneered, the flaming sword raised above his head.

She started to dodge, but Jophiel lashed out with a kick that caught her on the chin, and Eve fell.

"Did you know He actually believed that you could be saved?"

She heard the angel's voice through a sea of pain. She gazed up through the haze to see Jophiel looming over her like a vulture.

"It's true," the angel continued. "Even after Abaddon's seed infected you, turning you into this." He gestured toward her, wrinkling his nose. "He still believed in your redemption."

The words were like a white-hot brand searing her brain.

What the fuck is he saying . . . that God is still watching me?

Eve pushed herself to her feet.

"Guess we'll never know if He was right," Jophiel said, genuine amusement in his voice. "Personally I'd have smote you the moment you touched the fruit, but that's just me."

She heard the crackle of heavenly fire as the blade descended.

He still believed in your redemption.

What did it mean? If she died now, she'd never know.

Eve shifted just enough that the burning sword pierced her shoulder instead of her heart, cutting through flesh and bone with ease.

Had she evaded him completely, he wouldn't have been close enough. Taking that wound hurt like a son of a bitch, but it gave her just the edge—the moment—she was looking for.

"Smite this," she growled, slashing her talons into his groin, tearing through his clothing and the angelic flesh beneath.

She ripped him open from crotch to chest.

Jophiel stumbled back, taking his sword with him. Eve wasn't sure what hurt more, the blade going in or being pulled out. The messenger dropped to his knees, struggling to keep his viscera from spilling out onto the ground. But it wouldn't be long before Jophiel pulled himself together. Angels healed quickly. Divinity was the ultimate Plan B.

"You miserable bitch," he rasped, over and over again, slimy snakes of intestine slipping through his hands as he attempted to shove them all back inside.

Eve felt her legs begin to go.

"I would have made it quick," the angel said through gritted teeth. "But now I think I'll hurt you . . . very badly, then I'll give you to Abaddon."

He'd managed to get his guts back inside him, and the yawning gash was already starting to mend itself.

"Have you missed him, Eve?" Jophiel asked, venom dripping from his every word. "He talks about you all the time, about how proud he is of you, how you were his greatest achievement."

She wanted to go at him again, to rip him apart, but she was barely keeping it together. Eve dropped to her knees, the jarring impact shaking something loose. Blood and bile exploded in her mouth.

Jophiel was laughing again: that horrible fucking sound.

"I wonder if he'll just play with you for a while, have a little fun like the good old days, and eventually kill you. Or will he try to turn you again?"

The angel looked down at his torn clothing. The wounds had healed, leaving behind four angry, vertical scars where her claws had torn him open. And then he looked at her.

"I'd like to see that," Jophiel said. "I'd like to see how much you could take before the darkness claimed you again."

He started to rise, wings unfurling.

Eve knew this was it. She would kill herself rather than be given to Abaddon again, and she was looking around for something sharp, when she felt a jolt like an electric shock—the same feeling she'd had sporadically since coming to Eden. The Garden was alive, and it was telling her that it would not allow her to die.

Pushy bitch.

Thick vines erupted from the earth. Tentacles of vegetation wrapped about the angel's wrists, legs, and neck, pulling him back down to the ground. The harder he struggled, the more vines slithered up from the Garden's fertile soil, coiling around the thrashing angel, holding him tightly in their grip.

A gift for you, Eden whispered inside her head.

And Eve suddenly realized what was being offered to her. She was weak, probably even dying. If she were to survive, feeding was an absolute necessity, and even then, wounds so severe would take time to heal.

But to feed on the blood of an angel.

Eve dropped to her hands and knees. She crawled toward her ancient enemy, listening to him scream.

Jophiel knew what was coming, and she moved extra slowly to prolong his terror. She had fed on him before, and was looking forward to doing so again.

"Just like the good old days," she said, lying atop him, gazing down into his terror-filled eyes.

Then she could hold it back no more, the hunger inside her like a wild beast, eager to be released.

Eager to be fed.

She sought out the place where she had bitten him before, the scar tissue there the only ugliness marring his perfect flesh. It called to her like an old friend, as she buried her teeth in the soft skin of the angel's throat.

As she began to drink, Jophiel screamed for God to help him.

No one answered.

CONAN Doyle was fatigued, but he wouldn't let on to the others. He felt Ceridwen's gaze upon him and turned to give her a reassuring nod. The spell they had used to bring them to this limbo realm—even with the addition of Ceridwen's elemental magic—had exhausted him, but he did not have the luxury of rest.

The Menagerie stood in awe upon that strange middle ground between Heaven and Earth, before the Gate to Eden.

The place of humanity's birth.

Jelena sniffed the breeze, eyes closed as the scent of the place filled her nostrils. Clay stood beside the naked wolf woman. He wore his natural earthen form, his large, powerful hands clenched into fists, anticipating the struggle yet to come. Dr. Graves drifted in the air beside Squire, both of them staring at the formidable Garden Gate.

"It's not as impressive as I thought it would be," Squire said, idly scratching the side of his face.

The ghost of Dr. Grayes looked askance at the hobgoblin. "Not impressive?"

"Yeah, had a buddy back in the twenties, did a lot of work for the old-time Hollywood types, y'know, fences, walls, gates the whole shebang. He could put up something that would really blow your socks off."

Graves cocked an eyebrow. "Maybe you could put the Creator in touch with him. Your friend could help Him with future designs."

"Not a bad idea," Squire agreed, the sarcasm lost on him. "But Vito died of the ass cancer in '52." The goblin shook his head sadly. "Poor bastard. I think he might've owed me money."

Ceridwen approached the Garden Gate, her silken robes blowing in the gentle breeze. She looked at home here, among the green grass that carpeted the ground outside Paradise. As if she belonged.

"Approach with caution," Conan Doyle warned her.

She crouched in front of the Gate and laid a pale hand upon the ground, communing with the nature of this place.

"They were here," the Princess of Faerie said after a moment. "Evil has come to Eden."

"How many?" Conan Doyle asked.

Ceridwen ran her hands through the blades of grass. "Many feet," she said, head cocked to one side as she listened to the voice of the green. "A small army by the sounds."

Clay strode away from the group, moving toward the Gate. "If they were able to get inside, we shouldn't have any trouble."

He stopped just in front of the beautifully polished wood, studying its surface before raising his hands to place them on the door. Clay pushed, the muscles in his arms and back rippling with effort.

The Gate did not open, but it did push back.

Clay was hurled away from the obstruction, narrowly missing Ceridwen, who still knelt in the grass. The shapeshifter scrambled to his feet, a combination of rage and embarrassment in his dark eyes.

"Holy crap!" Squire shouted.

Conan Doyle saw Jelena cover her mouth, masking her amusement.

Clay strode back to the Gate as if to challenge it again. But he paused before them and cocked his head, studying its construction. "If I can't get inside, how did they?"

Dr. Graves looked at Conan Doyle. "There must be some sort of key. Something we're not aware of."

Squire trotted over to the gates. "No problems there, chief," he said. "Let me take a look." The goblin got very close to the door, searching for some clue.

"Could we not scale it?" the she-wolf asked.

"I'm afraid not," Conan Doyle replied. "Look carefully, you can see the shimmer of something powerful in the air. To avoid that, I imagine we must pass through the open Gate unimpeded. Also, I imagine that even if we did climb over it, we would find the other side little different from this spot. It is traveling through the Gate that gives entrance to Eden."

Squire turned away from the Gate. "Don't see shit," he said. "No runes, no keyholes. Nothing."

Conan Doyle nodded thoughtfully. None of this came as any surprise to him. It would not be something so simple as an ordinary key. And yet Abaddon and his allies had entered somehow. He had missed something important. As he wondered what that was, he glanced over at Ceridwen, who seemed to be conversing with the grass intently.

"Ceri," he said. "What is it?"

She looked up at him. "The blood of the first," she said. "The blades say the invaders spilled the blood of the first before the gate."

Jelena responded instinctively, dropping to all fours, nose pressed to the ground, her fur cloak falling like a curtain around her. She crawled along on hands and knees, sniffing the grass and the earth beneath.

"She's right," the she-wolf said. "There was blood spilled here recently." Jelena stopped suddenly, her muscles taut. "Here," she said. Her features had become more lupine, her teeth more pronounced, sharper.

They all approached the spot she had found. Graves kept shimmering, his translucent form becoming by turns more and less distinct. The ghost ignored their new discovery, still focused on the Gate.

Where Jelena crouched, the grass had withered to a sickly yellow. The ground looked damp, as if refusing to absorb what had been spilled there. Clay knelt beside her on the dying grass. He put his fingers into the dark, damp ground and brought them to his nose, breathing in the scent.

"Eve's blood," he said, glancing up at Conan Doyle.

"Aw, shit!" Squire grumbled. They looked over to see the hobgoblin standing on one foot, examining the other. Something black and foul smelling dripped from the sole of his boot.

"No pooper-scooper law here, evidently," he muttered.

The she-wolf approached the goblin, leaning down to sniff the foul substance. "This is not what you think, little gob. Not offal."

"Smells pretty fucking awful," Squire replied, his upper lip curling.

Jelena nodded, wrinkling her nose. "Yes. I mean it is not . . . droppings. Not shit. It stinks of corruption."

Blood and corruption, Conan Doyle thought, wishing that he'd brought a pipe with him. The answers were here; all he had to do was place them in their correct order.

"Clay," he said, and pointed to the blood. "If you would be so kind as to assume the shape of whoever it was that lost that."

The shape changer rubbed the blood between his fingers. His flesh began to ripple, becoming almost fluid. The sound of shifting bone and mass filled the air as he assumed the exquisitely naked form of Eve.

"Sweet," Squire said with a grotesque grin. "I could get used to these new uniforms."

The ghost of Dr. Graves studied the shapeshifter. "When she hears about this, we're all going to have some explaining to do."

Squire shrugged. "I'll happily take a beating in exchange for the view."

Conan Doyle studied the woman's lithe and muscular form. Eve was the mother of all vampires, but also the mother of humanity.

The blood of the first, Ceridwen had been told by the green. Conan Doyle looked back to the Gate, to Clay wearing the guise of Eve, then to Squire. The substance Squire had stepped in reeked of blood and corruption. It reeked of sin.

Discarded sin.

"Of course," Conan Doyle muttered, feeling the familiar, intoxicating twinge of revelation pass through him.

"What is it, Arthur?" Ceridwen asked, placing a hand on his shoulder.

"To pass through the Gate of Eden, one must be of the Garden," he started to explain. "Eve was part of this place before her fall, but in order to enter it would require her in the purest of states."

Squire scratched his large, gourd-shaped head. "I'm following you, boss, but I'm not getting how she could get them inside. Eve's blood hasn't been pure in a long, long time, and I doubt they had the time to give her a transfusion."

Conan Doyle smiled. "Yes, but if our adversaries had with them a shapeshifter, as we have started to believe, then it could have done the same as Clay here, becoming Eve by coming in contact with her blood, and purging that form of its corruption. Original sin."

He pointed at Squire's shoe, and the black, stinking substance on the ground.

"I don't know what's worse," Squire grumbled, rubbing his foot on the grass. "Tell ya the truth, I'd rather've stepped in shit."

Dr. Graves stared at Clay, who still wore Eve's form. "Can you feel it in her blood, the sin?"

Clay concentrated, bending over slightly as if in sudden pain. "Yes. It's like a cancer."

Conan Doyle nodded his appreciation to the ghost and turned to Clay. "Isolate, and expel it from your system. Purify her form, and we'll have our key."

The duplicated Eve dropped to her knees, clutching at her stomach as she bent over. A stream of putrid, stinking fluid was spewed up onto the grass, and she became wracked with dry heaves.

"Isn't that special," Squire chided.

Jelena moved away from the wretched black fluid, her bestial senses tormented by the stench of sin in its purest state.

"That should do it," Conan Doyle said, reaching down to help Clay rise. "Now if you would be so kind as to verify my suspicions."

He directed Clay toward the Gate. They all followed close behind Eve's naked form. "Casper's right. When she hears about this, she's gonna be pissed," Squire said with a chuckle, as he hefted the weapon-filled golf bag over one shoulder.

Clay raised his hands again and placed them upon the door. The wooden Gate swung inward to expose the beauty of Eden.

The Menagerie crossed the threshold and entered the Garden, the Gate shutting behind them with a ghostly silence. They stood in awe, gazing about at the primordial wilderness that sprawled around them.

Clay resumed his inhuman guise, shedding the form of Eve now that they had found their way inside.

"Nice place," Squire said.

The she-wolf was the first to sense it, her body stiffening beneath her fur cloak as she looked down to the ground beneath them.

"There's movement beneath the earth," she warned, lifting her feet and jumping back.

Before Conan Doyle could react Squire had taken a spear from within his bag and plunged it deep into the ground with a savage grunt. The hobgoblin gripped the shaft of the spear and pulled, withdrawing the head of a Drow soldier from beneath the rich, black soil, its eyes wide in the surprise of death, fat tongue lolling disgustingly from his large, open mouth.

"Drow," Squire spit as he wrinkled his nose in disgust. "I hate these guys."

Raised lines bulged up from the ground, then Drow warriors exploded up from the earth, carrying maces, axes, and clubs.

Conan Doyle cast a defensive ward about him and murmured an incantation, magic churning up around his fists. Ceridwen raised her elemental staff, icy wind and fire swirling around the sphere at its tip. Clay dropped into a combat stance, his earthen form radiating a formidable strength, and Jelena pulled her wolf skin tightly around her and fell to all fours, revealing her true form, that of the enormous, ravenous wolf.

Squire looked at Conan Doyle, clutching the hilt of another large sword.

"Got a plan?" the hobgoblin asked.

"Kill as many as you can," the mage said, lifting his hands and setting free a wave of destructive magic. His spell melted the bones of the nearest Drow.

"Works for me," Squire replied, charging toward an axe-wielding Drow, his sword raised.

The Menagerie swept into battle.

12

THE angel was dead.

Abaddon pulled his leathery wings tightly around his body, peering out into the dark tangles of vegetation, and knew the messenger of Heaven's fate. Eve had found him and seen to his end.

The demon tilted his horned head back, raising his nose to the air. The blood of an angel had a most distinctive aroma, and he could smell it now, dancing on the gentle exhalations of the Garden.

He couldn't say that he would miss Jophiel. Abaddon didn't have the capacity to care for anything other than himself. But he certainly had enjoyed watching the Lord's servant sink to ever-increasing depths of depravity.

What selfish beings He had created, and how easy it was to drag them down.

Abaddon detected motion to his left and turned to find Duergar slipping up beside him. The half-blood warrior had stealth that belied his size. His cooperation in this endeavor had been quite welcome. Here was a beast with voracious hungers and desires, and a penchant for cruelty that rivaled his own. Duergar had proven a valuable ally.

"Conan Doyle and his zoo have arrived," Duergar growled.

Abaddon nodded. This was to be expected. He turned to gaze at the most recent arrivals, the legions of demons and monstrosities from a hundred dimensions that had answered his invitation.

"The Menagerie?" a gigantic, maggotlike nether beast asked, having overhead. It was supported on the backs of smaller, pale-skinned creatures that cried and moaned, their skin eaten away by the acidic ooze that sweated from their master's pustulant flesh.

"Yes," Abaddon replied, watching anxious looks spread through the gathering of horrors.

"No need for concern," he reassured them.

A beautifully feathered bird soared down from a nearby tree, its shape starting to change and grow before it alighted upon the ground. Legion grew to his full, ominous height, a frightening smile upon his face.

"Is *he* with them?" the shapeshifter asked Duergar.

The Fey-Drow monster nodded.

"Excellent," Legion said, his black, marble eyes glinting excitedly as a ripple pulsed through his malleable flesh.

But Legion seemed the only one among them pleased at Conan Doyle's arrival. It seemed that his reputation spread far and wide throughout dimensions, though Abaddon suspected it was based more on his association with Sweetblood than the exploits of the Menagerie themselves. Unless he had underestimated them, which he quite doubted.

Still, that anxiety swept through the gathering like fire. Abaddon listened to the squeaks and burps of unearthly tongues as they nervously muttered among themselves.

He unfurled his wings, raising his arms to silence the otherworldly gathering. "Is that the stink of fear I smell?" the demon asked, wrinkling his nose as he bared his yellow fangs. "For if so, perhaps it would behoove you all to return to whence you came. There is no place in my new Kingdom for those who know fear."

The demon fixed them all in his unflinching gaze. "If we are to survive what is to come, all hesitation must be purged from our beings. Conan Doyle and his agents . . ."

Abaddon pointed out into the deepest part of the Garden, a jungle of wild growth, toward the Gate.

"They are the least of our concerns. The Devourer draws nearer."

A pack of Coinn Iotair, their thick black fur matted with old mud and blood that could have been there since the

Twilight Wars, forced their way from the back of the crowd to glare at him.

"And how will *you* deal with this threat, demon brother?" the pack leader asked, as the other doglike beasts nodded in agreement. "Will you send others to do the filthy work?"

Abaddon glared at the pack's leader, then at the others.

"I will do what is expected of me as the orchestrator of this gathering, and as a Lord of Hell," the demon said as he spread his arms and flapped his wings.

Ancient spells of devastation procured from many an unwilling source danced upon his lips. Black markings that seemed as deep as the ocean depths, and which screamed in the voices of the mages from whom he had stolen those magics, appeared upon his flesh. Abaddon made sure that the monstrous rabble saw each and every one—heard each of those despairing voices.

"I will make them cry out for mercy."

He spun on his cloven hooves and strode away from the gathering. He marched into the jungle with Legion and Duergar flanking him, off to combat the enemies that had followed them into Eden. There wasn't room in Paradise for all of them. In the air there still wafted the smell of an angel's blood.

Eve's scent carried on the breeze as well. *She could be a problem,* Abaddon thought. First they would deal with Conan Doyle and his followers. And then he would deal with the temptress.

Personally.

SOMETHING *is wrong with this picture.*

Squire charged at the first wave of Drow soldiers, hacking and slashing through them, but something wasn't right.

The bad guys aren't dying.

The hobgoblin spun around after killing—or at least he thought he had killed—a particularly fat Drow. The lumbering monster's armor barely covered his protruding gut, and the thing had called him something in the Drow language that translated to *fucker of shadows* just before Squire ran him through with his sword. Now the hobgoblin turned around to discover that all the Drows he had believed slain were getting up from where they had fallen, minus limbs and showing off some pretty major wounds.

The way they moved, the vacant look in their beady eyes said one thing: reanimation.

"Fucking zombie Drow," Squire spit, as he hacked and slashed. He couldn't really think of much worse.

Until the vampires began to emerge from the shadows of the jungle.

SO much evil in such a beautiful place, Ceridwen thought as she summoned twin spirals of wind that danced upon the palm of each delicate hand.

The sorceress had felt awareness from Eden, as though the Garden itself was alive, as though it had a soul. She felt fear.

Now she unleashed the swirling winds, letting them leap from her palms to the ground, where they began to grow. In their bloodlust, the dull-witted Drow attempted to attack her magic, stabbing the twin maelstroms with their axes and clubs, and were sucked into the growing vortexes. The breath was pulled from their lungs, and their bodies were savagely discarded by the whirlwinds, shattered on the ground or against the trunks of trees.

The earth behind her began to roil, and Duergar exploded from the ground as if vomited up by the holy Garden. The princess barely had time to react, spinning around even as she felt a psychic cry of warning that seemed to come from Eden itself.

If only she had been quicker.

THE vampires' flesh tasted of rot.

Jelena attacked with blinding speed, never giving them the opportunity to attack her en masse. The she-wolf in her natural state was an efficient killing machine, but the killing of the undead was another matter.

No matter how savagely she struck them, or tore the flesh from their bones, they were still alive, and murderous. She pushed herself, constantly in motion, swifter than she had ever been before. Jelena darted between and behind them, lunging for attack, then quickly moving on to the next. She tried to cripple as many as possible, ripping out the delicate tendons at the back of their legs, hobbling them so that they fell to the ground.

And though the she-wolf fought valiantly, never tiring as she brought down one vampire after another, as well as the occasional Drow that had come to the leeches' aid, she could not help but feel afraid of what the future held.

The Devourer was coming; no matter how hard they fought, how many of their enemies were vanquished, it still did not alter that fact.

The Devourer is coming.

A vampire bared its fangs with a ferocious hiss, springing at her. They wrestled upon the ground, and she buried her muzzle into the soft flesh of the vampire's abdomen. He shrieked in surprise and agony as she sank her fangs in, tearing away chunks of cold, undead flesh.

Her muzzle stained crimson, the she-wolf climbed to her feet, licking putrid blood from her face. The vampires were no longer attacking, and she wondered what mischief they could be perpetrating now.

Then she felt it, a warm tingling sensation in her belly, traveling like fire into her veins. She crumpled to the ground, all feeling in her extremities quickly draining away.

The sounds of fighting were all around her as the vampires slowly converged. The one whose stomach she had tasted had joined his brothers and sisters. He was smiling down on her, his teeth razor-sharp, glistening wetly.

In his hand he held a glass vial, the contents of which reeked very much like the contents of the vampire's belly.

It stank of poison.

DR. Graves's ectoplasmic pistols barked repeatedly, phantom bullets finding their targets as he drifted above the battlefield.

He was trying to help in any way that he could, but it all seemed so overwhelming. Vampires, Drow, and other unearthly things peered from the thick jungle, watching eagerly, as if waiting for their moment.

Waiting for the Menagerie to fall.

A fresh group of Drow exploded from the primeval forest, moving across Eden to aid their fellow warriors. Graves directed himself downward, a scream of fury upon his lips. The ghost aimed his guns, firing at the startled Drow soldiers. Their bodies twitched and danced as the ectoplasmic bullets hit them, but they did not die.

Something was protecting them.

The Drow chattered at one another in their guttural tongue, one of them producing what appeared to be some kind of net.

An unnerving sensation rippled through his spectral form, some kind of cautionary sense warning him of danger. Alarmed, the ghost of Dr. Graves started to make a swift retreat so that he could assess any dangers, but his instinct came too late. The Drow moved with astonishing speed, tossing the strangely woven net toward him.

The specter felt the effects of the net the moment it fell on him. Impossible as it seemed, he had been captured. The Drow dragged him to the ground by the weighted ends of the unusual snare.

Lying beneath the mesh he felt his body grow solid, and a weakness that rendered his limbs useless. Pathetically he struggled, trying to free himself, but to no avail.

The Drow laughed, amused by the plight of the helpless ghost.

THE battle raged.

One spell after another left Conan Doyle's lips, powerful blasts of magical fury that caused the attacking Drow and vampires to ignite into flames.

But it didn't stop them.

Powerful magic was at work here, some spell that locked the life force of these pathetic creatures in place, allowing them to attack, even after their bodies had been damaged beyond repair.

Powerful magic indeed.

Attacking as well as defending, he chanced a quick glance around the battlefield that Eden had become, wanting to check on the progress of the others. It was much the same with them. No matter how many were struck down by superior strength, weapons, or powerful elemental magics, their attackers continued to come at them.

He wanted to offer words of encouragement, to urge them to carry on with their struggle, but it all seemed pointless. Of course they would continue to fight—it was what they did.

It all seems so much harder of late, the mage thought, calling forth winds so fierce that they tore boulders up from the ground, crushing Eden's invaders beneath their weight. The closer the Demogorgon drew, the greater the evil, and the mightier the struggle.

The ground trembled beneath him. Magic crackled at his fingertips as he spun toward the disturbance, and he felt his heart cease to beat.

The half-breed, Duergar, held Ceridwen aloft by her throat, her feet dangling above the ground.

The monster will die for this.

About to unleash a spell that would have stripped the meat from Duergar's bones, Conan Doyle was struck from behind by a hex of such dark power that it hammered him forward and shattered his concentration. His own magic dispelled harmlessly into the soil.

Jacket smoldering, he dropped to the ground, rolling onto his back to extinguish the searing flames.

Abaddon towered above him, red, leathery flesh animated with the sigils of magic that Conan Doyle knew all too well. Many of those sigils had once belonged to friends and allies whose lives and magic had been stolen by the demon.

"Monster," Conan Doyle growled. The demon would be ready for brute force or blunt sorcery, so he summoned a spell that would have caused a brood of spiders to appear in the meat of Abaddon's brain.

The magic erupted from his hands and dark swirls scoured the air between them, like static on the face of the world. That cloud of buzzing energy struck Abaddon, but the demon was merely staggered.

Conan Doyle stared. The Hell-Lord's infernal power had deflected the spell easily.

"Is that the best you can do?" Abaddon asked.

With a savage grin, the demon hooked his fingers into talons and seemed to tear magic from the air itself. The hex hurtled downward and Conan Doyle hastily erected a defensive ward. The demon's power shredded his defenses, crushing Conan Doyle to the ground.

A suffocating blanket of darkness fell over him as he fought to remain conscious, the thought of Ceridwen in the clutches of a monster his last pitiful thought before it all went to black.

Ceri.

I've failed you.

NO matter how many Clay crushed, maimed, or tore limb from limb, vampire and Drow alike, they kept coming at him. The Drow horde stabbed at him with spears and swords, vampires sinking their hungry fangs uselessly into his hard, cracked flesh.

Clay roared, his thundering voice echoing about Paradise.

The more he tried to kill, the more enraged he became. The bodies were piling up at his feet, bloody and broken, but still they tried to fight him. He wanted to know where Eve was, but the creatures he fought remained silent, speaking only in the language of violence.

"Where is she?" he bellowed, snatching up a Drow soldier by the top of his head. The huge creature squirmed in his grasp, ugly face twisting in pain.

"Tell me!"

But the Drow remained silent, squealing and grunting as he tried to free himself. Clay exerted just a bit more pressure and felt the soldier's skull give way like an eggshell. He tossed the nearly headless body aside, ready to try again . . . when he saw her.

Eve emerged breathlessly from the jungle, coming to a sudden stop when she spotted him.

Clay called her name. With a burst of energy, he ripped his

way through the remaining attackers to get to her. "Are you all right?"

She stood staring at him, a strange smile dancing at the edges of her perfect mouth.

"One by one they fall," she said, gazing out at the carnage unfolding in Eden.

Clay looked away from her, observing his teammates' fate. Squire was lost beneath a squirming mass of attackers, Graves had somehow been trapped within a net, and the she-wolf lay still upon the ground. Even Ceridwen and Conan Doyle seemed nearly beaten. The Fey princess dangled in the clutches of a giant, warrior beast. Conan Doyle lay still upon the ground as the demon Abaddon loomed above him.

"Time to pull their asses from the fire," Clay said, turning toward Eve.

But Eve had vanished and been replaced by another—a creature who seemed Clay's own mirror image. The doppelgänger had the same earthen flesh, the same build, the same face. Entirely the same.

Except for the eyes. Something was missing in the eyes. There was coldness there, a black void that drew him in.

"Who?" Clay started to ask.

The other struck with the speed of a cobra, his fist connecting with Clay's forehead, fingers slipping into his skull. Clay could not see the point of impact, but he felt it. The enemy's touch had not shattered his earthen flesh, but melded with it—merged.

"I am Legion," the other said, flexing the fingers of his hand inside Clay's skull. "And I'm very glad to meet you, brother."

And everything went black.

Black as his brother's bottomless gaze.

CLAY remembered.

Like layers of sediment churned up from the bottom of a lake, he remembered each stratum of his long existence. The most recent were the easiest to recall, his years fighting alongside Conan Doyle and his Menagerie, fighting for the good of the world. With the mage he had found a reason to exist, his talents given purpose.

Was this why he had been abandoned by the Creator and cast adrift into the flow of the world. He would like to think it was.

The next layer was murkier, filled with poison—the dangerous recollections of a time when his mind was not his own. There was so much that he would rather not recall, but it was part of his history nonetheless. He had been sent to murder any who opposed his government masters—enemies of the state they had been called. Scientists, spies, or dictators, it didn't matter. Controlled by his captors, Clay saw them as prey, a mission to complete before moving on to the next, and the one after that. How many had he killed? He saw countless faces in his mind. Expressions etched in terror emerged from the billowing silt of his memory, but there were far too many to count.

He was not proud of that stage of his existence and found himself delving deeper into the next. Clay saw how he had come to be under their thrall—the army as they brought him down. But he wanted to be past this, sinking deeper.

Deeper.

Clay had wandered the planet searching for a purpose—using his unique nature to help those in need, believing that this was what He would have wanted, why the Almighty had left him alone.

Alone.

But it hadn't always been that way.

And deeper still.

SQUIRE was flattered. All this hullabaloo over one hobgoblin.

As the vampires and soldier Drows fell upon him, Squire wondered at the fate of his friends. There was some powerful magic going on here. It came off his attackers in stinking waves.

Which sucked big time for all of them.

He didn't have the room to swing the sword anymore; they were too close, grabbing at him with clawed hands. He dropped the blade, switching to a Gemini dagger instead. He didn't give them time to grab him, constantly moving in a circle, gouging out eyes and slashing throats.

Fat fucking lot of good it's doing.

Squire could hear sounds of struggle all around him, but couldn't take his eyes off this bunch for a second.

The dagger cut through their flesh like tissue paper, the special iron-and-silver alloy of his own design once again proving its worth. He didn't know how much longer he could keep this up, though. The years of nachos, donuts, and pork rinds had slowed him down considerably.

Conan Doyle had always warned him about the excesses.

He jabbed the dagger deep into the eye socket of a vampire that had gotten too close. The leech's shriek of pain was like an injection of nitrous oxide to his slowing engine, supercharging him for just a bit more of the ultraviolence.

From the back of his mind a thought bubbled to the surface. He and the boss had talked about situations like this. If things looked bleak—like they were all going down hard—his job was to escape at all costs, find reinforcements, and make the enemy pay.

He had dismissed his employer's request, not believing there would ever come a time when Conan Doyle would be on the ropes. It had been a ridiculous thought, but that had been before the coming of the Devourer.

A lot had changed since then.

A trio of the attackers that encircled him lunged at once, and as he spun to deflect their assault, others came from behind. It wasn't a good situation, and he could see himself going down for the count.

And where would they be, then?

Conan Doyle had told him that in the darkest of moments, his ability to walk the shadows might make him the variable between humanity's survival, and its extinction. It was an awful lot of weight placed upon a hobgoblin's shoulders, but what was a guy to do?

A vampire took hold of his knife arm and sank her fangs into his hand to get him to drop the blade. Squire screamed and released the dagger. The only upside was that there were more where that one had come from.

There wasn't much time. It had to be now.

They were all over him, forcing him to the ground. The stink was awful. Some of the vampires' heads descended, their fangs elongating in anticipation of a little hobgoblin juice. Squire reached into the pocket of his cargo pants, searching for one of the accessories he'd brought along when he learned that there might be vampires in the equation.

His fingers fumbled over loose pieces of candy, a pack of gum, a bottle opener, and a pack of Tic-Tacs, finally finding the object of his frantic search.

"There you are," he mumbled beneath his breath.

The grenade was tiny, but that didn't mean it wouldn't be effective. It was modeled after the Special Forces Thermite grenades, but with a little pinch of mojo.

"Got a surprise for you fuckers," Squire said, bringing the golf-ball-sized explosive up to his mouth. They tried to take it from him, to tear it from his hands, but luck just wasn't on their side.

He pulled the pin and let the banger roll from his grasp.

Most of his attackers looked down to see what he had dropped as he closed his eyes tightly and attempted to scramble away.

Squire rolled onto his stomach and started to crawl just as he heard the grenade explode. A blast of heat seared his back, like a piece of the sun had landed in Eden.

Their screams were music to his ears.

He'd worked long and hard designing those grenades, experimenting to find the right amount of magic to duplicate the heat and intensity of the sun for the right amount of time so that only the leeches present would be reduced to extra crispy.

The legs of his pants ignited, and he felt the skin beneath immediately begin to blister. Squire instinctively rolled around on the damp ground, extinguishing the flames. The burns would be added to the other injuries that throbbed painfully on his body.

When he opened his eyes, Squire saw that the grenade had been effective. Most of the vampires were gone, reduced to ash, and Drow lay burning upon the ground. He forced himself to stand, and saw the most terrifying of sights. Even though he didn't want to believe it, his worst fears had become a reality.

They had all fallen.

The demon Abaddon loomed above the body of Conan Doyle. Squire's heart did a little flip at the sight, never imagining that he would ever see such a thing. It was no better for Ceridwen, her limp body being dragged across the Garden by the son of a bitch, Duergar.

This is bad; this is real bad.

It looked like Graves was somehow trapped within a net, Jelena unconscious or dead upon the ground, and Clay . . .

Squire stared in disbelief at what he was seeing.

"Oh, shit," he muttered beneath his breath.

He wanted to help them, but knew that it had gone well beyond that. The best that he could do right now—much to his chagrin—was to run.

To escape.

He made his move toward the thickest part of the forest, his body screaming from more injuries than he even knew he had. Squire's head began to swim, and it took all that he could muster not to pass out.

The darkness of the trees was calling to him, but he knew that this, too, would be fraught with danger. He couldn't think about that now. He had to get away, to plan the next step, to find others to help rescue Conan Doyle and the Menagerie—and if that wasn't possible, to find some way to make sure the demon's plans were derailed.

Abaddon spun around just as he began to back toward the jungle.

"Going somewhere, troll?" the demon asked, black sigils slithering around on his crimson flesh.

"You know where you can shove your troll, pig fucker," Squire yelled, trying to keep from passing out as he threw himself into the forest.

He saw the patch of shadow and stumbled toward it.

"You're going nowhere!" he heard Abaddon call.

A wave of magical force pursued him, destroying everything in its path as he stumbled toward the pool of shadow.

Squire flung himself toward the shadow cast by the overhanging leaves of a gigantic, prehistoric fern, the fetid breath of destruction hot upon his neck.

13

ABADDON had the Menagerie dragged back to the encampment and put on display. As Duergar, Legion, and assorted vampires and Drows brought Conan Doyle into the camp, a strange hush fell over the demons and abominations that had answered his summons to become part of this revolution in Paradise. The Hell-Lord felt their awe. Faces—and what passed for faces—turned to watch him as he passed. They knew he was the author of this glory, and now his control over them was complete.

The Menagerie were dropped onto the ground and beaten insensate. Most had been unconscious already. Now Abaddon walked among them, admiring what his plans had wrought. He had studied them, each and every one, learning of their strengths and weaknesses, and had planned accordingly.

"We should kill them now," Duergar said, hefting his axe as he stood above the unconscious Ceridwen. "Shouldn't even be giving them the chance to wake up again."

The demon glanced over to see Legion squatting beside the frozen body of the other shape changer. He appeared fascinated by what lay upon the ground before him.

"It would be like killing a piece of myself," Legion said, reaching down to brush the tips of his fingers almost lovingly across Clay's brow.

"There will be no killing," Abaddon declared, flexing his powerful wings as he folded his arms across his chest.

Duergar snorted and stormed up to him, axe in hand.

"It's madness to leave them alive," he snarled. "There's always the chance that—"

"They remain alive until I decide otherwise," the demon said. He moved nearer to Duergar, lowering his voice and glancing around, letting the half-blood monster think that he viewed him as an equal. They were conspiring together. At least, Abaddon wanted Duergar to believe they were. "It is a matter of power, my friend. Our allies see that we have brought to heel those who would oppose us—those who frightened them—and they drool with anticipation. They see the great Conan Doyle and his illustrious Menagerie cowed, kept like animals or trophies, and they yearn to march beneath our banner. We are a force to be reckoned with, Duergar. And leaving them alive proves this to the disbelievers."

Abaddon closed his wings tightly about himself.

The half-blood narrowed his gaze. The edges of his hideous mouth raised in a twisted grin that bared even more of the yellowed tusks jutting from his lower jaw.

"You are cunning, Abaddon."

"It's in the blood, my friend."

Duergar nodded.

Satisfied, Abaddon glanced around and saw that the vampires and the Drows seemed to look upon him differently, now, just as the demons did. He reveled in it. He *had* defeated Conan Doyle, one of the great champions of the Twilight Wars. It was not an achievement to be taken lightly.

One of the newly arrived abominations shambled forward to gaze upon the prisoners. Multiple eyes that weaved in the air upon thick, muscular stalks surveyed each of the mighty that had been brought down.

"This is not all of them," multiple orifices in a sea of soft, flaccid flesh burbled. "The collection is not complete."

Abaddon grinned, more snarl than smile. "The hobgoblin is of little worry."

The thing shuddered, its flesh turning from pink to a rot-colored gray. "It is not the hobgoblin of whom I speak."

Others within the invited began to whisper, nodding.

"It is the mother," the creature's multiple mouths voiced. "Where is the one called Eve?"

The mention of the vampiress brought a hush to the gathering.

"Temporarily, she eludes us," Abaddon replied.

The eyestalks of the beast bent down to study again the unconscious Menagerie.

"The collection is not complete," it stated again.

Understanding the implication, the demon slowly nodded. "Of course it isn't," he growled. "And the value of collection would be severely affected without the final piece."

"Exactly," the nether beast gurgled.

Abaddon turned to the vampires, many of whom still felt the effects of the battle with the Menagerie, still alive only thanks to the power of his dark magics.

"Find her," he commanded, pointing a clawed finger out into the thick jungle of the Garden. "Find her and bring her to me."

SHE'D wanted so desperately to remember.

So much had been lost to her over the millennia that her loss of memory had seemed part of the Creator's punishment. With the passage of time, Eve had remembered less and less of what she had been, before Abaddon had infected her. Eventually, however, she had come to realize that perhaps this was a blessing.

Now, with the blood of the angel Jophiel coursing through her veins, she remembered it all.

Every fucking bit.

Pushing herself away from the angel's corpse, Eve was bombarded by painful recollections. It was all so perfectly clear, as if it had just happened mere moments before.

She curled into a tight ball on the ground, blades of wild grass gently caressing her cheek. But there would be no consoling her, for she remembered every detail of what she'd once had, and what she had lost . . . for herself, as well as for humanity.

What would it have been like for the world if she had resisted temptation? Eve wondered, contorting into a still-tighter ball, as if trying to make herself disappear. But something told her that even if she succeeded, the pain and guilt would still be there.

It could have been so perfect, so wonderful. If only she hadn't listened.

She remembered the sight of the serpent moving through the grass. Eve focused upon the memory of the serpent, the reptilian emissary of a much darker power. She doubted if there was anybody still alive that remembered that they had once had limbs.

That had been the Almighty's punishment for the serpent's involvement in her temptation . . . her fall from grace. He had cursed the animal, and all its future progeny, to crawl upon its belly for what it had done.

Partake of the fruit, be truly one with your Lord, the snake had hissed, as it climbed up the side of the tree.

Eve opened her eyes, looking past Jophiel's withered corpse at the Tree of Knowledge, its base wrapped in the thorny brambles. Large pieces of the strangely shaped fruit, plump and ripe, dangled from the highest branches.

Remembering the taste of the fruit, she began to gag. It had started out sweet, the most delicious thing she had ever tasted, but it soon turned bitter as poison.

Bitter as betrayal.

Eve buried her face in the dirt and grass, no longer wanting to remember. First she had betrayed the Creator, then, with nary a moment's hesitation, she had betrayed her mate.

And the serpent had laughed and laughed.

She heard it all again, clamping her hands to her ears to block out the sound, but still she could hear the awful laughter.

With Jophiel's blood flowing through her, Eve remembered it all, every single detail of her past, no matter how small.

"Careful what you wish for" was the old adage, but she had never truly grasped its full meaning until now.

She climbed to her feet, the blood of the messenger like fire in her veins. The tip of her tongue flicked at the pronounced canines inside her mouth as the claws upon her hands grew long, the tips of her fingers tingling in the anticipation of prey.

There was only one way to quench the unbearable fire.

Eve tilted her head back and sniffed the air. The angel's blood had charged her, had healed all her wounds, enhanced her every sense, and her strength and speed as well.

There were certain people she needed to talk to, and now seemed as good a time as any. Then, just as she was about to begin her hunt, she caught it on the breeze.

The smell of the undead.

The stink of her children.

Eve smiled, backing into the cool darkness of the forest to hide.

How considerate, she thought, waiting for them to arrive. *This saves me the trouble of looking for them.*

I T had been a very long time since he felt like this.

Palu stopped in the tangle of the forest as the others continued to hunt around him. The hairs on the back of his neck were standing on end, alerting him to danger. Long ago, while hunting a wild boar with his brother on Samoa, he had experienced a feeling very much like this.

How odd it was that he would recall it now.

They had stood in the jungle, their spears in hand, searching for signs of their injured prey. The animal had been swift, vicious, gouging a deep, bloody gash into his thigh with one of its tusks. But they had also injured it.

Palu and his brother Afua were their tribe's greatest hunters and had promised the village elders that the animal would be slain for a great feast. The raging boar had become legendary in his village as well as the surrounding villages. The number of Samoans it had injured—even taking the life of a child—was growing with the passing of seasons. The beast was growing too bold, too powerful, and the elders of his tribe dispatched their greatest hunters to dispatch the savage pig.

Though ages had passed since that time—his brother, and the rest of their tribe, having fallen to Palu's vampiric hunger—the memory seemed strangely fresh. On that day in the jungle, he and his brother had become the hunted. He had felt the eyes of the maddened predator that day.

He felt them again now.

Palu was about to yell a warning, but it was too late.

The beast exploded silently from the concealment of some shadows, its movements so swift—so deadly—that his eyes had trouble following its deadly course.

For the briefest of moments, he had trouble distinguishing between the then and the now, the images of Eve and the memory of the beast blending together in his mind as one, terrible, ferocious force.

Palu couldn't move, watching as she moved from victim to victim, her slashing claws so razor-sharp—cutting so deep—that they brought instantaneous death to his horde, even though they were protected by Abaddon's sorcery. There was only so much magic could do when dealing with something like the *mother of them all*.

He considered running, as he had done so many times in the past when Eve had confronted him. How many times had he managed to evade her wrath? He was looked upon by his kind as one of the lucky ones, but he'd always harbored a secret shame about his survival.

To run from fear was to dishonor one's lineage.

He hadn't run from the boar, even though his leg had been badly injured. He had confronted the beast and, with the help of his brother, finally killed it, watching the life go out of its black eyes.

As Eve came closer, a horrible grin upon her blood-spattered face, Palu saw that she had the same dark eyes.

The eyes of the beast.

Was it possible that boar somehow lived in her, now, and sought revenge for the death he had dealt it those many years ago? Gazing into the woman's eyes as she killed his brethren—*her children*—one after another, he believed it.

He had almost died from the injuries sustained in the jungle those ages ago, as day turned to night and he bled into the earth. He had lost so much blood, and infection had begun to poison him. Palu knew he would have died if not for the stranger who had come out of the night, promising to make him well, and to make him the greatest hunter his tribe had ever known.

For a simple price.

How could he have possibly refused such an offer? Through the delirium of fever he'd accepted, and died horribly, painfully, before what had been promised to him was delivered.

Now the vampires tried to escape her, as Palu himself had done in the past, but none of them were successful. Eve was relentless.

Palu would not flee.

Eve dug her talons into the flesh of one of the older females—an ancient thing named Samsessa—and dragged her to the ground. With tooth and claw, the mother tore Samsessa apart, digging into her and tearing out black, twisted organs and, finally, her heart. Samsessa burst into a cloud of oily smoke and ash, drifting upon the winds of Eden.

On all fours, Eve lifted her head, those dark, marble eyes connecting with his. Palu was startled to see that he was all that was left from the hunting party Abaddon had sent to find her.

"Hey, Palu," she rasped, her body tensed to spring. She was expecting him to run.

He glanced at the ground, searching for anything that might serve as a weapon. Not far from where he was standing he saw a broken tree limb.

It would have to do.

"So, what's the story?" Eve asked him, still crouched, watching him with an unwavering gaze. "Are you going to try again?"

He'd always looked at the others slain by her as sacrifices to a greater cause. In the laws of nature, there were always others of the herd that were slower, allowing the swift to escape while the predator took down the weakest.

Now, he was alone. A herd of one.

"Go on." She smiled at him, running a pointed, pink tongue across beautifully white teeth. "I'll even give you a head start."

His mind traveled back across the years again, and he was in his hut, the stink of infection drifting up from his injured leg. Palu knew he was going to die, and was afraid. His fear had drawn the stranger . . . the vampire. As he had looked upon the corpse white face of his savior and caught the stench of his breath as he opened his mouth to reveal jagged fangs, Palu had understood that what he feared was oblivion. He had welcomed the vampire's bite, if only to stave off the unknown.

Palu thought that he had moved beyond the fear of death, that the centuries of walking the earth had cured him of his malady. Now, he knew better.

Fear blazed up within him. All he wanted was to survive. If he went for the tree limb, tried to fight her, he knew how it would end. Palu spun and hurled himself into the forest, running as swiftly as he was able. Branches whipped at his face and eyes, but he would not allow himself to slow.

If I can reach the camp, I will be safe. Palu pushed on, listening for the sounds of pursuit, but he heard nothing.

A glimmer of hope rose within him, then was extinguished as Eve dropped down from the treetops to land in front of him, naked and gloriously feral. Before her bare feet had touched the ground, her talons slashed his throat, tearing through muscle and tendon. She gripped his head in both hands and began to pull. In the last moment of his undeath, he felt his spinal cord snap.

And then, oblivion.

14

CLAY lay on the ground, unmoving, but not entirely unconscious. His mind eddied upon the currents of thought and memory and dream. Whatever his counterpart had done to him, it had shocked his body so badly that he had physically shut down. If not for the mind and spirit within him, he would have been little more than a fallen statue, formed of clay. Outside, he remained completely still. But within, all was chaos.

Here, he was closer to the source of his creation than he had been in all the ages since he had first been set down upon the Earth. And as he lay there, mind a maelstrom, the grass and roots and soil seemed to pull at him. Eden itself *touched* him.

HE *can feel the attention of the Creator. The intent and focus. The whimsy and curiosity. That attention is the totality of him. For he is the Clay. There is light, an infinite array of glittering points that he understands are stars. There is darkness, and the weighty presence of earth and sea, of a sphere of potential, floating in the infinite. How can he know this? The Creator's hands give him form again and again, but the touch of the Creator is all that he knows. He floats in the infinite, flesh and bone flowing and twisting, hair and fur and feathers rippling across his hide, then vanishing again as creatures are imagined and either met with contented approval or discarded.*

How can the Clay know anything at all?

Yet even this he has begun to understand. As the Creator shapes and reshapes him, molding, inventing each of the birds and beasts that will populate this world, awareness has woken in him. This cannot be an accident. The Creator has lent him this awareness with some intent, but it is only a spark of knowledge, and he understands so little of the infinite.

An eternity of light and shadow passes before his eyes . . . his many eyes. On the planet that spins below, time passes. The Clay feels the Creator considering, enjoying the art of this work as His hands reshape the Clay yet again. He lingers for a time in that drift-state and he can see the world below, and watch as trees and plants begin to grow, as landmasses take form, as the animals his flesh has been used to model are born for the first time upon the surface of the world. They are fashioned by the Creator from the stuff of the infinite, and yet the Clay feels tethered to them all, as though they are all a part of him.

The world spins. The Clay drifts. The Creator considers. Time passes, and now the evolution of the planetary sphere below seems to slow.

Through the ages he has remained the Creator's plaything, His template, the physical manifestation of His minor imaginings. As time slows, however, the Clay has begun to awaken to detail. The awareness implanted in him by the Creator has blossomed, like the world below, and grown wildly. He feels bliss at the sight of the beauty of the world, admiration as he perceives the growing awareness of the first man, whose awakening seems to parallel his own.

Yet he also feels impatient and frustrated, even fearful.

Has the Creator finished with him? Would He give the gift of awareness only to leave the Clay to drift eternally across the infinite? No. He cannot believe this. He has felt the hands of the Creator, has felt His regard and purpose. Surely He must have some plan.

Still, he drifts. The Clay can never be alone, so long as the Creator is near, yet he longs for the weight of His attention once more. Life has stirred all across the spinning world below. It grows and thrives with the rutting and killing, the cries and struggles of the beasts of water, earth, and sky. He has been each of these creatures, had their form in his flesh before the Creator deigned to introduce them to the world, yet he is a prisoner, of sorts. Aware, but unable to wake. Alive, but unable to live.

The Clay is of two minds. He envies the beasts of the world the Creator has made and wishes he could be among them, longs to walk and fly and swim with them, to cherish all of Creation. Yet, somehow, at the same time, he despises it all. His frustration has turned to anger and jealousy. He wishes he could descend upon the world and destroy all that he cannot be or have.

The Creator knows this. Of course he knows. The Clay feels the return of his attention, of his regard, and rejoices. Yet part of him shrinks away in spite.

He feels the hands of Creation upon him, molding and shaping his flesh once more, and some of the turmoil within him is eased. This is as it should be. He feels the love and purpose of the Creator again, but beneath it he senses a return of the whimsy and curiosity he has felt so often as inspiration forged him anew, and anew, and anew.

Two natures have begun to war within the Clay, but in this moment they are joined in their exultation.

And then the hands pull at his flesh one final time, and he is torn in twain. The Clay screams with two voices, drifting through the infinite. But the hands of the Creator have not released them—the two of them. Ripped asunder, they can see one another there in the void, the two halves of the Clay, the one who longed to be a part of the world, and the one filled with jealousy and hatred.

The Clay can no longer see the infinite. Bright colors wash past his eyes, the blue-and-white sky, the green of forest and hill, and he feels himself falling. He strikes the Earth and his eyes flutter closed and for a brief time, he is aware of nothing.

When he awakens, he can hear the trickle of a stream and smell the rich scents of the Garden, which is itself the seed from which the world was grown. Of his other half—the part of him torn away by the hands of the Creator—he can find no *sign. The beauty of the world suffuses his soul, yet with it there comes a sadness.*

Curiosity and whimsy. He felt it in the purpose of the Creator, a desire to separate the two voices in the heart of the Clay, to set them upon the world and see what would become of them. Like so much of this world, and of the infinite, the Clay and his brother have become an experiment.

Loneliness fills him. He wonders what will become of him, and of his brother, but he fears that this last, at least, he already knows. There will be no loneliness in his other half— only rage.

The Clay rises and surveys the Garden. The world's star, its sun, shines brightly on the horizon, gliding across the sky. He starts toward it, hoping he will meet his brother, and they will be together once more. It is only much later that he will realize what an error he has made. His brother will see the sun and turn his back upon it, and set off in search of his own path in the direction of the encroaching darkness in the east, vanishing into the night.

SQUIRE woke to pain. As consciousness crept like the dawn across his mind, his body began to contort, as though it could escape the parts of him that had been injured. His right shoulder dropped, and he curled almost fetally in upon himself, trying to shield a slash across his upper arm and chest from any further harm. His legs were seared with hellfire or whatever magic the demon Abaddon had been hurling at him.

As his eyes opened, he pulled a breath in through his teeth.

"Fuck, that hurts," he whispered to the darkness around him.

Squire blinked. Darkness. His chest rose and fell painfully with each breath, but he would heal quickly enough. Nothing fatal or damning. As long as he had the time to heal. Unfortunately, he had a terrible suspicion he wouldn't have that luxury.

He recalled those last few moments in Eden, running for the shadows, the bitter taste of retreat in his mouth.

Hobgoblins weren't brave, by nature. Brave meant halfway to foolish, and Squire didn't consider himself a fool. But he also wasn't a coward. When the chips were down, the fool was the one who wouldn't stand and fight. Some human had once scribbled a bit of sloganeering about how all that was required for the bad guys to win was for the white hats to do nothing. Sounded like a bunch of propaganda, but it was also the truth.

Squire didn't like running. But sometimes strategy meant you had to run. Common sense. The better part of valor. All that shit. True enough.

So he'd gotten out, hit the Shadowpaths. Now that the Garden Gate was open, he'd be able to travel the paths back to the Blight. He'd never have been able to find Eden from the human world—even with the Gate open—but coming from this world and heading back to the other, he was confident he'd make it.

Or he would have if he wasn't bleeding all over the damn place, and if the serpent wasn't slithering out there in the shadow realm somewhere, searching the paths for his scent.

How long was I out? he wondered. *A few minutes, okay. But a few hours, pally, and you're screwed.*

He forced himself not to think about whether or not any of his friends were already dead. If they still lived, they were likely prisoners. Squire had only a single Gemini dagger on him as far as weapons went, and that wasn't going to be a hell of a lot of help. He needed to get to his workshop, and he needed reinforcements—whatever troops he could muster on short notice.

But the Murawa was here, somewhere. *Damned shadow snake.*

Squire lay half on the path and half in the churning gray maelstrom beyond it. His lower torso and legs were barely visible to him, obscured by that thick cloud of shadows. When he moved his feet, the pain in his burned legs jolted him. The surface that passed for ground beyond the edge of the path seemed even less solid here than elsewhere. It gave way as he tried to drag himself fully onto the path, and for a moment he felt as though he might slip down into the fabric of the shadow realm, swallowed whole. He could walk in there, travel there, if he had no other choice. But it would be a terrible risk. He might never emerge.

Groaning with pain, Squire pulled himself onto the path and for a long moment, he only lay there.

Something moved in the darkness farther along the path. He snapped his head up, gritting his teeth at the pain from the gashes in his arm and chest and the burns on his legs. Maybe it was the serpent, and maybe it wasn't. But Squire knew one thing—pain meant he was alive. If he had to haul himself between worlds, across whole universes of shadow, with this pain drilling into him, then he would do that. Death was the only other option, not only for himself, but for the rest of the Menagerie.

Not gonna happen.

Thick, dark blood ran from the gashes in his flesh and dripped onto the Shadowpaths. Even to his own nose, the scent of hobgoblin was unmistakable. If the shadow serpent hadn't already sensed his presence, it would notice soon; and then it would be coming.

Squire started along the path, trying to push away images of what his friends might be enduring. He focused on his objectives—the weapons at his forge and help for the others.

A wave of pain went through him. He shuddered and went down onto his knees. Cursing, he rose again and pressed on, but too slowly. Too damned slowly. He hissed through his teeth as the pain rattled him again. He staggered on. The healing had already begun. The waves of pain were a part of that, his body reacting to both the injury and the trauma of its repair.

The Shadowpath was firm as stone underfoot, but these were wild edges of the matrix of dark roads in this realm, and the gray-black clouds of shadow substance encroached upon the path. Up ahead, it narrowed so much that he would have to take great care not to stumble away from the trail.

Fresh pain jolted him. Squire froze, waiting for it to pass. *Not working,* he thought. In the roiling dark, he felt sure he heard something in motion. If not the serpent, then some other creature he did not want to encounter in his current condition.

And now he could not escape the fear he felt for the fate of his friends. He imagined a dozen gruesome deaths for them in the space of as many seconds. His situation was hopeless. No way could he gather up reinforcements like this, never mind weapons. The serpent would be on him before he reached any useful destination.

He could practically hear Eve's voice in his head. *Move your ass, runt, or you're snake food.* But moving his ass wouldn't solve the problem. Squire simply didn't have the strength yet, and the Murawa would not give him the time to recover. Neither, he felt sure, would Abaddon and the other monsters who'd invaded Paradise.

Time for another plan.

The fabric of the shadows pulsing on the left side of the path ahead seemed to rustle like a curtain about to part.

Squire had no choice. He wasn't going anywhere. The Legion of Doom—Abaddon's ugly bastards—had planned it all too well. The hobgoblin was a wild card, but the Murawa trumped him. Even if he could get through to find help, who would he go to first? Who could he be absolutely certain would help them, would not have been compromised already by Abaddon?

Only one person came to mind: Danny Ferrick. And the demon kid didn't have the most reliable record. But this job was just the sort of thing Danny loved. *See bad guy, tear bad guy to ribbons.*

If it just came down to Squire and Danny, they'd at least make a fight of it. Sneak in through some shadow in Eden when no one was looking, free whichever of the Menagerie were still alive, and stop Abaddon. Danny had shown a capacity for manipulating shadows in a way even Squire did not understand. The hobgoblin could travel by shadow, could slip in and out of them, but he couldn't control them, couldn't wrap himself in them or twist them to suit his purposes, and the demon kid had turned out to have hints of that kind of power.

He could walk the Shadowpaths, if he could figure out how to get in.

"What are you thinking?" Squire whispered to himself. He couldn't get to Danny. The kid was back in Boston, hellhound-sitting for Shuck. There were far too many paths to walk between here and there. Squire would never reach him without the serpent catching up to him.

He peered around, gazing into the roiling darkness on all sides. Gray-and-black wisps reached out from the void, inviting, caressing. Squire knew, then, with total certainty. He didn't have a chance of making it to safety, never mind to any destination that could provide a way for him to help the Menagerie.

The hobgoblin grinned.

Thoughts of Danny back at Conan Doyle's brownstone had given him a glimmer of hope. He didn't have to go get help. Not when there was a chance he could get help to come to him.

Putting a pair of grubby, leathery fingers into his mouth, he took a deep breath and whistled, as loud and long as he could manage. Pain shot through his chest, and he coughed a moment, then did it again.

Slipping the Gemini dagger from its sheath, he stepped off the path and let the primal darkness embrace him. In the maelstrom, soft shadow sifting underfoot, all he could do now was wait and hope he could stay close to the path.

The blood had stopped seeping from his wounds. But it had created another path, there in the dark realm—one that would be simple for any shadow beast to follow.

AWASH in the flickering light from the television, Danny lay sprawled on the couch with the remote control clutched in his hand. The heavy curtains were drawn in the living room of Conan Doyle's brownstone, and he had long since lost track of the time of day. A glimmer of light glowed at the edges of the curtains, but that might have come from the streetlights out in Louisburg Square just as easily as early morning or late afternoon.

Since the visit from Sanguedolce—which had totally freaked him out—he'd barely moved from the sofa. Several times he'd nodded off, but he had lost track of how much time he'd slept. His jeans and black hoodie sweatshirt had a stale smell that told him he ought to get up and take a shower pretty soon. But he couldn't bring himself to do that.

From the moment that Squire had taken off to help the others search for Eve—leaving Danny dog-sitting for

Shuck—a feeling had been growing in him. Dread comprised only a part of it. Hour by hour he had become more certain that he had a role to play in the current crisis, that he had some task to perform beyond just sitting on his ass and watching the enormous shadow hound pace the halls, sniffing at corners and breaking putrid wind.

He'd never had a feeling like this before. More than just gut instinct—or his fervent wish to have something to pummel—this gnawed at the back of his skull so much that he'd had to force himself to relax. This was something more, genuine precognition. Danny had never had any kind of psychic powers and usually thought they were a lot of bullshit. But he couldn't deny what he felt.

Whatever might be unfolding, it pulled at him, as though the need to act was imminent. But time dragged on, and still nothing happened, forcing him to tamp down any excitement that might be brewing in him.

Instead, he was bored out of his skull.

Listlessly, Danny thumbed the remote control, surfing the channel guide, hoping to come up with something that involved evisceration or lots of naked girls or, in a perfect world, both. News. Gardening. Reality crap. Seventies cop shows. At last he stumbled across an old movie that had Bill Murray mugging for the camera. Probably no tits, but at least he could have a laugh.

His stomach growled. Barely aware of it, he ran his tongue across his teeth. He wanted something hot to eat, not something he could snatch from Squire's snack cabinet. But getting that would mean ordering takeout to be delivered, and that would mean getting up off the couch. If Danny did that, he feared he might start pacing the halls like Shuck. Never mind that he didn't even know what time it was and if there was anyplace open that would deliver.

He started bouncing his left leg up and down, a nervous habit he'd had since childhood. With a sigh, he started switching channels. Bill Murray might as well have been the Marx Brothers for all he could hold Danny's attention. Anything made before he had been born automatically had two strikes against it.

"Stir-crazy," he muttered to himself. "You're gonna lose it."

An itch started, right behind his left horn, and he reached up to scratch at the leathery skin there. After a few seconds, he tossed the remote aside and practically leaped up from the couch.

"Screw it."

He wanted to go up onto the roof, check out the windows of the buildings around Doyle's. People watching had become an obsession. It was best when he could catch girls naked or in their underwear, but sometimes he liked to watch no matter who it was or what the situation. Peeking in other people's windows was the only glimpse he ever got of normal life these days. It hurt some to watch them, but in a strange way it soothed him, too.

Danny strode down the corridor, steps squeaking on the hardwood. He hit the stairs and started up, noticing that the carpet runner on the stairs was slightly worn. The lights that were on downstairs didn't reach this far, and as he set foot on the third step, he crossed into shadow.

A frown creased his brow. He'd heard something, a high, shrill sound, like a whistle. He paused a second to see if it would come again, but when it didn't, he started up the stairs again.

Back on the first floor, Shuck began to bark. The massive shadow beast came running from the back of the house, probably the kitchen, bellowing a thunderous clamor. The house shook. Danny could feel the place tremble through the wooden banister.

Shuck tried to slow down and reverse direction as he reached the bottom of the stairs, his claws scrabbling on the wood, scoring it deeply. The shadow hound nearly tripped over himself, but then he recovered his step and started up the stairs toward Danny.

"Whoa, boy!" Danny called, holding up both hands.

The hound came on.

"Hold on! Back off, you stupid mutt!"

But then Shuck leaped at him. Danny went down on his butt on the stairs. He tried to push the big, ugly dog off him, but Shuck caught his sleeve in his jaws and pushed past him, dragging him farther up the stairs. For all Danny's demonic strength, the shadow hound was too powerful for him. Danny spun around on the stairs and cooperated.

"All right, all right. I'm coming. What, Timmy's down the fucking well?"

The hound led him to the second-floor landing, tugging the entire way. Shuck kept growling and the sound rolled like distant thunder. If it didn't seem obvious that the monstrous dog meant him no harm, he would've thought Shuck intended to eat him or something. But then the growling turned to whining, a desperate sound, and Danny knew whatever the hound wanted him to do, it had to be done fast.

"What is it, mutt?" he asked, no longer joking. "What's going on? Danger coming? What do you want from me?"

Down at the end of the hall, a light burned in Conan Doyle's study. The rest of the floor was cast in gloom. But on the landing, there was a jog in the wall that created a dead corner, almost entirely devoid of light. The shadows gathered there.

Shuck dragged Danny toward that darkened corner, edging backward. In moments, the hound reached the point where he ought to have bumped into the wall. Instead, he kept going, the entire rear half of the creature vanishing into the shadows.

A trickle of fear went down Danny's spine. "Wait. Hey, cut it out." He tried to pull away, but the dog's jaws were clamped tight on his sleeve. "I can't go in there. Squire's the shadow-walker, not me. Even if I could get in, how the hell would I find my way out?"

The dog growled and bent low, muscles rippling beneath oil black fur as it tried to drag him unwillingly into the liquid shadows.

"Cut the crap!" he snarled. With all his strength, he tore his arm away from the hound. His sweatshirt ripped, and a swatch of the fabric remained in the beast's jaws. "Look what you did!"

Shuck took a step toward him, partially emerging from the Shadowpaths. Now there was danger in his growl, a warning. The pleading whine had left his repertoire.

"What the hell's set you off?" he shouted at the hound.

Danny blinked. What had gotten into Shuck? When he'd stepped into the shadows, he'd heard that weird whistling noise. This creature was from the Shadowpaths. Maybe the whistle had been some kind of summons. Something he recognized. He needed to go, and he wanted Danny to come along. Timmy-down-the-well didn't seem so off base all of a sudden. He'd never seen that old show about the dog rescuing the kid all the time, but he'd heard the reference made hundreds of times.

Maybe this is it, Danny thought. *Maybe this is the thing that's been causing that feeling.*

Shuck growled low, cocked his head, and stared at Danny. He barked once, as if telling him to move his ass.

"Look, I can't go in there. I told you. Even if this is my fucking psychic-flash come true, I can't walk the shadows like Squire."

But even as he said it, Danny started to wonder how he knew it was the truth. He'd learned months ago that he could vanish in shadows, wrap the darkness around him like a cloak to make himself practically invisible. In shadows, he could make himself unseen. His demonic abilities manifested themselves at different times and in different ways, and Squire had said that there were creatures other than hobgoblins that could walk in shadows.

The massive hound ducked his head forward and reached up, snatching Danny's hand gently in his jaws. The points of a hundred sharp fangs pricked his skin, but he did not try to pull away. He stared into the darkness beyond the hound, and when the beast tugged on him, he went along. Fascinated, he watched Shuck disappear into the darkness. When he stepped forward, following, and his arm slid into the shadows, he could feel himself breaking through the membrane between worlds. The Shadowpaths resisted his intrusion, closing around his arm, scraping at his flesh. Pain seared his skin, but did no damage.

Danny hissed through his teeth at the feeling, but then he gave a throaty laugh. A lot of times he despised his demonic nature. But the whole nearly indestructible thing didn't suck at all.

"All right, mutt," he snarled, forcing his way into and through the darkness, stepping into the shadow realm. "Lead the way."

15

SQUIRE held his breath.

Something moved in the maelstrom behind him. He could feel the churning darkness ripple with its passing. Slowly, so as not to create ripples of his own, he turned to look over his shoulder, and he saw a disturbance passing through the shadows, leaving a wake like the contrail of a jet across the sky. But its trail followed a curving pattern.

Serpentine.

Inwardly, the hobgoblin swore. But he would not utter a sound that might draw the snake's attention. His chest rose and fell, and he could feel his pulse racing fearfully, a primal reaction, bred into his kind over millennia spent in terror of such creatures.

Carefully, Squire tested his injured arm. It hurt to move, but not terribly. His legs had gone practically numb from standing still for so long, but he suspected the burns on them would be healing nicely by now. On his arm and chest, the bleeding had stopped.

The Murawa had followed the scent of his blood to this spot, and perhaps his piercing whistle. But the darkness played tricks on the senses. The winds that moved unexplained, eddying the shadows, would shift the scent and distort the sound, at least for a while. But not for very long. The snake hunted—that was all it did. The predator knew its territory. Soon, it would be upon him. Unless he moved.

Squire slid one foot forward, toward where the Shadowpaths had been before. The toe of his shoe touched nothing but soft, shifting darkness. Panic raced through him, and he forced himself to take a breath, calming down. The maelstrom always shifted. The question was, how far away had he shifted?

With the other foot, he felt in front of him. Still nothing. As he began a third, silent step, he felt the ripple of motion through the darkness behind him once again, and he froze. Squire squeezed his eyes closed, waiting for another wave of motion. His right hand closed on the handle of his Gemini dagger, and he slid it quietly from its sheath.

The ripple passed.

Again, he pushed a foot out ahead of him. This time, it came down on solid surface. A Shadowpath. He couldn't even be sure that this was the one he'd been walking before, but that mattered little. Even without being injured, he wouldn't have been able to outrun the shadow serpent. Thus far, he'd had great luck in outsmarting it. If he could race along the path, find a fork or a sharp turn and hurl himself into the maelstrom again, he might be able to elude the snake again. He was no longer bleeding, so there would be no fresh blood to leave behind a trail.

The hobgoblin had no choice at all.

Squire took a deep breath and stepped out onto the path, sliding from the churning shadows. To the left would—he thought—be back the way he'd come. Dagger in hand, he bolted along the path to his right. Pain shot through his legs, not from burns but from having stood still so long. He grunted softly and gritted his teeth but kept going, moving from a staggering run to a sprint.

Hobgoblins had always been faster than they looked. Squire thought it was from all the time they'd spent over the ages trying not to get eaten. The grim humor gave him no comfort. The weight of the Gemini dagger in his grip provided even less.

His muscles ached as he ran, barreling forward, forcing himself to such speed that he felt entirely out of control. Misty shadows drifted across his path, but the ground stayed solid beneath him. To either side he saw churning darkness that could hide the serpent, but he spared only a glance. The path curved to the left up ahead. A clock had been ticking in his mind. Twelve seconds had passed since he burst onto the path. The serpent would have heard him, would have sensed him moving. It would be coming for him now. Squire thought he could feel its cold presence at the back of his neck, about to strike.

That curve would be the place. He would have to leave the path. Get a running start and a good push off the solid ground and just hurl himself into the maelstrom, hoping the shadow snake would lose his trail.

Squire had almost reached the turn in the path when the Murawa emerged from the coalescing darkness just ahead of him. It did not dart at him, only slid its head from the shadows and stared at him in silent menace, as grimly inevitable as death itself. The serpent had been tracking him all along. It had paced him, gotten ahead of him, and now it slithered onto the solid Shadowpath, coiling in upon itself, its head never wavering in that glare.

Logic fled. Squire came to a total halt on the path, only the Gemini dagger for protection. He held the blade weakly in front of him. The serpent's heavy head began to sway, its entire body formed from silken darkness. Its black tongue flickered out.

With a deep breath, Squire raised the dagger and straightened his back. He couldn't see any way to survive beyond the next minute, but the notion provided a certain freedom. Death had arrived. The only facet of it he could control was the manner in which he comported himself in its presence.

"I'm gristle and bone," the hobgoblin growled. "I hope you fucking choke."

The snake reared its head back so far that the churning darkness caressed its upper body, embracing the creature in a shadowy fog. It ceased its swaying, about to strike. Squire tightened his grip on the dagger's handle.

Around the curve in the path, something roared.

The Murawa twisted itself around and whipped its head toward the sound. Squire took the moment to attack, crossing the nine steps between himself and the snake in as many heartbeats. He thrust the Gemini blade into its underbelly, gripped the hilt with both hands, and sliced downward. Moist darkness spilled out, thick, oil black organs slapping the ground.

The snake hissed its pain and turned on him, darted its head down to gobble him up. Squire sidestepped and thrust the blade up into its lower jaw. The Gemini dagger became lodged there, and the snake whipped its body around, careening into Squire, knocking him to the ground.

The hobgoblin looked up to see Shuck hurtling along the Shadowpath with Danny Ferrick at his side. The demon boy's countenance terrified Squire, etched with madness and ferocity unlike anything he'd ever seen. For half a moment, he wondered how the kid had gotten onto the Shadowpaths, how he could even be here.

Then Danny leaped at the Murawa, and all rational thought left Squire's head. He could only stare as the snake darted its head toward Danny, fangs bared and dripping venom, and the handle of the Gemini dagger jutting from its lower jaw.

The demon boy collided with the snake in midair, the impact knocking them into the maelstrom, which swallowed all but the shadow serpent's lower body in churning blackness. Shuck howled and bounded toward the snake, snagging its bottom coils with the claws of his forepaws. The hound dipped his head and tore into the serpent, burying his muzzle in the creature's flesh.

The shriek that filled the Shadowpaths could never have come from any ordinary serpent—of any size.

"Shuck, be careful!" Squire called.

The hound glanced up at him.

The curtain of darkness parted as Danny rode the serpent's upper coils down to the solid path. As he struck the ground, the shadow snake darted its head again and snapped its jaws closed on the demon boy's shoulder. Danny shouted in pain, but the serpent's fangs shattered and venom stained the kid's sweatshirt, thick as tar.

"Shit!" Danny snapped.

He spun and drove his fist into the shadow snake's right eye with a wretched sucking noise. Danny straddled the serpent, dug in his knees, and started to beat the snake against the solid darkness of the Shadowpath.

"Enough with ruining the hoodie!" the kid screamed. His eyes gleamed yellow in the darkness of the shadow realm, and his face was split with a giddy grin.

Even with all he'd seen Danny going through, he'd never seen the kid this ferocious, or realized how strong he really was. Sometimes, Danny Ferrick scared the shit out of him.

"It's dead, guys," Squire said.

Shuck had torn its lower coils so completely apart that only shreds of darkness remained, slipping off the path, merging with the mist of the maelstrom, becoming nothing but shadow again—if anything in this world could be considered to be something as mundane as an ordinary shadow.

The hound backed off. Danny did not.

The demon kid withdrew his fist and began to use both hands to hammer at the snake's head, then he opened his fists and began to tear at it instead. Ripping it apart.

Squire strode over and grabbed his shoulder. "Kid! That's enough!"

Danny rounded on him, eyes wide with that same ferocity. His expression flickered, and he blinked, then took a breath. When he smiled, now, it was only the lazy, sarcastic grin of the wiseass teenager he'd always been.

"Relax, Squire. You whistled us up, didn't you? Shuck tracked you down, and we saved your ass. You can't blame me if I want to have a little fun after being cooped up at home all this time."

The hobgoblin almost argued with him. But as long as Danny was on their side and stood with them when the bad guys tried to eat the world, how could he blame the kid for being what he was born to be?

"Fun's over, Dan. Thanks for the save, but we've gotta get moving."

Squire bent down, put one shoe on the already deteriorating darkness of the serpent's head, and tugged out his Gemini dagger. He slipped it back into its sheath. Shuck came over and sat on the path next to him, bumping the hobgoblin with his big head, wanting to be patted.

"Thanks to you, too, buddy," Squire said, scratching Shuck behind the ears.

"So where are the others? Where are we going?" Danny asked.

Squire glanced up at him. "They're in trouble. Hard to say how much, but I'd guess a shitload. They're in Eden, kid, but I've got an anchor there, now. A shadow I've already passed through. They couldn't close me out if they wanted to, unless they had a dark-elf mage, and that's just about the only freakin' thing they don't have on their side. No, I can take us there anytime I want to, now.

"First, though, we're going to my workshop, maybe even back to the brownstone, and we're getting every damned weapon we can carry. Abaddon—the asshole behind this whole scheme—he's gonna learn an ugly lesson, pal. He figured why the hell bother with the hobgoblin . . . how much trouble can one little runt be?

"But the bastard made a huge mistake, Danny. He should've killed me first. Nothing in any world holds a grudge like a hobgoblin. And now it's time to take the fucker down."

EVE'S heart sang with the blood of the angel. Light filled her eyes, changing her perceptions. Her senses had always been extraordinarily acute, but now she saw the world around her in a strange, slanted light that somehow managed to make the colors of the Garden both muted and vibrant at the same time. When she moved, walking or darting silently from branch to branch in the highest of trees, the air seemed to flow around her, caressing her, carrying her forward. There were scents more intoxicating and stenches more vile than she had ever imagined existing. The feeling was transcendent.

Now she perched in the crook of a branch in a tall tree of a type that no longer grew in man's world. Its leaves were broad and long and its branches hung heavy with succulent golden and scarlet fruit. Once it had been just another tree in the midst of the endless sprawl of lush garden, of flowers and fruit and wild things capering joyfully. Now it stood just at the edge of a wide swath of the Garden that had transformed into blasted tundra, a ruin of dark earth and yellowed grass, withered plants and trees that had fallen to rot in a matter of hours. Some of the trees had fallen, but others were pale, chalky gray, or charcoal black, skeletal fingers scratching at the bright, sunless sky of Eden.

The corruption of Abaddon and Jophiel's intrusion—of the arrival of their putrid army—had scarred the heart of the Garden, and that rot continued to spread. The infection's growth had slowed, but not stopped. Even the azure sky seemed dimmer above that awful encampment.

The Hell-Lord and his confederates had wrought a hideous change upon this patch of Eden. A mound of earth stood at the center, excavated from below, so that it resembled some nightmarish anthill. Insectoid demons crawled in and out of its peak, and at the base, an other-dimensional horror lay half-burrowed like a giant tick in the loose dirt, its tentacles lifting and sensing the air whenever another creature passed.

A cairn had been built from stones dug up from the ground, a doorway left open so that the half-breed Duergar could come and go. His Drow warriors, lumbering primitives, awaited outside like faithful dogs, most of them sleeping on the ground. An array of tents spread around the perimeter of the tainted area—military surplus and stolen camping tents—and from scent alone, Eve knew these had been pitched by the vampire horde.

Yet the most disturbing sight—the most hideous intrusion into paradise—towered above the others. In scarcely enough time for the vampires to finish setting up their tents, one or more of the demons that Abaddon had brought into Eden had created a massive structure the size and relative shape of a circus big top. It had not been built, however. From what Eve could see, the material had been woven like a spider's web, or spun into a kind of cocoon. The cocoon had not been completed. White jets of gossamer flew up through holes in its shell and continued to fill in those breaches. It might have been the womb for something unimaginable. This had been her first thought. But when she saw how many of the creatures worked industriously to shore up its foundations, pushing dirt up around the sides and carving window slits in its face, she realized it served a different purpose.

The demons were building a city, and this would be its center, gathering place, and seat of power. Abaddon would rule here. Some kind of new kingdom was being created, with him as its monarch.

Not going to happen, she thought.

Bastard thought he could hide out from the Demogorgon right here in Eden, that maybe somehow the Devourer wouldn't be able to pass through the Garden Gate. And perhaps he was right. They'd needed her blood—her pure, untainted blood from the days at the birth of the world—to open the gate. Maybe they truly would be safe here when the Outsider arrived at last.

But they'd made a terrible mistake. They'd brought Eve into the Garden with them, and they wouldn't be safe from her.

Perched on that branch, she closed her eyes and raised her face to the breeze. The odors that rose from that ruined part of Eden made her retch. Blood and bile rose up in the back of her throat. The lovely scents of other parts of the Garden were perverted by the stench of what evil had wrought.

But in among those odors, she found others. Her skin prickled with strength like she had never known, and her veins burned with Jophiel's divine blood. Even in the midst of the sensory overload that Eden and its intruders provided, she could sift and search. From the moment she had scrambled into that crook in the tree, she had caught a familiar scent. Eyes closed, she inhaled the wind and confirmed her belief. The aroma of rich, Turkish pipe tobacco reached her. Other odors mingled with it; Fey magic, ancient, unmistakable clay, and the musk of a she-wolf. This last was unfamiliar, but it combined inextricably with the others.

The Menagerie had been captured.

The scents came from the cairn-hut the Drows had built for Duergar. Conan Doyle and the others were being held there, and they were still alive. Of course, the ancient clay she smelled might belong to the shapeshifter called Legion, but with the other scents, she doubted that. It must be Clay. The thought made her skin prickle even more, her body tensing with anticipation. She wanted to see Clay again, quite desperately. Now that her memories of Eden had returned—

now that Jophiel had indicated that she hadn't been forgotten by the Creator at all—she had to talk to Clay. In all the worlds in existence, he was the only one who would understand all of the things in her cold heart. It did not beat, but she had at last come to understand that it had never really been dead.

Clay. Conan Doyle. Ceridwen. And what of Graves, Squire, and Danny?

No more time for thinking. There were far too many enemies for her to face alone. Eve needed allies, now. And she couldn't leave her friends in the hands of Abaddon. No one knew better than she how much a body and soul could be ruined by the demon's touch.

The wind blew cool across her naked flesh. The last time she had run naked across Eden she had been filled with shame. Now she felt nothing of the kind, filled instead with righteous determination. For a fleeting moment, she wondered if this return to the Garden without shame could be considered progress, or further corruption. She found she didn't much care.

Eve studied the encampment of the enemy a few seconds longer, then raced along a branch that should not have been able to support her weight. She leaped from it to a lower limb of another, thicker tree. She scrambled up through its tangle of leaves and leaped again. From tree to tree, up trunks and across branches, she traveled around the perimeter of the dying, withered clearing without a rustle or sway that could be attributed to anything but wind.

Her fingers extended into talons, she lowered herself hand over hand down through the screened interior of an evergreen born at the dawn of the world, then dropped to the ground. Eve landed in a crouch, suffused with the rush of angel blood. The wind whispered in her ears, yet it felt to her that it had slowed, that she moved now in between moments.

One of the vampire tents—a nylon camping setup spattered with dark bloodstains—stood thirty feet away. Eve scanned her surroundings. Demons moved in the Garden, sampling its delights, but none were nearby. The soil had become more arid, the grass more withered, in just the few moments since Eve had first taken measure of the camp. The edges of the tainted area continued to spread. As she paused, it touched the tree from which she'd just descended, and the bark facing the camp began to rot, then blacken. Leaves fell from the branches above her.

Hatred filled her with terrible venom. Eve darted from beneath that doomed tree and raced across the intervening space toward the vampires' tent. She scented them inside, two of the hollow leeches. Swift and sure as an angel, she slipped inside and brought them final death. Young, brash things they were. One of them sighed upon spying her, and she tore off its head. The other saw her—saw the changes the angel's blood had made in her—and sank to his knees wearing a look of surrender and damnation. Her talons raked its throat, then plunged into its chest and crushed the frozen, hardened nut of its heart.

She sliced open the back of the tent to reveal the view of Duergar's cairn that she had planned. This spot on the perimeter lay nearer to the stone dwelling than any other. A pair of vampires—messengers or scouts—raced across the tortured ground toward the cocoon, where Abaddon must even now have been holding court. On this side of the cairn were perhaps a dozen Drows. Two of them sat not far from the entrance of the cairn eating a once-proud stag, a beast of Eden, crunching bones and all in their teeth. Several others stood close together a short distance away, punching one another with their huge fists in some kind of game or ritual. They laughed in gravelly voices and grunted, and Eve almost felt sorry for them. Stupidity and belligerence were their only real sins. They followed Duergar because of his strength and cleverness, because he was both one of them and one of the magical Fey, and to the lumbering trolls this made him a natural leader. They followed him because they feared him, these innocent, idiotic things.

But they would die just the same. Their savagery came from not knowing any better, but they could not be reasoned with. Only death could stop them.

And sometimes not even that. For now that she had come closer, Eve saw that the Drows that were sprawled on the ground, those she'd thought were sleeping, were silent and still. They were dead. Their stink as corpses had been no worse than it had been when they were among the living, so she had missed that small fact. Undead Drows, roused, no doubt, by the demon's infernal power. Those that still lived were up and around. Those that lay inert on the ground were dead and would rise again when they were needed.

Eden would never be pure again.

Once again, Eve tested the air and found the scents of her friends even stronger. The soft light of the sky seemed almost not to reach the ground here, but it was nothing like night. Still, she could not wait for real darkness. Truly, she could not wait a moment. Another glance told her that, other than the Drows, there were no enemies within sight of the tent.

She bolted, keeping low to the ground and her tread light as could be. Otherwise, stealth be damned. Eve raced toward the Drows, wondering if the dead would stir. They did not. The laughing, muttering trio continued their odd game of punching one another. The two by the door, eating the stag, had begun to pick bone shards from their teeth with filthy fingers. As she sprinted for the cairn, they glanced up.

A figure loomed out of the darkness of that doorway. Duergar stood blocking her way, massive axe hanging in silhouette at his side. The white streak in his hair and his green eyes gleamed in the shadowed interior of that stone hut, and a swirl of Fey magic began to crackle around the blade of his axe.

Eve did not hesitate. She flicked her fingers outward and her talons lengthened even more. Blood sang in her ears, a choir of dead angels. From within the cairn she caught the scent of her friends and comrades even more strongly.

The dead Drows began to stir.

One of the two eating the stag smiled at her, and she saw terrible intelligence in its gaze, far greater than any of its ilk ought to have. Its flesh ran like mercury, and it became earth as dry as the soil beneath her feet, and it wore that garment peculiar to ancient Egypt that seemed so much like a skirt.

The moment she realized that Legion had been waiting for her, Eve knew it was a trap. Of course it was. She'd been so drunk on Jophiel's blood that it had never occurred to her that Abaddon would have been expecting her.

And just as his name entered her mind, as if summoned,

black wings blotted out Eden's sky above her. She cursed herself and the Creator and Jophiel and Abaddon and even Conan Doyle for letting the Menagerie get captured when they'd obviously come here to try to help her. Her glorious plan to free her allies and begin a counteroffensive to destroy the putrid creatures who'd tainted Eden unraveled in her mind.

Only one choice remained to her. Flight. Eve knew this, and yet for an eyeblink she hesitated, hating the idea of running. Why not stand and fight and make an end to things? If she could destroy Abaddon, the incursion of rot in Eden might fall apart. But she knew that was no solution. The high she'd gotten from the angel's blood had made her careless, not stupid. Full of hate and frustration, she made her decision.

At the last second, the wind blew and a new scent reached her—one with which she was all too familiar. A smile touched her lips. Above her, Abaddon drew a bloodred sword and stared at her in confusion, surprised by her grin.

Eve veered toward the three idiotic Drows—too foolish to be let in on the plan and only now becoming aware that anything odd was unfolding around them. The dead ones reached for her as they rose, but Eve easily eluded their grasp. The trio of moronic troll-beasts tried to grab at her as well, and Eve leaped into the air, somersaulting between two of them. As she flew by their heads she lashed out with her talons, tearing out their throats. The two fell, and the third became tangled with them, roaring in fury.

"Legion, no!" Eve heard Abaddon shout from the sky above her. "Leave her to me. I've waited too long for this. The final depravity."

She glanced back only once to see that Duergar had never left the doorway of his cairn-hut. Legion had closed to within a dozen feet of her but now stopped near the carnage of the two Drows she had murdered and the third, still buried beneath them, arms waving.

Then she sprinted, and once again it felt as though the winds of Eden were aiding her, sweeping her along. Several vampires had emerged and now moved to block her way. Eve only laughed as she sped through them, blood spraying the arid, ruined ground.

Black wings beat the air above her. She felt the presence of Abaddon as he swept down, closing in on her, as though his shadow coated her with the filth of his hideous purpose.

"Run, bitch," the demon sneered, his voice a whisper in her ears, as though he was right beside her. "But I'll have you again, in ways that will make the last time seem sweet and gentle."

He ought to have kept silent. She felt him descend upon her as she reached the perimeter of the encampment, and she dodged his grasp. Abaddon would not get a second chance. Eve entered the Garden, then, and this was her home, the place she walked in her dreams, whether she recalled them or not. She remembered now, though. Every step. Every hill. Every stream.

The demon cried out in rage and dropped to the ground. Abaddon could not fly through the tangle of trees and flowering plants that grew nearly as high. Now the veneer of humanity he sometimes wore disappeared. Like a bull, he crashed through the lush Garden, hooves pounding the ground, splintering tree roots, horns breaking branches, slowing him down.

Eve laughed, knowing it would infuriate him even more.

"Your friends will die!" Abaddon snarled. "Without your help, they'll be eviscerated. Their blood will feed the Garden."

She kept silent, twisting around trees, running amidst the flowers. Birds screamed and took wing. Animals rushed into the undergrowth in terror. Then Eve arrived at her destination, the stream. She dived in, submerging, and swam with the current. Her body knifed through the water and she knew that Abaddon would have heard the splash, would be hunting her even now.

When the current diminished, she knew she had reached her goal. Naked, water sluicing off her, she stood up from the stream and stepped out onto the soft bank. Abaddon burst through a screen of tangled plants, ripping orange blossoms and magenta flowers from their stalks. Chest heaving, the demon saw that she had stopped running. In his grin, she could see all the devils of Hell.

Eve grinned back.

Abaddon's gaze tracked upward, finally noticing just where their chase had led him.

She stood before the Tree of Knowledge, its base surrounded by prickly briar still splashed with the blood of Jophiel.

"Come on, Abaddon," Eve said, spreading her arms, letting the light glisten on the droplets of water sliding down her breasts and belly and legs. The fruit hung ripe from the tree, only feet away from her fingers.

"It's everything you've always wanted."

CONAN Doyle lay in the dark on the rough earthen floor inside Duergar's cairn. The half-Drow, half-Fey warrior had been reminiscing with him and regaling him with tales of what he would do to the mage as soon as Abaddon no longer had need of him. Conan Doyle's arms and legs were bound with something alive—black, slick things that wormed in and out of his fingers and between his wrists and ankles. Whatever these Hellspawn were, they leeched the magic from him somehow.

Far worse was the white, writhing maggot that plugged his mouth, swelling larger anytime he tried to move his tongue or speak past it. He breathed through his nose, trying desperately to keep from suffocating. Abaddon had kept them all as bait for Eve—and perhaps he had some other use for them as well—but Conan Doyle felt sure the demon would not weep if he were to choke to death on the vile, pulsing thing in his mouth.

He'd had no choice but to sit and listen to Duergar's mutterings and to endure the half-breed's sneer. When the monstrous Fey had knelt and run his hands roughly over Ceridwen's body, cupping her breasts, insinuating themselves inside the silk of her clothing, a murderous rage had filled him like never before. But he could do nothing, and neither could Ceri, who had been trussed up in the same fashion.

Iron chains bound Jelena, naked save for the wolf skin she wore like a cloak. Yet her sensuality had vanished with her captivity. No dignity remained for her. Not here. The ghost of Dr. Graves had been captured in a strange net that seemed constructed of ectoplasm, and in silent moments, Conan Doyle thought he could hear the net screaming. Somehow, it had been woven in Hell from the souls of the damned. Graves appeared to be unharmed and conscious, but he did not speak, nor would he raise his eyes when addressed.

Among them all, Clay was the only one who had not woken. He lay as he'd fallen—and been dropped here inside the stone hut—like an ancient statue, upended by vandals.

Duergar had left them alone in the gloom, only dim light filtering in from outside relieving the darkness. Something transpired beyond the door of the cairn—figures in motion, Duergar holding his axe as though ready for combat—but only when Conan Doyle heard the voice of Abaddon calling out did he realize that Eve had tried to reach them, and the demon now pursued her.

The irony struck him, but he could not laugh, could not even grin in amusement, with the bulbous maggot squirming in his mouth. He took several deep breaths through his nose and glanced over again to see that Duergar had disappeared from the doorway of the cairn-hut. For the moment, they were alone. Surrounded by enemies, yes, but within those stone walls, they were unobserved.

Conan Doyle tensed against the bonds that twisted themselves around his wrists and fingers. If he could slip even one hand free . . . but he could not. They tightened whenever he moved. When he tried to contort his fingers to form a sigil or to scratch runes in the dirt, they reacted, jerking his digits into other positions. A quick glance told him Ceridwen had started the same process but had no greater luck than he. She ought to have been able to summon ice or fire from the air or roots from the ground to do her bidding. Conan Doyle had deduced that this tainted ground—the part of Eden soiled by the presence of demons—had simply been killed. All the elemental spirits that had been here had been destroyed or driven out. And the eel-like things that bound him and

Ceridwen both, sapping their magic, prevented her from drawing the elements to her from elsewhere in Eden.

He began to wonder what would happen if he bit into the maggot in his mouth. Its blood and other fluids would spill down his throat, and he would likely vomit. Coughing would not eject the intruding creature, but perhaps he could regurgitate it, if its blood did not poison or taint him forever and if it did not use the opportunity to thrust itself down his open throat, clogging his airways entirely.

All of this crossed his mind in seconds. The risk seemed foolish, but under the circumstances, he felt he had little other choice.

Then a frown furrowed his brow. Conan Doyle blinked. He felt a presence in the cairn-hut with them and a breeze that did not come from the open doorway. His nose wrinkled with the scent of wet dog, and he heard heavy breathing.

"Wow, you guys are totally screwed, huh?"

Had he been able to do so, at that moment Conan Doyle would have cheered. He twisted his head to get a better view of the door. In the shadow of the stones that made up the arched doorway stood a small, misshapen figure, bedecked with weapons. Squire came toward him, and Conan Doyle saw motion behind him. A moment later, Danny Ferrick stepped out of the darkness similarly armed and followed by the shadow hound, Shuck.

Danny's arms were full of swords, daggers, axes, and a shotgun-style weapon Conan Doyle had never seen before. Its short barrel had a wide mouth that made the mage think of an old-fashioned blunderbuss.

Squire unsheathed a dagger that caught the glint of the light from the door. A Gemini Blade, Conan Doyle felt sure, made of the hobgoblin's own metal alloy combining iron and silver. It would kill vampires, Fey, and Drow alike . . . and the demons wouldn't enjoy the kiss of one of those blades either.

"Enough of this lying around shit, boss," Squire muttered, a grin on his face. He sliced the wormlike Hellspawn from Conan Doyle's legs, then from his wrists.

"Oh, and by the way . . . big fuckin' raise. I'm just saying."

As Danny raced over to do the same for Ceridwen, Conan Doyle raised both hands, his fingers surrounded now by blue-tinted fire that crackled in the darkness. He started to reach for his mouth, for his throat, then changed his mind. Narrowing his eyes he turned away from Squire and the others and a gout of cobalt blue magic shot from his mouth, disintegrating the maggot the demon had placed there.

He glanced over at Ceridwen in time to see her rise, the thing in her mouth spilling out in shards of shattered ice.

Her violet eyes gleamed, and a cold wind eddied around her. Icy mist formed around one fist and pure fire around the other. Her powers were weakened on this spot, but not gone.

"I want to kill them all," she said.

Conan Doyle reached out a hand to her, and his magic touched elemental sorcery. He nodded.

"Excellent plan. Simple. I like it."

Shuck had trotted over and closed his jaws on the net of souls that held Dr. Graves. The shadow beast dragged the net away, and, for the first time since their captivity, the ghost met Conan Doyle's gaze. His spectral translucent form shimmered in the dark and twin holsters appeared, one under each arm. He drew his phantom guns and nodded without speaking.

Conan Doyle gestured toward Jelena. Her iron chains fell away, clanking to the ground. Her eyes narrowed with such ferocity that it overshadowed her nudity. Danny didn't fail to notice, however. He stared at her breasts and gently sloping belly the way only a teenaged boy ever could, entranced.

Jelena drew the wolf skin tightly around her, pulled it over her head, and dropped to the ground on all fours. When she looked up at him, her golden eyes were the she-wolf's once more.

Ceridwen chose weapons from the pile Danny had left on the ground. Conan Doyle did the same. Their magic ought to be enough, but against an army, an arsenal could only help. He reached for the blunderbuss.

"Ah-ah, I don't think so," Squire said. The hobgoblin grabbed the big-mouthed gun. "That one's for me."

Only Clay remained.

"What's up with him?" Danny asked, staring down at the

shapeshifter, not so interested in Jelena now that she was no longer a naked woman.

"He's sleeping."

Conan Doyle knelt beside Clay, fearful that his answer was woefully inadequate. If the creature they'd seen—Legion—really was Clay's brother somehow, there was no telling what sort of trauma their contact had caused. He held up a hand and summoned a light, which shone down on Clay's immobile face. Some of the dry, cracked earth that made up his forehead had altered its color, and there were ridges that had not been there before. It looked almost as though something was attached to Clay's face.

"Hello, old friend," Conan Doyle whispered, bent down beside him. "Time to wake up, now. We need you, Clay. More than ever, I fear. Trust me, you don't want to sleep through this."

Nothing happened.

Troubled, he glanced around at the rest of the Menagerie. Shuck whined low. Conan Doyle glanced outside, then nodded to Ceridwen and Graves and tilted his head toward the door. Someone moved back and forth in front out there, shadow blocking the light. They had only seconds.

The she-wolf growled softly.

"What now?" Danny asked, jittery and anxious, ready for a fight.

Conan Doyle took the blunderbuss from Squire's hands. The hobgoblin started to protest, but shut up when the mage leveled the barrel of the big gun at Clay's forehead and pulled the trigger.

Iron and silver pellets blew off the top of Clay's head. The sound boomed through the cairn-hut, echoing off the walls, even as Danny started screaming at him, asking what the hell he'd done. Other shouts came from outside. The ground shook with the approach of their enemies.

In the dirt, different shades of clay sifted away from one another. Clay's head re-formed, though very roughly. Then his entire body shifted, earth flowing into flesh as he transformed into a creature unlike anything Conan Doyle had seen before—a strange mixture of bear and rhinoceros, and something else he couldn't name.

Clay staggered to his feet and shook himself. He glanced at Conan Doyle. "Thanks for that."

The mage gave a small bow of his head as he handed Squire back the blunderbuss.

Jelena threw back her head and let loose a howl that shook the stones of the cairn, a cry of anguish and fury. From a distance, even through the walls of the cairn, they heard the cries of a thousand beasts of Eden, howling in reply.

"They're coming," the she-wolf snarled.

"Arthur," Ceridwen said, his name a caress.

Conan Doyle looked up to see Duergar stepping into the stone hut, axe raised. He lifted his other hand, and the earth around them began to tremble, about to split and perhaps swallow them all.

Ceridwen raised both hands and shouted a summons to the spirits of the wind. They answered. She gestured toward Duergar, who gnashed his teeth, glistening tusks already covered in the blood of some poor creature. The wind struck him with such force that Conan Doyle heard bones breaking. The entire wall around the door collapsed, stones tumbling down as Duergar tumbled end over end across the ravaged patch of the Garden of Eden.

Dust flew up from the collapsed wall. Vampires and Drows came at a run. Coinn Iotair, the dog-beasts they'd fought in the Twilight Wars, raced at their sides. The demons would arrive in moments—already something hideous circled above their heads.

Duergar rose to one knee. He nodded as though pleased that the moment had finally arrived. As one, weapons raised, magic swirling around them, phantom bullets flying, the Menagerie erupted from the wreckage of the stone hut.

The true battle for Eden had begun.

16

THE wind kicked up dust from the dry, loose soil beneath
Ceridwen's feet. A glance over her shoulder revealed the beginnings of some hellish city being built. Demons from a
dozen theologies and cosmologies worked at the base of the
bizarre cocoon-structure that overshadowed the volcanic-
looking earthen tower beside it. Some walked on hooves,
heads heavy with horns. Others were headless things with
saw-toothed mouths gaping in their bellies. There were insectoid things and larval crawlers, moist, half-melted things
and others that defied description.

But the demons either had not noticed the disturbance or
were in no hurry to respond.

The air filled with shouts and cries and the distant howls
of the beasts of the Garden of Eden. At the edges of the
wretched camp, birds of prey darted out from the trees and
began to circle. The odd shotgun Squire had brought barked
loudly.

Conan Doyle called to her. She nodded without turning
his way. They were in battle together, again. No matter what
they felt for one another, they would not allow their love to
distract them. If the melee went badly, and death seemed imminent, only then would they come together, reaching for a
final embrace before the end. Until then, they would bring
their wrath upon their enemies, swift and merciless, for evil
had no mercy in its heart or no heart with which to cradle
mercy.

Clay charged the undead rotting Drows that tried to attack

them, shouting his brother's name, an anguish in his voice Ceridwen had never heard before. The ghost of Dr. Graves flitted across the battlefield so quickly her eyes could not track him. Only the shots that rang from his phantom guns pinpointed his location for her. A band of vampires, ancient by the look of them—and only creatures of such age would be allowed by Abaddon to station themselves this close to the center of camp—swept in from the left. Jelena howled again, then bounded into the air, claws stripping away faces and slashing throats. Hawks and huge eagles dived from the sky and clawed at the vampires' eyes.

Twenty feet away from her, Duergar rose to his feet. His fingers opened and closed on the handle of his axe, getting a better grip. It glowed dully in the dim light that filtered down from Eden's sky. His orange-red hair flowed in the wind, its white stripe like some kind of scar on his head. The tribal marking on his forehead seemed not black but bloodred.

"Kill her," the half-breed snarled, teeth gnashing as though he could not wait to tear into her with the tusks that jutted from his lower jaw.

The Drows were not intelligent creatures, but they understood killing well enough. Their dead were even slower than the living. Even so, they closed in around her.

Ceridwen tensed. Across her back she had slung a Gemini sword that Squire had forged. Where he'd hidden these weapons all of this time, she had no idea, but she had never appreciated the hobgoblin more. In her right hand, she held a katar forged from the same mystical alloy. The blade was long and wide, and she held it in her fist as the Drows came toward her.

"You waste my time with such as these," Ceridwen called to Duergar.

The first Drow lunged for her. She swept the katar in front of her and sliced off its right arm, the silver-and-iron blade cleaving rough leathery flesh and bone with ease. The Drow screamed and clutched at her with its left hand. Ceridwen spun inside its grasp and drove her elbow up into its gut. As it groaned and bent over, gasping for breath, she spun again and whipped the katar around, slashing its throat.

A second Drow tromped toward her. The Princess of

Faerie pistoned her legs and dived at it, katar held before her in both hands. The monstrosity was slow and could not grab her before the blade split its abdomen. The katar sank to her wrists in its guts and Ceridwen twisted it. A hot torrent of blood and viscera spilled onto her arms.

The corpses fell simultaneously, the dry soil greedily drinking the stinking ichor that bled from them. Abaddon's power would raise them soon enough, but not yet.

Ceridwen faced Duergar. Annoyance contorted the warrior's features.

"You're more formidable than I recall," the half-blood said, green eyes narrowing. "But your magic is diminished here, cousin, and you won't find me as slow and stupid as the Drows."

A smile touched the corners of Ceridwen's lips. The wind gusted, blowing strands of her blond hair across her face.

"Not as slow, perhaps, but no less stupid, Duergar. Magic diminished is not magic erased. Are you truly such a fool? I killed your lackeys by hand because I wanted to wash in their blood. I'm Fey by birth, an elementress by nature, but the Twilight Wars made me a warrior as well. I've more weapons than sorcery. And as for my 'diminished' power . . ."

Ceridwen dropped to one knee, driving the katar deep into the dry soil. The scent of fresh, sweet earth rose up from within.

"The taint of your demonic allies has not spread as far as they would like us all to think."

Duergar began to speak, muttering some denial, she felt sure. But Ceridwen did not listen. The elemental spirits of Eden flowed up from the soil and into her. With a single desire, she located the roots of a tree that had once stood here and teased it upward, nurturing it in seconds. The tree thrust up through the ruined earth, leaves rustling as they grew, dry ground cracking as it was pushed away. Sweet, lush fruit weighed down the branches. New, healthy grass burst from the ground around the tree, and the restored area began to spread, transforming the land all around her. In the space of a few heartbeats, the dead Drows lay on a patch of Paradise.

Ceridwen left the katar buried in the ground. She snapped off a branch and in her hand it grew into her elemental staff.

Fire flickered at its head, and an ice sphere formed around that flame.

The half-blood creature, Duergar of Faerie, laughed at her. "Sorcery or not, I'll have you, princess. You survived our last encounter only because I was told to distract you, not to kill you."

"Perhaps," she replied, staff in hand, Gemini sword slung across her back. The spirits of the wind danced around her, whipping at her hair and her dress. The ground shifted under her feet as roots spread, and more of the tainted soil was reclaimed. She could feel the presence of water running far below the surface. The fire elementals sparked in the air around her.

"But circumstances have changed."

Moments ago, Ceridwen had been diminished, just as her enemy believed. But she had connected with Paradise once more. The elements here were more pure than anything she'd ever felt, and she felt suffused with their power.

"I'm an elemental sorceress in the Garden of Eden, you fool. And Eden is on my side."

DANNY fought side by side with Conan Doyle. Danny had known that Doyle was one of the most powerful mages in the world, and he'd seen the man's magic in action, but never anything like this. A couple of zombified troll-dudes came at them. Conan Doyle raised a hand, and a flash of purplish light flowed from his fingers. The Drows rotted down to bone, then even the bones crumbled.

"Hey, boss!" Danny called, mimicking Squire. "Leave some for me!"

Off to the right, the hobgoblin shouted something the demon boy couldn't hear over all the shouting and killing.

Vampires had started to surround them, the bloodsuckers rushing in from all sides of the camp. They were an array of leeches from filthy to regal, of every race and style of dress, but they were all the same to him—all maggots with their mouths open like lampreys, waiting for something to suck on.

Danny didn't give Conan Doyle a chance to hog all the

fun. He ran to meet the leeches as they swarmed around him
and the mage. In his hands was a long, curved scimitar made
with the Gemini alloy. Danny swung the blade in an arc that
decapitated the first vampire to get near him and chopped
through the torso of the second. Then three of them were on
him. One sank its teeth into his throat. Danny drew a silver-
and-iron dagger from a sheath at his hip and shanked the
vamp through the right eye. The ones he'd killed exploded in
a burst of ash that eddied away on the wind.

They were many. Another vampire grabbed him from behind. Danny shot his head back, shattering her face with his
skull, then twisted in her grasp and drove the small points of
his horns into her cheek. He struck her with the dagger so
hard that it broke through her chest and burrowed into her
heart. Danny twisted around, but then the dagger was
knocked from his left hand.

Fine by him. The sword was easier to wield with two
hands.

Out of the corner of his eye, Danny saw movement at the
edge of the camp. A glance made him pause in amazement.
Animals raced out onto the ruined ground, some of them still
howling in response to the wolf-babe's voice. He saw a pride
of lions, huge elks or something, gorillas—freakin' gorillas—and all sorts of other animals. They started trashing the
vampires tents and chasing down some of the leeches.

Danny laughed out loud.

Claws raked his back.

He spun to find a demon looming above him. It had
curved horns like a ram that were bigger than its head,
weighing its skull down so that a huge hump stuck up from
its back. Its arms hung by its sides, and its matted fur dripped
with some foul ooze. Its withered, vestigial lower body
twitched, dragging behind it, little more than a husk, so that
it floated in the air. Hundreds of beetles clicked and crawled
on its face, eating the flesh and each other.

It spoke the language of some ancient Hell—and Danny
understood.

"You should be with us, child," the demon spit.

"Yeah, no," Danny said. "Been through all that, but
thanks."

He drove the Gemini sword into its face and twisted, coring its skull. The demon faltered and sank to the ground, flopping around. The blade had lodged in the bones of its head, and as Danny tried to remove it, the beetles raced up the metal toward his hands. He let go and backed off.

"Fuck it, take the sword. Close up and personal is more fun."

Conan Doyle shouted something, and Danny turned in alarm. But the words were a spell and as the demon boy spotted him, a ripple of sorcerous power swept from the mage's hands, and the vampires all dropped to their hands and knees and began to puke up blood. It streamed from their eyes and noses and ears. As the blood left them, they withered until their flesh was as dry and cracked as the ground beneath them. One by one, they crumbled to chalky dust.

"Nice!" Danny called.

Conan Doyle glanced at him, then ran toward him. Danny turned to see a couple of demons flying down at them from above, wingless things with scorpion tails. More vampires were gathering for another rush. A couple of dead Drows lumbered their way.

"So, am I gonna be in trouble for disobeying, skipping out on house-sitting duty?" Danny asked, arching an eyebrow.

Conan Doyle actually grinned. "Not bloody likely."

The monsters kept coming. Danny laughed and, side by side, he and Mr. Doyle prepared to give them a bit of monster in return.

CLAY felt aware of every atom in his body. He grunted, chest heaving, and marched across the ruined ground. Undead Drows—resurrected again and again by Abaddon's demonic power—tried to slow him or to kill him. The tallest of them stood fourteen feet, but in this form Clay himself was only a few feet shy of that mark. The Drows grappled with him, and Clay tore them apart. He drove the horns on his rhino head into their chests and backs to rip them open, then thrust the matted, hairy claws of a bear into their bodies and broke them up into pieces, scattering their remains.

That would take awhile to recover from. Even Abaddon's power might not be able to repair them now.

Squire shouted something to him. Clay glanced over and saw the hobgoblin and his shadow hound, Shuck, under attack by a pack of Coinn Iotair. The dog-beasts didn't stand a chance. Shuck picked one up and shook it in his teeth so fiercely that pieces of it tore off and flew around the hound's head. Squire shoved the wide barrel of his shotgun into the open jaws of another Coinn Iotair and pulled the trigger, evaporating its head. Then the hobgoblin started swinging a Gemini-bladed axe around—a double-sided war axe that Clay coveted. The little bastard might not know sorcery, but he was a magician at the forge.

With a growl, another Drow lumbered toward Clay. As he started toward it, a shadow passed over his face. He glanced upward to see a falcon dropping down from the sky. A pair of lions leaped on a vampire a stone's throw away, and Clay felt hope spark in him. Jelena had summoned the animals of Eden to their aid, drastically improving their odds.

But the falcon didn't veer off toward one of his enemies. It dropped toward Clay, talons raised and aimed at his face. With a single beat of its wings, the falcon rippled on the air, growing, shifting its form into that of a massive gryphon, the mythical beast with the body of a lion and the wings and head of an eagle.

Legion.

Clay braced himself and raised his bear claws just as the gryphon slammed into him. They crashed to the ground together in an earth-shaking tumble of claws and horns, talons and wings. The eagle's beak dug into the matted fur of his chest and tore away a strip of skin and muscle. Clay let out a roar as he struggled with the shapeshifter who'd masqueraded as him. Blood spilled onto his fur.

With a thought, he changed. A silverback gorilla with a tiger's head. Powerful, feline jaws clamped down on the foreleg of the gryphon, and he ripped tendon and meat, muzzle soaking in blood. They struggled against one another. Legion raked gryphon claws across Clay's chest and back, opening up foot-long gashes that spilled even more blood, which the dry, ravaged ground greedily absorbed.

Clay twisted the gryphon around, got an arm around its throat, and jerked, snapping bones in its neck. With all of his strength he forced the shapeshifter over, slammed one foot onto its spine, and tore off one of its wings with a crackle of marrow.

Legion screamed. The sound made Clay rejoice and grieve at the same time.

His brother—and he felt sure now that this was true, that somehow the other shapeshifter truly was his brother, for what else could he be?—transformed into a serpent and coiled instantly around his leg. Clay reached down to tear the thing from his body, and Legion changed again, taking the form of an outback dingo. Jaws clamped on Clay's hand and tore away fingers. The dingo swallowed without chewing.

They were at one another then in a flurry of claws and blows, beneath a rainstorm of spattering blood. Their flesh changed so swiftly—breaking, ripping, healing, and re-forming, reabsorbing what had been carved away—that neither could gain the upper hand. Clay caved in the chest of a dragonlike beast even as it incinerated his face with fire and ripped off his left arm with a swipe of claws like scythes. Legion transformed into an enormous python, and Clay used alligator's jaws to snap the thing in half.

Still, the bloodshed continued. They healed and inflicted hideous injury on one another again and again until their battle transcended time and flesh. To Clay, it seemed there had never been a time when agony did not sear his every fiber. Once, he had been limited to the creatures that had existed in the human world, but Legion's touch had changed that, perhaps awakened a memory of other worlds the Creator had breathed into life, or unshackled possibilities in his mind that Clay had not allowed himself to pursue.

It only meant there were infinite ways for them to hate, and to hurt, one another.

Then Legion leaped away, putting space between them, and his flesh flowed into earth once more. He stood before Clay in the Egyptian garb he favored, a hairless, earthen creature much larger than any man. Clay took a breath, waiting for Legion to attack again, but when that did not happen, he reverted to what he had always considered his true form. He became a mirror image of Legion, this time right down to the color and texture of the Egyptian clothing.

His brother leaped at him. Clay raised his arms to defend himself but that was what Legion had hoped for. Their hands joined, clasped together in an impossibly equal test of will and strength. Teeth gritted, they struggled like that, each trying to force the other back or break the grip.

When the dry, cracked clay of Legion's palms merged with his own, he felt it happen. A tremor went through him, and he nearly collapsed. But it wasn't like the feeling he'd had when Legion had plunged a hand into his head. That contact had stunned Clay into catatonia and unlocked memories of the infinite inside of him. Once done, it could not be done again. This time, the contact did not harm him, but it had a more insidious effect.

Images battered his mind and soul. *The burning of Alexandria. The rape of street urchins in Babylon. Screams and flayed skin and scarlet splashes. The thrill of the torture devices of the Spanish Inquisition, breaking and tearing and crushing accused witches. Eating the flesh from the bones of Christians in the lion pits beneath the Coliseum. The smell of burning, diseased corpses in the death fields of plague-stricken Europe. Striding through the gas chambers at Birkenau, grinning down on the withered and dying, laughing at them as they died.*

And more. And more. And more.

"No," Clay whispered.

"Oh, yes," Legion replied, their hands still locked together, sealed flesh to flesh, clay to clay. "He cast us out, brother. Tore us apart from each other and tossed us away like garbage."

Clay shoved against him, drove him back a few steps. He squeezed his eyes closed as he recalled the memories that had visited him while he'd been catatonic. Legion's words were not quite truth, but they were not lies. The Creator had ripped them in two—one the loving, questioning spirit and one the fury and frustration—and that had been how they lived their lives down across all the ages of mankind.

In all that time, not once had the Creator returned to them. Not to bless Clay or to damn Legion.

His brother shoved back, and Clay stumbled, went down on one knee.

"That's right, brother," Legion rasped, pushing down from above him. "Surrender. Die. End the Almighty's repulsive experiment. Isn't it worth sacrificing yourself just to find out if it'll make the son of a bitch sit up and pay attention?"

Clay looked up into those hate-filled eyes, and pistoned himself upward. He slammed his forehead into Legion's face, and the two of them broke apart, a scattering of dirt falling from their hands as they separated.

"I have questions," Clay admitted. "But I won't have them answered at the expense of my friends' lives or the fate of infinite worlds."

Legion laughed, acid in his tone. "Daddy's good boy."

He launched himself at Clay, and the carnage began again.

THE ghost of Dr. Graves helped where he could. Phantom bullets had little effect on the Drows, but those dull-witted monstrosities could do nothing to harm him. Vampires and demons were another story. His ectoplasmic bullets tore their flesh, spun them around, knocked them down, and just generally pissed them off. The bloodsuckers could be killed if he eradicated their hearts. Some of the lesser demons died just as strong men would have. But there were other demons that might have ripped his soul apart and tossed it into the air like confetti, denying him eternity. He avoided them and tried to tell himself he wasn't a coward.

Spectral and devastating, he visited all of his allies, coming to the aid of Conan Doyle and Danny, then Ceridwen. He obliterated a bulbous-eyed, disgusting demon carried by a dozen lesser abominations that looked almost like babies, destroying them all before the demon could cover Squire in the boiling, putrid mucus it vomited as some kind of weapon. Dr. Graves helped Jelena, the she-wolf, and the beasts of Eden wherever he could. The animals were brutal and swift, and soon the vampires were few and far between, and nearly all of the Coinn Iotair had been dragged down and slaughtered.

When he came upon Clay and Legion, the ghost knew he had to help. Just watching them tearing each other's flesh and breaking bones, plucking out eyes and organs, he felt as though he might be sick. Long dead, Graves knew his revulsion and nausea could amount to nothing, but it hurt his spirit to bear witness to their carnage.

He stood there on ground that had been ravaged and scarred only moments before but which now sprouted with new green grass and flowers—Ceridwen's doing, he felt sure. The ghost of Dr. Graves leveled his phantom guns at the dueling shapeshifters and could not discern a single clue that might have told him which of them was his friend and which his enemy.

"Clay!" he shouted. "Give me a sign!"

Both of them tried to speak, but neither allowed the other a word. More blood flew.

An eerie keening filled the air and Graves glanced past them. A quartet of demons raced at the shapeshifters. They were awful things, with tentacles where their faces should have been, gnashing jaws in their chests, and mosquito wings. Their arms ended in three-fingered claws with what appeared to be strange proboscises that would suck the fluids from their victims.

"Damn it!" Graves muttered.

He started firing. Bullets tore into the demons. Chest shots seemed to have the desired effect, slowing them down. Soft, pustulant flesh split, and sickly yellow, viscous fluid drooled from the wounds.

One of the shapeshifters turned to try to fight them off.

The other only laughed and used the opportunity to rip open his brother's abdomen.

Graves swore and gritted his teeth. He had his answer.

Abandoning any pretense of solidity, the specter darted toward Legion, swept up like a wraith behind him, and raised both guns. Dr. Graves pulled both triggers again and again, splattering bits of Clay's brother onto the attacking demons. As Legion fell, Graves shot him a dozen more times in every part of his body.

He turned to the demons, helping Clay to finish them off, waiting for an attack from behind at any time. Legion wouldn't be dead. The ghost could practically feel the hatred of the shapeshifter on his back.

But when the four demons were dead, tentacles and proboscises twitching on the ground, Graves and Clay turned to find that Legion had vanished.

"Where—" the ghost began.

"No idea," Clay said, glancing around desperately, searching for a continuation of a vicious struggle neither brother could ever win.

"We'll catch up with him," Graves replied, though he felt little confidence that they would. Not if Legion did not want them to catch up.

Together, ghost and shapeshifter waded into the battle once more, going to the aid of their friends. Dr. Graves looked at the horizon and saw that the demons Abaddon had invited to infiltrate Eden had begun to spill from the strange constructions of their encampment in greater numbers.

The Menagerie had taken the upper hand, but only for the moment.

Now they faced the renegades of a hundred Hells.

EVE stood in the shadow of the Tree of Knowledge and licked her lips with the memory of tasting its fruit, of the nectar that ran down her chin and blossomed the light of sweet epiphany in her mind. It had woken her spirit. She ought to have felt hatred for the serpent in the Garden, whose forked tongue had seduced her into disobeying the Creator's will, but she had never been able to blame the devil. Once she had bitten into the fruit, though the sin stained her with every drop of juice that dripped from her lips, she could not bring herself to regret.

She had never been sorry. Not when she brought Adam to the Tree and tempted him to taste its fruit so that he would feel himself full of wonder just as she had; not even when the damned angels had driven her and Adam from paradise. It had taken her eons to confess that to herself, but she felt free, now. Somehow, she felt free.

"Come, Abaddon," Eve sighed, running a hand over her curves and glancing up at the Tree, its succulent fruit so close, though the briars made it unobtainable. "You know you want it."

Never had the demon looked so hideous, even in the midst of the depravity he had perpetrated against her. All traces of the elegant façade he sometimes wore had been scoured away by his hatred and determination. Eve felt sure, though, that this was not even his true face. What she saw was only scratching the surface of the real evil Abaddon represented. Beneath his exterior there lay an endless cesspool of filth and disease, an abyss filled with malice.

Abaddon's chest rose and fell. Crimson-black flesh rippled with movement of corded muscles underneath, and perhaps other things that slithered inside his skin. His horns had sprouted offshoots, seventy-seven prongs, so that they were now more like heavy antlers. Tiny things, demonic parasites, capered in those antlers or hung from the prongs like leeches.

When the demon grinned, jaws unhinging, hanging wide, his rows of fangs pushed outward, jutting to extreme lengths.

"There's nothing here I want, temptress, except for your suffering," Abaddon said, his voice a leer. "I will see you plead for death; and then I will strip away all hope and spirit and belief that there's a scrap of goodness left in this existence, and I will see you suffer more until the light finally goes from your eyes, and the madness and bloodlust sets in. Then I will wait as long as it takes for you to free yourself, to awaken to what new carnage you might have caused. I'll see the self-loathing and despair in your eyes, and it will begin again. Only when I'm certain there is nothing left of you but the evil, the hunger, will I snuff your flame."

Eve heard the words, but did not listen. She saw the way the demon's eyes flickered from her body to the Tree, to the forbidden fruit.

Abaddon took a step toward her, but there was caution in that step.

"Look at you, quivering like a schoolgirl," Eve said, laughing softly. "You talk big, but I see the temptation in you. You're transparent. I'm not the tender-fleshed creature I was when we first met. Are you sure you can kill me. If you don't, you'll never get to the fruit."

"I didn't come here for that, or for you!" the demon

protested in a snarl, shaking his head like a bull about to charge.

"No. You didn't. I know why you came. Because you're a fucking coward, and you wanted someplace to hide from the Demogorgon and you figured if there was anyplace that might truly be inviolate, this would be it. But the Tree's right here in front of you, Abaddon, and so am I. Come on. Take what you want. Taste it. I'll give it willingly."

That startled him. The demon narrowed his eyes and took half a step back. "You think I'm a fool?"

"Well, yeah!" she said, grinning. "But that's not what this is about."

Abaddon roared and started toward her. His hooves splashed in the stream, and he stopped there, raised both taloned hands, and gestured at her. Black fire ballooned into a sphere around his hands, then exploded outward, searing the air toward her.

Eve slipped aside as though the wind moved her. And perhaps it had.

That discharge of demonic power—of hellfire—burned past her and struck the tangle of briars surrounding the base of the Tree. They crackled and charred black in an instant, then fell away to nothing but cinders.

"See," Eve said, arching an eyebrow, moving in a sort of willowy glide that accentuated her body. Her voice dropped an octave, suggesting everything a Lord of Hell could imagine. "You didn't want to destroy me. Not with that attack. Had you meant to, I'd be dead, wouldn't I? You're the demon Abaddon. You kill what you intend to kill. Which tells me what you really wanted was to destroy those briars, open yourself up a path to the Tree."

"You're mocking me!" the demon roared, stomping his hooves and stepping from the stream, talons opening and closing. Black pus drooled from the corners of his mouth as he stared his hatred at her. "Have you truly forgotten, Eve? Did you forget what it was like the last time I had you at my mercy? The last time I—"

"Enough," she said, voice soft and low.

As she said it, she stepped through the section of charred bramble and reached up to the Tree. Her fingers caressed a piece of fruit, and she heard Abaddon give up a gasp that sounded like Hell's version of a prayer.

Eve plucked the fruit from the Tree and turned to Abaddon. There beneath the boughs of the Tree of Knowledge, she held the fruit out toward him, just as she had done once before, at the beginning of the world.

"Think of it," she said. "You defiled the mother of humanity and despoiled Paradise. You pretend otherwise, but isn't it all about spitting in the Creator's eye? Ruining what is most precious to Him? Now you have a chance to taste that which has always been forbidden, to your kind most of all."

Abaddon hesitated, almost mesmerized by the ripe fruit.

"You call me temptress, but you know there's more to it than that. I was the first to be tempted, yes. But He put the Tree here to tempt us all. Take it, Abaddon. Taste what He wishes to deny you, like you always have. He must have a plan, even for Hell, even for your kind. Eat of the Tree and your eyes will open. You'll see God's plan for the universe and understand your place in it. How can you resist?"

The ripe fruit lay upon her palm, ripe and dappled with moisture. Its aroma filled the clearing, richer and sweeter than the mead of Asgard, pure as Eden itself. The fruit exuded the scent of paradise, of divinity and perfection . . . of Heaven.

Abaddon's desire writ itself upon his features. He leaned toward her, somehow diminished by his lust for the fruit—for the knowledge she had tempted him with.

"You've some trick planned," he said, his voice a rasp and his gaze riveted upon the fruit in her hand.

"Really?" Eve asked.

She lifted the fruit to her lips and sank her fangs into it, breaking the tender skin and tearing the ripe flesh. Its juice ran down over her chin and dripped treacle upon her breasts. Eve shuddered with pleasure and anguish. She had tasted of this fruit before, and it had cost the world Paradise. The cost had been even higher than that. Yet still the taste rippled through her with bliss and an unparalleled arousal that transcended the sexual.

"Mmmm," she murmured, letting Abaddon see her shiver, and the way it made her body arch.

Mesmerized, Abaddon came toward her. Eve took a step back and reached up for the lowest branches of the tree. She pulled herself up and perched there in the crook of the tree, holding the fruit out toward him. The demon plucked it from her hand, raised the fruit to his lips, and bit into it.

He tasted the knowledge that God had forbidden.

The demon stiffened and threw his head back, sucking air into his lungs as though it were his last breath. His red eyes went wide, and the fruit tumbled from his hand to fall to the ground, soiled by dirt and the ashes of the brambles that had surrounded the tree.

Abaddon's mouth fell open, and he began to whimper. The demon fell to his knees, jerking spasmodically.

The words he choked out were in the language of angels before the Fall, a language he'd not been allowed to speak since the Creator had cast him out along with Lucifer and all of his traitorous brethren. It had been the language of Paradise as well, once upon a time.

"How can this be?" Abaddon asked.

The question was not for her. Eve understood that it had been directed at the one who had sown the seeds of Paradise . . . sown the seeds of everything. Twice, now, she had eaten of the Tree and she knew that the knowledge its fruit provided was a rose with thorns. That knowledge was understanding . . . awareness of the self.

As she watched, Abaddon buckled and fell to the ground, still twisting in anguish. Tears of liquid fire and blood raced down from the corners of his eyes—perhaps the first time a demon had ever wept.

"You understand now, don't you? Bastard," Eve whispered as she slipped down from the branches of the Tree. "You've a glimmer of what it means to have a soul and to suffer the things you did to me."

"I . . . I remember," Abaddon said.

Weakly, hideous mouth twisted in agony, he forced himself to his knees. The demon glared up at her from beneath knitted brows and the heavy, vicious horns upon his head. All of the evil Abaddon had ever perpetrated now returned to him, but he'd been awakened to the horror of his deeds.

Eve smiled, licking the juice from her fingers. "What you feel now, demon, is remorse."

Abaddon snarled at her. One corner of his mouth lifted to reveal black fangs, and he managed to rise on one knee. "You overestimate your God, bitch. He made me. He had a plan for me, and for all of us. And that plan included rebellion. It included our Fall. He knew what we would become. Demons were a part of the plan from the start. Whatever I am, Eve, He made me.

"Remorse? Perhaps. But hatred, and fury? Oh, yes. Most certainly. If evil is what I am, then He is to blame. If redemption is possible, I don't want it. I spit in the face of the Creator. Piss on Him. Fuck forgiveness."

Slowly, off-balance, Abaddon began to rise.

Sorrow enveloped Eve as she stared at the demon. She did not understand. Forgiveness was all that she had ever wanted.

"Have it your way," she said.

Eve lunged at him. Abaddon raised his arms to try to defend himself, but the taste of the fruit had overwhelmed and drained him. One talon raked her chest, dragging furrows in the tender flesh of her breasts. But it began to heal almost instantly, even as blood mingled with the juice that had dripped on her.

Then she had him. Eve tore her claws along both sides of Abaddon's face, slicing his eyes, which burst and dribbled black-red fluid. Abaddon screamed and doubled over, hands going to his face. Eve drove her knee into his head, and something in his skull cracked. She wrapped the fingers of one hand in the tangle of his horns and drove her fist into his chest over and over, breaking bones.

Abaddon tried to strike out at her with a hoof. Eve twisted his head to get him off-balance, exposing his legs, and shattered one with a hard kick. Again, the demon screamed.

He thrust upward with such strength that one branch of his horns snapped off in her hand. Blinded, the pits of his eyes gouting foul ichor, Abaddon reached for her. Eve thrust out her right hand, slipped her fingers into the sockets where his eyes had been, and dragged him to the ground once more. Her body still sang with the blood of the angel, but even if she had been withering with hunger she would not have drunk from Abaddon.

Eve crouched above him, his life hers to destroy, the demon at her mercy at long last. It took all of the strength she could muster to keep herself from killing him.

"Bitch," Abaddon rasped in the language of angels.

She lifted him effortlessly from the ground, twisted, and hurled him into the Tree of Knowledge, impaling the demon upon its branches. For the third time, Abaddon screamed. Limply, he hung there.

Then he uttered a low, gurgling laugh.

"You think this will kill me?" Abaddon asked.

Eve moved nearer to him, crushing a fallen piece of fruit under her foot. Hatred and revulsion welled up within her so fiercely that she shook with it. Abaddon was correct. Though he might not be able to extricate himself from the tree's branches, he would not die. He might hang there for eternity.

With a trembling breath, she released all of the venom that had built up in her heart. Eve reached up and touched the side of Abaddon's ruined face.

"I . . ." she began, and faltered.

She hung her head.

"I forgive you."

The demon howled his rage and refusal, but he could not deny that which she had given him. A burden lifted from her. It had been the most difficult task of her immortal life, but it had been done.

Perhaps she had not earned the Creator's redemption yet. Or maybe she had, and He had simply not deigned to share the news with her. Regardless, she had found her own redemption within her own heart. Eve had put the past behind her. She had forgiven herself.

That would have to be good enough.

A smile touched her lips. Once again, she had visited this place and become newly aware of her nakedness. Some clothes would be nice. She would set off back toward the encampment that the demon's confederates had set up and, hopefully, along the way she would find a vampire whose clothes would fit her. The idea troubled her. The damned leeches never had a lot of fashion sense. It was too much to

hope that she'd be able to kill one who was wearing something stylish.

Eve turned on one heel and strode from the glade where
the Tree of Knowledge grew, newly adorned. Abaddon
shrieked after her, but she found it was simple enough to shut
out his cries and listen instead to the wind and the cries of the
birds of Paradise.

17

DUERGAR roared and raised his axe. In response, the ground in front of him rose in a wave, huge stones surging up, rushing toward her like a battering ram.

Ceridwen raised her elemental staff. Pure, golden light swept down from the head of the staff and splashed across that wave of churning earth, and it stopped. Green grass and vividly colored flowers grew from the mound left behind.

With her free hand, she reached up into the air. The winds rushed away from her, swept across the encampment to the tallest tree at the edge, and the tree bent like a reed, its branches reaching for her even as her fingers beckoned.

Duergar spun, eyes wide, and raised his axe, but too late. The tree hammered him against the ground.

The half-blood warrior heaved his body upward, trying to free himself from the weight of the tree that, like a mortar and pestle, ground him into the dirt. Ceridwen took the moment to cast a quick glance around her. The vampires had been either driven off or exterminated; only a few of them lingered there in the demons' camp. Whatever dark magic Abaddon had used to keep the dead Drows shambling around had been extinguished. They lay in heaps of rotting flesh.

Beneath them, new grass and flowers bloomed.

Ceridwen took a deep breath and inhaled the pure air of Paradise. The wind gently tousled her hair and ruffled the silken gown she wore. Never had she felt so entirely a part of nature. The elements seemed to flow through her, to touch her heart and soul, and her spirit spread out across all of Eden.

In the sky, a gigantic, golden-feathered bird tore into the flesh of an amorphous demon that hung in the air like a jellyfish, poison tendrils dangling to the ground. The bird could only be Clay. Ceridwen reached a hand up and summoned the winds of Eden. Powerful gusts rushed against the translucent demon and pushed it farther skyward. She drove the bottom of her elemental staff into the new grass beneath her feet. The fire that churned within the ice sphere atop the staff burned brighter, then seared out in an arc of raging flame that engulfed those deadly tendrils. The fire raced up toward the hanging belly of the thing as though each was a fuse.

A piercing shriek tore across the clearing, and Ceridwen spun to see that it came from a trio of hideous, gigantic hags who were attacking Dr. Graves. The ghost dived clear of their reach and fired his spectral guns in a staccato thunder that blew holes through the monstrous creatures, scattering their raw, pink flesh in gobbets across the clearing.

Squire, Danny, and Shuck were arrayed in the midst of a savage battle with the onslaught of insectoid demons that had begun to swarm toward the Menagerie. Animals summoned by Jelena, the she-wolf, ran rampant through the encampment, tearing at demons and the remaining vampires and trampling underfoot the stinking hounds from Faerie, the Coinn Iotair.

"Ceri!"

The sorceress whipped around to see Arthur running toward her. His hands and arms were coated in green-black demon blood, and crimson stained his clothes. Beyond him lay the scorched and twisted remains of several demons, and farther in the distance others had begun to emerge from the gigantic cocoon that had been spun in the center of the encampment. But Conan Doyle wasn't crying out to her for help.

He extended one long finger, pointing past her.

Ceridwen's eyelids fluttered, and she drew a deep breath. She could feel the ground beneath her tremble, translating a message, even as the wind gusted against her back. Much as she appreciated Arthur's concern and his warning, they were unnecessary.

"Die, Fey witch!" Duergar roared as he careened toward her.

With a whisper to the elements, Ceridwen summoned the wind. It lifted her, swept her from his path, and pushed Duergar, increasing his momentum so that he stumbled and crashed to the ground, tusks and chin digging up the new grass.

Conan Doyle arrived at her side.

"He would have attacked from behind, the blackguard!"

Sometimes she loved how old-fashioned Arthur could be. Ceridwen arched an eyebrow and looked at her lover.

"He's through," she said, her tone strangely light, almost foreign to her ears, as though she were speaking with the voice of Eden herself.

Duergar snarled, snuffling in the dirt like a wild boar, and forced himself up on arms that rippled with muscle. The effort made him groan. His face was torn and bloody. His leather armor had been cracked by the tree she'd hammered him with, and Ceridwen could only assume that his bones had taken similar damage.

His huge fist still clutched the axe with which he had slain so many of her kinsmen during the Twilight Wars. Its blade had been stained with the blood of her aunt and many cousins, some close and some distant. He'd been a traitor and a conniver, a rapist and murderer. Always, he called himself a warrior, but Duergar had never had the honor to bear that title.

"Damned fairy whore!" the half-blood creature said, with the dull-witted cruelty of his Drow kin in his eyes.

"Bastard," Conan Doyle sneered, orbs of dark blue magic pulsing around his fists.

Duergar rose. "Oh, of course, let the magician come to your rescue. It won't help, Ceridwen. The two of you tried to kill me time and again in the Wars, and never could manage it. Not even after I split your aunt in two with prick and axe."

"Times have changed," Ceridwen said softly. "I have changed."

Conan Doyle cursed loudly as he attacked, crackling indigo leaping from his hands and striking Duergar, driving the half-blood staggering backward. That dark light enveloped him in an eyeblink and, as Ceridwen watched, stripped the thick, tough hide from Duergar's face, hands, and arms. All of his exposed skin scraped away, and the warrior roared in an agony like nothing the sorceress had ever heard. Even the lids of his eyes had been peeled from his face.

Duergar never dropped the axe. As he screamed, his eyes seethed with hatred, and he took a step forward, raising the blade. Conan Doyle swore and began to cast a new spell, one comprised of some guttural language, a piece of dark magic she would never wish him to stain his soul with.

"No, Arthur. I told you, he is through."

The half-blood laughed even as he choked with agony. He staggered forward.

Ceridwen felt the presence of Eden in her very soul. She whispered to the soil, to the heart of Paradise, and with a gesture, roots thrust up from the ground beneath Duergar. With his armor already cracked and torn and his thick hide scoured away, he had nothing to protect him. The roots impaled him through the legs and chest and throat. They twined themselves around him and dragged him down. Bones shattered and organs burst wetly as the roots pulled Duergar down under the soil, tearing him apart.

Moments later, he had disappeared, leaving only splashes of blood on the grass and on several trees that had begun to grow to replace parts of the Garden that had once stood on that spot.

The axe lay on the grass, the only proof that Duergar had ever existed at all.

"Ceri," Conan Doyle began, hesitant, perhaps surprised by the savagery of the half-blood's destruction.

"I wasn't alone, Arthur. I summoned the elements, but Eden destroyed him, in the end. Though I, for one, would call it self-defense."

Conan Doyle nodded and reached out to take her hand. His simple presence at her side gave her comfort and reminded her of the warmth and weight of flesh, of life beyond the touch of elemental spirits.

She touched his face and parted her lips to speak his name

again, but new cries of rage and pain filled the clearing. Demons shrieked in voices unlike anything ever heard by human or Fey. Side by side, they turned to see that the demon hordes had not been thinned nearly enough to claim victory. Things crawled along the ground and floated in the sky, and where they passed, the purity of the Garden became freshly despoiled.

"It isn't over," Ceridwen said.

"It's only begun," Conan Doyle replied.

Voices called to them. Ceridwen turned to see Danny and Squire running toward them, still armed with Gemini swords and daggers, and the hobgoblin carrying that great, heavy blunderbuss. Shuck bounded along behind, snapping at demons that tried to give chase.

The Menagerie began to gather, there in the clearing where the dregs of a hundred Hells had invaded Eden and still fought to conquer it. Dr. Graves's phantom guns barked again and again, and the ghost drifted in from their left. From the right came Clay, wielding Gemini Blades and wearing the cracked-earth form he considered his natural face.

Falcons, ravens, eagles, and dozens of other birds soared through the sky, tearing at the demons that could fly. Jaguars and apes, cobras and rams attacked on the ground. Seeing the Menagerie clustering in one place in the clearing, the huge she-wolf broke off from the battle and loped toward them, rising on her rear legs and pulling open her skin like a cloak to reveal Jelena's face and body beneath.

"The odds are against us," the she-wolf growled as she ran toward them.

"Yeah, ya think?" Squire snapped.

The Menagerie formed a circle, backs to one another. The demons began to surround them. A monstrosity covered with eyes, each of its six arms wielding a fiery weapon forged in the pits of some stygian sewer, let out a cry and raised its hands. The fire snuffed out instantly, all of its weapons going dark, and it collapsed to the ground.

Eve stood behind it. She'd torn open the back of the demon and cored out whatever piece of filth acted as its heart.

The vampiress trampled the demon's gelid remains. She

wore loose, ill-fitting leather and black silk, clothes borrowed from some defeated enemy.

"The gang's all here," she said, a grin suffusing her face with bliss and an ethereal beauty even she had never managed before. "Now the party can start."

A chorus of demonic wails and roars went up, and they started toward her. Eve joined the Menagerie at the center of the onslaught.

"Abaddon?" Conan Doyle asked.

"Taken care of."

"You killed the son of a bitch?" Danny said.

Eve smiled. "No. But he's off the board, and he's suffering."

"Good enough," Dr. Graves said.

The demons began to shuffle closer. A splintering sound crashed across the sky. They all turned to see the strange cocoon structure cracking and pieces of it falling away to shatter on the ground. Trees grew up from within it, reaching for the sky, branches spreading. The earthen mound the demons had built began to tremble, and a moment later, branches began to shoot up from beneath that as well.

Squire whistled. "Holy fuck."

Clay stared at Ceridwen. "When did you become this powerful?"

"It isn't me," she said. "It's Eden."

The demons seemed unsure for a moment what to do, then, slowly, their ranks began to break.

"Hey, boss," Squire said. "We've got company."

Ceridwen looked at the hobgoblin and saw that he stared off toward the edge of the clearing. In the thick trees and wild undergrowth of the Garden, figures had begun to emerge. At first there seemed only a few, but as several of them started out of the trees and across the clearing, dozens of other silhouettes appeared in the dark shadows of Eden. At least two of the figures that strode toward them were familiar. One was Nigel Gull, the mage who had once been Conan Doyle's friend and ally and whose face had been twisted by dark magic so that his head was like that of a horse.

The other was Lorenzo Sanguedolce.

"Sweetblood," Conan Doyle rasped.

"Oh, shit," Squire muttered.

A muttering of his name went through the clearing. His legend hung with dread over the denizens of a thousand realms. It seemed to Ceridwen that even the demons held their breath. If Sanguedolce was here, with Gull alongside and who knew how many followers, there was no telling what he might be up to. Had he come to ally himself with Abaddon and Jophiel, but arrived too late?

When Sanguedolce approached the outer ring of demons that surrounded the Menagerie, one of the creatures sniffed and turned to glare defiantly at him.

The archmage glanced at the tall, thin, batlike demon. Fire erupted from Sanguedolce's eye—from the Eye of Eoghain, which he'd once plucked from Conan Doyle's skull—and incinerated the demon where it stood. The fire was rimmed with orange but had a black core, as though the center of that inferno was an oil slick, or an eye itself into an abyss even demons wished not to view.

More of Sanguedolce's followers—his army—stepped from the wilds of the Garden and started toward the demons. They scattered from the path of the mage who had once been mentor and teacher to both Conan Doyle and Nigel Gull.

In moments, Sanguedolce and Gull stood with the Menagerie, facing the demons. Not a word was spoken.

The demons fled. Their ranks broke, and they flew and lumbered, slithered and darted back toward the Garden Gate in an exodus from Eden like nothing the angels who'd driven Adam and Eve from the place could ever have imagined.

Everyone turned to stare at Sanguedolce and Gull, even as Sweetblood's many followers filled the clearing. There were creatures from many realms, many breeds, some hideous and some beautiful. The members of the Menagerie seemed ready for a new battle.

Then Ceridwen noticed Conan Doyle's face. She narrowed her eyes and studied his expression in astonishment. He did not seem at all surprised.

Conan Doyle smoothed his blood-stiffened jacket and ran his fingers through his hair. He took a deep breath and patted his pockets idly, as though he expected to find his pipe.

"I wondered when you might arrive to show your hand,"

he said, almost to the air, although all those gathered fully understood that he spoke only to his former mentor.

Sanguedolce smiled. "You've been expecting me? How could you have known I would come?"

"All the pieces fit, Lorenzo. Elementary, sir. Elementary."

EDEN continued to reclaim the area that Abaddon's invasion had caused to rot and wither. A single tree grew up in seconds from beneath the cairn-hut the Drows had built for Duergar, shattering it and scattering stones into the tall grass and flowering plants that had begun to thrive there. Demon and Drow corpses were swallowed up by the earth or hidden by the tangle of the Garden's swift growth. Soon, there would be almost no trace at all of the taint that the demons had brought to Paradise.

Conan Doyle surveyed the small army that had arrived with Sanguedolce and Gull. Many of them he recognized—sorcerers, necromancers, mediums, and an array of monsters that humanity considered nothing but legend. Several of those who followed Sweetblood the Mage had been at the council Conan Doyle had convened in Dubrovnik.

"Arthur," Ceridwen said, her voice low as she touched his arm and moved nearer to him. "What, precisely, is going on here?"

The question made Sanguedolce smile and glance at Conan Doyle as though he hoped for an answer to the same question.

Many of the members of his Menagerie had recently taken a decidedly hesitant stance on the issue of trust. More specifically, Conan Doyle had become aware that they did not precisely trust *him.* The ghost of Dr. Graves had spent decades lingering in the fleshly world upon the promise that Conan Doyle would help him solve the mystery of his own murder, but upon at last solving the mystery himself, Graves had discovered that Conan Doyle had known the truth for ages and not shared it with him. He had kept it secret in order to save the ghost from heartbreak, but that explanation did not sit well with Dr. Graves. The demon child, Danny, looked at the mage with the wary eye any teenager has for the authority figures in his life. Clay had come to doubt the purity of Conan Doyle's motivations during the situation with Graves. Jelena was an unknown element. Of them all, only Ceridwen, Eve, and Squire would normally trust him without hesitation.

Yet now, even those three—even the woman who loved him—fixed him with a doubtful stare.

Conan Doyle stroked his mustache and returned his focus to Lorenzo Sanguedolce, the man who had transformed him from magical dabbler into archmage. The most dangerous man in the world. If Conan Doyle often kept his own agenda close to the vest and was reluctant to take even his allies into his confidence, Sanguedolce had set the example.

"What's going on here, Arthur?" the ghost of Dr. Graves asked. He still brandished his phantom guns and showed no interest in returning them to their holsters.

"Arthur?" Clay prodded.

Squire crossed his arms.

"Yes, Arthur," Sanguedolce said. "By all means, enlighten us. What is it that you find so elementary about my arrival?"

Conan Doyle slid his hands into his pockets and glanced a moment at the horizon. In the distance he could see a small mountain and a waterfall spilling down its face. The birds had begun to return to the thickest parts of the Garden. The darker hue that had tinged the sky cleared and the light of Eden shone down fully once more, bringing out the colors of the flowers more vividly than ever.

"You have dogged our steps every moment since we helped to release you from the amber sarcophagus within which you had imprisoned yourself," Conan Doyle said.

"When you doomed the world of men, you mean?" Sanguedolce said, one corner of his mouth lifting in the semblance of a smile. "If not for your misguided heroics, the Demogorgon would never have located Earth."

"So you say," Conan Doyle replied with a wave of his hand. "Be that as it may, you've used every opportunity since your revival to keep watch over us, and to use our activities to your advantage. Among your prizes have been the Eye of Eoghain, the Forge of Hephaestus, and a renewed acquaintance with Mister Gull, who I note now seems to be your aide-de-camp."

Gull sniffed in derision and stared at Conan Doyle. Though it was clear he had become nothing more than Sanguedolce's lackey once again—this afflicted sorcerer who shared Conan Doyle's status as one of the most powerful mages in the world—Gull would never have admitted it.

"Yet you couldn't have expected our arrival here," Sanguedolce replied, curiosity lighting his eyes. "You've never been nearly as clever as you think you are, nor as cunning as the detective in your scribblings. I only learned of Eve's predicament and your journey to Eden on a visit to your home. I had a little chat with young Master Ferrick that was quite fascinating."

Conan Doyle turned to Ceridwen and smiled. He touched her cheek and gazed into her curious, violet eyes. Normally he was not one to express his affection publicly, but he needed her to see in his own eyes that nothing had changed in his heart or his mind. For the moment, he ignored the narrowed eyes and knitted brows of his other comrades. Among them, only Jelena smiled, amused by the interplay between the two old mages.

The winds of Paradise carried the rich aromas of earth and flower, of fruit and musk.

When Conan Doyle gazed at Sanguedolce again, he abandoned all pretense that this was nothing more than repartee. Indigo magic crackled around his fingers and shimmered in his eyes so that his vision was shaded blue.

Gull stiffened and raised his hands, ready for a fight. Sanguedolce cautioned him with a raised hand. It seemed as if the entire Garden took a breath and held it.

"It doesn't take a genius or a detective, Lorenzo," Conan Doyle said. "You've been keeping tabs on us all along. You took advantage of Gull's obsession with Medusa in order to get your hands on the Forge of Hephaestus so that you could make weapons that might actually do some damage against the Demogorgon. You manipulated us, left us at the mercy of mad gods in order to achieve your goals. Bravo, you bastard.

"When Abaddon and Jophiel gathered so many of our enemies together and snatched Eve, I had no doubt that you would become aware of our current circumstances and that you would realize, as I did, that they might very well be correct in their presumptions about Eden. It only stood to reason that you'd be along shortly. Frankly, the only thing that surprised me was that you didn't wait until the battle had been fully decided to make your appearance."

Sanguedolce executed a curt, low bow. "We came as fast as we were able, Arthur, to aid you if we could."

Conan Doyle did not extinguish the magic that churned around his fists. "I very much doubt that, but no matter. You're here now. I suspect your allies have already carried the Forge into Eden. Soon enough, the production of weapons and armor will begin—"

"Oh, it's begun already," Sanguedolce confirmed. "You didn't think these past months I'd been idle?"

"Of course not. Nor has Squire, I assure you."

The hobgoblin grunted in confusion and stared back and forth between his employer and Sweetblood. "What the hell are you two talking about?"

"About you, Master 'Goblin," Sanguedolce replied. "I've got the Forge, yes, and have done as well as possible with the making of new weapons, just as Arthur says. But I know of no weaponsmith who can match your skill, and we've been the poorer for the lack of your participation."

Squire shot a hard look at Conan Doyle. "Boss, what the fuck is this about? Translate that for me, will you?"

The mage glanced around the gathering of his friends, allies, and enemies and saw confusion, anger, curiosity, and fear.

"Simply put, Squire, the demon Abaddon and his confederates have done us all an enormous favor. In fact, they might have saved our lives and given us the key to saving the human world and every plane of existence that borders upon it."

All along, Eve had been listening carefully, studying him. Conan Doyle had felt the weight of her regard and of her expectation. Now she stepped forward, fingers still lengthened into deadly talons, and put herself almost between him and Sanguedolce. The vampiress stared at Sweetblood, then turned her gaze to Conan Doyle.

"All of this? What they did to me, and to the rest of you, and—hell, Doyle, listen to yourself—to Eden . . . you're saying this is all a good thing?"

He did not blink or turn from the intensity of her gaze. "It is."

"Just how do you figure?" Danny sneered, crouched on his haunches, eyes gleaming. The hellhound, Shuck, sat beside him, silently watching the proceedings with his tongue hanging from his mouth.

"Isn't it obvious?" the ghost of Dr. Graves asked.

"It should be," Conan Doyle replied, nodding to him. He spread his arms, taking in all of Eden with the gesture. "The demons and their allies were correct, you see. The Garden Gate can be closed again, and we can control when and if it opens. With the will of the Creator Himself protecting this place, Eden may be the only safe spot in the universe from the Demogorgon. It's the perfect staging area for a war against the Devourer. The perfect place to establish a beachhead, to gather allies and to plan, and to stoke up the Forge of Hephaestus and try to make sure we're prepared for its arrival."

Clay moved past Jelena and stood across from Eve, effectively creating a smaller circle of four—the two mages, and the two oldest living beings to walk the world of man, both of whom had begun their lives in Eden.

"And you expect us to work with Sweetblood?" the shapeshifter said. "After everything he's done?"

Sanguedolce did not so much as glance at him, his eyes locked on Conan Doyle's. "Petty differences must be put aside for the good of all. If there isn't a world left, what then is the point of squabbling over how we live in it?"

Conan Doyle glanced at Ceridwen. He saw the distaste she felt for the entire conversation, but she gave an almost imperceptible nod.

"Agreed," he said, and he held out a hand.

Sanguedolce shook it, and the pact was made.

After all that had happened, it seemed that they themselves had become the invaders of Eden. Intruders in Paradise.

Silence reigned. Gull wore a grim expression on his equine face that perhaps only Conan Doyle, who knew him better than anyone, would have recognized as smug. A susurrus of whispers began among Sanguedolce's followers, but they were carried off by the wind, and Conan Doyle ignored them. The members of the Menagerie did not object, but he could not fail to see the tension in his comrades. He had made this decision without their approval and hoped that they would come to realize that there had really never been any other choice. Allies and enemies alike would stand or fall side by side when the Demogorgon came. They would help one another live or help one another die.

"All right," Eve said, nodding grimly. "I get it. Long term, it makes sense. I don't like it, but I get it. Before we all go running hand in hand through the fucking poppies, though, let me ask you one question."

Conan Doyle felt much of the tension go out of him. The magic diminished around his hands and eyes, then vanished altogether, drawn back into himself. If Eve backed him, the others would go along, even if they had their doubts.

"What is it?" he asked.

Eve nodded toward Sanguedolce. "This asshole set us up to die for his convenience in Greece not too long ago. And I know he talked to Danny, and that makes it look like he just got the bright idea about fighting our little war from here not too long ago. But how do we know that's the truth? Were Abaddon and Jophiel clever enough to figure that out on their own, the idea of hiding out here from the Demogorgon, or was it maybe suggested to them by someone a whole lot more devious? How do we know the whole thing wasn't a setup from the start?"

Conan Doyle stroked his mustache again, contemplating this.

Gull snorted, and Eve turned to glare at him.

"An excellent question," the mage said with his twisted mouth. "But even if it was a setup, how do we know who orchestrated the situation? Arthur could have manipulated us all just as easily as Lorenzo. How do we know, really?"

"We don't," Conan Doyle replied, then turned to Eve. "And for now, it doesn't matter. As long as we all want to stay alive, how we do so matters not at all. Believe me, Eve, I have no intention of investing any trust in Sweetblood beyond our mutual goals."

Sanguedolce laughed darkly, the Eye of Eoghain glittering with the blackest of magics.

"Well said, Arthur. I see that we understand each other perfectly."

"We do," Conan Doyle replied. "All too well."

The mages stared at one another. A gust of wind danced around them, carrying the distant sound of a demon's anguished cries from somewhere in the wilds of Eden. The voice, Conan Doyle knew, belonged to Abaddon, who had achieved precisely what he'd set out to do and gotten exactly what he deserved.

EPILOGUE

EVEN with the light breeze blowing in from Boston Harbor, the spring night was unseasonably warm. Not a cloud hung in the sky, leaving it clear enough to see an endless array of stars in spite of the city lights. Quincy Market was alive with the laughter and chatter of milling tourists, twenty- and thirtysomething professionals, and the infinite horde of college students who had become Boston's trademark. Glasses clinked in the patio restaurants, and street performers busked, playing guitar and juggling, riding unicycles and singing a capella.

No clowns, though. That was good. Most people hated mimes, but they didn't bother Eve much. Her enmity was reserved for clowns. Greasepainted freaks. And those eyes— always seemed bigger than human eyes. She'd face down an entire pantheon of gods or demons, but clowns just freaked her out.

"Wow," a voice said, as she walked past.

Eve glanced back to see a couple of college boys checking out her ass. She smiled and put an extra swing into her step. This was exactly the kind of night she needed. Lost in the swirling current of humanity, bathed in the scents of a dozen restaurants, an outdoor florist, and the chocolate chip cookies baking at the Chipyard, she felt the kind of contact with humanity that she'd been cut off from ever since Abaddon had come back into her life.

Lovers walked hand in hand. Two twentyish girls, one black and one white, had stopped outside a restaurant whose open doors let the music from their live entertainment sail out across the cobblestones of the marketplace. They danced together, fingers intertwined, kissing gently and laying their foreheads against one another. An older couple looked their way. Eve expected them to scowl in disgust, but instead they only smiled knowingly and slid their arms around each other while they walked.

This place—this world—was alive. These people had hearts and souls and ideas. Right here, this was worth fighting for. This was worth dying for.

At a small bar on the corner, where the glass walls had been accordioned back to let the warm spring night breeze through, a piano player sat and tapped out a jazzy version of "East of the Sun, West of the Moon."

Story of my life, Eve thought.

For a long moment she stood and listened. The piano player noticed her out of the corner of his eye and looked up. As he sang, he smiled, appreciating her. Eve gave him a flirtatious wave, but she really wasn't in the mood to start anything tonight, so before he could finish the song, she turned to continue her stroll.

Clay stood a dozen feet away, watching her with his hands jammed into his pockets, leaning up against one of the trees that grew up out of squares of dirt in the cobblestone street. He wore jeans and imported leather sneakers and a light cotton, button-down shirt. His chin was lightly stubbled. The human face he chose to wear most often was damned handsome, something she'd been unable to stop noticing of late.

Eve blinked. He had to have followed her from the house. For a fraction of a moment she felt herself growing annoyed, but then it passed. In the time since their return from Eden, they had become very close. They had wandered several cities scattered around the world together, sharing the memories that their experiences in Eden had unlocked. In that time, they had learned how much they truly had in common.

Clay and Eve were both God's castoffs, at least the way they saw it. From the Sacre Coeur in Paris to the Hagia Sofia in Istanbul and the gardens of Kyoto, they had discussed the central question of their lives, which was whether the Creator had a plan for His nomadic outcasts, or if He was simply an absentee God who'd forgotten them the moment He'd abandoned them.

"Hey," Clay said, as Eve strode toward him.

"Hey."

"You took off. Did you want to be alone, or would you like some company?"

Eve gave him a half smile that lifted one corner of her mouth. In all the worlds, no one could ever understand what she had endured. But Clay could come damned close. For the two of them to go on, to keep living their eternities, they had to believe that there *was* a plan.

They had to have faith.

Having Clay around made that easier for Eve, and she knew that her presence did the same for him.

"I'd love company," she said, offering her arm. He linked arms with her, and they started off across the cobblestones. "You know what I'd love even more, though?"

Clay raised an eyebrow and glanced sidelong at her. "What?"

"Chocolate chip cookies. I mean, damn, do you *smell* those? I'm practically moist just thinking about them. There oughta be a law."

"You want cookies?" He grinned.

"Oh, yes."

"Well, by all means. Never let it be said that I didn't give a lady what she most desired."

"Are you flirting with me?" Eve asked.

"Could be."

"Cookies," she demanded.

"As you wish."